HOMELAND

HOMELAND

E.V. THOMPSON

ROBERT HALE · LONDON

© E.V. Thompson 1991

First published in Great Britain 1991
This edition 2013

ISBN 978-0-7198-1035-0

Robert Hale Ltd
Clerkenwell House
Clerkenwell Green
London EC1R 0HT

www.halebooks.com

The right of E.V. Thompson to be identified as author of this
work has been asserted by him in accordance
with the Copyright, Designs and Patents Act 1988

2 4 6 8 10 9 7 5 3 1

Printed in the UK by Berforts Information Press Ltd

CONTENTS

CAMERON family

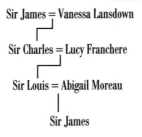

Sir James = Vanessa Lansdown
Sir Charles = Lucy Franchere
Sir Louis = Abigail Moreau
Sir James

ROSS family

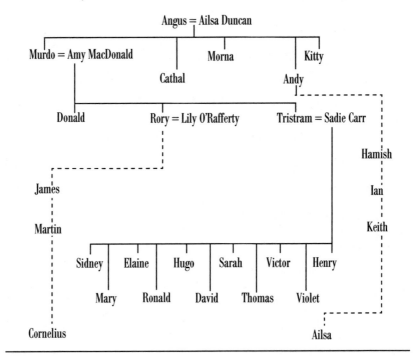

Angus = Ailsa Duncan

Murdo = Amy MacDonald   Morna   Kitty

Cathal   Andy

Donald   Rory = Lily O'Rafferty   Tristram = Sadie Carr

James   Hamish

Martin   Ian

Sidney   Elaine   Hugo   Sarah   Victor   Henry   Keith

Mary   Ronald   David   Thomas   Violet

Cornelius   Ailsa

MacCRIMMON family

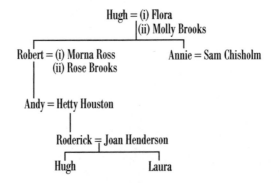

Hugh = (i) Flora
      (ii) Molly Brooks

Robert = (i) Morna Ross   Annie = Sam Chisholm
       (ii) Rose Brooks

Andy = Hetty Houston

Roderick = Joan Henderson

Hugh   Laura

ONE

Glenelg 1817

The threat of eviction loomed over the small Scots peninsular of Glenelg like a black, malignant, November cloud. It lowered over the rock-strewn heights of Forcan Ridge and cast a long, dark, ominous shadow along the secret depths of Glen More, touching cottar and crofter, tacksman and householder.

In his small, free-stone cottage, Angus Ross, sub-tenant of Hugh MacCrimmon, knew he would be among the first to experience the effects of the gathering storm. Father of seven living children, Angus and his prematurely worn-out wife, Ailsa, had laid four more to rest in Glenelg's tiny churchyard. Eviction would take little from the Ross family — but it would be their all.

Eviction also threatened Hugh MacCrimmon himself. Tacksman, full tenant and distant kinsman of the clan chief of Glenelg, MacCrimmon grazed a herd of black, half-wild cattle on the mountainsides above the river that ran through Glen More, although he had enough land spare to sub-let to the equally wild Highland men.

The great love in Hugh MacCrimmon's life was the pipes: the great war bagpipes of the Highlands. On these he repeated tunes that had been played by MacCrimmons for centuries among the mountains and glens of Glenelg.

Men declared that Hugh MacCrimmon was the finest piper the remote Highland area had ever known, and when Charles Cameron of Glenelg had raised a regiment to take to the Peninsular War, he chose Hugh MacCrimmon as his Pipe Major. Together they were part of the victorious army of the Duke of Wellington, which fought its way across Portugal and Spain to the Pyrenees and finally bearded Napoleon Bonaparte in his own land.

On a hillside outside Toulouse a musket ball from a sharp-shooter's rifle had struck down Pipe Major MacCrimmon while he played Glenelg's own regiment into battle. Propped against the shattered wheel of an abandoned wagon, Hugh MacCrimmon had continued to play the rousing music of the Highlands of Scotland, waving men past him into the fray and offering comforting words when they returned, bloody but victorious.

One of those more seriously wounded at the battle of Toulouse had been Angus Ross. A cannonball had left little work for the amputating surgeon to perform; by the time the battle for Toulouse was over, Angus Ross's arm was among the gruesome contents of a wooden bath outside a church-turned-operating-theatre on the edge of the field of battle.

That hard-won victory had been three years before, in 1814. Now the spectre of eviction was the enemy. By reaching out a little further it might even touch Cameron of Glenelg himself, in his fine home on the green slopes of Ratagan, to the east of the Glenelg peninsular. Not that the landowner was aware of the approaching threat. Cameron of Glenelg looked only downwards upon his tacksmen and tenants; not upwards towards the heavens.

This was not the Cameron of Glenelg who had taken his regiment to Toulouse. That brave man had fallen at the very moment of victory, struck down during the last desperate moments of the enemy's resistance. Angus Ross and Hugh MacCrimmon had wept bitter, burning tears at the graveside of the Laird of Glenelg and there would have been more had either man realised what they were witnessing. Far more than the mere body of a Highland chieftain was being lowered into a grave in this foreign land. The sad, wind-borne music of Hugh MacCrimmon's pipes played a dirge for a way of life, the scattering of a whole breed of people. That day, on a windy hillside near Toulouse, Hugh MacCrimmon's lament marked the passing of 'The Highlander'.

Angus Ross was weeding in his garden when Hugh MacCrimmon came visiting. Wielding a hoe dexterously with his one hand, the ex-soldier had watched the approach of his near-neighbour along the valley. MacCrimmon walked with the slow, weary gait of a much-troubled man and there was no warmth in his greeting.

'A blessing on you and yours, Angus.'

'And on you too, Hugh MacCrimmon. But I've paid the rent and you haven't walked the length of Glen More to wish me and my family well. You'll have something to say – and there's little good news travelling the Highlands these days.'

Both men spoke in Gaelic, as did most of those who lived hereabouts.

The pain on Hugh MacCrimmon's face might almost have had a physical source, but his words hinted at the truth.

'You've paid your rent to *me*, Angus, but when it comes down to it I'm a tenant too.'

'Ah!' Angus Ross began chopping at the low green weeds with the hoe as though it had suddenly become the most important task in his life. 'So Cameron has finally sent for you. Did he have the same message as he had for the others? Must we leave the glen?'

Hugh MacCrimmon nodded, not trusting himself to speak. Rosses and MacCrimmons had been living in Glenelg for generations before a long-ago Cameron had come along and married the only daughter of the Chieftain of Glenelg. She had been a MacCrimmon.

'How long has he given us?' Weeding crops seemed a futile waste of time now, yet still the one-armed ex-soldier jabbed away at the ground although he no longer looked at what he was doing.

'I've until next year to find extra rent for only half the land I have now. He wants this end of the glen cleared by Midsummer Day. That's when they'll begin moving in the sheep.'

The hoe dropped to the ground as Angus stared at the other man in disbelief. 'Midsummer Day? That's only six weeks away! My crops will be no more than half-grown by then.'

'Cameron says he'll pay fair compensation.'

'Fair? James Cameron's never learned the meaning of the word. He'll offer a tenth of what the crops are worth – then find reasons for paying less than half that. It's what he did to Macleod in Glen Beg – and Widow Matheson fared even worse. What of my house . . . ? I've a family and a sick woman inside. Where am I supposed to take them?'

'Cameron says he'll rent you a piece of land over by Ardintoul. You can take your roof timbers with you . . . .'

'Can I now?' Angus Ross's voice was charged with both sarcasm and anger. 'He's moved so many families to Ardintoul the place has more folk than stones – and there's enough of *them* in Ardintoul to build a city.'

'I said as much to Cameron, Angus, but he'll not listen to me, or to anyone else. He's set his mind on letting out the land for sheep walks.'

'That's likely the only way he'll ever pay off the debts run up by that English wife of his.' Angus spoke bitterly. 'It's a pity his father didn't have the same idea years ago. He could have taken a flock of sheep to fight for him at Toulouse – and I'd have two arms to help keep my family.'

'Young Cameron's not the man his father was,' said Hugh Mac-Crimmon. He hesitated a moment before adding, 'I'm not a rich man, but I'll not see you or your family starve, Angus.'

'I thank you for that, Hugh, but you'll need money for yourself. What if you can't find the rent young Cameron is wanting from you?'

Hugh shrugged. 'I'll need to move south, or take a boat to America, maybe.'

'*Damn* James Cameron — and that wife of his!' Angus picked up his hoe, only to fling it petulantly to the ground once more. 'If it wasn't for my family I'd fight him, one arm or no.'

'It would do no good, that way's been tried elsewhere. Cameron has the law on his side. I'm sorry, Angus.'

'Aye, I know you are, Hugh. We've seen glorious times, you and I, and our families go back a long way together. We've both been proud to serve the Camerons of Glenelg too — but not this one. It's greed, not pride in his people, that drives James Cameron.'

'Go and look at Ardintoul, Angus. Choose your plot and let me know when you want to move. I've a horse and wagon you can use.'

Angus Ross nodded acknowledgement of the offer. 'I'll need to go in and break the news to Ailsa. She'll be upset.' He nodded to where wooden crosses and rough granite tombstones were visible above the low wall of Glenelg churchyard, visible at the far end of the glen where the cottage stood. 'Four of our children are buried here. She visits them every week.'

Turning away so the tacksman would not see his tortured expression, the red-haired, red-bearded man ducked his head and passed in through the low doorway of the rough-thatched cott that had been his home for so long.

*

As Angus Ross led the horse pulling Hugh MacCrimmon's loudly protesting cart along Glen More, a vast sea of sheep spilled from the hills into the glen behind him. But Angus did not look back, and it would not be necessary to make a second trip. One journey was sufficient to carry all the worldly goods of the Ross family and still leave room on the creaking cart for his wife. He would never visit this glen again.

Ailsa Ross lay at the back of the wagon on a ragged mattress stuffed with wiry, sweet-smelling heather. She was not a strong woman and it took her longer each year to recover from the rigours of the long, Highland winter. Sharing the mattress with her were the two youngest Ross girls, the oldest only thirty months old. Both had been bom after Angus's return from the Peninsular War. For them, moving house and riding on a cart was a great adventure; neither could understand why the remainder of the family did not share their excitement.

Ailsa saw the sheep pouring down the steep slopes to the land they had just left, and she wept silently and long. She wept also for the way of life she was leaving behind. It had been hard and filled with drudgery, yet it was possible to gain comfort from its unchanging familiarity. She wept for her children, who faced an uncertain future. But most of all she wept for the man who trudged ahead of the cart, leading the horse. The man she had married.

Angus Ross had inherited nothing from life but his pride: a fierce, hungry, merciless pride. It had driven him into the army when he could see no other way to improve the lot of his family. Once in the army he had set out to earn quick promotion. His father had reached the rank of Sergeant-Major before he died, and Angus was determined to achieve the same. A cannonball had come between Angus and his ambition, but he had returned from the war with his pride intact, having acquitted himself well. His arm had been sacrificed in the service of a Cameron of Glenelg. It was customary for bravery and sacrifice to be rewarded by a gift of land; this had been the way of the Highlands for countless generations. But the new Cameron of Glenelg had not been brought up to Highland ways. Schooled in Edinburgh he had then gone south and taken an English wife. He had none of the gratitude or sense of duty of his predecessors, and Angus had been allowed to keep the tenancy of his cott only through the generosity of Hugh MacCrimmon.

James Cameron's first act as Chieftain of Glenelg was to begin clearing cottars from the area in order that he might rent the lands to sheep-owners. For three years MacCrimmon and a few other tacksmen had stood between the landowner and those he wished to dispossess by meeting rent increases themselves, but Cameron was becoming ever more greedy. The cottars were being ousted and unless MacCrimmon and the other tenants-in-chief could match the impossibly high rents offered by the sheep-men, they too would find themselves homeless.

Ailsa Ross raised herself in a bid to catch a glimpse of her husband as he plodded along beside the horse's head, but their possessions were stacked precariously high, hiding him from her view. Many aspects of the move to Ardintoul caused her great concern. They would be living on a small plot of land surrounded by other dispossessed Highlanders. Her husband had a hot temper and was not used to making allowances for others. It had not mattered in Glen More where they had no neighbours; the only one Angus could vent his temper on there was her, and she understood him. He was a good and caring man, but the frustrations in him caused by the loss of an arm needed to come out sometimes.

He remained a man with unfulfilled ambitions, thwarted by birth and disability. The army was to have been his way out, but that opportunity had been taken from him when he had followed a Cameron of Glenelg to war. Now another bearing the same name sought to take away what little pride and independence remained.

Almost a hundred thousand acres of Glenelg land had already been cleared. Those at Ardintoul were clinging to the last vestige of a Highland way of life. Some were determined never to leave Glenelg, and a few could not. Others, losing all hope, moved south to the cities or to England. Many more joined dispossessed Highlanders from other parts of Scodand and boarded wooden-hulled sailing ships to seek a new life in Canada, America, Australia or New Zealand.

Angus had built a new home for his family with the help of his neighbours. It was a simple dwelling with no windows and only a single wall of stone, the other walls being made of dried mud. Turf and rough thatch were laid upon roof timbers brought from the old cottage and weighted down with heavy stones as protection against the fierce winds that blew along Loch Alsh from the Atlantic.

12

Ailsa Ross's heart came close to breaking when she first saw the house, but she did not allow her husband to see her distress. Instead, she said, 'It will do us fine,' and rising from her mattress directed where their furniture should be placed.

The Ross family consisted of three sons and four daughters, their ages ranging from eighteen months to eighteen years. It was going to be difficult to feed such a large family from the land they rented on the shores of Ardintoul. The soil was no more than a few inches deep and bore a heavy crop of stones, yet despite the many disadvantages, Angus worked hard.

He kept his patience when the salt-laden wind from the sea turned the young crops brown. He did not give up when the sheep strayed down to Ardintoul, scrambling over the low walls surrounding his piece of land and eating what little crops the wind had spurned.

A complaint to the owner of the sheep brought the retort that he should build his walls higher. The sheep-man had rented grazing, it was not his responsibility to build walls around any properties within his grazing area. Indeed, Cameron of Glenelg had promised there would be no cottars in the vicinity of the sheep walk. Cottars and sheep-men were like fire and water. Neither could live with the other.

At the end of that summer of change, the Ross family cow died. It was a slow death, brought about by starvation. Grazing was sparse in the vicinity of the waterside plot of land and on the surrounding mountain slopes the close-cropping sheep had eaten every blade of grass down to the roots.

The cow had been the one possession that set Angus Ross above his fellow cottars, marking him as a man of some achievement, at least. Only now did he decide that he must take his troubles to Cameron of Glenelg. With him he took two of his three sons: eighteen-year-old Murdo, and Cathal, who had almost reached his seventeenth birthday.

It was a seven-mile walk to Cameron's house at Ratagan. As the path climbed high from Ardintoul it afforded breathtaking views of the Highlands to the north and east. Far below, the waters of Loch Alsh captured the sunlight and lacquered it with a silver sheen that hurt the eyes. In spite of his troubles it made Angus want to stand and breathe it all in, to thank God for giving him life.

Father and sons walked along the path that passed the Point of Totaig and then swung south and east, when Loch Alsh became Loch Duich, dipping to the very edge of the water. Here the mood of the day changed dramatically. High cloud drifted between Highlands and sky, the waters of the loch changed to the colour of a storm and the high hills on either side seemed to draw closer to one another.

It might have been an omen. At Ratagan, Angus learned that James Cameron had a party from London staying at the house, and neither host nor guests were early risers. No one was available to deal with the cottar's problem, but Angus said that he and his sons would wait.

James Cameron emerged from his bedroom late in the morning, in no hurry to speak to the Ardintoul cottar. Not until late in the afternoon were Angus Ross and his two sons escorted through the corridors of the big house to a room that could have held two of the Ardintoul cotts. James Cameron stood at one end of the room, brandy glass in hand, chatting to friends. Others in the room watched two men who leaned over a green baize-covered table, playing billiards.

The game and all conversation ceased as the Rosses entered. Angus was wearing the tartan kilt of the regiment raised by Charles Cameron. Those worn by his sons were plain grey. Each carried a weather-faded plaid slung over one shoulder. For the Londoners this was their first glimpse of the men they had expected to find in the vicinity of Glenelg: the Highlanders.

Angus felt as out of place inside Ratagan as the occupants of the room might have been in his mud-floored cott at Ardintoul. But no one who saw him walk the length of the large room, head held high, would have guessed he was ill at ease, and his sons took their cue from him. Halting when still more than a pace away from the owner of the house, Angus inclined his head in a gesture of allegiance to Cameron of Glenelg.

'God's blessing be upon you,' Angus greeted the other man in Gaelic because that was the way he had always greeted James Cameron's father.

The greeting was wasted – James Cameron spoke no Gaelic.

Yet, looking about the room, he was well satisfied with the impact the visit of a genuine Highlander had made upon his guests. It had created an amusing diversion, but now he wanted the Rosses out of the room as quickly as possible. They had brought the smell of peat-smoke and dung-smeared floors into his house with them.

'State your business and be on your way, Ross. You're interrupting a gathering of friends.'

Warning his eldest son with a glance so swift it was missed by others in the room, Angus said, 'I'm sorry to trouble you – and your friends – but it's the land we've been moved to at Ardintoul. The soil is too thin to grow crops and sheep climb the walls as though they don't exist. Now my cow has starved to death because the sheep have eaten all the grass . . . .'

'What do you expect *me* to do? You're fortunate to have been rehoused – and in a prime fishing-spot too. If you can no longer graze cattle or grow vegetables you must learn to fish. There's a good living to be earned from the sea by a diligent man.'

'A boat costs a deal of money — and it's not easy for a one-armed man to learn a new way of life . . . .'

'I suppose, because you followed my father into battle, you feel I owe you something, Ross? May I remind you that it was your King for whom you were fighting – and I venture to suggest that my father's sacrifice was greater than yours.'

'Had your father not been killed he'd have returned to his own home. He'd not have found his wife turned out onto the hills as so many other Highland women were. But if he had come back, perhaps no one would have been turned out.'

The outburst came from Murdo Ross, his face as red as the hair he had inherited from his father.

'That's *enough*!' Angus Ross could see that there was still a great deal of anger in Murdo, and wanted to silence his son before he went too far.

'I strongly advise you to take heed of your father and not interfere in matters about which you know nothing.' James Cameron's expression was one of fierce anger, but he tried hard to keep his temper in front of his London guests.

'I stopped the boy because it's not polite to insult a man in his own house. I have no argument with the truth of what was said. I went to the war because your father went to war, and he was Cameron of Glenelg and a brave man. I had no other reason to fight for an English King. When we charged the enemy your father was at the head of his men, as a brave officer should be. I followed as close as any man, so close that the shot that killed him was the same one that took off my arm, yet I mourned his death more than I did the loss of a limb. I mourn it more than ever today, but I take comfort in the knowledge that when I die I leave behind brave sons who will bring honour to the name of Ross. The Cameron name died at Toulouse with the death of your father – Charles Cameron was the last true Cameron of Glenelg.'

Turning his back upon James Cameron, Angus Ross walked from the room looking neither to left nor right. Murdo and Cathal followed, pride in their father showing in their bearing.

As the three Highlanders left, the billiard room erupted in a babble of astonished voices. All agreed that Angus Ross had been unforgivably insulting, yet none had noticed that he was dressed in little more than rags. Repeating the story to friends, as they often would, each would describe Angus Ross as a tall, proud Highlander, wearing the full uniform of a Highland soldier.

Five days after Angus Ross's visit to the Ratagan home of James Cameron of Glenelg, a sheriff's officer rode to Ardintoul. In a pouch at his side he carried eviction orders for every occupant of the loch-side cotts. For the second time in a matter of months they were being forced to leave their homes.

The cottars had made no trouble on the first occasion and the sheriff's officer was expecting none now – but he had misjudged the mood of the Highland women. Since being forced to leave their cotts among the mountains and glens they had tried unsuccessfully to eke out a wretched existence on the stony lands of Ardintoul. They had sunk as low as their Highland pride would allow. There was nowhere else to go, nothing more to lose.

By the time the sheriff's officer had served four notices, word of his errand had reached every one of the lochside cotts. He returned to his horse to find it surrounded by a crowd of angry women. When he tried to push between them they refused to budge. Ordering them to stand aside in the name of the sheriff he represented, he waited confidently for them to obey his official demand.

Instead, the women seized hold of the sheriff's officer and stripped him of his clothing, and moments later, man, clothes and pouch were pitched into the cold waters of the loch. As the sheriff's officer cursed the women and shivered in the water, embarrassed by his nakedness but otherwise unhurt, the women of the Ardintoul cotts set fire to the notices of eviction.

Unwilling to report the truth, the incident grew in the mind of the sheriff's officer on the long, shivering-wet ride to Inverness. By the time he reached his destination the incident had become an insurrection: the long-expected reaction to the wholesale Clearances in the Highlands.

Messages went out from the sheriff to every gentleman in the area. The militia were called to arms. Meetings took place in the sheriff's office during which battle plans were drawn up and discarded, drawn up again and amended. Men, whose only experience of cold steel was serving out a pound of nails in their hardware shops, strutted around the town wearing swords at their belts. The less illustrious residents of the town noted with amusement that the clatter of a sword scabbard on the cobblestone pavement seemed to have a magical effect, causing a hitherto unassuming man to puff up with a sudden, unaccustomed importance.

When the plans had finally been agreed, the landowners and militiamen assembled in the town centre for a blessing from the minister of the church before riding off on the King's business. Their route to Glenelg took them across miles of empty Highlands. Where there had once been a whole network of communities to pass on news of their coming, there was now only the plaintive warning call of the eagle, echoing between high, rocky peaks with no man to hear.

At Ratagan, the gentlemen were made welcome by Cameron of Glenelg and the militiamen given billets in the barns and outhouses. The next morning they were roused before dawn and Cameron's land agent guided them along the path to Ardintoul.

Descending from the heights above the village they took the cottars completely by surprise. In Angus Ross's cott they found the one-armed ex-soldier with two of his sons seated around a fire, over which a small joint of lamb spluttered on a spit, its mouth-watering aroma filling the single room. In one of the dark and damp corners their youngest son Andy lay on a blanket, his skin burning with the heat of a fever. Only his obvious illness saved Andy from suffering the fate of his father and brothers. It was no use Angus insisting he had chased two eagles from the carcass of the lamb and brought it home for his starving family. The sheriff had heard many such stories; the only way a cottar could provide lamb for his family to eat was to steal it. Father and two sons were arrested and the family, including the feverish son, evicted.

Outside, the Highlanders were herded together and placed under a heavy militia guard. Then, as the women wailed and the men cursed the sheriff, the furniture was dragged from each house and the thatch and roof beams put to the torch. Yet even this did not satisfy the sheriff and his men. Before being burned some of the wooden beams were used as battering rams with which to break down the mud walls of the one-roomed hovels. Meanwhile their horses milled about in the small gardens, trampling crops into the ground. The sheriff's men performed their work well. By the time they left Ardintoul not a single cott was left and the smell of smoke hung like a heavy pall on the air.

Angus Ross and his sons Murdo and Cathal were brought to trial before the Circuit Court in Inverness three weeks after these latest evictions. Seated on the bench at the side of the presiding judge was the sheriff who had ordered their arrest.

The verdict was never in doubt. The court felt no more inclined to believe Angus Ross's story than the sheriff, although the judge proved more merciful in the end. It had been the sheriff's hope that the judge would grasp the opportunity to make an example of the Ross men, thus causing the Highlanders to think twice before flouting authority in the future. Instead, the judge pointed out that no one had come forward to claim ownership of the lamb that had found its disputed way to Angus Ross's miserable cott at Ardintoul. All he had been able to ascertain was that the animal did not belong to the Ross family, neither did they possess the means of purchasing a lamb for food. In view of this missing link in the chain of their guilt, the judge felt justified in being merciful: he sentenced Angus Ross to fourteen years' transportation, and his sons to seven years each.

Angus Ross was carried from the court calling down curses upon the judge, the sheriff, and the landowner who had brought about the ruination of the Ross family. At the back of the court many of the

Highlanders who had come to see justice done joined in the shouting and were driven from the court by the cudgels of the sheriff's constables.

No one paid any attention to the young boy who sat at the back of the courtroom in a state of shock, his mind in turmoil. Andy Ross had walked the fifty miles to Inverness believing justice would be done and that he would be returning to Glenelg in the company of Murdo, Cathal and their father. He had told his mother so, persuading her not to leave the crude shelter he had built among the rocks on the Ardintoul shore. He had told her that things would be better when his father returned; that somehow they would have food again, and his father would find somewhere for them to live. Now Andy did not know what he would do. The whole situation was more than a twelve-year-old boy should have had to cope with . . . .

By the time the gaoler allowed Andy Ross to see his father in the cells beneath the courtroom he had regained his composure.

'It'll be all right, Pa,' he assured the distraught Angus, 'we're managing fine. The gaoler says you'll be going to Botany Bay. As soon as I get some money put by I'll bring Ma and the girls out there to you. The gaoler says if a man's family follow him out there he's allowed to go free. He's even given land to work. I expect they'll free Murdo and Cathal too. The gaoler knows, Pa. He went out there on one of the transports; was there for five years. He says a family man's better off at Botany Bay than he is in the Highlands today.'

'Well, he can hardly be worse off . . . but your mother . . . she's not strong. How's she bearing up under all this? Where are you living? Are the villagers of Ardintoul taking care of you . . . ?'

For a moment or two Andy Ross looked down at the dirty stone floor at his feet. Ailsa Ross was little more than a skeleton. Living out in the open with scant shelter from wind and rain was sapping what little strength she had left. She would not survive a winter – and there was not a householder in Ardintoul who would dare to take them in, or even give them food. James Cameron of Glenelg had threatened immediate eviction for anyone who helped the homeless cottars. Helping a Ross would bring about a burning as well . . . .

'Everyone's doing all they can, Pa. Don't worry about us. Ma would have come today but she needed to stay with the girls.'

Angus Ross nodded, not trusting himself to speak as he thought of his wife and the girls he feared he would never see again. After a long silence he managed to say, 'Take care of them, Andy. Take care of them all – and if you are ever really in need of help go to see Hugh MacCrimmon. He's a good man. He'll not let you starve.'

Andy Ross nodded. He did not want to tell his father that he had already sought the help of Hugh MacCrimmon and that neither the tacksman nor his twenty-year-old son Robert was at home. MacCrimmon was a widower, and only his daughter had been there. She had informed Andy that both men were driving their black cattle southwards to the annual market in the Lowlands. They were not expected back in Glenelg for at least a month.

'I'll remember, Pa. Take care of yourself. . . . Take care of all yourselves.'

Then Andy was being held to his father's chest and he could see nothing for the tears that blurred his vision. It was the first time in his young life that his father had hugged him, and he feared it might be the last. It was followed by brief hugs for both brothers as the gaoler called impatiently for him to leave.

On the way out, Andy passed a blacksmith carrying chains and fetters and a heavy hammer with which to secure them. The chains and fetters securing a man's wrists and ankles would be a permanent, degrading reminder of the Highlands and would remain with the transported Ross trio for as long as they were convicts.

For most men sentenced to transportation, this meant that they would wear the chains until they were lowered into a convict's shallow grave.

The hundred-and-fifty-mile cattle drive to the south took much longer than Hugh MacCrimmon had anticipated, even though his son Robert was there to help him. There had been a time when herds from the Highlands and Islands of Scotland would converge to form a slow-moving river of wide-horned cattle, all flowing in the direction of the Lowland markets, but the old ways were disappearing fast. MacCrimmon's small herd of black cattle followed in the wake of a much larger herd which had been swum across the narrows of Kyle Rhea from the Isle of Skye, and problems were encountered almost immediately. The days were past when cattle drovers were welcomed on the long trail by cottars and Highland tenants, all eager to sell their produce and glean the latest news from the north.

Indeed, most Highlanders had left the glens and the mountain slopes along the route taken by the cattle. The land was now rented out to sheep-men and they complained that the Highland cattle ate grass for which they were paying rent. Heavy wooden fences appeared along the narrow, steep-sided glens and sheriff's officers warned the cattle drovers away from boundaries that had never been accurately defined.

So difficult did the drive become that Hugh MacCrimmon sought a new route to market in a bid to avoid further trouble. Taking to higher ground solved his problems to a great extent, but grass was scarcer here and, as a result, the cattle required extra grazing time in order to reach the market in prime condition.

By the time the two MacCrimmons concluded their business in the Lowlands and returned to Glenelg, a full month had elapsed since the conviction of Angus Ross and his two sons at the Inverness court. Hugh MacCrimmon's immediate reaction to news of the Clearances and arrests was to ride to Inverness. He hoped he might find the imprisoned Rosses still being held there, but he was many weeks too late. Only twenty-four hours after their trial, Angus Ross and his sons were placed on board a ship and carried to the rotting prison hulks lying at anchor off the foul-smelling mudflats of Woolwich.

On his return from Inverness, MacCrimmon learned that he had been summoned to play the pipes at a reception due to be held at Ratagan the following evening. It had always been a condition of the MacCrimmon tenancy that the head of the family would play for Cameron of Glenelg whenever a piper was required.

It was to be a grand occasion. James Cameron was entertaining a large party of important people from London, and two Ministers of the Crown and a royal duke would be attending the reception. James Cameron was out to impress his guests and 'Pipe Major' MacCrimmon was ordered to appear wearing the full dress uniform of the regiment raised by Cameron's father for his King.

In normal times such a summons would have been regarded as an honour and the reception at Ratagan have been an occasion for great excitement. Tenants and cottars would have flocked to the vicinity of the great house and watched from a respectful distance to see all that went on and to listen to the pipe music. As the source of such entertainment, Hugh MacCrimmon would have spent days practising; but right now he had other matters on his mind.

On the morning before the reception, Hugh MacCrimmon set out for Ardintoul to learn what had happened to the remainder of the Ross family. What he saw at the site of the eviction shocked him – and Hugh was not a man who was easily shocked.

There was not a house left standing along the shore and at first he could see no sign of life anywhere. Then he noticed a thin wisp of smoke rising from the blackened shell of a cott. He went to investigate, hoping to find the Ross family, but the ruin was occupied by two women. One was at least sixty years of age – and the other was her mother. Hugh had seen the younger woman before, but there had been a family gathered about her then. When he asked where they were now, the woman pointed vaguely in a southerly direction.

'Gone. To find work, they said, but I doubt I'll see them again. By the time they return I'll be dead. Me and mother both.'

'Why didn't they take you with them?'

'I'd ha' gone soon enough, there's nothing for me here any more, but there's no moving Mother. She can't hear, can hardly see and is able to walk no more than five yards at a time. She'll die here and be buried at Glenelg, where she belongs – and I'll die with her.'

As she was speaking the woman idly stirred the contents of a pot which was rested at a dangerous angle upon the fire. The smell that rose from the disturbed ingredients smelled foul.

'What are you cooking?'

'Mussels and seaweed. It's more than we had yesterday, or the day before.'

Hugh MacCrimmon was appalled. 'What of the people of Ardintoul – the old village? Haven't they given you help?'

'None – but who can blame them. Cameron has threatened to evict any man or woman who helps or feeds us. He'll keep his word and well they know it. That man calls himself a Cameron, but he's like no Cameron we've seen in Glenelg before.'

'Here, woman. Take these.' Hugh MacCrimmon thrust a handful of sovereigns at the woman. He did not count them, the amount did not matter. 'Have one of the fishermen take you somewhere better than this place. Away from Cameron land. When the old woman dies you can bring her back to bury her. James Cameron hasn't let out the graveyard to sheep yet.'

As the old woman bit into each guinea to test it was genuine, Hugh MacCrimmon said, 'I came here looking for the Ross family – those that were left after Angus went to prison. Do you know where they are?'

'Gone to the Lowlands.' The woman tucked the sovereigns in a hidden pocket somewhere beneath her skirt.

'Are you certain?'

'I'm not certain of anything any more, but I haven't seen Ailsa Ross or her brood for a week or more. Everyone else has gone south, so no doubt that's where you'll find them.'

Hugh MacCrimmon got the same answer from the residents of the old village of Ardintoul, although most were reluctant to even talk of the evicted cottars.

Hugh did not return to his home immediately, but instead he wandered among the blackened ruins of the cotts, becoming more and more depressed at what he saw there. The charred remains of treasured furniture strewn outside some of the houses was an indication that the occupants had been given no time to remove all their belongings to safety before Cameron's men moved in.

There were trampled crops here too, sufficient to keep a family alive during the harsh months of winter. It was usual in cases of eviction for a cottar to be allowed to remain in his home long enough to gather his crops. This had been a sudden and brutal dispossession.

Prowling about among the ruins of the settlement Hugh twice thought he detected a movement farther along the coastline, among the rocks beneath a towering cliff. When he saw it for a third time he was certain; someone *was* there. Scrambling over rocks and a section of fallen cliff he came to a tiny grassed headland. Worn by wind and sea it was now a tiny island, no more than ten feet across. Beneath this headland, on a ledge of similar size, a crude shelter had been erected. Around it was an assortment of empty shells. Here, squatting on the ground hunched over in pain, was Andy Ross.

23

The boy looked up in alarm at Hugh's shout and tried to drag himself inside the shelter.

'It's me, Andy, Hugh MacCrimmon. I've been looking for you.'

The boy's fear was replaced by anxiety as Hugh MacCrimmon scrambled down from the small headland. 'Don't come too close to us, MacCrimmon. I think . . . I think we've the cholera.' Hugh stopped twelve feet from the young boy. There were rumours of cholera in the cities of Edinburgh and Glasgow, but he had heard of no outbreaks in the Highlands.

'What makes you think you're suffering from cholera?'

Doubled over in agony, both arms crossed over his stomach, Andy Ross described his symptoms.

'That's not cholera,' Hugh MacCrimmon spoke with the assurance of a soldier who had seen more than one outbreak of the dreaded disease, 'it sounds to me as though you're suffering from poisoned food. What have you been eating?'

'Nothing for most of the week. Then yesterday I went down to the rocks gathering shellfish and one of the girls found some mushrooms up on the cliff . . . .'

'There are no mushrooms hereabouts! Toadstools, yes.'

Hugh advanced to where Andy rocked on the ground. 'Where are the others?'

Andy jerked his head towards the rough shelter, then bowed his head low, his teeth clenched to keep in a cry of pain. The makeshift home was no more than three feet high from grassy floor to turfed roof. Hugh ducked inside and was immediately aware of an unhealthy stench.

Ailsa Ross and her four daughters were lying on the floor, but not one of them so much as twitched a muscle as he crawled among them. At first, Hugh MacCrimmon thought they must all be dead. Then he heard a moan.

'Andy! Come in here. Help me get everyone outside.' The boy was ill too, but he would feel better if he tried to do something instead of sitting with nothing to think about but the pain he was in. When Andy crawled in through the entrance Hugh set him to work immediately. 'Drag everyone outside so I can see them. Quickly, now. There may not be much time . . . .'

Time had already run out for two of the girls. The youngest and second eldest were dead. Another was in a bad way, so too was Ailsa Ross. Hugh knew that there was no more he could do here.

A wooden bucket half-filled with water stood outside the crude shelter and Hugh thrust it at the boy. 'Try to get some of this inside them. I'm going to the village for help.'

The water would make little difference to anyone, but it would keep the boy occupied while Hugh was away.

In Ardintoul, Hugh MacCrimmon knocked on door after door, berating the occupants of each house and acquainting them with the condition of the Ross family. Eventually he had gathered enough men to bring the surviving Rosses to the village. In answer to their fears of what Cameron of Glenelg might do to them, Hugh informed them curtly that James Cameron would never know. All he required from the Ardintoul villagers was help in bringing the Ross family to the village and the loan of a cart. He would then use this to convey them to his own home.

The Ardintoul villagers had good reason to be afraid of James Cameron, but they were not without human feelings. When they saw the sorry state of Ailsa Ross and her family, all thought of their own danger was forgotten and mother, daughters and son were taken inside the houses where they were given food and drink.

The poisoned food had not affected Ailsa or Morna, the eldest daughter, as severely as it had the others. All they needed was warm food in their bellies. One of the elderly village women also brewed up a concoction of herbs for the whole family and within an hour Andy was able to stand without clutching his stomach. The survivors were on the road to recovery.

It was midday when Hugh MacCrimmon set off from Ardintoul with the wagon and the Ross family. Behind them they left two fresh mounds in the bleak, windswept Ardintoul graveyard. Inside the open wagon Ailsa Ross had recovered sufficiently to weep at the loss of another two children. As Hugh walked beside the wagon, his mind was filled with black thoughts of James Cameron. The landowner had done more to destroy the Highland way of life in a couple of years at Glenelg than the English had been able to accomplish in four hundred years of warfare.

*

25

Hugh MacCrimmon was late arriving for the reception at Ratagan and James Cameron was not pleased. Resplendent in a kilt of Cameron tartan and a jacket with gleaming silver buttons and buckles, Cameron was waiting impatiently in the entrance hall of his imposing house.

Petulantly, he snapped, 'Where have you been? You should have been here an hour ago . . . . No, never mind explaining now, I'll deal with you later. Go into the ballroom. When my wife and I take to the floor strike up a reel and keep it going until I signal you to stop. Get along, man – and look sharp about it.'

The ballroom, or great hall, was packed with guests, and it seemed each had tried to outdo the others in splendour of dress. Hugh MacCrimmon had attended many parties and gatherings at Ratagan, but never one such as this. James Cameron had decorated the great hall at vast expense and the light from a hundred-candle chandelier struck fire from the jewellery worn by women attending the grand occasion.

Smiling, as though the evening was going exactly as he would have wished, James Cameron led his English wife to the centre of the cleared floor, accompanied by the applause of his guests. Nodding curtly in the direction of Hugh, the landowner prepared to lead the guests in the reel he had been practising for weeks. As the bag filled with air, the discordant wail of the pipes filled the room. Suddenly a melody spilled from the pipes and Hugh MacCrimmon played as he had never played before – but it was not a reel. Slowly he marched down the great hall between James Cameron's guests, to the sound of a forlorn lament.

Behind him the landowner's leg was poised for the first step of the dance. It remained in this position until Cameron realised how ridiculous he must look and lowered it to the ground. At first he thought MacCrimmon was playing an overlong prelude to a reel. Only when the piper had slow-marched halfway down the hall did James Cameron realise that Hugh's choice of music was deliberate.

Releasing his wife's hand, the angry landowner strode the length of the room, his face suffused with fury. Gripping the piper's arm, he pulled MacCrimmon around to face him and the lament faded away in a wail of protest.

'What the devil do you think you're doing, MacCrimmon? I ordered you here to play for a ball, not a funeral.'

'I hope your guests will forgive me, Cameron of Glenelg, but I've been to both today. Here, in this fine hall, I see people who have everything. Jewellery and grand homes, fine food and drink, and a warm fire. Yet not many hours since I attended a sad funeral at Ardintoul. The funeral of two small girls.'

Hugh MacCrimmon stood a head taller than James Cameron and he looked down at him with an expression that no landlord would expect to see on the face of a tenant.

'They died because they'd eaten poisoned mushrooms and barnacles. It was the only food they'd had for a whole week.'

As a gasp went up from some of the assembled guests, Hugh MacCrimmon went on, 'I found their bodies in a shelter of sticks and grass on the side of a cliff with sick members of their family who were too weak to move them. Their home had been burned down about their heads. *Deliberately* burned down – on your orders, James Cameron. They died because you'd threatened the same treatment to anyone who dared feed or help them. Well, *I've* helped them. I've fed the family and they're beneath my roof at this moment. When they're well I'll give them money to travel to relatives in Glasgow – except for young Morna. She'll be staying on and will likely marry my son. I've defied your orders, James Cameron. I've saved the lives of a woman and children you'd have seen die – and now you can do your damnedest!'

'*How dare you speak to me in such a manner!*' For a moment it seemed James Cameron would strike the other man, but he controlled himself in time. 'You'll regret this, MacCrimmon . . . .'

'No. You have the power to make me suffer for my actions, but not regret them. If I have any regret it's that I've lived to see the son of Charles Cameron cast aside all that his father held so dear. You've destroyed your father's people and shamed his memory.'

'Get out! Leave this house *now*! I'll deal with you later . . . .'

'Before I go, there's something I need to do that will hurt me more than anything *you* can think of, Cameron of Glenelg.'

Hugh MacCrimmon took the pipes from beneath his arm and looked down at them lovingly. 'These were given to me by your father when he made me his Pipe Major. They led his regiment into battle on the day he fell and I played them over his grave in France. They've been my proudest possession – a reminder of a brave man – such sentiment is meaningless now.'

Before anyone could guess his intention, Hugh MacCrimmon walked to the fire burning in the huge grate and committed the pipes to the flames.

Turning back to James Cameron, he said, 'I've destroyed the pipes just as you've destroyed your heritage. Never again will a Mac-Crimmon play for a Cameron of Glenelg.'

Hugh MacCrimmon gave James Cameron a shallow bow.

'Good evening to you. Now you can continue with your ball – if you've the stomach for it.'

TWO

Transportation 1817

The foul stench of the prison hulk reached Angus Ross long before he saw the dismasted, obsolete man-of-war. The odour offended his nose and caught at the back of his throat. It was an evil, unhealthy smell. The smell of fear, degradation and despair. It was the breath of a once brave ship, that now had a terrible disease in its belly. Beside his father, sixteen-year-old Cathal shivered from both cold and apprehension and Angus Ross rested his hand on his son's shoulder for a moment.

The ship carrying the prisoners from Scotland had anchored in the River Thames during the hours of darkness. By morning a thick, clinging fog was swirling along the river, billowing off the sea. It brought with it an unseasonal chill and the chained prisoners took their places in the waiting boat, cursed and berated by cold and irritable sailors. There were fifteen prisoners being transferred to the hulk, all former inmates of Highland gaols.

After twenty minutes of hard rowing, the boat bumped against a ship's gangway and the dark, stained bulk of the prison hulk loomed above them. Indistinct faces appeared behind stout bars fitted to a number of small portholes in the ship's side. From inside rose a chorus of derisive howls and cynical advice was shouted to the new arrivals: 'You'll be sorry!' 'Hide your money now or the Captain will pinch it.'

The next hour was every bit as degrading as the prison ship authorities intended it should be. In a cage-like structure under the eyes of half-a-dozen guards, each man was forced to hand over any valuable he still possessed. Next, his chains were momentarily removed and he parted with his clothes. This was followed by a crude medical examination carried out by a surgeon whose breath was heavy with brandy despite the early hour. When the surgeon was satisfied that the Highlanders had brought no new disease with them, they were forced to take a bath in cold river water.

Still shivering, each prisoner was issued with a coarse shirt that scratched his skin, a pair of canvas trousers, and shoes. All were thrust upon them with a contemptuous disregard for size. When each man was dressed, chains were replaced on wrists and legs and a giant of a blacksmith fitted an iron weight of at least fourteen pounds about the right ankle of each man. This, one of the guards informed them, was in case any man should take it into his head to swim ashore.

Finally, the new arrivals received the attentions of a prisoner-barber, whose aim appeared to be to see how close he could crop each victim's hair without actually removing the skin from his head.

Suitably equipped for their new status in life, the prisoners were escorted to their 'quarters'. Moving awkwardly and painfully and chained to each other, the men were taken to a spot where a heavy, iron-bound hatch cover was set into one of the lower decks. Not until the hatch was surrounded by guards, each wielding a heavy wooden club, was it swung open.

The first of the newly-arrived prisoners was ordered inside. However, the babble of sound escaping from below was accompanied by such an overpowering stench that the man reeled back. He was immediately seized by two of the gaolers, who literally pitched him into the unseen dungeon with a total disregard for the man who was attached to him by a, fortunately, long chain. The howls from below indicated that the man's fall had been broken by his fellow prisoners, but by now the other Scotsmen were clattering awkwardly down the steep ladder to join their dazed companion.

Angus Ross was the last to step onto the ladder and he had to duck his head quickly to avoid having the heavy hatch cover slammed down upon him. It was as though the gaolers were in fear of being tainted by the foul odours escaping from within the evil-smelling prison hold.

Inside, as the new arrivals huddled together, other prisoners crowded around, firing questions at them about the outside world, their home towns and the crimes for which they had been convicted. At the same time, hands skilled in the art of pickpocketing were exploring their pockets in the hope that the prison hulk authorities might have allowed them to keep something of value.

There seemed to be only one other convict from Scotland. A small, bright pickpocket from the slums of Glasgow, he was pathetically pleased to have the company of some fellow countrymen. Picking out Angus Ross as the natural leader of the group, he looked about him quickly. Then, winking, he said in a low, conspiratorial voice, 'Don't you worry, I'll see you're all right while you're in here. There's nothing that Charlie Campbell doesn't know about life on board the *Ganymede* – and a man can't have too many friends on a prison hulk.'

'Have you been here long?'

After a lengthy silence Cathal Ross felt obliged to say something to the friendly Glaswegian as none of his companions seemed inclined to make conversation with him.

'Aye, three years.'

'Three years? Does it take that long to arrange transportation?' Angus put the question sharply.

'No, you'll be gone by the end of the month – but not me.' The furtive glance and the wink were repeated. 'If the court sentences a man to serve his time in Botany Bay it stands to reason he's not expected to enjoy life there. I've got influence around here. Friends in the right places. I'll serve out my seven years right here on the *Ganymede.*'

Murdo Ross growled, 'I'll take my chances with Botany Bay. At least we should be able to breathe. I can't imagine anything worse than being cooped up here like a worm in the ground.'

'Don't you worry, laddie. You'll be out in the air – and today. You've timed your arrival badly. When the night shift of gaolers goes off and the day shift arrives we'll all be taken ashore to work. I hope you're good at breaking stones, because that's what you'll be doing. Breaking them and heaving them into the river to make a breakwater over by the docks.'

'What about Pa? He's only got one arm. He can't break rocks . . . .'

'He'll need to learn to wield a hammer in his one hand – every man on a rock-breaking gang does his full share. There'll be no shirkers, not while I'm in charge of the gangs.' A big, shaven-headed man with red-rimmed, watering eyes broke into the conversation.

'I'll do as much as any other man – but no more.'

'See you do – or you might lose the use of your other arm.' The big man's laugh was echoed by some of the other prisoners.

The man turned his attention to Cathal. Suddenly reaching out he caught Cathal's cheek between thumb and forefinger. 'You're a likely looking boy. How'd you like to be chained to me instead of that sorry-looking bunch? I'd see you were well-looked after. You'd never go hungry – and there'd be a noggin or two for you to enjoy. Yes . . . I think you should come under my wing.'

As the pinch became a gentle pat, Angus Ross stepped forward quickly. Before the big man could guess his intention, he swung his arm and the steel cuff hit the other man on the side of the jaw. The big man dropped to his knees, momentarily dazed, but shaking his head, he let out a bellow of rage and began to rise to his feet, his eyes fixed on Angus. He never saw the blow from the double-cuffed hands of Murdo Ross which came down upon the top of his hairless head.

The big man pitched forward and lay unconscious among the dirty straw, scattered sparingly on the wooden floor.

Accompanied by the small Glaswegian, the three Highlanders retreated across the cell as a number of convicts advanced towards them, but the other convicts advanced no further than the unconscious man lying on the deck. Lifting him beneath the armpits they dragged him across the cell to where a water butt stood in a corner.

Charlie Campbell looked terrified. 'You shouldn't have done that, Bill Bloxham's a bad man to cross. Even the gaolers try to stay on the good side of him. He's a rough handful.'

'He's a bully,' declared Angus. 'The army had a fair share of 'em, but I never met one who didn't back off if he thought there was a likelihood of getting hurt himself.' Angus raised his one arm and hit the fetter on his wrist against the thick wooden wall. 'This is as heavy as the one on Bloxham's wrist and can do as much damage. He'll think twice about coming too close to us again.'

Charlie Campbell was not entirely convinced. 'All the same, you'll do well to take care. He'll try to get his own back for what you did to him today.'

At eight o'clock that morning the convicts from the *Ganymede* were led out from the hold and after being chained in groups of four were placed in boats and ferried ashore. There was no selection of the men for each group, they were taken as they came from the hold, but Charlie Campbell managed to join the three Rosses.

It soon became apparent that Bill Bloxham was going to make life as difficult for the Highlanders as he possibly could. His unofficial designation as prisoner-in-charge of the stone-breaking gangs meant that although he was still fettered, he took no part in the hard physical work. While the guards sat drinking tea and playing cards some distance away, Bill Bloxham walked among his fellow prisoners, a heavy stave in his hands. It was his task to detail the prisoners for their work and then to ensure that there was no slacking. He allocated the largest pile of rocks to the Rosses, and spent much of the day nearby, preventing them from taking any unauthorised rests.

Late in the afternoon, Murdo Ross accidentally dropped his heavy hammer. When he picked it up again he paused for a moment to rub the back of a hand across his forehead. Bloxham was there immediately, shouting at him to get on with his work and wielding his stick to some effect. The hot-headed Murdo would have rounded on the big man had Angus not restrained him.

'Forget it, Murdo. Don't give him any reason to complain to the guards about you. You'd be in the wrong, no matter the cause.'

'That's right, one-arm, you give him some fatherly advice, but it won't be long before one of you steps out of line. When it happens I'll be there, you can be sure of that.'

'You can be sure of something else, Bloxham. The day that happens – you're a dead man.' He held up his fettered wrist. 'I hit you with the flat of this wristband yesterday. The staple would make a fair-sized hole in a man's head, no matter how thick his skull. Pick on any one of us and it will be your skull, I promise you that.'

Bill Bloxham raised his stick as though he might strike Murdo once again. Instead, he suddenly turned on his heel and stalked away to another group of convicts who had been listening to the exchange. Going among them with his stick flailing, he called on them to get on with their work before he called on the guards.

Cathal Ross's expression showed the pride he felt in his father as he said, 'You were right, Pa. He is scared of being hurt.'

'That doesn't mean he's any less dangerous, for that. We'll need to watch Bill Bloxham very carefully in the future. He'll not miss any opportunity to take his revenge on the Ross family.'

The next few days were difficult ones for the Ross family. Every day they went ashore to work Bill Bloxham always allocated them the largest pile of rocks to break, and they were forced to work harder than any of the other convicts. Nevertheless, no more threats were made against them. Then, on Sunday, only six days after their arrival on board *Ganymede,* startling news sped around the hulk. A transport ship to carry them to Australia would be arriving the next morning. The revelation took everyone by surprise, the convicts having been led to believe that there would not be a ship available for at least another month.

Although the news was received with very mixed feelings, there was an air of great excitement on board the hulk that night. Elaborate and totally impracticable schemes for escape were abandoned – much to the relief of many who had committed themselves to take part in them. For convicts who had been on the hulk for months it was a time to rekindle hope that had almost died inside them. Others squatted on the floor and, squinting in the feeble light, wrote to loved ones whom they would never meet again.

Cathal was among the letter writers. He wrote to his mother, brother and sisters and addressed the letter care of Hugh MacCrimmon. He told them not to despair, but to look to the future with hope. The Rosses were good men and hard workers; they would prove themselves in the new land and as soon as they were released, they would make money and send for the remainder of the family. It would be an opportunity for a fresh beginning in a new land for every one of them: a new life together.

It was a hopeful letter, a young man's letter. It contained none of the fears that beset Angus Ross as he lay unsleeping in the filthy hold for much of that long night. He feared for the future of the two sons who lay on either side of him, and for the wife and young family left behind to fend for themselves in Scotland. He had no false optimism that they would ever meet again. All he could do for them was pray that young Andy might prove a better provider than his father.

The next morning, the men were mustered in the grey light of dawn on the upper deck of the prison hulk. Much to the surprise of Angus Ross, Charlie Campbell, the diminutive Glaswegian, mustered with them.

'I thought you had friends who'd keep you in this country until you'd served your sentence.' Angus spoke in a whisper when the guards were out of earshot. Talking among themselves was forbidden when convicts were parading, and anyone found infringing this rule received a hard blow from a guard's stave.

Charlie Campbell looked sheepish. 'It's the first time there's been anyone on *Ganymede* I'd like to travel with to Australia. It's made me realise how much I miss Scotland and my own kind. Besides, I don't want to have to get to know a fresh batch of convicts. With the exception of you and your boys they've been getting steadily worse. I couldn't survive another one like Bill Bloxham.'

Both convicts fell silent as the warden of the hulk and his senior men came along the chained ranks. With them was a choleric-looking man whom whisper quickly identified as the master of the transport, the *Hercules*.

The reason for his visit became clear as sick and elderly prisoners were weeded out and returned below, many in tears. Their return to the cells of the hulk marked them as doomed men. If the ship's master did not think a convict would survive the voyage to Australia he was unlikely to last long amidst the filth and disease of the hulk. But this was of no concern to the master of the *Hercules*. He was paid a bonus for every man he delivered alive in the penal colony, and a dying man was unprofitable. For such a man, imprisonment would end only when he was pitched unceremoniously into an unmarked grave in the mud of the Woolwich flats.

Not until a man who had lost the fingers of one hand was rejected did Angus Ross realise with a sense of shock that there was a distinct possibility he too would be returned to the hulk's cells.

'Close up against me, tight now.' The command was an urgent whisper to his sons.

Obeying the order, Murdo and Cathal shuffled closer as the master of the transport began to inspect their rank. He reached Murdo, eyed him from head to toe, and was about to pass on to Angus Ross when there was a sudden howl of pain from Charlie Campbell, chained on the far side of Cathal. The eyes of everyone in the official party turned immediately to Charlie Campbell and the master of the transport ship moved towards him.

'What's the matter with you?'

His face contorted with pain, Charlie Campbell held one foot clear of the ground. 'It was him . . .', he indicated the man standing on the side of him farthest from Cathal, 'he shifted his foot, to scratch the back of his leg or something, and dropped his weight on my toe.'

'I did no such thing!' The man accused by Charlie protested his innocence indignantly.

'Is this man a known troublemaker?' The ship's master pointed to Charlie. 'I'll have none of them on my ship.'

'He's a model prisoner,' the senior warden assured the sailor. He was anxious to be rid of as many prisoners as possible. 'You . . .' The warden dealt the man beside Charlie a vicious whack on the shoulder with his stave. 'Be more careful what you're doing . . . . And you . . .' This time Charlie Campbell felt the blow. 'Don't make so much fuss. You'll suffer more than a sore toe by the time you've completed your sentence.'

The inspecting party passed on and Angus Ross breathed his relief. The dangerous moment had passed. He was in Charlie Campbell's debt.

Two hours later the four Scotsmen were in a boat waiting off the gangway of the transport *Hercules* with twenty other prisoners. They were the first of ten such convict cargoes due to be conveyed from the *Ganymede* hulk.

The reason for the delay in boarding was the cause of much excitement on board the small boat. A barge had come down the Thames from London town with a hundred and fifty female convicts on board. They too were to take passage to Australia on the *Hercules*.

The convicts in the waiting boat were being viewed with equal interest by the women. Incarcerated in prisons, some for many months, they had been liberally fed with rumours of life in the penal colony on the far side of the world. One such rumour promised that if they married a convict immediately upon arrival, both would be freed and given land to farm. As they climbed the steep gangway extending up the ship's side, the women pointed and waved as they debated the qualities of the men destined to be their shipmates for many months to come.

Among the last women to go up the gangway was a girl of no more than fifteen or sixteen. Her pale, pinched face was turned towards the boat, now practically alongside the *Hercules*. She neither waved nor smiled, yet it seemed to Cathal that she was looking directly at him. There was something about her that caused him to draw in his breath with sudden unprecedented wonder. 'That girl . . . nearing the top now. She *can't* be a convict . . . .'

Murdo Ross smiled in amused affection at his younger brother. 'Did you hear that, Pa? Our Cathal's been smitten for the first time in his life – and by a *convict* girl! Mind you, I have to agree with him, she's a pretty one.'

'Because she's with them doesn't mean she's a convict too. She might be . . . well, someone's daughter.'

'Oh, she'll be *someone's* daughter all right. I can promise you that, young Cathal. But, in case you didn't notice, she has a chain on her wrists, same as all the others. She's a convict, right enough.'

'She won't have that innocent look on her face by the time she gets to Botany Bay, I can tell you that.' One of the seamen, leaning on his oar, had overheard the conversation. 'As soon as the women go on board the crew are given a choice of 'em. Captain first, officers next, and then the crew. Live like sultans, they do, on a transport voyage. As many women as they can manage. My brother's just come back from a voyage to Australia. Reckons if he'd had one more he'd have died of exhaustion. There was one ship spent so long becalmed it took nigh on a year to reach Botany Bay. By the time they got there they had a hundred more on board than they'd set out with — all of 'em newborn babes.'

The disbelieving laughter from convicts and crew that followed this story brought a stern command for silence from the boat's coxswain. The laughter caused the young girl to look round once more and Cathal watched in a furious silence as the girl disappeared over the ship's side to the upper deck.

By the very nature of its role, no ship in the transport fleet could be deemed 'a happy ship'. Fitted out to carry the maximum number of convicts in the minimum comfort needed to keep them alive, the role of the transport ships was to remove those convicted of breaking the law as far from their native land as possible. Yet even among this unhappy fleet the *Hercules* was known as a 'bad' ship.

The fault lay with the ship's master. Captain Hywel Jones was a weak officer in love with the bottle. At sea, on board ship – *his* ship – he was able to indulge his weakness. His crew had served with him for a long time. There were those among them who would never receive promotion, but who might even have suffered *demotion* on another vessel. Yet, for as long as Captain Jones remained in nominal command of the *Hercules,* they knew they could enjoy all the privileges afforded to officers far above their rank.

During the master's prolonged drinking bouts, responsibility for the ship rested with First Mate Hugo Skinner, and it was the only taste of command he would ever enjoy. Indicted for causing the deaths of three convicts on an earlier voyage, the charges against him had been dismissed even though he was unquestionably guilty. Nevertheless, he would never command his own vessel and Hugo Skinner vented his permanent resentment on those he blamed for his fall from favour: the convicts.

The Isles of Scilly were still in view on the horizon when the First Mate gave the convicts a taste of what they could expect on the long voyage. They had not yet been allowed to come up on deck, and as many had never before been to sea, conditions below deck were particularly foul.

The convicts were accommodated in heavily barred 'cages', built against the side of two lower decks, approximately fifty to a cage. Between these were narrow alleyways to allow the guards to maintain a constant watch on their fettered charges.

First Mate Skinner came below and stalked up and down the space between the cages, glaring in at the inmates. Most of the convicts recognised the First Mate's expression; he was spoiling for trouble and they kept their glances averted. One man, a simpleton, did not.

Skinner stopped opposite the cage where the man was fettered and glared in through the bars at him. 'You . . . convict. Why are you staring at me like that?'

The simpleton, unused to being singled out for attention, grinned. To the watching convicts it looked for a few moments as though First Mate Skinner was about to suffer an apoplectic fit. Yet all might have been well, even now, had not an unseen convict laughed.

Enraged, the First Mate pointed at the simpleton. 'That man will feel the lash! I'll teach him to try to make a fool of me. It's insubordination of the worst kind. Bring the convicts on deck to see it. I want them to know what to expect if they step out of line on this ship.'

The gaoler knew better than to argue with the First Mate. 'Yes, sir . . . how many lashes?'

'A hundred . . . . No, *two* hundred. Half today and the rest tomorrow.'

There was an angry gasp from the convict cages and First Mate Skinner smiled from one to the other triumphantly. 'He'll think twice before being insubordinate again – and so will the rest of you when you've seen what the lash does to him. All right, get him up top and have these gaol-scrapings brought on deck. The women too. They're the most spiritless lot it's ever been my misfortune to carry to Australia. The sight of a man's blood might liven them up.'

As convicts spilled from the dark prison-holds of the *Hercules* they were dazzled by the brightness of the sun high in the sky above. Waiting on deck with increasing impatience, First Mate Skinner shouted for the guards to 'Hurry them along!'

Anxious not to incur the displeasure of the bad-tempered ship's officer the guards wielded their long wooden batons freely in a bid to speed up the temporarily blinded convicts.

As their eyes grew accustomed to the bright sun the convicts could see that the women had already been brought on deck. A silent group in dresses of drab grey material, they stood on the far side of the man whose unfortunate lot it was to be the central figure in the afternoon's 'entertainment'.

Stripped to the waist, the simpleton's wrists were secured to the rigging above his head. So taut was the rope that he was forced to stand on tiptoe, his body muscles fully stretched. It was an unnecessary extension of his punishment and the convicts murmured angrily, only to be hastily silenced by the flailing batons of the guards.

Before the whipping commenced, First Mate Skinner came to stand between the two groups of convicts, his back to the simpleton. Glaring about him at the convicts, he said, 'You've been brought up on deck to witness the flogging of a convict for insubordination. The same punishment will be meted out to anyone — man or woman — who steps out of line whilst on this ship. You're convicts, scum! No one cares what happens to you. If you were all to die and be thrown overboard for the sharks not a soul would look on it as anything but a blessing. But you won't die – though some of you might wish you have by the time this voyage is over. You'll live, even if I have to send you ashore to Van Dieman's Land with all the flesh flogged from your bones. I'm Skinner by name, and skinner by nature. Remember it.'

Nodding to a powerfully built seaman who stood nearby running the leather thongs of a cat-o'-nine-tails through his hands, the First Mate nodded. 'Commence the flogging.'

When the first blow was struck and the leather thongs of the cat-o'-nine-tails cut into his back, the simpleton's body jerked in pain and shock. He looked around at the man who had inflicted the pain and his expression was one of bewilderment.

The second blow produced a whimper, the third a cry. By the time ten strokes had been laid on his back in practised, evenly spaced red weals, the simpleton was crying like a child. First blood was drawn at fifteen strokes and now the unfortunate victim was writhing in agony and pleading for the punishment to come to an end. By the time half of the hundred strokes had been delivered, the simpleton was frothing at the mouth and blubbering incoherently. His back was a bloody mess, the skin cut to ribbons by the blood-stiffened thongs of the cat-o'-nine-tails.

The punishment was being witnessed by convicted criminals, but it would be many months before they became inured to the sight of a flogging. Many of the women were in tears and tried to avert their eyes. But Skinner was watching, and a bellow from the First Mate was enough to bring a guard to the spot, wielding a stave.

Mercifully, the simpleton lost consciousness somewhere between the sixty-second and sixty-fifth stroke of the lash. It was impossible to tell more precisely because although the moaning stopped after the thongs of the cat-o'-nine-tails cut into the simpleton's back for the sixty-second time, the flayed muscles continued twitching while three more blows fell.

Even now the punishment was not over. When the seaman lowered the lash and looked towards the First Mate, Skinner reacted angrily. 'Carry on! If a punishment was stopped whenever a man feigned unconsciousness they'd all be passing out before they had a mark on their backs. I said he'd have a hundred lashes today and a hundred it'll be. If he tries the same trick tomorrow he'll take another hundred the day after as well.'

This time the growl that rose from the convicts could not be traced to any one man, and while Skinner ranted at them the guards waded in, lashing out indiscriminately with their heavy staves. When order had been restored the flogging resumed. Thirty-five more lashes were laid on the simpleton's torn back before he was cut down. The savage punishment had lasted for thirty minutes, but the memory of its brutality would remain for ever in the memories of those who saw it.

When the simpleton was laid face down on the deck, the First Mate expressed satisfaction with the seaman's handiwork, adding, 'Give him a dose of King Neptune's liniment before you lock him below with the others. I want him good and healthy for tomorrow.'

'King Neptune's liniment' turned out to be a bucket of sea-water, thrown casually over the simpleton's bloody back. Then he was linked to his fellow prisoners and carried by them below to the convict cages.

Most of the prisoners on board the *Hercules* had some experience of prison life in addition to the time they had spent on the hulk. If they had learned any lesson at all, it was that a convict needed to put his own survival above all other considerations. A fellow man's misfortune was something to be exploited, not pitied. Nevertheless, that night when the evening meal was distributed, any man who found a reasonably edible piece of meat in his bowl passed it on to the young simpleton.

Angus Ross took it upon himself to spoon food into the flogged man's mouth, while Cathal held him up. Cathal's task was not easy. Not a square inch of the simpleton's back had been spared by the cat-o'-nine-tails and he moaned in agony, all hunger forgotten whenever it was touched.

Later that night, Cathal lay unsleeping beside his father listening to the pain-filled whimpering of the simpleton.

'They won't really whip him tomorrow, will they, Pa? Not with his back the way it is?'

'It wouldn't have been done in the army – and God knows they were ready enough to flog a soldier for little enough reason. But this isn't the army. First Mate Skinner holds the power of life or death for us and don't you ever forget it.'

'But . . . surely we can do *something*?'

'Cathal, one of the most important lessons of life – and one of the hardest to learn – is knowing what a man can change and what he needs to leave well alone. Here, on this ship, you're a convict. In

First Mate Skinner's eyes that means you're on a par with a cockroach. He'd stamp on you and squash you just to admire the mess it made. We've done all that can be done. Leave it there, son.'

Cathal knew the wisdom of his father's words, but he lay awake for much of the night, his mind a turmoil of futile thought.

Early the next morning the cage door was opened and a party of guards entered. They examined the simpleton and the senior guard shook his head sorrowfully. 'This lad should be seen by a surgeon.'

Another of the guards snorted derisively. 'We haven't got a surgeon, as well you know. He never came back on board after that last night ashore in London. Anyway, we're well rid of him. He killed more men than the Mate.'

'All the same, this convict ain't fit enough for another flogging today.'

'*You* try telling that to the Mate – I won't. If he's made up his mind to have a flogging he'll not be particular who's on the wrong end of "the cat". I've spent thirty-two years growing the skin on my back. I intend to keep it there.'

'So do I – and we're not down here to play nursemaid to no convict. There's work to be done . . . .' Looking about him at the convicts the first sailor said, 'I want twelve good strong men – who's it to be? – and don't all rush to volunteer.'

Nothing pleasant had occurred in the lives of the convicts for a very long time, and it was hardly likely that their luck would change on a transport ship run by First Mate Hugo Skinner. Not one convict responded.

The sailor who had spoken sighed in an exaggerated manner. 'That's pretty much what I thought. Right. I'll have you . . . and you . . . you . . . .' Walking around the iron-barred cage, the sailor chose twelve convicts, Murdo and Cathal among them. As each man was pointed out another sailor unfastened the chain securing him to his companions, leaving fetters on wrists and ankles.

'Where are we going?'

Cathal plucked up the courage to put the question to one of the sailors as he followed him awkwardly up the steep ladder to the upper deck.

'So you have got voices.' The sailor spoke sarcastically, but when he turned to look at Cathal his expression was not unkind. 'This is your lucky day, lad. You're to have a morning in the healthy fresh air, holystoning the deck.'

'What's that mean?' Cathal asked the question querulously, fearing what might be involved.

'You'll find out soon enough.' One of the sailors behind Cathal banged his stave noisily against the wooden ladder. 'Step lively now. You'd better be working hard by the time the First Mate does his rounds or you'll suffer the same fate as your simple friend.'

Cathal quickly discovered that 'holystoning' involved nothing more than scrubbing the upper deck, using sea water and a block of limestone, the 'holystone', in place of a scrubbing brush. It was a task the sailors were happy to delegate to convicts, the rough surface of the stone being apt to rub skin from fingers and hands when used with any vigour.

The convicts had not been working for long when the sailor to whom Cathal had spoken on the ladder returned. After asking Cathal his name, he wanted to know the reason for his transportation.

'We'd had little to eat for days when we found an eagle feeding on a dead lamb. We took the lamb home and cooked it. The sheriff's men came calling and said the lamb was stolen. Maybe it was, but they couldn't take the eagle before the magistrate, so they took us instead.'

The sailor nodded in sympathy. 'You'll be a Highlander, then. We had a couple of dozen on our last voyage. From all I've heard it should be the landowners going to Van Dieman's Land in chains, not your people . . . . But I don't make the laws of the land. My job is to see this ship's kept clean. I've a special task for you, lad – and it's not one for a thief – bring a bucket of water and your holystone, and follow me.'

The sailor led the way to the stern of the ship where he ordered Cathal through a hatchway to what he referred to as 'the officers' quarters'. For Cathal it was as though he had entered another world. Nothing could take away the stench of a convict transport. Effluent from the convict decks seeped through to the bilges and permeated the whole vessel, but it was far less odious here – and everything was *clean*. The glass in the lamps, brass handrails, the wood of the bulkheads . . . .

'Set to and scrub this passageway, lad – and be sure you make a good job of it. That's the Mate's cabin along there . . . .' The sailor pointed to a closed door at the far end of the passageway. 'He'll be

43

out soon to carry out his rounds. Be sure he finds you working hard – and keep your nose out of the cabins. If anything goes missing you'll be strung up from a yardarm. You understand?'

Cathal *did* understand and he wished he were back up on the deck with Murdo and the others, but he nodded.

'Good! Now set to and start scrubbing. I'm trusting you to work on your own, but I'll be back to see how you're doing.'

Cathal set to work as though his life depended upon what he was doing. A few minutes later he was convinced it did. He heard a door open and close behind him and knew it was the door to the First Mate's cabin. Not daring to look round he scrubbed with renewed vigour. When footsteps came along the passageway, Cathal moved over to make room without slackening his pace.

Hugo Skinner walked slowly past Cathal and on across the newly scrubbed floor until he reached the foot of the ladder. Turning around, he eyed Cathal's handiwork critically for a few moments. Then, much to Cathal's relief, he climbed the ladder to the upper deck and disappeared from view.

Cathal was still working hard when he heard another door open behind him. He did not look around, expecting someone to pass him by at any moment, but no one came. Eventually he risked a glance over his shoulder – and the heavy holystone dropped to the deck with a clatter. Standing in a cabin doorway was the young girl he had first noticed when she climbed the gangway of the transport with the other female convicts at Woolwich. Suddenly Cathal remembered the stories the convicts told about the crew members on the transports having their choice of the women convicts to while away the days, weeks and months of a long voyage. This girl must have been taken by one of the officers who might still be in the cabin. Recovering the holystone, he resumed his scrubbing furiously.

'Do you want some bread and cheese?'

The girl repeated her low-voiced question twice before Cathal realised she was talking to him. Looking round at her he nodded, not daring to speak, although his mouth watered at the thought of the almost forgotten taste. He had not eaten cheese since the Ross family cow died. Before then his mother had made cheese frequently; delicious, Highland cheese.

He took the hunk of coarse bread and an equally large piece of cheese from the girl, almost afraid it would disappear before his eyes.

He wolfed down a huge mouthful, then broke off a chunk of cheese and thrust it in the pocket of his trousers to be shared with his father and Murdo. Hastily mopping up the crumbs he had dropped on the wet deck, he scrubbed furiously with the holystone, aware that at any moment a ship's officer might come from one of the cabins to find out why he had stopped working.

'What's your name?'

Cathal almost choked as he attempted to swallow the last piece of bread and cheese in his mouth in order to give the girl an answer.

'Cathal Ross. What's yours?'

'Amy MacDonald.' She sounded delighted. 'You're a Scot. My father was a Highlander from Inverness. He was killed in the war, at Waterloo.'

'My pa was in the war. That's where he lost his arm. Inverness is where we were sentenced to be transported. Pa, Murdo and me . . . .'

Looking up at the girl Cathal found himself suddenly at a loss for words. Her eyes were an incredible blue.

'Would you like a drink? There's some wine in the cabin.'

Cathal felt uneasy. 'What if the – your man, finds it missing?'

Amy laughed and it was a wonderful sound, one he had not heard for such a very long time. 'What if he does? I'll say I drank it.'

Seeing the expression on Cathal's face, Amy MacDonald stopped laughing and gave Cathal a long, calculating look. 'What would you say if I told you Sam Jolly, the Second Mate, is not my man but . . . my *uncle?*'

'Is he your uncle?'

When Amy nodded Cathal felt ridiculously pleased. He was also confused. 'Then . . . you're not a convict like the rest of us? But I saw you coming on board in chains.'

'Oh, I'm a convict, all right.'

'What did you do?' Cathal had stopped scrubbing and now re-sumed his work again with considerable energy while he waited for her reply.

'We were short of money when my father died and I was put into service. I was a servant in a big house in the country when a letter came to say Ma was very ill. The lady of the house wouldn't let me go home, so I ran off. I took some food with me – and some money – but only what they owed me in wages. I was taken up before I got home. By then it was too late anyway; my ma had died

45

and I was sentenced to seven years' transportation. My uncle – my ma's brother – offered to pay back the money and pay for the food I'd taken, but "my lady" wouldn't accept it. My uncle is a sailor, so when he learned I was being sent on the *Hercules* he got taken on as Second Mate. He said it wasn't difficult, no officers want to sail with Skinner. My uncle says he's going to report him when the ship gets back to England.'

Amy MacDonald seemed to be awaiting a reaction to her story from Cathal. When there was none she passed him a tankard half-filled with watered rum. 'Why are you here?'

Between sips he told her the story of the Rosses' convictions and she nodded sympathetically. 'My father used to tell me about the Clearances. I think it happened to some of his brothers while he was away at the war.'

Cathal handed the empty tankard to her and she took it back inside the cabin. The drink had left a warm glow in his stomach and he attacked the deck of the passageway with renewed vigour. When she returned to the cabin doorway, he spoke without pausing in his task. 'What's going to happen to you when we reach Botany Bay?'

'My uncle says he'll make sure I go to a good family. What about you?'

Cathal shrugged. 'I haven't thought too much about it, but I hope Pa, Murdo and me can stay together . . . .'

'Is Murdo the tall, red-haired one, with a beard . . . ?' Suddenly they heard voices at the hatchway leading down to the cabins. Amy barely had time to close the cabin door before the seaman who had detailed Cathal for his task clattered down the ladder.

'Come on, lad. I thought you'd have it all finished by now. It's almost time for you to go below again.'

'I've nearly done.' Cathal kept his head bent low over the holystone. He could taste the rum and water and felt sure the seaman must detect the heady fumes he was breathing out.

'Hm! Well, you must have been working hard when the Mate came out. He says you're the only one ever to have done the job properly. You're to do it as a regular job. It's the first time anyone has managed to please him this trip. You keep him happy, and me and my mates will save a little something for you at grub times, all right?'

Back in the cell-cage Cathal gave the cheese to his father and Murdo, and they savoured it much as he had done. Murdo was sceptical about Amy MacDonald's story, but he merely said, 'I haven't tasted cheese like that since we lost our old cow. You keep that girl happy, Cathal.'

Suddenly looking pensive, he added, 'I wonder what our ma's doing now?'

The pleasure of this unexpected titbit faded as Angus Ross thought of the wife and family he had left behind in Glenelg. 'Thinking about your ma and the others keeps me awake nights, Murdo, even though I tell myself there's nothing more I could have done. We'll just have to rest our trust in Andy and Hugh MacCrimmon. There's no one else can help 'em.'

The simpleton survived his second hundred lashes only through the skill and belated humanity of the seaman wielding the cat-o'-nine-tails. The blows were delivered on the least affected parts of the unfortunate victim's body, with the minimum force necessary to satisfy the sadistic First Mate. Even so, the victim sank into unconsciousness before the ordeal was over and the convicts' murmur of anger became a full-blooded roar, with the women's voices joining in.

The seamen and their staves were unable to silence the noisy convicts and Skinner, his face scarlet with fury, roared for them to be taken below. His orders were passed on by bellowing seamen, but the convicts defied them, even though blows were being rained upon them. A sudden thrill of unaccustomed power surged through the ranks of the chained prisoners, but it was shortlived. First Mate Skinner called out all the watches of seamen and armed with cutlasses and muskets, they surrounded the noisy convicts.

Raising his voice so that he could be heard above the din, the First Mate shouted, 'The order to go below will be given just once again. If you still refuse, I'll take four men from the front rank and give them each a hundred lashes. If that fails, I'll select four from the next rank and give them *two* hundred. I don't care if I have to give every man and woman on this ship a *thousand* lashes – you'll go below.'

Walking along the front rank of convicts he selected four men, saying, 'You'll be the first to feel the lash. Now, are you going below?'

An uneasy silence fell upon the ranks of convicts. Such a threat coming from another man might possibly be a bluff, but no one doubted that First Mate Skinner would carry out his promise. Without looking at his companions the first man selected for a flogging began shuffling towards the hatchway leading to the convict cages. The second man had the choice of pulling back on the chain that connected them, or going with him. He chose to follow and the remainder of the convicts went with him. The half-hearted 'mutiny' was over.

For the next few days the men waited for the First Mate to take his revenge on them — but nothing happened. The only change in routine was that the convicts were not taken on deck for exercise and the sailors holystoned the decks themselves. The only convict to leave the cages – and to see First Mate Skinner, was Cathal Ross. Called out to scrub the passageway in the officers' quarters, he made his way from the convict deck to the jeers and catcalls of his fellow inmates. While Cathal was carrying out his task the First Mate came along the passageway as before, passing Cathal without acknowledging the convict's presence in any way.

There was a very good reason for the First Mate's surprising failure to take immediate action against the convicts on the *Hercules*. Tenerife, the next port of call, was just over the horizon and it was time to sober up Captain Jones. There were duties for the ship's Captain to perform during the week they would be anchored off the Spanish island. Nevertheless, First Mate Skinner had not forgotten the convicts' disobedience. He would make them suffer for their misbehaviour.

Time was on the Mate's side. Ten days out from Tenerife the *Hercules* would clear the Cape Verde Islands and the ship would begin the long voyage across the Atlantic Ocean to Rio de Janeiro. For perhaps two months they would be out of sight of land. During these weeks the scales of justice would rise or fall according to the whim of the *Hercules's* First Mate. Time enough then to flog all rebelliousness out of the ship's convict cargo.

The *Hercules* dropped anchor off Tenerife, one of the Canary Islands, also known as the 'Fortunate' Islands. The sweet and heavy scent of the island's many flowering shrubs and trees failed to reach into the hold of the convict transport. Indeed, the convicts were kept firmly locked in their cages for the first few days of their stay. Only Cathal was taken out to perform his daily task and each day when he returned to the convict cage he was closely questioned about the island by the other convicts. He had an eager audience for his description of the island's mountains and lush green vegetation, but few of them believed him when he spoke of the vivid colours of the island's many flowering shrubs, which were plainly visible from the deck.

Cathal also reported a squadron of British men-of-war anchored nearby and although the convicts could not look into the future, these ships were to have a profound effect upon their miserable existence.

The chief naval surgeon serving with the British fleet chose to pay the transport ship a visit on the third day of the *Hercules's* stay at Tenerife. Cathal was at the bottom of the ladder in the officers' quarters, Amy MacDonald with him, when the surgeon came on board.

The naval officer was of sufficient seniority to have the *Hercules's* Captain greet him at the gangway and act as his escort. The two men paused at the top of the hatchway that led to the officers' quarters and Cathal and Amy MacDonald overheard their conversation sufficiently well for Cathal to pass it on to his fellow convicts later.

'. . . I wanted to come on board because I was beginning to worry. I haven't seen any of your convicts exercising on deck. I feared you might have sickness on the ship. If so, I've no doubt your surgeon would welcome some help.'

'We have no sickness . . . neither do we carry a surgeon. May I introduce my First Mate, Mister Skinner, he's in charge of the convicts. He also caters for their medical needs.'

'This is most irregular, Captain! You are aware that the regulations laid down for the transportation of convicts require you to carry a surgeon? It's a very wise ruling, if I may say so.'

'We had a surgeon when we began taking on convicts. Unfortunately he went ashore and failed to return. There was no time to find another. But this isn't my first voyage on a transport. There's little you can tell me about convict illnesses.'

Cathal thought the First Mate sounded arrogant, and it seemed the naval surgeon was of the same opinion.

'It takes little knowledge to recognise their illnesses, sir. I doubt you have the skills to give them the necessary treatment.'

'Convicts are not pampered on this ship. They're convicted felons, not fare-paying passengers.'

'I see.' The naval surgeon's words were clipped. His disapproval of First Mate Skinner's statement was evident. 'In that case, I must ask you to allow me to inspect your convicts and the conditions in which they are being carried. If you doubt my authority I have a letter here from the Admiralty . . . .'

'That won't be necessary.' Captain Jones's tone was conciliatory. 'We have nothing to hide on the *Hercules*. Mister Skinner will be pleased to escort you round the ship. Should you have any cause for concern, I trust you will come and tell me.'

'I will, Captain Jones, I assuredly will.'

Cathal and Amy retreated hastily. Slopping water on the floor, Cathal began holystoning noisily in case someone should come below. At the same time Amy spoke to him through the open door of the cabin.

'I wonder what will happen when he finds the poor man who was flogged by Skinner?'

'Perhaps he'll have Skinner removed from the ship.'

'He might even be arrested!'

'He deserves to be.'

It was the eager, unworldly chatter of two young people, speaking of what they hoped might happen rather than what could be expected from the naval surgeon's visit.

Later that day when the surgeon was shown the flogged man he expressed neither interest nor sympathy, suggesting only that the man's wounds should be bathed at least three times a day in seawater. Flogging was an accepted punishment in both navy and army, and the surgeon had seen worse backs than that of the simpleton.

However, the surgeon's tour of inspection did improve the lot of the convicts during the remaining few days they spent at Tenerife. He was concerned about the state of the prison cages and the fact that the convicts were not being exercised on deck. When the First Mate said the convicts had been in a mutinous state on their arrival at Tenerife, the surgeon dismissed the danger this posed. He pointed out that if the convicts were allowed on deck one prison cage at a time, an armed crew could contain them with ease.

The surgeon also thought the odour of the ship left a lot to be desired. He took his observations to Captain Jones with the result that the convicts were brought up on deck in groups that same afternoon to enjoy the fresh air, sun, and views of Tenerife. While they were on deck, selected groups of prisoners scrubbed out the cages with a mixture of vinegar and water. When this was done, salt water was pumped into the bilges and the accumulated filth floated out. It was a full twenty-four hours before the whole operation was completed, and the foul stench would never entirely disappear, but it was agreed that the ship was a much more pleasant place than before. The improved conditions for the convicts and First Mate Skinner's failure to punish them for their brief rebellion lulled the prisoners into a false sense of security.

Cathal's burgeoning relationship with Amy was disrupted only when her uncle was in the cabin while Cathal was working, and as a result, he grew careless. One day, when most of the officers including First Mate Skinner were ashore, Cathal completed his holystoning with more speed than usual and at Amy MacDonald's insistence went with her into her uncle's cabin. It was small and cosy in there and she had laid out a feast for him. It was more food than he had seen since his arrest – and for a very long time before that – cheese, meat, bread and fruit were set out on a side locker.

'What's all this? Where's it come from?' Cathal's fear was that it had been stolen and she would get into trouble as a result.

'It's all right, my uncle bought it for me – for us. Today's my birthday . . . .' She looked suddenly shy as she said, 'I wanted it to be something special . . . for you as well as for me.'

Eyeing the food, Cathal thought he had never seen such a wonderful spread. There was drink too – brandy, no less!

'Well, don't just stand there, eat something. If you don't hurry up the First Mate'll be back.'

She did not need to tell him again. He began cramming food in his mouth until he suddenly realised she had eaten nothing.

'I'm sorry . . . . Here!' He passed her a hunk of bread and a piece of meat. 'After all, it's *your* birthday.'

'I don't mind. It must be awful for you, shut away down below for most of the day.'

'It was much worse before I got the job of scrubbing the passageway and met you.'

'I'm glad we've met and been able to talk to each other. I like you, Cathal. I like you very much.'

Her hand found his and for a few minutes the silence in the cabin was such that Cathal stopped chewing on the piece of meat in his mouth because of the noise it made.

'Have you thought any more of what you hope to do when you get to Botany Bay?' Amy released his hand and broke the silence, much to Cathal's relief. He had been afraid that he would choke if he kept the large piece of meat in his mouth for very much longer.

Chewing and swallowing the meat quicker than was good for him, he said painfully, 'It's not much good hoping for anything when I get to Botany Bay. I've heard it's not too bad if you're not put on a road gang – I suppose that's what I hope – not to be put on one of them. How about you?'

She shrugged. 'I don't know. They say there are "factories" at Botany Bay that are no more than brothels. It's even worse in Van Dieman's Land. I . . . my uncle says he'll try to get me put out to a married woman, but he doubts if there are many there.'

Amy paused and looked away from Cathal. 'The women say that if two convicts marry they're given a piece of land and put on parole.'

'You mean . . . if two people get married they're not convicts any more?'

'Well . . . they're still *sort* of convicts, but if they keep out of trouble nobody bothers them.'

'It sounds much too good to be true.'

'Why?'

Amy had thought long and hard about this; she was not about to allow Cathal to dismiss it out of hand.

'We're *convicts*. Why should they bother to give us anything?'

'Because they want to do something with the land. Make things grow, feed everyone who's there and let 'em bring up families. So it becomes like an ordinary country.'

Cathal doubted whether any of what Amy said was true. Why should they take land from a man in the Highlands, force him to do something wrong and sentence him to be transported to Australia in chains — only to give him land and freedom once more? It seemed a most peculiar way of going about things.

'What if it *is* true? Wouldn't you like to be free again? You and me together? *I* would.'

When the implication of her words got through to Cathal his mouth dropped open. 'You mean . . . you and me . . . married?'

'Would it be so bad?'

It sounded like a very good idea — a wonderful idea. But still too good to be true.

'You might even be able to have your father and brother working on your own land. One of the women knows someone who did that.'

Speechless, Cathal looked at the girl before him. She seemed to have learned a great deal about life in the penal colonies to which they were heading. She was a bright girl. A bright *and* attractive girl.

'Do you agree, then?'

Cathal was taken aback by the speed at which Amy was taking matters. As though reading his thoughts, she said, 'We may not have another chance to talk about it.'

She was right. Cathal nodded. 'It's . . . it's all right with me. I'd like to talk to Pa about it first, though.'

It made him sound weak and indecisive, Cathal knew, but he was not a quick thinker, and this was far too important a matter to be settled by a hasty decision. He tried to put his thoughts into words, but Amy silenced him.

'It's all right, Cathal. I understand. I've thought of little else since we started meeting like this, but it *is* important – for *all* of us. I hope I haven't spoiled your appetite . . . .'

Fifteen minutes later, his stomach full and with more brandy than he was used to, Cathal reached a decision.

'I don't think I need speak to Pa about marrying you, Amy. It's a great idea and I admire you for thinking of it. I . . . . admire you anyway. I have from the time I first saw you walking up the gangway of the ship at Woolwich. I *want* to marry you, Amy.'

'I'm so glad! I saw you at Woolwich too, and I want to marry you, Cathal Ross.'

It was the first time Cathal had ever kissed a girl. It was made more difficult by the chains he wore on his wrists, but he kissed her until they were both gasping for breath.

Cathal was still holding Amy MacDonald when First Mate Hugo Skinner threw open the cabin door. Cathal had only half-turned towards the sound when a blow from the Mate of the *Hercules* knocked him to the ground. His last memory before he was kicked into unconsciousness was of Amy screaming.

Cathal Ross spent four days incarcerated in the dreaded 'black hole', deep in the bowels of the *Hercules*. It was a windowless box four feet square, with stinking water from the bilges sloshing across the floor with each movement of the ship. The primitive construction had been especially made to house recalcitrant convicts and designed so they could neither stand upright, nor stretch out full-length.

When Cathal was released and prodded up the ladders from the punishment cell, his cramped muscles caused him excruciating pain. The ship was underway once more and as he emerged onto the upper deck, the bright light of the sun seared his eyes. Cathal was aware that there were others about him and he was roughly grabbed, his shirt torn from his body and his arms raised above his head and secured to the rigging. By now his eyes were becoming accustomed to the light and he was able to see that every convict on board the ship was assembled on deck. Then Amy MacDonald was brought forward and made to stand only a few feet away from him. She too was fettered and appeared to have been weeping.

By twisting his head Cathal was able to see the First Mate standing nearby.

'She did nothing . . .' his voice sounded thick and unfamiliar, 'it was my idea . . . everything.'

'Very noble of you, I'm sure,' the First Mate's voice mocked him with heavy sarcasm, 'but I've got the truth from the girl. You've been caught committing a criminal act – stealing food. I won't tolerate thievery, and as for the other things you've both been doing . . . . It's bad enough when brats are born to convict women and sired by seamen who should know better. I'll not have bastards fathered by *convicts* on board my ship!'

First Mate Skinner was pacing up and down in front of the assembled convicts as he spoke. Now he stopped before Cathal. 'I'm going to make an example of you. No one plays Hugo Skinner for a fool. You'll receive *one thousand* lashes. Two hundred every other day . . . .'

The announcement brought an angry roar of protest from the convicts. Cathal was stunned by the First Mate's words, yet he could hear his father's voice raised above the others.

'. . . And don't think the girl is getting away scot-free. She'll receive fifty lashes – and she can think herself lucky she's not getting more.'

Now it was Cathal's turn to protest, but the First Mate bellowed at him to 'Shut up!' Beckoning to the sailor who stood nearby nursing a cat-o'-nine-tails, Skinner ordered him to commence the flogging. The sailor was reluctant – but his reluctance did not stem from humanitarianism.

'I don't know as I'll be able to lay on two hundred, Mister Skinner. If it hadn't been for them other four we just flogged I might, but I don't rightly know . . . .'

For the first time, Cathal became aware that the deck at his feet was wet with blood. It seemed that First Mate Skinner had *not* forgotten the convicts who had defied him before the arrival of the ship at Tenerife.

'. . . I'll do it for you – and make a good job of it.'

Horror was added to the sickness Cathal felt in the pit of his stomach as he recognised the voice of Bill Bloxham. He could expect no mercy at the hands of this brutish fellow convict.

First Mate Skinner sized Bloxham up approvingly. 'You certainly look as though you're capable of carrying out a satisfactory flogging – but if I'm not satisfied you'll feel the bite of the lash yourself.'

'You'll have no complaint about *my* work — and when I've done I'll still have strength enough left for the girl.'

Now Cathal heard Murdo's voice above the general din; he was shouting threats at Bill Bloxham.

'Very well. Someone release this man from his manacles and we'll see what he can do.'

When Bill Bloxham was free of his chains and was handed the cat-o'-nine-tails, Cathal held his breath, his body tense. Determined not to make a sound, he was unprepared for the shock of pain that coursed through his body when the leather thongs of the cat-o'-nine-tails struck and curled about his ribs. It took his breath away and left him gasping for air, like an old dog tethered in the sun. His teeth drew blood from his tongue when the next blow fell and although his resolution held, his body writhed in agony. At the tenth blow he was unable to hold back the screams any longer and by the time the count reached twenty-three he was sobbing, vaguely aware that somewhere close at hand a woman was crying too.

Cathal's body felt as though it were on fire and he stopped registering new pain after receiving sixty lashes. Yet he did not lose consciousness until twenty more blows had fallen. Bill Bloxham continued the punishment until the count reached a hundred and fifty. By this time no skin remained on Cathal's back and his ribs and backbone resembled the bones on a hung carcass in a butcher's shop. Angry in the knowledge that Cathal had sunk beyond pain, the First Mate ordered Cathal be cut down, declaring that the missing lashes would be added to the total of those still to come in ensuing days.

The seamen who cut Cathal down were those who had set him to work in the passageway. They carried him with unexpected gentleness to the rear of the convict ranks where Angus and Murdo Ross waited. As they chained his unconscious body to the others, one of the seamen said sympathetically, 'He's hurt real bad, but I've seen 'em live through worse. Mind you, if he has to take another eight hundred, or so . . . !'

'Get some sea water for my son . . . .'

A seaman lowered a bucket over the side of the ship at the end of a rope. Hoisting it on board he threw the contents over Cathal. The mutilated young Scot did not so much as twitch a muscle and the seaman left with a shrug of his shoulders.

Suddenly there was a roar of anticipation from the assembled convicts and they surged forward, leaving Cathal behind on the deck, secured to Angus, Murdo, and their fellow Scot Charlie Campbell.

Standing up, Murdo saw that Amy MacDonald had taken Cathal's place secured to the rigging. Her cheap, cotton prison-dress had been ripped down from her shoulders and left hanging in tatters about her naked waist.

'They're about to flog the girl . . . .'

The lash fell upon Amy MacDonald's bared back and she screamed. As the male convicts pushed forward for a closer look at the proceedings they cheered and shouted as though witnessing a dogfight.

Kneeling by the side of his younger son, Angus Ross stroked Cathal's forehead and mouthed words that no member of his family had ever heard him speak before.

Suddenly a shadow fell across Cathal's prostrate body. Looking up, Angus Ross saw the First Mate standing over him.

'Leave the boy. Stand up and see what his whoring has brought on the girl . . . .'

The First Mate's words were lost as Amy MacDonald writhed in agony and the excited convicts shouted bawdy and unsympathetic remarks.

Angus Ross came up from the deck in a swift movement that caught the First Mate off guard. Even as he opened his mouth to shout, the long chain looping Angus to Murdo Ross was looped about his throat and a quick movement of Angus's foot brought the First Mate to the deck.

'Pull, Murdo! Pull hard. *I want him dead before help arrives!'*

Murdo needed no urging. As Charlie Campbell looked on in ashen-faced alarm, father and son strained at the chain about Hugo Skinner's neck and the First Mate struggled in vain to tug the iron noose from his throat. As his face changed colour and his eyes bulged alarmingly, he made a few strangled gurgles and his heels drummed feebly on the wooden deck, but the sounds were lost in the uproar caused by Amy MacDonald's flogging.

'He's dead, Pa. We've killed him!'

Murdo's elation passed and his face became the colour of Charlie Campbell's at the realisation he had killed a man – even though that man was Hugo Skinner.

Angus had no such qualms. He had fought in a bitter war and had killed men with musket and bayonet. He had seen death in every possible form. He felt *nothing* for the dead First Mate; unlooping the chain from about his neck he stood up to accept what must come from Skinner's seamen.

But none of the ship's crew were running to arrest the two Scotsmen, or beat them to the ground and subdue them. The crew were as engrossed in the flogging of Amy MacDonald as were the convicts. Just then one of the convicts turned towards them. An older man, he had a daughter of Amy's age and was sickened by the sadistic flogging. When he saw Skinner lying on the deck and the Ross father and son standing above him, the convict's mouth dropped open and he turned to the man to whom he was chained.

More heads turned in their direction from men who shared a cell-cage with the Ross men. Hardened criminals for the most part, they would not raise a shout and attract the attention of their seamen-gaolers. Instead, there was a sudden, wordless movement of the convicts towards them and the body of Hugo Skinner was quickly lost amidst the grey and yellow uniforms of the convicts.

Some of the seamen saw the unexpected movement of the convicts, but at that moment Amy MacDonald fainted. Her back bloody and torn, her unconscious form sagged from the rigging. Women convicts began screaming for her to be cut down. Brushing their gaolers aside they pushed forward, intent upon releasing her themselves.

By the time order had been restored on the upper deck the body of Hugo Skinner was already in the sea astern of the *Hercules* and word was being passed among the convicts that the sadistic First Mate would maltreat his charges no more. Although many convicts were a party to the disposal of the body, no more than three knew *how* he had died. They would never tell.

After the women had been beaten back from the unconscious Amy, Bill Bloxham stood uncertainly awaiting orders from the First Mate before resuming the flogging. Only now was it discovered that Hugo Skinner was nowhere to be found. A search was hastily carried out without success and it became increasingly evident that something untoward had happened. It left the Second Mate, Amy MacDonald's uncle, in charge of the ship.

While Amy was cut down, the Second Mate ordered that all the prisoners be taken back to their cells and secured, and he posted double guards on all hatches. Only when this was done did he commence a thorough search of the ship.

No trace was found of Hugo Skinner even though the ship was turned about and a vain search made of the area through which they had just sailed. An attempt was also made to sober up the ship's Captain, but after his enforced sobriety during the vessel's stay at Tenerife he had been making up for lost time. It would be days before he was in a fit state to make any decisions about the ship's future.

That evening the Second Mate called the ship's officers together and told them that he intended taking the transport back to Tenerife, to where they had left the British fleet. He would tell the senior naval officer of all that had occurred on board and ask for his assistance. It was to be a time of reckoning.

The Admiral in command of the British fleet anchored at Ten-erife ordered a board of inquiry to look into the circumstances surrounding the loss of the First Mate of the *Hercules*. At the same time the board would investigate all that had occurred previously.

Nothing was learned of the fate of Hugo Skinner, but the fate of one man paled into insignificance when the board realised the power Skinner had been able to wield over his fellow men, and how he had abused that power. Conditions on board the *Hercules* were compared with those on the slave ships trading between Africa and the West Indies – and found wanting.

So damning were the findings of the board of inquiry, that every officer was dismissed from the *Hercules* – including the Second Mate, who had brought the ship back to Tenerife.

A naval Lieutenant was put in command of the ship, with junior officers to help him and a naval surgeon to attend to the needs of crew and convicts. In addition, a party of marines was drafted on board and given the task of guarding the convicts for the remainder of the long journey.

There was great jubilation among the convicts when news of the changes filtered through to them. There was at least a chance now that most of them would arrive in Australia to begin a new life with a whole hide.

Not everyone joined in the celebrations. In the women's cells Amy nursed her sore back and wept for Cathal Ross, who had died during the night of the *Hercules's* arrival in Tenerife. Taken ashore, he was buried without ceremony in a tiny Spanish graveyard overlooking the busy harbour. Cathal Ross's grave was marked by no headstone and he left little behind him but memories for those who had known him.

THREE

America 1818

Standing on the Manhattan quayside looking towards the bustling, dirty city of New York, Hugh MacCrimmon felt small, insignificant, and hopelessly out of place. It was a feeling that often came over him in large towns and cities. Yet before there had been the knowledge that he would one day return to familiar surroundings – to the Highlands. This time there was no comforting thought of return. The Highlands belonged to the past. America – although certainly *not* New York – was where the future lay.

Farther along the quay Robert and Annie MacCrimmon, with Morna Ross, were part of a huge crowd watching a paddle steamer. Churning the brown water of the Hudson River to a muddy froth, the ungainly craft was making heavy work of docking. Eventually the bosun of the strange, new vessel was obliged to call upon the help of those on shore. Minutes later, heaving enthusiastically on the ropes, the watchers brought the vessel alongside. The release of steam as valves were opened sounded like a giant, mechanical sigh of relief. Soon afterwards the three youngsters ran back to Hugh MacCrimmon, bubbling over with excitement.

'Did you *see* that, Pa? We brought the boat alongside. Have you ever seen anything like it in your life before? This is a *wonderful* country!'

Hugh MacCrimmon smiled, wishing he were able to share in their excitement. He had expected there to be people here to meet the immigrants from Scotland: to offer accommodation, work, or merely to pass on information. Such help had been promised by those who had taken the passage-money from them in Glasgow. But Glasgow was now many thousands of miles away across the Atlantic Ocean. On arrival in their new country, however, the immigrants had been subject to a minimum of formalities before being deposited on the quay without so much as a 'Welcome to America!'

Hugh thought the residents of New York must be very prosperous not to want to separate the new immigrants from what little money they possessed, by offering to sell their knowledge. All around the busy quay small groups of Scots men, women and children stayed together. They were reluctant to break friendships forged during a transatlantic voyage of ten weeks' duration that had not been short of alarms and dangers.

Most of the new arrivals were far worse-off than the MacCrimmons. Some knew nothing of the land to which they had been sent by their late landlords. Few had sufficient money with which to embark upon a new life. They had agreed to make the voyage only because the uncertainty of a new land was preferable to the unrelieved poverty they were leaving behind.

'We'll not find a place to stay standing about here. Let's go and see what New York has to offer.'

Hugh shouldered a bundle of clothing and stooped to take the handle of a canvas and wood trunk. Robert MacCrimmon took the other handle, his own clothes tucked beneath his other arm. The whole family and Morna Ross had brought only as many possessions as they could carry, but beneath their outer clothing each wore a vest to which gold coins were stitched like the scales of a suit of golden armour. It was a great weight to have to carry around, but it gave the wearer a comforting feeling.

In addition to this ready cash, Hugh MacCrimmon had arranged for money to be transferred to a bank here in America. Compared with his fellow immigrants, the former Glenelg tacksman was a wealthy man. His cattle had held their weight during a winter that was mild by Highland standards, and driven south in the spring, they fetched a high price in the meat-hungry Lowlands.

MacCrimmon had sold his furniture to a southerner who had bought land across the loch from Glenelg. This same man had also purchased the windows and roof-beams from the house for a price Hugh would never have asked from his neighbours.

By the time James Cameron's anticipated eviction notice was served, Hugh was ready to leave. He was able to smile at the large force of sheriff's men mustered for the occasion and invite them to do their worst with all that remained of his lifetime home. Nor was the sheriff given the satisfaction of harassing him on the road south. Respect for the one-time Pipe Major extended far beyond Glenelg and the lands of James Cameron. Men came from all the adjacent communities, some travelling thirty miles, in order that they might tell future generations how they had escorted Piper Hugh MacCrimmon on the journey that was to take him from Scotland for ever.

Shamed by the example set by strangers, the residents of Glenelg left their own homes and took to the road to escort the departing tacksman. By the time the procession passed by the Ratagan home of Cameron of Glenelg, three hundred men and fifteen pipers were escorting Hugh MacCrimmon on his way.

It had been a proud yet sad moment for the Glenelg piper, and he resisted the urge to turn and take a last look at the land that had bred generations of MacCrimmons. There must be no looking back. It was impossible to forecast what the future held, but he had laid his plans with much thought. He faced life in the New World with more confidence than did others forced to leave the British Isles.

Hugh MacCrimmon also travelled with a dream. For far too many years he had held a tenancy which was subject to the whim of changing generations of landlords. In America he intended purchasing his *own* land; there was enough here for everyone. With hard work he hoped to pass on an inheritance to his son, Robert, and daughter, Annie. He was determined that they should have a future more secure than any they would have known in Scotland.

Nevertheless, Hugh MacCrimmon would never let them forget the land from whence the MacCrimmons had sprung. Scotland – Glenelg – would always be 'home', even though not one MacCrimmon remained there outside of the small, grey-walled churchyard. To this end he had brought a set of pipes so they would never forget the tunes that had always meant so much to the family generations.

Exactly where this new beginning would take place was some-what less certain. No one he had met in Scotland knew anything of the New World. Emigration agents had told of the wonderful life to be found in America, yet none he met had ever set foot in the country. They could offer no advice on the best areas in which to buy land. However, the problem was not too serious. Hugh MacCrimmon was a careful man. He would assess the country and its prospects before making any decision on where to settle with his two children and Morna Ross.

The small group made its way in the direction of the residential part of New York. Here, on the edge of the trading area, Hugh MacCrimmon found lodgings in a clean and respectable house owned by a German woman who spoke only a little English.

The next few days were spent in a fruitless attempt to find someone who knew anything of the country beyond New York. Finally, Hugh and Robert MacCrimmon paid a visit to a man named Garfield Ferris who advertised in a New York newspaper, offering cheap land for sale in America's largely unexplored 'Western Territories'. The advertisement claimed that the soil in these lands was so rich that a man had only to scratch the surface to plant his seeds; the climate so warm and equable, a man could grow two crops every year if he chose.

Hugh and Robert found the 'land salesman' living in a squalid hovel. Over the doorway a rough-painted sign advertised Garfield Ferris's 'vocation'. With the land agent was a woman with features and colouring that Hugh MacCrimmon would one day recognise as belonging to an American Indian. Ferris had obviously been drinking, but in answer to Hugh's questioning it was apparent he knew the country to the west of New York, although he seemed less certain of its potential for cultivation. After being asked a number of searching questions, he sent the woman hurrying from the hut, giving her brisk instructions in an unintelligible tongue.

'Come now . . . Mister MacCrimmon, d'you say? Just sit down a while and help me empty this jug of whisky. I've sent for some friends. They'll be able to answer all your very intelligent questions. Not only that, them and I will set you on the trail to a land that has more to offer a man than Eden ever had. Why, there are Indian women out there just waiting to throw themselves at your feet for a fistful of beads. A man need never be short of a woman in the west. . . .'

'I'll be taking two young girls with me. What has the country to offer *them*?' Hugh was not impressed with Mr Garfield Ferris, but this was the first man he had met who claimed to know anything at all of the land to the west of New York.

'Two young girls? Well now, with me and my men to take care of 'em they'll enjoy the trip, I promise you *that*. Once you're settled and folk start flocking out west to take up land, your two girls will be able to find rich young husbands to take care of 'em. How old did you say they are . . . ?'

'I didn't.' Hugh MacCrimmon was new to America, but he had seen enough of life to recognise danger when he met with it. He was beginning to feel increasingly uneasy in the company of this man. Ferris was no businessman; neither was he the type of man upon whose word Hugh MacCrimmon would stake the futures of himself and his family.

Standing up suddenly, he said, 'I thank you for your time, Mister Ferris, but me and my family will be looking elsewhere for land.'

'Now, now. Don't be so hasty, Mister MacCrimmon. You ain't even heard about the territory yet. When my friends get here and start telling you about the opportunities out west, you'll be begging for me to take you there. It's a chance you mustn't miss, Mister Mac-Crimmon, believe me.'

'I'll take a chance on what I might miss. Good day to you, Mister Ferris.'

'Now just you wait a while . . . . You've been wasting my time – *valuable* time. I reckon you should pay for that. It's the way we do things out here.'

'You advertised land for sale. It seems to me that you know nothing at all about selling land. So if you don't move from in front of that door I'll show you how we do things in *Scotland*.'

Garfield Ferris stood his ground only until the Highlander took a pace in his direction. Moving hastily to one side, he said, 'Look, let's talk about this some more . . . .'

Hugh MacCrimmon brushed the land agent to one side, then pushed Robert out through the door ahead of him. Once in the rubbish-strewn street, he said, 'Let's get well away from here before Ferris's friends arrive.'

They had not turned the corner when four men came into view at the far end of the narrow, mud road. Standing in his doorway, Garfield Ferris called to the men, at the same time pointing in the direction of Hugh and Robert MacCrimmon. The men began running and Ferris joined them as they passed by his 'office'.

'Run for your life!' Hugh MacCrimmon set an example, his son at his side.

Dodging along narrow side streets, the two Scotsmen tried to give Garfield Ferris and his friends the slip, but they were Highlanders, not townsmen. It did not take them many minutes to realise that they were hopelessly lost. Hugh had expected the last turn they made to bring them out on to a busy road close to their lodgings. Instead, the two men found themselves in a street filled with noisy saloons, beyond which was the river and the busy quayside. While the two MacCrimmons hesitated, uncertain which way to go next, two of their pursuers emerged from a narrow alleyway a hundred paces ahead. When Hugh MacCrimmon turned he saw Garfield Ferris and the remainder of his men behind them.

There was a saloon nearby. Grabbing Robert by the arm Hugh pulled him towards the open door, beside which a man was seated on a chair, hat tilted over his eyes and nursing a scattergun in his arms. Hugh thought he was dozing, but the man rose to his feet and barred the way before they made the sanctuary of the saloon.

'You'd best find somewhere else to settle your quarrels, friends. I'm paid to see there's no trouble in here.'

'We'll not be starting any trouble . . . .'

'Maybe not, but your friends might. Like I said, you'd best be finding somewhere else.'

The scattergun had a bell-shaped barrel that opened out as wide as a cannon's mouth. Hugh MacCrimmon did not doubt that the saloon guard would use it if the need arose.

It was too late to seek safety elsewhere. As Garfield Ferris and his men closed in, the 'land agent' murmured, 'Edge 'em down the next alleyway. It don't go nowhere except to the livery barn.'

'Keep your back to the wall and stay as close to me as you can,' Hugh MacCrimmon instructed his son.

A man lurched from the saloon, peered at the scene outside and called, 'Hey! There's a fight about to start out here with two men wearing skirts. Come see!'

His words brought an immediate response. Men spilled from the doorway like beans from a bag, surrounding the two MacCrimmons and Garfield Ferris and his four friends.

Hugh MacCrimmon breathed a sigh of relief. Onlookers would not prevent father and son from taking a beating, but their presence should ensure that at least they were not robbed.

Backs to the wooden wall of the saloon, the MacCrimmons stood shoulder to shoulder as Ferris and his men closed in cautiously, each side waiting for the other to throw the first punch.

'Come on, if it's a fight you're looking for let's make a start and have it over with.' Hugh MacCrimmon tried to goad Ferris's men to action. If the fight did not soon begin the onlookers might lose interest and return to the saloon.

Hugh MacCrimmon's words brought an unexpected response. A huge, red-bearded man standing a head taller than any other in the crowd pushed his way towards them. Another man walked in his wake. He too was big and powerfully built, but he was scarcely noticed behind his huge companion.

'The odds are pretty much in your favour, Ferris. Mind if me and Gil take a hand?'

There was the trace of a Scots accent in the voice and Hugh Mac-Crimmon's spirits soared.

'This is none of your business, Sam. Keep out of it.'

'Hell, who's talking of business? Me and Gil are joining in for fun. You help the older man out, Gil. I'll side with the boy.' Looking down at Garfield Ferris, the big man said, 'What's it about this time, Ferris? These two come asking for their money back? Or are they kin to them settlers who went west with you and was never seen again?'

'Hold your tongue, Sam Chisholm. You're not talking to a band of ignorant savages now. This is New York and there's a law against slander . . . .' There was anger in Ferris's voice, but there was something else too. Hugh MacCrimmon thought it might be fear.

'Go right ahead and find a judge, Ferris. After we've both had a talk with him we'll see which of us comes out of the courthouse smiling.'

'One day you'll push me too far, Sam Chisholm. Then you'll realise how big a target you make.'

Turning angrily away from the big man, Garfield Ferris pushed through the disappointed crowd and walked away stiff-legged along the road. Sheepishly his companions backed away from the saloon and followed in his wake. They were pursued by howls of derision as the crowd dispersed.

Extending a hand to the big man, Hugh MacCrimmon introduced himself and his son, adding, 'We're in your debt, Mister Chisholm – and unless I'm mistaken I place your accent as originating not too far from Glenelg.'

'You're not mistaken. I was born in Glenmoriston.'

Hugh MacCrimmon's expression registered delight – Glenmoriston was only a few miles from Glenelg.

'But I came out here as a boy. You won't have been here long or you'd have known better than to fall foul of Garfield Ferris.'

'He claimed to be an agent selling land somewhere out west.'

'The only land anyone's had from Ferris is a shallow grave somewhere in Indian country. No one who's set off with him and his men has ever been seen again. Come inside and have a drink. It's a long time since I spoke to a fellow Highlander.'

'I'd enjoy that, but I need to send Robert back to the place where we're lodging. The girls will be worrying about us.'

'Girls? Never mind, we'll talk about them later.' Sam Chisholm dropped a hand on the shoulder of the man who had accompanied him through the crowd outside the saloon. 'Gil here will see your boy home safely. Gil Sherborne's my partner. He's just about the best partner a man could ever have. Never a word of reproach from him, no matter what damn-fool scrape I get him into. Matter of fact, Gil's never said a word to anyone since Choctaw Indians took him prisoner and cut out his tongue.'

As Robert stared open-mouthed at Gil Sherborne, Sam said to him, 'Just tell Gil where you want to go, son. He'll take you there – but make sure you stay right with him. Garfield Ferris is not a man to forget and forgive in a hurry.'

When Robert MacCrimmon and Gil Sherborne had gone off together, Sam led the way inside the saloon and men moved from his path respectfully. It was noisy in here and men stood three-deep at the bar. However, it was impossible to ignore a man of Sam Chisholm's bulk. Reaching over the heads of other waiting customers he took a bottle and two glasses from the hands of a harassed bartender.

In a corner of the room two men sat in silence at a small table, staring morosely down at empty glasses. Flipping them a coin, Sam Chisholm boomed, 'Go get yourself a drink and find somewhere else to sit.' One of the men caught the coin and he and his companion weaved an unsteady course towards the bar.

The big man filled the two glasses from the bottle and pushed one towards MacCrimmon. 'This is what men drink in New York. A man with a recipe for good Highland whisky would make a fortune here . . . talking of which, what's brought you to America?'

The two men talked for some hours, during which time Hugh MacCrimmon's respect for the big man grew. Sam Chisholm was a 'frontiersman'. Spending most of the year in or beyond the small settlements that constituted America's far western frontier, he traded with the Indians for buffalo hides and furs. The frontier, Sam explained, was constantly being pushed farther and farther westwards, yet he suggested to Hugh that nothing that had occurred so far would equal the expansion America seemed likely to make in the next few years.

'There's a whole *continent* out there,' he said enthusiastically, 'empty land just crying out for people. The government's bought a chunk of land from the French that's damn near as big as the whole of Europe yet the only people there are a handful of wandering Indians. I tell you, there are wonderful opportunities for an ambitious man.'

'If this land is so good why doesn't everyone leave New York and make their way there?'

'I'm surprised you need ask such a question, MacCrimmon. Why do Highland cottars sit in their homes pretending there's no world beyond their four walls until the landlord arrives to pitch them out? I'll tell you why . . . because they're scared of the unknown. They may be dissatisfied with what they have, but it's *familiar. Safe.* Tell them there's a fortune waiting for them – but it's out *there* . . . .' Sam Chisholm waved his great arm expansively. 'Tell 'em that and they'll find a hundred excuses for staying right where they are. It's only when more folk come in – men hungry for land – that they'll spill over into the emptiness between the Missouri and Mississippi Rivers.'

'Mississippi?' Hugh MacCrimmon smiled. 'It has a certain ring to it. "Mississippi" and "Missouri". They're names I could grow to like.'

'No, there's no one *likes* the Mississippi or the Missouri. You either hate 'em, or it's love at first sight.'

Sam Chisholm looked over the heads of the nearby drinkers for a long time. Suddenly he rose to his feet and looked down at Hugh MacCrimmon.

'I think you're a man after my own heart, Hugh MacCrimmon. A man I could like and trust. If "Mississippi" and "Missouri" sound the same to you tomorrow, when neither of us has a drink in his belly, we'll talk of what the future might hold for all of us. Here's Gil coming in, he'll see you home. I need to say hello to a girl who won't have seen the outside of a saloon since before winter broke.'

*

68

The MacCrimmons, Morna Ross, Sam Chisholm and Gil Sherborne set off from New York in July 1818. They took along two wagons loaded with tools and equipment with which to carve a new life from the lands beyond the Mississippi River.

To reach their first destination, Fort Pitt, on the Ohio River, they needed to cross more than three hundred miles of constantly changing country. The first hundred miles of the great journey, from New York to Philadelphia, gave them no taste of what was to come. Early immigrants had settled here many years before. It was rich farmland and the area abounded with prosperous farms and villages. There were even one or two firmly established towns with churches and schools.

In this area Hugh MacCrimmon purchased good, sound live-stock to take with him to the new lands. A young bull and four cows – one with a small calf; eight sheep and a ram; hens, and a litter of piglets. Penned in a box strapped to the back of one of the wagons, the piglets kept up a constant squealing that Sam Chisholm grumbled would attract 'Every damn Indian for ten miles around'.

Sam Chisholm and Gil Sherborne rode horses. Sam told Hugh he'd spent so much time on one since coming to America that he'd come to feel naked unless he was sitting a horse. All the same, he advised Hugh to wait until they reached St Louis before buying mounts for himself and the family. St Louis was the river port where most 'frontiersmen' caught a boat to return them to civilisation. The cost of shipping a horse was not worthwhile. They found it simpler to sell their mounts for good drinking money, in the hope that they would have enough money left from the sale of their furs, or whatever they were taking back to civilisation, to purchase a new horse on which to return west – as most of them would.

After leaving Philadelphia, the countryside began to change. Almost imperceptible at first, it soon became more evident. There were fewer farms to be seen and those there were seemed to be hiding amidst the trees, as though their owners hoped they might remain inconspicuous, unnoticed.

The travellers had reached heavily afforested country now. Sometimes it seemed they saw nothing but trees for days at a time and whenever a small community was sighted it came as a surprise.

Hugh MacCrimmon noticed something else. Every man they met carried a rifle. In the few fields which had been carved from the forest land, where a man needed two hands to tend his crops, there was always a long-barrelled musket or rifle propped against a tree, no more than a few paces away.

When Hugh commented upon this to Sam, the frontiersman nodded gravely. 'Only a fool goes far from home without a gun, hereabouts. The Indians have been pushed off to the west, but the country's big and empty for the most part. Raiding parties have been known to come this far east when something's stirred 'em up, or if they have something special in mind.'

'Are we likely to meet up with any Indians?'

'Sure to.' Sam smiled at Morna Ross's wide-eyed question. 'But don't you worry, they aren't going to bother you while I'm around.'

Along the trail Hugh MacCrimmon had told the big frontiers man the story of the tragic break-up of Morna's family. As a result, Sam Chisholm had gone out of his way to pay Morna special attention. He did not find it difficult – Morna was a lively and intelligent girl.

'You mustn't get to thinking that all Indians are out to lift your scalp,' Sam added, 'although until you get to know 'em better it's not a bad thing to treat 'em as though they might.'

Morna shuddered in an exaggerated manner. 'I don't think I *want* to meet any Indians.'

'Every settler says the same, and some have done some pretty powerful praying on the subject, but if you head west you're bound to meet up with an Indian sooner or later. They're not all bad. Look at it this way . . . you and your folk have been thrown out of the Highlands by your landlord because he wants your land – and you know how you feel about it. The Indian feels the same way – and for the very same reason, but he has no long-standing clan kinship with us to stop him from fighting to keep what's rightly his anyway. If you think about it you can almost get to feeling sorry for him.'

Two days later the westward-bound party met up with another frontiersman travelling in the opposite direction to themselves. Riding on a wiry little pony and leading three heavily-laden mules, the newcomer greeted Sam and Gil with a whoop of delight that sent up a flock of crows from some nearby trees.

After much back-slapping and good-natured pummelling, Sam introduced the other man to Hugh as Ben Calloni.

'If you've any questions about Indians, this is the man to ask. Ben knows more about Indians – Shawnees in particular, than they know themselves. Ain't it so, Ben?'

'I've taken a Shawnee wife or two,' admitted the frontiersman. 'A man shouldn't do that more than once 'less he understands something about 'em.'

Ben Calloni became serious. 'Talking of which, rumour has it that old Broken Lance has crossed the Ohio. He won't find buffalo this side of the river, so it must be trouble he's looking for.'

'How many braves are with him?'

'No one knows for sure, but if he's come through Seneca country he'll have brought enough warriors to keep trouble away. I thought he might be after the wagon train, but they're travelling with enough men to fight off the whole Shawnee nation.'

'Wagon train? Where?'

'You don't know? Hell, they're carving a trail towards Fort Pitt that's wide enough for a city man to follow on a dark night. If you haven't found signs of 'em yet they must have come on the old trail – but you'll see their signs where the two trails join, a mile or two ahead. They've eaten the grass clear down to the roots for a mile on either side of the trail.'

Sam looked concerned. 'Maybe we should cut south for a few miles. What's the land like on that side?'

'Much the same as this. Plenty of trees and a few more farms, perhaps, but there aren't enough of you to upset any earth-chewers you come across. Anyways, you'll be better off keeping clear of the wagon train. There's a man with 'em I'd ride a few extra miles to stay clear of, even if I wasn't looking for good grass. You ever run across Garfield Ferris?'

Ben Calloni saw Hugh's expression change and he grinned. 'I see you *have* heard of him. You haven't wasted your time in this country, Mister.'

'Hugh had a run-in with Ferris in New York. That's how we met . . . .' Sam told the frontiersman of the incident between Garfield Ferris and the MacCrimmons.

Ben nodded and it was clear he was reappraising Hugh Mac-Crimmon. 'That explains why he's with the wagons. He couldn't do any business in New York. He'll be hoping to pick up a party of those who don't know any better from the wagon train. He might, at that.

It's the largest party of settlers that's ever passed this way. There's always some of 'em eager to settle land before they've learned to tell east from south, or friend from villain. You watch your back if you ever meet up with Ferris again, friend. He's long on memory and short on forgiving.'

Ben Calloni ran his tongue around his lips noisily. 'Goddammit, I can't remember when I ever talked quite so much 'less it was to cuss my miles. I'd forgotten how thirsty talking makes a man. You folks wouldn't happen to be packing a jug of whisky on one of your wagons, would you now?'

When Ben Calloni and the westward-bound travellers parted company the next morning, every man among them was convinced *his* was the worst headache ever suffered by a survivor from the night before. The frontiersman had also heard bagpipe music for the first time in his life and he was still shaking his aching head in wonderment as he rode on his way.

Away from the main trail, the going was harder than it would otherwise have been, but there was no shortage of grass for the animals. They found the farms of which Ben Calloni had spoken, but most had been abandoned, some for many years.

Gil Sherborne had taken to riding ahead of the wagons for most of the day, but on the fifth day after the meeting with Ben, the tongue-less frontiersman rode back to the wagons in the early afternoon and had a brief but animated exchange with Sam, using sign language. When the silent exchange ended, Sam looked about him quickly. They had been travelling beside a narrow river for some miles. Just behind them the river ran shallow for about a mile. On the far bank was a high bluff, from which the floodwaters of tens of thousands of years had scooped out pocket-handkerchief-sized beaches, strewn with pebbles and larger stones.

Pointing to one that was large enough to take the two wagons, Sam ordered, 'Get the wagons across there as fast as you can – but without overturning either wagon in the river.'

Before Hugh could ask any questions, Sam was turning the oxen of one wagon towards the river. The slow, ungainly animals were reluctant to take to the water, but Sam Chisholm's strength and determination was matched by his skill with a bullwhip and he won the day. As the swaying wagons pulled clear of the river on the far bank, Sam spoke to Hugh. 'Check your guns. Make sure they're loaded and primed. The spare guns too. Keep 'em out of sight, but put 'em where they can be reached in a hurry, if need be.'

'What is it? What's happening?' Hugh MacCrimmon was lifting guns from one of the wagons even as he asked the questions.

'We can expect a visit from Indians in a few minutes. Shawnee. This used to be their country, but they don't come back just to enjoy the view. If we're lucky they'll do no more than try to cadge food, but we're too small a party to take any chances.'

Ten minutes later the MacCrimmon party had its first sighting of an American Indian. No more than a dozen of them, they were mounted on wiry, rough-haired little ponies. The Indians rode neither with saddles nor stirrups, their only riding aid being a thin, plaited rein. On the far bank they halted, uncertain whether or not to cross the river to the two wagons.

Sam Chisholm had chosen his spot cleverly. There was ample room on the pebble beach for the two wagons and their oxen, but twelve Indians with their horses would have packed the small space tighter than sheep in a pen.

It was now that Gil Sherborne demonstrated his proficiency in the sign language. From the edge of the water his hands and arms wrote question and answer upon the air, while an Indian across the river responded in kind.

Sam understood sign language well enough to translate the silent exchange for the benefit of Hugh MacCrimmon and the others.

'The head man with 'em is called "Stone Cutter". He's been told where we're heading .... Now he's asking for food and drink. *Strong* drink.'

'Will we give it to 'em?'

'A little food, maybe – but no drink. It doesn't take much to get an Indian drunk, and he doesn't just get fighting drunk, he gets *killing* drunk. Gil's inviting only four of 'em to come over here.'

'What shall I give them?' Morna asked the question as she settled the cooking-pot more firmly on the fire. She had lit the cooking fire as soon as they stopped. Dry wood was always gathered along the trail, wherever it was found, and Morna had taken it upon herself to cook for the party. Hot from the task of lighting the fire, she brushed back a rebellious lock of hair. 'I've prepared only enough food for six. It won't go far if I have to stretch it for another twelve!'

'Add more water, and something to thicken it up – use anything. Indians aren't too fussy about their food, and they've no manners to speak of, but they're mighty strong on etiquette. Out here a man's expected to share his food with anyone who says he has need of it. Anyone who doesn't go along with this is likely to have it taken anyway – usually at the point of a gun. But *you* won't give it to 'em, Morna. When it's ready take out enough for us and they can help themselves to what's left. If they want to take some back across the river for the others, they will. If not, they'll go hungry. But I want you and Annie to stay well back, out of the way. There's a river between us right now, but even from here I can see that Stone Cutter is taking more than a polite interest in you – and that's not good news.'

As Sam spoke, the Indians' leader and three of his men drove their horses into the water and began to splash their way towards the wagons.

'What can we expect from them?' Annie MacCrimmon was as composed as though they were receiving a visit from neighbours they had known for years.

'They'll learn all they can about us, without telling us anything in return. If we stay on top of the situation they'll ride away again without so much as a grunt of thanks.'

'What if we *don't* stay on top of the situation?' This time the question came from Robert MacCrimmon.

'We'll need to shoot the first Indian who steps out of line. Bring your gun and come with me, and don't forget to give 'em a smile of welcome.'

Robert began a grin, thinking Sam was being humorous. By the time he realised the frontiersman was in deadly earnest, Sam was walking to the water's edge, the long barrel of a hunting rifle supported in the crook of his left arm. Lifting his own gun from a wagon, Robert followed the big man.

The four Indians brought their horses to a halt in the water just short of the riverbank. There was no fear in their expressions, yet they reminded Hugh of a quartet of Highland deer, ready to take flight at the slightest alarm.

When Gil Sherborne signalled an invitation for the Indians to dismount, they rode to the bank. Sliding from their horses to the shingle they handed the reins to Sam and squatted down in a seemingly uncomfortable position. While Sam tethered the nervous horses to a wagon wheel, Gil continued his silent exchange with the Indians.

'What are they saying?' Robert lacked the patience of his father and his question came after many minutes without a sound.

'They don't believe we're not carrying whisky in the wagons.' Sam spoke without shifting his gaze from the conversing men. 'The chief says he's never known white men travel in wagons without whisky.'

'What's Gil's answer to that?' Hugh put the soft-voiced question as Gil's hand pointed to sky, heart and mouth in continuing explanation.

'He's saying it's against our religion to allow strong liquor to pass our lips.'

Sam aimed a stream of brown tobacco juice at a lizard edging cautiously out from beneath a large flat stone. The reptile ducked back quickly.

'If the Indians start walking about and nosing inside the wagons, chase 'em away. We don't want them finding any drink. An Indian takes as kindly to being lied to as he does to being shot at.'

Gil brought the Indians to the cooking-pot when it had been boiling for no more than a few minutes, inviting them to help themselves, even though Morna Ross protested the food had hardly begun to cook.

The Indians ate their fill and left without taking any for the others on the far bank. They went protesting everlasting friendship.

When they had gone out of sight, Gil broke into a flurry of sign language once more. This time it was directed at Sam. Occasionally Sam interrupted with a question, but as it usually consisted of no more than a single word, the others were unable to follow what was being communicated by the speechless man.

When Gil had passed on all his information, the others waited for Sam to relay it to them. Instead, he said, 'Annie, Morna . . . have the Indians left anything worth eating in that pot? If not I'd be obliged if you'd put something on to cook for me.'

Instead of doing as the frontiersman asked, Annie stood in front of Sam, hands on hips and an expression of exasperation on her young face. 'If that's your clumsy way of getting me and Morna out of the way so you can tell Pa and Robert something you don't want us to know about, you can forget it. We're all in this together. If there's going to be trouble we want to be prepared too.'

Sam looked towards Hugh and received a brief nod. Grinning ruefully, he said, 'One day a man's going to marry you and find he's tied himself to a mountain cat.'

'He'll find I can purr as well as I can spit. What trouble are we going to run into?'

'None, if we're lucky. But there's trouble brewing for someone. Like I told you when the Indians were still on the far bank, Stone Cutter had his eye on you and Morna. He wanted to kill us and take the pair of you off with him . . . .'

This information brought an incredulous blink from Annie Mac-Crimmon, and a stifled gasp from Morna Ross.

'Don't worry, another of the Indians suggested you weren't worth getting killed for. He was reminded that he'd soon have all the white women he wanted! It's a good thing the Indians didn't realise that Gil understands Shawnee as well as he does sign language. If they did, they'd have had to kill us.'

'What did he mean? What white women were they talking about?' The questions came from Hugh MacCrimmon.

Sam Chisholm shook his head. 'I wish I knew. I'd say the wagon train was far too strong for the Indians to risk an attack. They probably intend attacking a settlement somewhere.'

'Shouldn't we warn someone?'

'We'll pass the word on to any settlers we meet, but I don't think the Indians will do anything around here. The pickings are far too slim.'

Gil made a grotesque noise in his throat to attract his partner's attention. When he had it he broke into another flurry of sign language.

'Hmm! Could be you're right, Gil.'

Sam rubbed his chin thoughtfully. 'Gil seems to think all this has something to do with Garfield Ferris and his friends. That could be the reason Stone Cutter's here. Ferris trades with the Indians, giving them whatever they want. It's known that he's supplied 'em with guns in the past. He'd not be above trading women to them too.'

'You can't trade . . . in *people*!' Morna was red-faced with indignation.

'You've a lot to learn, Morna. England's stopped trading in slaves, but you'll find plenty here in America – and men ready to go to war to keep things the way they are.'

'But . . . it's *unchristian!*' It was the worst thing Morna could think of to say.

'Perhaps, but you'd best keep such opinions to yourself until you're settled in and accepted as having a right to speak your mind.'

'We were hounded out of Scotland for speaking our minds against Cameron of Glenelg, and it sounds as though things are no different *here.*' Annie put in her opinion.

'I think what Sam's trying to say is, you've every right to speak your mind – once you *belong* to the country. We're still strangers.'

'I'm not at all sure I *want* to belong.'

'There's a part of you that never *will* be American, Annie. A part that will always belong to Scotland,' Sam spoke seriously and respectfully to Annie MacCrimmon now, 'but just wait until you see the country beyond the Mississippi. You'll fall in love with the land there, I guarantee you will.'

Sam Chisholm guided the two wagons to the Ohio River, at a point a few miles below the busy riverside town of Fort Pitt. Fort Pitt was the head of the river for the paddle steamers that had recently begun working this far upriver, all the way from New Orleans. It was also the starting point for settlers and trappers heading north and west. Fort Pitt was a busy, noisy, hustling town, whose growth had outstripped law and order. Sam Chisholm swore that if they took the wagons into town without an escort they would be stripped 'cleaner than a honeycomb in an ants' nest'.

Another reason for avoiding the town was because the large wagon train Ben Calloni had warned them about had reached Fort Pitt two days before. For a while prices in the riverside town would be outrageously high.

Sam Chisholm informed Hugh MacCrimmon that the two wagons and their occupants would travel down the Ohio River on a huge raft which the men would build from felled trees. The forest was retreating farther from the town with every passing week and such trees could only be found away from Fort Pitt. Every member of the party took part in the construction of the raft and as it began to take shape, Hugh MacCrimmon thought it looked more like a floating island than a man-made raft. When the animals went on board, Annie declared that it was more in the nature of a Noah's Ark.

The wagons, with their wheels taken off, would provide sleeping space for the girls, while a canvas sheet stretched between the two would provide a living quarter. Should they meet with hostile Indians the loaded wagons would also give them protection against arrows and bullets — but Sam did not pass this thought on to the others.

When the raft was almost ready, Sam and Gil took their horses and rode in to Fort Pitt to pick up some last-minute provisions and an extra stock of gunpowder. The two frontiersmen had still not returned when night fell, much to the consternation of Morna Ross, who felt something must have happened to them. Annie kept her own counsel. She believed, as did Hugh, that there was another explanation for the prolonged absence of the two men. Fort Pitt was a frontier town, with all the pleasures and temptations expected of such a place. In spite of Morna's pleading, Hugh declined to go to Fort Pitt to look for them, saying that the two men would probably not make the journey back to them in the dark, but would stay in town until the morning.

Hugh was proved right, and the two men returned to the riverside camp at breakfast-time. Gil was unusually cheerful, but Sam was considerably chastened. He had, he explained, met up with an old friend. They had much to talk about and when one drink led to another they had decided to make a night of it.

Sam Chisholm's explanation would have been received with more credence had his partner not been grinning behind his back and gesticulating with sign language that required no translation. His expressive hands described flowing, shoulder-length hair and a body far more curvaceous than the 'old friend' with whom Sam Chisholm would have them believe he had reminisced the night away.

However, Sam brought with him news that disturbed Hugh far more than the frontiersman's nocturnal activities. A number of Scots families travelling with the wagon train had employed Garfield Ferris as a guide. They intended travelling with him to the promised lands of the west where, according to Ferris, they would find a way of life to exceed all the dreams they had ever entertained of America.

'Are you telling me these people believe all that Ferris must have been telling them?' Hugh MacCrimmon was incredulous.

'That's the way of it. You said yourself that most are simple folk who've never come across a man like him before.'

'That's all the more reason for stopping them from going off with him. God only knows why he's bothering with them, they had little enough money to begin with. Most of it was spent before they reached America.'

'How d'you figure on stopping 'em? I spoke to the wagon master and he says he warned 'em about Ferris's promises. What more can anyone do? We're talking of grown men. They have to make up their own minds.'

'They're children compared to men like Ferris. I'll go into Fort Pitt this evening and speak to them myself. They'll listen to me.'

'They might, but you'd better take Gil along with you. Ferris has one debt to settle with you already. He'll not let you keep adding to your score.'

Hugh MacCrimmon never made the journey to Fort Pitt. Later that afternoon, when the men were working on the raft, they heard the unexpected sound of laughter – women's laughter. It came from the river, somewhere upstream towards Fort Pitt. As they paused to listen, the sound came again, a little closer this time. A few minutes later two rafts swept into view on the river. Neither raft was as large as that being built by the MacCrimmons, but each was heavily laden with provisions – and with people.

Hugh immediately recognised the two families, one on each raft. Both had travelled from Scotland with him on the immigrant ship. On the first raft was the Brooks family, mother, father and five girls aged between eleven and eighteen. On the second raft were the Johnsons. They had a boy of Robert's age and three younger daughters. Also on the rafts were Ferris and three of his friends.

If the land speculator recognised Hugh MacCrimmon and his companions he did not acknowledge the fact – but the Scots with him did. They shouted and waved as though they were setting off on a kirk picnic among the safe glens of the Highlands of Scotland.

'Hello, Hugh . . . Hugh MacCrimmon! You'll need to stir yourself or the best land will be gone long before you set off.'

'There's plenty of land for all . . . . Come ashore and have a drink of whisky to help you on your way.'

The Scotsman on the leading raft spoke to Garfield Ferris before replying, his voice carrying across a widening expanse of water that lay between them. 'We've no time now. We'll drink together when we all reach the promised land. Play us on our way, Hugh MacCrimmon. I'd hear the pipes . . . one last time.'

Minutes later, still waving, the families on the two rafts were lost to view as the river curved gently away from those watching on the bank.

Spitting tobacco juice into the waters of the river, Sam commented, 'Your friend's "promised land" is likely to be a six-foot plot covered by rocks – and that only if Ferris is in a burying mood. That raft he's on isn't built to carry them many miles. It would break up at the first hint of white water. I hope for the sake of the women they're carrying some money. Ferris and his men might be content to take it and head east – after they've had a little fun with the women.'

'And if they're carrying no money . . . ?' Robert asked the question.

Sam gave a non-committal shrug. 'They'll sell the women to the Indians.'

'What will happen to the women . . . if they're sold to the Indians?' Morna put the question hesitantly, not at all certain that she really wanted to hear Sam's reply.

'That's something you needn't trouble yourself about while we're with you, girl. Gil and me will never let Indians take you. We'd kill you first.'

The frontiersman's reply was intended to reassure the Scots girl but it served only to alarm her even more. However, Hugh's thoughts were still with the two families travelling with Garfield Ferris. 'We can't let anything happen to those families, Sam. You saw them . . . the young girls . . . !'

'So, say we catch up with them. What do we say – "Don't travel with Ferris and friends, they're bad men"? We'd be talking to grown men, Hugh. They've made their decision. Perhaps they can handle it.'

'You know damn well they *can't* – and so do I. I've travelled with them, on the ship from Scotland. They're Highlanders, shipped out here by landowners who wanted their croft and who led them to believe that putting fifty pounds in their pockets made them rich men. They'll trust anyone, because that's the way they've been brought up. If you won't help them, then I must. Robert, fetch the guns – and I'll need you to come with me.'

'Now hold on, Hugh. I know the country up ahead. You try to follow and you'll likely kill yourself fighting your way through the undergrowth. All right, if you want to go after them that's what we'll do – *all* of us – but we'll use the river. If we work hard we can have the raft completed, more or less, by nightfall and set off at dawn, we can't do it any quicker. It may be too late already. Stone Cutter and his Shawnees were expecting to meet someone pretty soon, as I remember . . . .'

The MacCrimmons, Morna Ross and the two frontiersmen set off next morning as soon as it was light enough to see any hazards that might be on the river.

There was plenty of water flowing in the river for the time of year, but the large raft was most unwieldy and difficult to manoeuvre. For much of the time the huge, removable rudder was of little practical use. It proved far more effective to push the craft away from danger using long, stout poles. It needed time and considerable strength to guide it around the occasional sandbank or island, and when it encountered shallow, fast-running water the primitive structure creaked and buckled alarmingly.

Hugh had hoped to catch up with the two rafts belonging to Garfield Ferris and the Scots families some time later that day, but it seemed Ferris was anxious to put as many miles as possible between the two rafts and Fort Pitt.

Not until the second day, when the sun was dipping beneath the tops of the tall trees that came all the way down to the river's edge, were the two smaller rafts sighted.

Sam Chisholm and Gil Sherborne were busy poling the big raft clear of a strip of broken water when Annie MacCrimmon suddenly put a hand to her forehead to shield her eyes from the low-slanting sun and peered into the shadows beside the bank.

Pointing to a spot deep in shadow, she called, 'Look! Aren't those the rafts, over there?'

Pulled in beside the riverbank, the two smaller rafts were partially concealed by low-hanging branches, and there was no sign of anyone near them. By the time the men were able to bring their own huge craft to the riverbank, the spot where they had seen the rafts of Garfield Ferris was almost half a mile behind them.

Sam told Hugh that this was to their advantage. Talking softly, he said, 'There's less chance of them hearing us and coming to pay a visit. It doesn't do to take chances with Garfield Ferris. I want you and Robert to stay here with the raft – you'd both be more hindrance than help in the woods. Besides, someone has to stand guard on the girls.'

Robert began to protest that he wanted a chance to take on Ferris, but he was quickly silenced by his father.

'Sam's right. We're more useful here than we would be blundering around in the woods. Get on and do whatever needs to be done, Sam. Robert and I'll look after things here.'

When the frontiersmen slipped quietly away into the forest, the two MacCrimmon men brought out their spare muskets and placed them with powder and shot in the canvas-topped shelter, between the wheel-less wagons.

Speaking to Morna and Annie, Hugh said, 'I want you two girls to stay in here so we needn't worry about looking for you if anything happens. If something unexpected occurs you'll have the guns close to hand. Don't hesitate to use them if the need arises. Robert and I will be at the end of the raft closest to the shore, but . . .'

Hugh broke off as the sound of a muffled shot came from somewhere deep in the forest. It was quickly followed by two more. Robert and Hugh exchanged anxious glances, but neither wanted to express his thoughts. Two of the shots might have come from the guns of Sam and Gil – but not a third.

'You think one of us ought to go and see what's happening, Pa?'

'No. Blundering around in the forest we're as likely to be shot by Sam or Gil as by Ferris and his men. We stay here.'

Behind them one of the hens began boasting that she had laid an egg. Hugh called back, 'Annie! Silence that bird – now. Wring its neck if you have to, but shut it up!'

He had hardly finished speaking when another shot was heard. This one sounded as though it came from much closer to the river, but it was difficult to tell in the dense forest.

'Something's going on out there. I wish we knew what it was.'

'Sam should have let me go with him.' Robert's voice betrayed his frustrated excitement.

'You needn't fret about missing out on anything. From what I've seen of this country already there's enough violence and killing for everyone to have a share. Don't be over-anxious to use that gun you have in your hand, Robert. There's no more to killing a man than squeezing a trigger. The work of a second, to destroy what the Good Lord's spent a long time in the making – and no amount of regret will bring a man to life again after you've killed him.'

There was a faint sound from the undergrowth and Hugh's long-barrelled hunting rifle came to the aim with a speed that was a complete contradiction to the advice he had just given his son. For a moment, neither man could identify the sound they heard next. Then the bushes parted not five paces from them and Gil Sherborne came into view. He was closely followed by three girls and Molly Brooks, wife of the man who had waved from the first raft two days before. The source of the sound the two MacCrimmons had heard was immediately apparent: one of the young girls was sobbing with fear.

Gil did not wait to set foot on the raft. Satisfied that the women had reached safety, he pointed first to himself, then indicated the way he had come. He promptly disappeared into the forest once more.

Hugh and Robert pulled the dishevelled Molly Brooks and her girls onto the raft, helped a moment later by Annie and Morna. Hurrying them back to the shelter of the wagons, Hugh asked the women, 'What's happened? What's going on out there now?'

Molly Brooks gathered one of the girls to her. No more than fifteen or sixteen, the girl was shaking violently and still making the sound Hugh had heard when the family were approaching the raft.

'Ferris and his men . . . they attacked us . . . .' Molly Brooks inclined her head in the direction of the girl she cradled in her arms. '. . . Jenny and me. They've still got Helen . . . and my eldest . . . .' Molly's voice broke as she said, 'God help them both – those men are . . . *animals!*'

The youngest of the Brooks girls began to cry and Molly reached out an arm to bring her into her arms with Jenny. 'They've got Marjorie Johnson and her three girls too. They shot her boy . . . and her husband.'

They heard more shots from the forest, much closer this time, and Hugh left the women and girls in the care of Morna and Annie. Returning to where Robert crouched at the front of the raft, they both peered anxiously into the dense forest undergrowth.

Before long they heard someone approaching in a great hurry. Moments later the huge bulk of Sam Chisholm appeared, closely followed by Gil Sherborne. Leaping onto the raft, Sam grabbed a pole and called for the MacCrimmons to do the same. Gil paused to slash the ropes with a knife from his belt then, after straining to push the raft off from the bank, he leaped on board. Gripping one end of the same stout pole, Hugh and Robert helped the two frontiersmen clear of the wooded bank.

Emerging from the wagon shelter, shedding children on either side, Molly Brooks cried, 'We can't leave yet. They've got my girls . . . and my Haemish!'

'They'll have us *all* if we stay. Go inside – and get the girls under cover. Someone's likely to be shooting at us before long.'

Hugh expected Molly Brooks to argue, or to plead with Sam to wait, but she did none of these things. Instead, gathering her three children about her like a mother with her chicks, she shooed them back inside the wagon shelter.

'Do you know what's happened to her other girls, and her husband?'

Sam's muscles bulged as he gave the final push that drove the big raft out into the current. Pulling the pole free of the water and laying it on the raft, he called, 'Robert, take the tiller. Steer well out from the bank – and stay out. If you come to an island, pass it on the far side.'

Not until Robert had gone to the rear of the raft to take the tiller that controlled the clumsy rudder, did Sam answer Hugh's question. 'The woman's husband is dead. No doubt the girls are wishing they were too. If Ferris's men have finished using them they'll have passed them on to Stone Cutter by now – along with the other woman and her three young 'uns – *get down, boy!*' Sam shouted the last instruction to Robert. 'Take the raft further out . . . you'd better learn to steer lying down . . . .'

Before Robert could ask for an explanation, Hugh saw a puff of smoke drift up from the bushes beside the river. Splinters flew from the tiller moments before the crack of a rifle shot reached the raft.

Wide-eyed, Robert crouched low as he steered the slow-moving raft farther away from the bank. Hugh fired a shot into the bushes where the gunpowder smoke was slow to clear, but there was no indication that he had hit anyone.

'There's an island near the far bank, about two miles downriver. We'll tie up there.'

'What if Ferris uses his rafts to come after us?'

'There's no fear of that . . . .' Sam saw the smoke of another shot and returned the fire as the sound reached them. '. . . Gil cut their rafts loose and pushed 'em out into the current. Ferris has lost his river transport. We might even be able to recover some of his stores if no one else gets to 'em first.'

'What about recovering the Brooks girls – and the Johnsons?' Hugh spoke quietly so the women would not hear.

Sam's face took on a grim expression. 'We haven't a hope in hell of getting any of 'em back even if we chased Stone Cutter all the way home. He's probably joined up with Broken Lance by now, and with the men he's got there's not enough white men this side of Fort Pitt to trouble them. If there were, he'd kill the girls and the woman before we could reach him. All that can be done is to pass the word around about them, and remember them for the future. If there's ever something Stone Cutter or Broken Lance need bad enough we might strike lucky and be able to trade for 'em. The other thing we'll do is to remember Garfield Ferris. If you ever meet up with him again, kill him. Someone should have done it years ago.'

'I can't go on . . . I keep thinking of what they're doing to my Helen and Eileen . . . .' Molly Brooks sat down heavily upon a rock, over-come by anguish. 'And there's Haemish . . . . What if he's *not* dead, but lying hurt somewhere?'

It was an argument Molly Brooks had put forward half-a-dozen times since dawn. The whole party should have been two or three miles downriver by now, but the Scotswoman had adamantly re-fused to leave the island.

'Molly, will you walk with me – to where the children won't be able to hear what I have to say to you?'

Hugh spoke to his countrywoman and, after a moment more of hesitation, she nodded her head. She followed the Highlander to the shade of a tower of weathered rocks, balanced by nature one upon the other. From here the raft was not only out of hearing, but out of sight too.

Here Hugh turned to the woman. 'Molly, you've suffered a griev-ous loss in Haemish, and what's happened to your two girls would have unbalanced any mother. It's not a time for thinking straight – yet you *have* to reach a decision, for all our sakes – and especially for the future of the three girls you still have. Jenny in particular needs to settle somewhere and build a new life around herself. She'll never be able to forget what Ferris and his men did to her, any more than you will. But with something to look *forward* to, something to *think* about, she can push it behind her. It's something she *has* to do – and so do the rest of you, if life is to go on.'

'I know what you're saying makes sense, Hugh. I have a responsibility to the children – all Haemish's children, but . . . I can't bring myself to believe he's dead. And Helen and Eileen . . . . What if they've not been taken off, but are out there in the forest? I can't desert them. I *can't!*'

Molly Brooks began to weep quietly. Hugh gazed down at her sympathetically for a few minutes, then he took her hand.

'Molly, what I'm going to say to you now is probably the cruellest thing I've ever said to any woman – to any wife or mother, but it would be crueller were it left unsaid. Haemish *is* dead. There's no doubt of it at all, because the man who killed him took his scalp, to sell to the Indians . . . .'

Ignoring Molly's cry of horror, Hugh continued, 'Gil shot Haemish's killer and took the scalp from him. He has it, if you still need proof.'

'No . . . no . . . !' Molly moaned in horror at his words, but Hugh was not through yet.

'Now you have to decide what you want to do, Molly. Sam is quite certain the Indians have already carried off your two eldest girls. He says they'll be on their way westward, the direction in which we're heading. But it's a vast country and I can't promise we'll ever find either of them. They might not live too long. Sam says that many girls taken by Indians kill themselves the first chance they get . . . .'

Molly moaned again, as though she was in physical pain, and Hugh squeezed her hand in sympathy and understanding. 'I'll never stop looking for the girls, Molly, neither will Sam, Gil, or Robert. But we need to face facts. What you have to decide is whether you want to go westward with us, or return to Fort Pitt, to those you travelled overland with. Or you can return to Scotland, maybe. If that's what you decide I can help you with the money.'

Molly shook her head. 'There's nothing for me in Scotland any more.'

'I don't know what there is to the west – except land. I intend carving a farm from the wilderness for myself, Robert, Annie and Morna. We'll help you build a cabin on your own land if it's what you want – and give you stock to get started. It will be a hard life, but you have three sets of hands to help, and Robert and I will be near at hand.

'If this doesn't appeal to you we could leave you in St Louis. Sam says it's a fast-growing town, especially now the riverboats are plying up from New Orleans. There'll be no shortage of work – respectable work, for yourself and the girls.'

Molly was thinking now, her head bowed, and Hugh released her hand. 'A woman shouldn't have to be making such decisions so soon after losing her man and part of her family . . . but they must be made, Molly, and made *now*. Will you go on, or shall we take you back to Fort Pitt?'

When Molly Brooks raised her head to look at Hugh MacCrimmon she had regained some of her composure, although the horror of the tragedy she had suffered showed in her eyes.

'I've tried to do what you've asked, Hugh, and think of my girls – all my girls. I can't go back to Scotland because Haemish and the girls are all the family I've ever had there. There are folks we know in Fort Pitt, but they'll be breaking up and going their separate ways – if they haven't gone already. Besides, every time I met any of them I'd need to recount what happened here, in the forest.'

Molly shuddered. 'Jenny would never be allowed to forget what's happened. I'd rather go on, perhaps to St Louis. We could start afresh there. We're none of us strangers to hard work; no one who employs us will have cause for complaint.'

'Good! So I'll be telling Sam you and the girls will be staying on with us for a while?'

'Aye, if you'll have us. It's a brave responsibility you'll be taking on, Hugh MacCrimmon – for you and the others. Escorting six women along a thousand miles of river, through a land that spawns men like Garfield Ferris and the savages who have the girls. I'll do my best to come to terms with what's happened — for everyone's sake, but Eileen and Helen will never be far from my thoughts. I'll never be able to forget them.'

'None of us will forget them, but the question of you coming with us has already been discussed. You'll be in good hands, Molly. Sam Chisholm and Gil Sherborne are two of the finest men I've met anywhere. Gil knows what it is to suffer at the hands of Indians, and Sam Chisholm's from good Scots stock.'

'You and your boy are fine men too, Hugh MacCrimmon. Haemish said so himself when we passed you on the river. He'd be well pleased to know we have you taking care of us.'

The river journey to the junction where the Ohio River relinquished its own distinctive identity to the Mississippi River took the party almost two months.

It was a journey filled with incident. At times, on wide, mud-flat shallows they were hard put to find water deep enough to float the great raft. At other places they were swept along between high rocky bluffs on floodwaters that carried them at awesome speeds. They lost ten-year-old Rose overboard in flood-swollen rapids – and were fortunate to recover her clinging to a spray-soaked rock, a mile down river.

The travellers survived a partial break-up of the raft in a series of rapids, and only two days afterwards shot their way out of an Indian ambush in a shallow and sluggish stretch of the river. It was here that Robert shot and killed his first man: an Indian who rode to the very edge of the raft and was about to hurl his lance into the broad back of Sam Chisholm.

The party survived a similar trap set by river pirates who fired upon them when they refused to be lured to the riverbank by the promise of a party.

There were lighter moments, too. One occurred when they were overtaken by two smaller rafts. On board were Scots families who had been in America for five years, but who had recently been lured from the safety of the Eastern Seaboard by the promise of cheap land in the west.

That night the three rafts moored together and the forest alongside the Ohio River was filled with the sound of bagpipes, played by Hugh and Robert MacCrimmon. The younger MacCrimmon was maintaining the family tradition and was, to quote his father, 'a promising piper'.

There was time on the journey too for the men and women of the two families to assess each other's character.

Molly Brooks was an intelligent, hard-working woman who was as ready to take a turn steering the great raft through a section of swift-running water as she was to cook a meal, milk a cow, or tell a story. The stories she told her children had Morna Ross and Annie MacCrimmon listening attentively – and more often than not the men listened too. She was also indomitably cheerful and used her cheerfulness to good effect in helping her three daughters to put behind them memories of the treatment meted out to the family by Garfield Ferris and his men.

However, Molly could not maintain the facade for the whole time. More than once in the late evening, whilst the girls were sleeping, Hugh MacCrimmon would see her seated alone at the back of the raft. She would be gazing back along the river, as though wishing that time and the river current might be reversed and she be carried back to Fort Pitt, her husband, and the two daughters she had lost. Hugh would allow her only a few minutes of such sad-memory time before making his way to her with a drop of whisky, ostensibly to chase away the chill of the night.

Pretending not to notice the tears that occasionally glistened in her eyes in the darkness, Hugh MacCrimmon would squat beside her on the rough-bark logs of the raft. Chatting about the countryside they had passed through, the animals they had seen, the weather, and other inconsequential matters, he would talk her through the loneliest hour of her day. Then, when she had retired to her own bed, he would remain behind smoking a pipe of tobacco as he thought the lonely thoughts he was unable to share with anyone.

One morning, shortly before noon, Sam called the attention of the others to a large cluster of cabins on the north bank of the river. It was the largest settlement they had seen since leaving Fort Pitt, with high levees and wooden quays leaning out over the sluggish water.

'That's Cairo, back of those quays. The damn-fool men who built the town will be sitting there right now, waiting for steamers and freight to come upriver to offload on their jetties, fill the warehouses and make their fortunes. They'll need to wait a very long time.'

'Why?' The question came from Robert MacCrimmon.

'Because no one can see any reason for putting in to Cairo, that's why. Folks heading west are either on the river, or travelling the south bank. Anyone heading east won't be travelling this way, and north-south river traffic has no reason to stop.'

'Then why was the town built right here?'

'Seemed a good spot to put it, I suppose. The place where two great rivers like the Ohio and the Mississippi meet.'

'The *Mississippi*?' This time the surprised question came from Hugh MacCrimmon.

'That's right. You see the change in the colour of the water over there . . . as though someone's painted a line down the middle? The clear water's the Ohio, the mud belongs to the Mississippi. The easy part of the journey's over, folks. We'll drift the raft to the far bank of the Mississippi and unload. There are one or two settlements over there where we should be able to sell the logs. If no one wants them one of the river-steamers trading up to St Louis will buy them from us for fuel. There should be no shortage of buyers – chances are we'll make a tidy profit.'

As Sam spoke, Hugh was watching Molly: her face had gone deathly pale. The woman who had been a pillar of strength to her family throughout the journey, and during the ordeal they had suffered in the forest, realised that the support *she* had come to rely upon was about to be taken away from her. She had to take full responsibility for the well-being of the three young girls once more, and Molly Brooks felt suddenly more vulnerable than the youngest of her children.

That night the whole party spent its first night on the soil of Missouri territory. When Gil Sherborne returned from a brief hunting trip with a sizeable buck borne across his shoulders, cooking began immediately. The whisky jar was brought out, Hugh MacCrimmon warmed up his bagpipes and a party got underway.

Later, Robert took over the bagpipes and played reels and dances in which the girls and the two frontiersmen joined with an energy and enthusiasm that made up for their lack of dancing skill.

While the dancing and whooping was at its height, Hugh saw Molly wander away from the firelight, heading down the bank to where the raft was moored. When she had not returned after about ten minutes, he set off to find her. There was only a thin sliver of moon balanced in the sky and high cloud hid many of the stars, but Hugh had no difficulty locating the Scotswoman.

Molly Brooks sat on the bank, gazing out across the wide confluence of the two great rivers. His footsteps had made no sound on the soft grass, but while he was wondering whether or not to disturb her, she spoke quietly, without turning her head.

'What's the matter, Hugh? Have you had enough of the jollifications too, or are you like me, needing to do some thinking?'

'How did you know it was me and not one of the others?' Hugh MacCrimmon was startled. He had made no sound approaching the riverbank.

Molly turned her face towards him and briefly he saw the white of her smile. He also imagined he could see the glint of tears on her face. If so, they would be the first he had seen for a while.

'If you ever hope to learn Gil Sherborne's skill in creeping up on folk you'll need to give up smoking that pipe, Hugh MacCrimmon. It's a comfortable aroma, for all that. I shall miss it.'

'Does that mean you've made up your mind what you want to do? You'll be leaving us?'

'It's not a question of what I *want* to do, Hugh. I need to decide what's best for the girls. Just thinking about it's kept me awake night after night on the raft. I've remembered the dream that brought us all to America, the dream that led to Haemish's death, and the loss of my poor girls: the chance to own land and farm it. I've thought about it until my brain is so clogged up with thoughts it can take no more. I can't do it, Hugh. I can't work a homestead on my own, and I can't tie the girls down to helping me. One day they'll want to marry and enjoy a life of their own.'

'I've already told you that Robert and I will help you all.'

'I know what you've said, Hugh, and I deeply appreciate your offer, but that's not the way a homestead needs to be run. You know it too, in your heart. You, Robert and your girls will have enough work to do on your own place if you're to make a success of it. No, I'll be obliged if you would stay with us until a riverboat comes by. Then me and the girls will take passage to this St Louis Sam talks about. We'll make out there. I don't have much money left, but it will suffice until we can find work. If St Louis is as busy as Sam says it is, we'll have no problem at all. There'll always be work for an honest, hard-working Scotswoman and her daughters.'

For a few minutes the only sound from Hugh MacCrimmon was the faint pull of breath on his pipe. Then he said thoughtfully, 'There's *another* alternative you might care to think about, Molly.'

'If it's returning to Scotland then I've already thought – and the answer is still no. I 'll not leave America while there's a chance that Eileen and Helen are still living.'

'I'm not suggesting you should leave America, Molly. As for the two girls . . . there's not one of us will ever give up looking for as long as we live. No, what I have in mind is something very different – and before you refuse it out of hand I'd like you to give it some deep and serious thought.'

'It might be easier for me to decide if you were to tell me what it is you're thinking of, Hugh MacCrimmon.'

'I'd like you to consider marrying me. I know it's soon after losing your husband, and I wouldn't expect to take his place in your affections right away . . . but we could make it work, Molly.'

Molly Brooks thought her gasp must have been heard above the sound of the pipe music coming from the camp.

'Why would you want to marry *me*, Hugh MacCrimmon?'

'You could do with a man in your life right now, Molly. A raw country like this is no place for a woman to try to bring up three girls on her own . . . and from what Sam Chisholm's said about St Louis I somehow don't think any of you would feel much at home there.'

'I'm not asking you to tell me why I should want to marry you. I could no doubt think of many more reasons than you can. I asked why *you* want to marry *me*.'

'We both need someone, Molly. Your girls need a father – and Annie and Robert have almost forgotten what it's like to have a mother. Soon I expect they and Morna will go their own ways, and a cabin in a new land will likely be a lonely place with no family around.'

'Is that it? You could hire a woman to provide the comforts of home – or buy a slave woman, maybe. Sam was telling me there are folks along the river keep slaves and sell them off like livestock. You've said nothing yet to persuade me to say yes to you.'

'I'm trying to convince you that such an idea makes sense, Molly. If I was to tell you straight away the *real* reason I want you to marry me, you'd likely tell me the sun has made me soft in the head, or some such thing.'

'Would I now? Tell me the "real" reason, Hugh, and let me be the judge of that.'

'I'm asking you to marry me because I've watched you during the weeks we've been on the raft. I 've come to admire you for what you are and to envy you your patience with the girls. You're one of the most gentle women I've ever known, yet there's an inner strength to you that refuses to let life beat you. I find myself thinking about you as I've thought of no other woman since I lost Robert and Annie's mother. The thought of having you go away from me now is making me very unhappy. It would leave a gap in my life that I'd almost learned to forget was there. The truth is . . . I've grown very fond of you, Molly.'

'Ah! Then you should have said that at the very beginning, Hugh MacCrimmon. It was *that* I wanted to hear. Marriage may be a solemn contract, as I've heard many a minister say – but it's more than that to me. Much more. It's not something to be entered into unless both parties are *fond* of each other.'

'I know, Molly, but you'd learn to become fond of me in time, I'm sure you would . . . .'

'You're a good man, Hugh. You have strength and courage, and yet I can see a gentleness in you too. It would be a strange woman indeed who could spend the weeks I've spent with you and not become fond of you.'

Hugh only just managed to save his pipe as his mouth dropped open. 'Does that mean . . . you'll marry me?'

'It does, but the loss of Haemish is still a raw wound. You'll need to give me time to get used to being . . . Mrs MacCrimmon.'

'You can have all the time you need, Molly! I – I feel like a young lad again! Shall we . . . can we go and tell the others?'

'We'll hardly be able to keep it a secret from them . . . but isn't there something you're forgetting? I'm not going to marry a man who's never even kissed me . . . .'

FOUR

Canada 1818

Clearing the long-established tenants and subtenants from his Glenelg lands did not provide James Cameron with a solution to his financial problems. He was far too heavily in debt. The restoration of the great house alone had cost him more than many gentlemen could expect to earn in a lifetime. The work had been supervised by the architect John Nash. Nash was currently basking in the favour of the Prince Regent and, as a consequence, was the most expensive architect in the British Isles.

In addition, James Cameron's English wife, Vanessa, was spending the rent collected from the sheep-grazers as fast as it was paid in.

The restoration of Ratagan and James Cameron's lavish entertaining were all part of a desperate bid by the Highland landowner to obtain an official appointment. He did not particularly care what it was, just so long as it carried with it prestige, or a degree of official power. It was his intention to use this as a foundation on which to rebuild the depleted Cameron fortune.

James Cameron entertained many men from Edinburgh and London who were in a position to offer him such an appointment – but none was forthcoming.

Vanessa's father, Cuthbert Lansdown, occupied a senior government post in London, but he too seemed peculiarly reticent about placing his son-in-law in any of the departments within which he had considerable influence.

Then, when James Cameron's many creditors were beginning to press him with particular determination, he was summoned to London by Cuthbert Lansdown, and the Scots landowner believed

94

that salvation was finally at hand. He wasted no time. Ten days after receipt of the long-awaited summons, James and Vanessa Cameron were passengers on board a ship riding the incoming tide to London Town.

At Woolwich, their ship passed close to the prison hulk *Ganymede*. Vanessa, standing on deck, turned away hurriedly and placed a handkerchief to her nose in a vain bid to shut out the stench which reached out across the water, polluting the air for a mile downriver.

'What a *dreadful* smell!'

The *Ganymede* behind them, Vanessa sprinkled scented water on her clothing to mask the clinging odour of the hulk. 'What must visitors from other countries think when they are greeted on their approach to the capital city of England by such an awful stench? I hope you are given a post which will enable you to have such hulks removed to places where they are not likely to offend decent, clean-living people. They could be moved to Ireland, perhaps?'

'It would be a popular move,' agreed her husband. He had been watching the other passengers, whose reaction had been the same as Vanessa's. He would mention it to Cuthbert Lansdown. It would show that he was taking a serious view of matters affecting the image of the country.

James Cameron brought up the subject that evening as he and Vanessa were dining with Cuthbert Lansdown and other members of the family, but it was not received with the approbation he had been expecting. Instead, it provoked an indignant outcry from the women and murmurs of protest from the men. Fixing his son-in-law with a look of stern disapproval, Cuthbert Lansdown suggested firmly that it was 'not a suitable subject for dinner-table conversation'.

The Scots landowner decided that the English had weaker stomachs than those who lived north of the Scots border. He was disappointed that he was not to be allowed to expound the ideas he had formulated on the subject of prison hulks in general. He was also somewhat peeved that as the dinner wore on, Cuthbert Lansdown made no reference to the reason for which James had been called to London.

Neither was there any of the deference he had been expecting from the husbands of Vanessa's three sisters. The girls had married well. One was married to the eldest son of a baron, another to an ambitious cavalry Colonel, the third to a wealthy ship-owner and merchant. All had always regarded the 'Laird' of an obscure Scottish estate with some amusement and James had often felt that Vanessa's father looked upon him less favourably than he did his other sons-in-law.

Not until the meal ended and the women had left the dining room did Cuthbert Lansdown suggest that he and James should retire to the library, for 'a chat'. It seemed the moment for which James had been waiting was finally at hand. Beaming amiably at his unsmiling brothers-in-law, James followed Vanessa's father from the room.

'Sit down, James.'

Cuthbert Lansdown indicated a large, leather armchair to one side of the polished marble fireplace, wherein burned a cheerful log fire. Instead of seating himself in the armchair's twin on the far side of the fireplace, Vanessa's father took up a position with his back to the crackling fire.

Cuthbert Lansdown had brought a full glass of port to the library with him and by the time he had taken a third sip without uttering a word, James was wishing he had not left his own drink behind on the dining table.

Flames had eaten away at the heart of the fire and a sudden collapse sent a funnel of sparks up the chimney and left a log hanging precariously over the edge of the fire basket. Cuthbert Lansdown moved to one side as his son-in-law took up a brass poker and eased the charred log back into the basket. Replacing the poker, he returned to the armchair and looked up to see the older man frowning down at him.

'James . . . . Why do you think I've sent for you to come to London?'

'Why . . . ? To offer me some official position. Is this not so?'

Cuthbert Lansdown's frown deepened. 'In a manner of speaking . . . . How deeply are you in debt, James?'

The question took James Cameron by surprise, but he tried to laugh off the alarm he suddenly felt. 'I don't suppose I owe more than any other Scots landowner. These are hard times. All I need is something to tide me over until things improve.'

Cuthbert Lansdown shook his head, his expression ominously serious. 'It's not what I've heard, James. In fact, I understand some of your creditors are contemplating bringing you before a debtors' court.'

James Cameron's surprise was genuine. *Gentlemen* were not sued by tradesmen. 'Why . . . that's *scurrilous*! They'll get their money . . . .'

'I can't take the risk of having my son-in-law thrown into prison for debt. It would do my career no good, no good at all. It might also have repercussions for other members of the family. On the other hand, none of us can afford to pay off the huge debts you seem to have accumulated . . . .'

Forsaking his place in front of the fire, Cuthbert Lansdown began pacing the room, followed by James's bewildered gaze.

Suddenly Lansdown stopped in front of his son-in-law. 'I've had a long talk with the others and we've come up with a solution.'

James was angry that his financial situation had been the subject of a family conference, but he was careful not to allow his feelings to show. One did not reveal anger in the presence of Cuthbert Lansdown.

'The first thing you'll need to do is sell your lands in Scotland.'

James stared at the other man in disbelief. 'Sell my lands! They've been in the Cameron family for centuries. Quite apart from any other consideration, these *are* difficult times. The land would fetch nothing like the price it's really worth. It might just satisfy my most pressing debts, but what of the future? I'd be left with no income at all. Such a state of affairs wouldn't suit your daughter. *It wouldn't suit her at all!*'

A pained expression crossed the face of Cuthbert Lansdown and he held up a hand to silence his son-in-law. 'Hear me out, James. I, and the others, have given this matter a great deal of thought, and not a little of our time. We have discovered a potential buyer — a Scotsman, Sir Alasdair Mackinnon. He's willing to pay the full value of your lands; enough to settle the bulk of your debts and leave you with a respectable sum of money. Sir Alasdair intends to enter politics and in consequence of this will shortly be resigning as director of a company he formed in Canada, the Upper Canada Trading Company.'

James Cameron opened his mouth as though to speak, but Cuthbert Lansdown waved him to silence.

'Allow me to finish what I have to say, James. I have caused enquiries to be made and the company he founded is a sound one, with considerable prospects. So much so that I have put in some of my own money. Because of this, Sir Alasdair is willing for you to become a director of the company. He will also make you a grant of six thousand acres of first class, afforested land – in Canada.'

'You want to send me and your daughter to *Canada*?' James shook his head. 'It wouldn't work. It just wouldn't work. Even if I felt there was a future for me there — and I *don't* – Vanessa would never agree to live in any primitive, faraway country. Things may be hard for me right now, but I can still give your daughter a comfortable home on my estate at Glenelg.'

'For how long?' Cuthbert Lansdown had to make a determined effort to control the exasperation he felt with his son-in-law. 'It only needs one creditor to take you to court and the remainder will follow like lemmings. You'll lose your home; furniture – and much of your land – and have nothing to show for the loss. Furthermore, you may expect no help from me. In order to safeguard my own position I 'll need to make it public knowledge that I disassociate myself from you. Regrettably, I realise that this will bring creditors clamouring at your door, but I will have no alternative.'

Moving to a cabinet in a corner of the room, Cuthbert took out a bottle and refilled his glass without offering a drink to James.

'So you see, James, you really have no alternative but to accept what is, after all, a remarkable opportunity for a young man. Especially one in such deep financial difficulties as yourself. I concede that Vanessa's extravagance will not have helped your situation. However, a stronger-minded man might perhaps have effectively kept her extravagances in check. Nevertheless, as my daughter is at least *partly* to blame for your situation, I have been able to procure a further incentive that should help in your future business dealings in Canada. It should also prove sufficient to persuade Vanessa to accompany you to Canada. When you agree to my proposition and arrangements have been made, you will be offered a baronetcy. You and Vanessa will arrive in Canada possessing an extensive land-holding – and a title – Sir James and Lady Cameron.'

*

Sir James and Lady Cameron travelled to Canada on board the emigrant ship *Lady Eileen* from Glasgow. It was neither a pleasant nor a comfortable voyage.

The vessel carried two hundred Highland emigrants in addition to the cabin passengers. The quarters occupied by the Camerons were vastly superior to those allocated to their impoverished countrymen and women, but even in the cabins the presence of the emigrants could not be ignored. The noise of their children and the stench from the overcrowded holds in which they were accommodated provided a constant reminder of the conditions in which they travelled.

Sixteen days out from Glasgow the grim-faced ship's surgeon addressed a gathering of cabin passengers. He broke the news to them that cholera had broken out among the unfortunate occupants of the overcrowded holds.

The spectre of cholera haunted every passenger who travelled the oceans of the nineteenth-century world – and with very good reason. From this day onwards the passing of time would be measured not in days, but by the number of bodies sent sliding down a tilted plank to a last resting place in an unmarked Atlantic grave.

Twenty-seven Scots emigrants died of the disease, seventeen of them young children, before the low, wooded coastline of Canada came into view.

Those who had survived dropped to their knees to offer up a heartfelt prayer, and as the ship drew closer the crew prepared the ship for docking. But the ordeal of the passengers and crew had not yet come to an end.

For seven days the ship was kept at an anchorage so close to the shore that two young men, impatient of waiting, went over the side to swim to their new land. Neither was seen again. Meanwhile, the ship was cleaned and disinfected from stem to stern. Not until no new cases of cholera had been reported for forty-eight hours did the Canadian authorities finally allow the remaining passengers to go ashore.

Although they had reached the new land, Sir James and Lady Cameron still had a great distance to travel before they reached their new home in Upper Canada. Landed at Fort Halifax, in Nova Scotia, their destination was the town of York, on the northern shore of Lake Ontario.

This part of their journey to York took almost as long as the voyage across the Atlantic. Almost all of the journey was made by boat, and the vessels used by the Camerons ranged from ocean-going sailing vessels, to canoes.

They found a thriving community in York. It was a township aware of its situation as the gateway to the vast and largely unknown tracts of Upper Canada. Here, for the first time since their arrival in the new land, Vanessa and her husband were accorded the respect she felt was due to a baronet and his lady. York had a distinct and accepted social stratum and James Cameron was delighted to learn that every office of importance in the community was held by a fellow Scot.

They remained in York for a full month and could quite happily have made their permanent home there, where the head office of the Upper Canada Trading Company was situated. But, although the King of England had granted James Cameron a baronetcy, he was only a *junior* director of the company. Before he could be of any real use, he needed to know how the company operated in the trading posts to the north.

With the short summer fast approaching its end, Sir James and Lady Cameron set off on their travels once more. This time they were heading for Murrayton, more than a hundred miles away in the region of the Kawartha Lakes. Named for Henry Murray, Principal Director of the company, Murrayton was the company's largest trading post. Here they would meet the founder himself and learn something of the business of fur trading.

The party set off in two huge, birchwood canoes, heavily laden with goods for the trading post. There were eighteen men in the party, all trappers, and they were led by a French-speaking Canadian named René Lesouris.

Whilst they were passengers in the canoes, the two newcomers to the party quite enjoyed the novelty of the journey, marvelling at the seemingly endless maze of waterways and forests through which they were travelling. Then, on the third day, the canoes were beached and their contents packed on the backs of the trappers. Then, shouldering the canoe, they set off across country, performing what Lesouris described as *portage*.

It became immediately apparent that, despite their heavy burdens, the trappers were setting a pace that would soon outstrip the speed of the inexperienced Scots couple. By the time the party had covered two miles, the Camerons were far behind and caught up with the trappers only when the men stopped for a brief rest.

When James Cameron protested, on his wife's behalf, René Lesouris said bluntly, 'If you lag too far behind you will both be taken by Indians. They will make you travel faster and longer than our speed – and between marches they'll keep your wife far too occupied to enjoy any rest. I suggest you make quite certain you *do* keep up with us.'

The trapper spoke with such a pronounced French accent that it took James Cameron a few moments to make sense of his words. When he did, he flushed angrily. 'I won't have you talking in such a manner in front of my wife, Lesouris.'

The Canadian shrugged. 'Then you might find the Indians more to your liking. They don't talk much — although I doubt if you'll care too much for their habits.'

With this cryptic comment the trapper shrugged the straps of his pack over his shoulders and waved the others on. Behind them, as James Cameron and his wife hurried to keep up, anxious not to fall behind, the baronet muttered, 'When we reach Murrayton I'll have Lesouris dismissed from the company for the way he spoke to us.'

'I doubt if he intended to offend.' Vanessa Cameron's opinion was expressed in an uncharacteristically reasoned manner. 'He was probably trying to be helpful.'

'Good intentions are no excuse for bad manners. But it's not only the way he spoke. I'll not have riff-raff like Lesouris looking at you in such a bold manner. My belief is that he was deliberately trying to shock you. Had we been at home – in Scotland – I'd have horsewhipped the man.'

'This is *not* Scotland, James – and I suggest you don't let René Lesouris overhear you talking of horsewhipping.'

Vanessa was looking to where René Lesouris strode ahead of the others. A big man, he was almost a head taller than any of the others, and hardly stooped beneath the weight of his heavy pack. Vanessa had never before been in close contact with men who had the coarse manners of these French trappers. They disturbed her in a strange way – especially their leader. René Lesouris was as blunt and uncouth as any of his companions, yet there was something about him that set him apart from the others; an air of authority that marked him as a leader. James may have been a director of the Upper Canada Trading Company and René Lesouris one of his employees, yet Vanessa was convinced that in any form of dispute between the two men, James would be the loser.

When they reached Murrayton three days later, Vanessa Cameron's worst nightmares were realised. The women she had spoken to in York had suggested she might find conditions in Murrayton somewhat primitive, but nothing they said had prepared her for what she found.

The small, stockaded township occupied a near-perfect position on a small rise. At the town's edge a wide river flowed into a tree-lined lake that extended as far as the eye could see – but the idyll ended here. Murrayton was no more than a huddle of functional cabins, built around an open space, or 'square'. The pallisade surrounding the community was built of ten-feet high pine logs and although the wooden gates were propped wide open it was evident that the trading post had been built with defence in mind.

As the travellers entered the township they were confronted by a scene of appalling untidiness. Ashes from long-dead fires had been strewn haphazardly around the whole area; canoes that would never again traverse the rivers and lakes of Upper Canada were abandoned against cabin walls, or left lying where the winds of past winters had carried them. Cast-out rubbish lay where it had been abandoned by long-forgotten owners, ignored even by the few rib-thin dogs that wandered aimlessly in a desultory, nose-to-the-ground manner around the trading post.

There were a number of Indians inside the stockade. Not the tall, clean-featured, buckskin-clad warriors of the popular drawings Vanessa Cameron had seen in British magazines. The Indians of Murrayton were dressed in a ragged collection of cast-off, European-style clothing. Many squatted forlornly outside the largest of the log-built buildings. This, according to a weather-warped sign, was the Trading Store.

There were many women among the Indians and as Vanessa watched she saw an Indian girl leave the store in the company of a man dressed in a similar fashion to the trappers with whom she had been travelling.

'You are surprised to see a European man with an Indian girl?'
Vanessa had not seen René Lesouris's approach.

Her glance shifted to where James had taken up a position at the
head of the party, before she looked again at the French-speaking
Canadian.

'What the men here do does not concern me.'

'Dan Urquhart is a countryman of yours, I believe. He is also a
trapper – one of the best. The girl with him is an Indian, a Sioux.
They are not often seen here. She will travel with him when he goes
off trapping, will take care of him, cook his food, make his clothes,
help him skin the animals he traps, and cure the furs. She might
even give birth to his child somewhere in the wilderness. When the
season is over he'll probably leave her behind with her tribe – or
perhaps trade her in for someone new.'

Vanessa believed that for reasons best known to himself, René
Lesouris was trying again to shock her. She *was* shocked, but she
was not going to allow this man to observe her feelings.

'It sounds as though it's high time someone brought a civilising
influence to Upper Canada, Monsieur Lesouris.'

The French-Canadian grinned. 'I seem to remember Dan Urquhart saying something very similar when he came to Canada six
years ago. He is from a good family, and was an officer in the British
army. He has changed – as will you and your husband. This is a
vast and untamed land. A generous land to those who adapt to its
ways, a harsh place for those who do not. It will break those who try
to mould it in the shape of the country they left behind in Europe.
Upper Canada is like no other place in the world.'

The grin reappeared and Vanessa Cameron realised for the first
time that in spite of the beard and a weathered skin, René Lesouris
was not as old as she had first thought. She put his age at no more
than thirty-five, or even thirty.

'Canada can be likened to a woman, Madame. One that must be
wooed and understood if she is not to break a man's heart.'

As on a previous occasion, Vanessa Cameron was not certain
whether or not she *ought* to be offended by this man, but she was
saved from the necessity of arriving at a conclusion by her husband.
A noisy crowd was gathering about the new arrivals to the trading
post. Old friends were greeted heartily and news eagerly sought of
the settlements to the south and east.

No one hurried forward to greet the Upper Canada Trading Company's new director, but James Cameron had spotted a cabin which carried a plaque identifying it as the office of the factor. Standing in the doorway was an elderly man wearing a linen shirt and fustian trousers, clothes that immediately set him apart from the other men in this isolated community.

Calling upon Vanessa to accompany him, James Cameron advanced towards the cabin. 'Henry Murray? I'm Sir James Cameron. This is my wife, Vanessa.'

The elderly man shook the extended hand and nodded in Vanessa's direction before saying, 'Andrew Farr is my name, Sir James.' The accent was as pronounced as any the Camerons had left behind in the hills and valleys of Glenelg. 'I'm the factor's clerk. Mister Murray is away just now. Some of our trappers have been attacked by the Nor'West Company's men and had their furs stolen. Mister Murray's gone to find out what it's all about. He left orders for you to follow as soon as you arrived here.'

'Me? How does he expect me to find my way to him in such country?'

James Cameron was thoroughly alarmed at the thought of heading off into the wilderness to help settle a dispute about which he knew nothing. He was also resentful that such orders should have been conveyed to a *director* of the company by a clerk.

'You'll be given a guide – and an escort, of course. We wouldn't dream of allowing you to wander around Upper Canada on your own, Sir James. Our trading company may not be as long-established as some of the larger concerns, but we've a reputation for taking care of our own. That's the reason Mister Murray went out himself to see what can be done for the trappers. If you're ready by morning I'll have René Lesouris and his men go with you.'

James Cameron did not relish the thought of spending more time in the company of the French-Canadian trapper. 'Is there no one else who can accompany me? I find Lesouris's manners extremely offensive. He has been particularly insensitive when speaking in Lady Cameron's hearing.'

Andrew Farr looked at James Cameron thoughtfully for a few moments. 'I could send you out with a great many trappers, all of whom are at home in the forest, but there's only one man I'd trust with *my* life if there was likely to be trouble – *Indian* trouble. That man is René Lesouris.'

'You must take Lesouris with you,' said Vanessa firmly. 'I'm quite certain he had no intention of insulting me. He was trying to make his warning as strong as possible, that's all, but where am I to stay while you're away?'

'That poses something of a problem,' said Andrew Farr. 'I wasn't expecting you to bring a wife along with you, Sir James. Most wives prefer to remain in York. Had I known in advance I'd have had a cabin raised for you. As it is, the only half-decent cabin is the one being used by Dan Urquhart and his Indian woman.'

'Lady Cameron is not sharing a cabin with *anyone* – certainly not with an *Indian* woman!'

'Perhaps I can solve the problem for you, Andrew.' René Lesouris had come up silently. He kicked mud from his moccasins as he stepped to the rough-wood boardwalk outside the factor's office. 'I believe you want me to take him to find Henry?'

James Cameron found the dismissive 'him' offensive, but he held his tongue.

When Andrew Farr nodded, René Lesouris said, 'I was just talking to Dan Urquhart. He tells me the Nor'West Company is being helped by a party of Iroquois Indians. This particular crowd is a bad bunch, but Tissee – that's Dan's woman – is related to some of them. I believe her sister married into the tribe. I'd like to take them both with me.'

Andrew Farr nodded, relieved at such an easy solution to the problem of finding accommodation for the new director's wife. 'That's settled then – but you'll need to share the cabin with Urquhart tonight . . . .'

Once again James Cameron protested vigorously, but the factor's clerk closed the argument by saying, simply, 'There's nowhere else. The rest of the cabins are single men's quarters. You either share Dan's cabin, or you'll need to sleep in the open and get eaten by mosquitoes. They're particularly bad this year.'

With James Cameron still protesting, the couple were led to the Urquhart cabin, where they discovered their huge quantity of baggage had already been piled in a corner of the cabin's single room.

Dan Urquhart greeted the disgruntled newcomers cheerily. Introducing Tissee, a young and extremely shy Indian girl, he held out his hand to James Cameron, saying, 'It will be a delight to spend the evening in the company of a countryman. Tissee's a good, hard-working girl, but she's no great conversationalist. It's been a long time since I spoke to someone fresh from Scotland.'

Ignoring the outstretched hand, James Cameron said brusquely, 'We're here under sufferance. When I set off for Murrayton with my wife I believed we would at least have a cabin to ourselves. Conditions here are *appalling*. Murrayton seems to be occupied by men who are determined to put all forms of civilised and acceptable behaviour behind them.'

'You're seeing it at the best time of the year,' commented Dan Urquhart cheerfully, apparently unconcerned that James Cameron had not taken his hand. 'Around thaw-time you'll find it knee-deep in mud. Yet after a winter spent up there in trapping country you begin to think about Murrayton as some Highland folk look upon Edinburgh. But you folks must be hungry. While you settle in Tissee'll serve you up something to eat. I might even be able to find some half-decent whisky for you. There's a still out back of the store. It's run by a Scotsman who worked in a legal distillery before coming out here.'

As Dan Urquhart talked he threw an occasional word in Tissee's direction, and before her man had finished talking to the new company director she brought a bowl of steaming stew across the room and proffered it to James Cameron. He took it from her with a barely perceptible grunt that might, or might not, have signified his thanks. The aroma from the bowl was highly appetising and James Cameron realised he was hungry.

He took a taste, and then a second.

'This is very pleasant,' he said grudgingly, 'what meat is it?'

Dan Urquhart shrugged. 'Difficult to say. Dog probably. There was one hereabouts that wasn't any too well yesterday. I suggested Tissee should cook it for us.'

James Cameron's head jerked up and he searched Dan Urquhart's face for the hint of a smile, but the young, red-haired Scot had apparently dismissed the subject from his mind and he was briskly rolling a pair of buckskin trousers, prior to stowing them inside a pack.

James Cameron's mouth clamped shut as his stomach heaved in rebellion. Placing the bowl on the room's only table he dived for the door.

As the door banged shut behind the hastily departing baronet, Dan Urquhart looked up in feigned surprise.

'Your husband left in an awful hurry, Lady Cameron. I was about to tell him it couldn't be dog. I remember seeing someone burying him this morning. It must be the buck I shot on the way in yesterday. Good prime meat. There's plenty of it about these parts.'

Sir James Cameron did not share his heavily armed companions' enthusiasm at the prospect of a fight with the men of the North West Company.

The men set off travelling in two canoes. René Lesouris, Dan Urquhart, Tissee and James Cameron were among those sharing the leading vessel. During the first night's camp the men let it be known that they had heard about the joke played upon the new Upper Canada Trading Company's director by his fellow Scot. As James Cameron placed a spoonful of a somewhat less-than-palatable food to his lips, one of the trappers, indistinguishable in the darkness, barked like a dog. The sound brought a hoot of laughter from the men gathered about the camp fire.

Cameron flushed angrily, but continued with his meal and René Lesouris said quietly, 'There is not much subtlety in their humour, M'sieur Director, but they are good men. Any one of them will fight and die for you, should it prove necessary.'

'Their humour – or lack of it, doesn't trouble me. As for dying . . . I came out here to help run a company, not to fight a war.'

'That's what the Hudson's Bay Company said when they first fell foul of the North West Company. They soon learned to behave in the same way as their rivals. Now there's nothing to choose between them and when you find a dead trapper who can tell which company paid for the gun that killed him? Especially as most of the Indians up here fight for both companies at some time or another.'

Uneasily pushing the thought of murdered trappers to the back of his mind, James Cameron asked, 'How do you know where to find Henry Murray? Did he leave word where he was going?'

All that day they had been travelling by canoe through densely afforested, trackless country. Twice they had made brief overland portages. James was uncertain whether they had changed to other rivers, or were merely avoiding tortuous river bends.

'We'll find him. But right now we need to get these fires built up with plenty of green wood. The smoke needs to be thick enough to choke a chimney if it's to drive off the mosquitoes. Without it they are likely to carry you off with them when dusk falls.'

James Cameron took this to be another of the Frenchman's jokes, but on this occasion his words proved to be uncomfortably true. Later that evening, when the Scotsman was unable to endure the choking, acrid smoke any longer, he left the vicinity of the fire and was immediately pounced upon by a great cloud of insects. There were so many it felt as though their stings explored every pore in the skin that was exposed to them. Eyelids, ears, lips – they even invaded his nostrils.

Stumbling back to the suddenly welcome smoke of the camp fires, James ignored the knowing, but not unsympathetic smiles of the trappers as he pounded arms and face unmercifully in a bid to dislodge the small, blood-sucking insects that had driven him back to the sanctuary of the wood-fire.

When James Cameron woke the next morning he peered at the world through narrow slits between grotesquely swollen eyelids. His skin itched as though he had been wrapped in a hair shirt all night. Before the party set off, Tissee came to him and rubbed an evil-smelling ointment into his skin. He complained of the smell grumpily, in the belief that the Indian girl spoke no English. To his surprise, she replied, 'The smell does not matter to anyone here and soon you will feel better.'

Feeling somewhat foolish, James Cameron asked, 'Am I the only one who's been bitten?'

'No, but it is much worse for you, your skin is soft.' Tissee rested her hand against his cheek to emphasise her words. She had just rubbed ointment into every part of his skin that was exposed to the air, but her touch felt somehow different this time, more gentle.

Coming up and seeing Tissee with her hand against the Scots-man's cheek, Dan Urquhart said, 'You'd do well to guard yourself against girls like Tissee, Sir James. Before you know it you'll realise there's a lot more to being a trapper than standing up to your waist in water setting traps. You might even learn to like the life.'

Taking offence at the trapper's words, James snapped back, 'I prefer to take my pleasures among *civilised* people, Urquhart.'

'Talk to an Indian and you'll learn that he believes *he's* the civilised one. He's got a point, too. I've yet to hear of an Indian chief rewarding the loyalty of his people by shipping them off somewhere just so he can rent out their lands and make himself a tidy profit.'

The eyes behind the puffed-up lids were hot with anger as Cameron watched the other man walk away with Tissee in step behind him. Yet the Scots baronet found his gaze was following the progress of the Indian girl and not that of the trapper.

The party from Murrayton found Henry Murray and the survivors of his party five days later in a crude log stockade on the shore of Georgian Bay. James Cameron marvelled that the French trapper knew where to come. This place looked no different to a hundred other places they had seen.

Henry Murray and his men were in dire straits. For ten days they had fought fierce, sporadic battles with the Indian allies of the North Western Company. Six of the fifteen-strong party had been killed and Murray himself was laid low with a fever.

The Indians had not been seen for twenty-four hours, but with Henry Murray ill the men of the Upper Canada Company had not known what to do for the best. They greeted the new arrivals with great relief, their cheers echoing back from the tall trees of the dark forest that came almost to the walls of the fort.

Clasping the hand of his junior partner warmly, Henry Murray said, 'This is not the way I'd intended greeting you, James, but given the present circumstances I don't mind telling you I'm damned glad to see you. I'd almost resigned myself to dying out here in the forest – and Canada's a place for living, not dying.'

'I wish the Nor'West Company thought as you do, Henry.' The speaker was René Lesouris. 'If you feel up to it I'd like to move off right away. I think you were attacked by no more than thirty or forty Iroquois, but Tissee says they have a lot more warriors in the area they can call on. I don't want to get caught up in a war we haven't a hope in hell of winning.'

'Which route were you thinking of taking back to Murrayton?'

'I'll head out on the bay as soon as it gets dark. That should start them guessing. Then we'll head for the old fort at Parry Sound. There are a lot of Nor'Western men in that area and it's the last thing the Indians will expect us to do. By morning we'll be well past the fort and into the lakes beyond. Once there they'll never find us among the islands.'

'It's risky, René. If we don't succeed in passing the fort in darkness they'll have us for sure.'

'It's just as certain that they'll have us if we stay here until morning.'

Henry Murray thought about it for only a few moments. 'You're right. There's just one thing, though. We had to hide two canoes loaded with prime pelts on an island about thirty miles north of here. I've no intention of leaving them there to rot. They could make all the difference between profit and loss this year.'

'You'll not be around to take credit for your success unless we get you to a doctor.'

'Dan Urquhart knows the island. If he takes seven men and his woman he can find the pelts and bring them back. James can go with them too.'

René Lesouris's glance at James Cameron held genuine concern. 'Your partner's new here. It's not fair to send him.'

'You brought him *here*, didn't you? Besides, fairness has nothing to do with it. The Upper Canada Trading Company has only two directors in this country right now. If your plan for our return goes wrong and we're attacked it would mean the end for the company. Besides, James and his canoes stand less chance of being attacked than ours.'

When Henry Murray turned to James Cameron his words allowed for no argument. 'You'll reach the island by dawn and you'd best hole up there until nightfall. Leave the bay and head south along Lake Huron, making for Detroit. You'll find Jim Collins there – anyone will tell you where his place is. He'll make you a fair offer for the furs and pay cash. If you have any doubts about anything, talk things over with Dan Urquhart. He's a good man, you can trust him.'

Henry Murray lay back; talking had tired him. 'Go away now and get ready to leave — but before you go see if you can find my jug of whisky. If I can't get rid of my problems, I'll damn well drown 'em.'

James Cameron did not relish the prospect of spending a few weeks in the close company of Dan Urquhart. He would have preferred to return to Murrayton with Henry Murray. A more courageous man might have told Murray that human life – especially *his* life, meant more than balancing the books with the aid of a few furs, but James realised that such a protest would brand him as a coward for the remainder of his life in Canada.

Four canoes pushed off from the lakeside stockade that night when darkness had fallen. Paddling silently away from the shore the canoes were steered northwards, the trappers taking their bearings from a star-strewn sky. When they were a long way from the shore a low hail from René Lesouris signalled that it was time for the canoes to part company.

When low-voiced farewells had been exchanged between the men, the canoes carrying Henry Murray and his party set a course for Parry Sound. The two canoes carrying James Cameron and Dan Urquhart continued on their northerly course, the paddling settling down to a steady, untiring rhythm.

After paddling all night, when the stars were fading and a faint, coloured tint of dawn had made its appearance in the eastern sky, Dan Urquhart brought his canoe alongside Cameron's canoe.

'We should be close to the island now. We'll stop paddling and when it's light enough to see what we're doing, we'll go ashore, find the pelts and rest up until dark. Come dusk we'll head for Detroit – and have a time we'll remember all winter!'

The statement brought a murmur of approval from the trappers paddling the canoes.

'You ever been to Detroit?' Dan Urquhart put the question to James Cameron.

'I journeyed straight to York from Nova Scotia, then went on to Murrayton. What's so special about Detroit?'

'It's American for a start – and one hell of a town! When we get there and you've sold the pelts, the men will expect an advance on whatever they're owed. Don't give 'em too much, or we might never see them again. We'll need to leave Tissee behind, of course. The Yankees are a bit touchy when it comes to Indians.'

'Leave her behind? Where?' James Cameron remembered what René Lesouris had told him about the relationship between Dan Urquhart and his Indian woman.

Dan Urquhart's shrug was just visible in the grey, pre-dawn light. 'Her sister's with the Iroquois. Here would be as good as anywhere else.'

'But . . . Henry Murray said the furs are on an island. How will she make her way to the mainland? And the Iroquois are fighting us. What will they do to her if they learn she's been travelling with us? With you?'

'Tissee's a resourceful girl. She'll think of some way to reach the mainland. Anyway, the longer she takes, the less likelihood there'll be of the Iroquois coming after us. That's if she decides to tell them she's been travelling with men of the Upper Canada Trading Company.'

'Don't you care what happens to her?' James Cameron's impassioned question surprised him as much as it did anyone else. 'I know I've only been here a short while, but from what I've seen Tissee is both loyal and hard-working. Doesn't that count for anything?'

'Any suggestion that loyalty and service deserves reward is a mockery coming from the tongue of a Cameron of Glenelg. *I'm* a Highlander too, Sir James Cameron. There are many of us in Canada. When we get together we exchange news of what's happening back home. The last I heard of Glenelg, loyalty and service were being trampled underfoot by Lowland sheep. Are you trying to tell me that "loyalty" means something when dealing with Indians, but can be disregarded when Highlanders are involved? Is that what you think? Not that it matters, I don't give a damn either way. When we leave the island bound for Detroit, Tissee stays behind. Now, let's head for the shore and find these furs.'

The exchange between the two men had been carried on in low voices, but it had been heard by most of the men in the two boats and Cameron seethed with anger. When they returned to Murrayton he intended making Urquhart pay dearly for speaking to him this way in front of the other trappers. Scotsman and fine trapper he might be, but *no one* spoke to James Cameron in such a manner.

As the large canoes nosed through reeds to run aground on the soft mud of the island's shore, the leading men in each canoe leaped over the side and hauled the two craft farther on land. As other men jumped ashore the craft were pulled well clear of the water and hidden amongst the trees at the water's edge.

'Where are the pelts?'

One of the trappers from Cameron's canoe put the question to Dan Urquhart.

'They should be about twenty paces in from that rock.' Urquhart pointed to a long, rounded rock jutting out from the island, at right angles from the shoreline. 'We'll load the canoes then make camp.'

By now the sun had dragged itself clear of the waters of the eastern end of the lake and was beginning its ascent into an almost cloudless sky.

'Tissee, get a fire going. We'll have something to eat . . . do you fish?' The question was put to James Cameron.

'Of course.'

'You'll find a couple of lines in my canoe. Take some corn for bait and try your luck.'

James found the lines, each fitted with a number of hooks, and he made his way along the wooded shoreline, seeking a spot clear of reeds.

It was a very large island, probably about seven miles long and equally as wide, and James had no difficulty finding a suitable place from which to fish. He chose a spot about a half-mile from the camp. Here there was a large, flat rock which extended out beyond the reeds into clearer water.

James had been fishing without success for some minutes when Tissee came along the edge of the treeline, gathering dead wood. Seeing Cameron, she stopped.

'You catch many fish?'

'Not one.'

Tissee laughed. It was a pleasant sound and it effectively dulled the edge of her next words.

'You do not belong here. You should be with your own people, in a place where others do things for you. But I teach you catch fish.'

Dropping the armful of wood to the ground, Tissee scrambled out on the rock to join James. It was narrow at the end where he was standing, and she had to clasp him about the waist in order to pass by.

Pulling in the line, she inspected the hooks. Making soft sounds of disapproval, Tissee stripped the bait from each hook, discarding the large, yellow grains of corn into the water. Speedily and efficiently re-baiting the hooks she swung the line, pendulum-style, back and forth a couple of times, before lobbing it with impressive accuracy to land within inches of the rushes. She jerked on the line almost immediately and hauled it in. James was mortified to see that Tissee had hooked not one, but two wildly flapping, silver-scaled fish.

The smile Tissee directed at him contained more delight than triumph, and James shook his head in rueful acceptance of her superior fishing skill. Tissee dropped the fish to the rock at her feet and was unhooking them when she and James heard the sound of two shots – they came from the direction of the camp. As Tissee straightened up they heard more shots. Sliding past him, Tissee jumped from the rock and began running in the direction of the camp. James followed.

Fortunately for the Scots baronet and the Indian girl, they were still in the shadow of the trees when they came within view of the lakeside camp. A whole host of Indians were swarming around the trappers, wielding axes and knives and discharging guns at point-blank range.

Cameron identified Urquhart immediately, his red hair and large build unmistakable among the trappers who still remained on their feet. He stood as solid as a great bear, wielding an empty rifle and surrounded by yelping, aggressive Indians. As James watched, the big Scotsman beat off three attackers in quick succession, but the odds against him were too great.

Watching in helpless horror, James saw a bloody axe raised in the air and brought crashing down upon the head of Dan Urquhart. The giant trapper sank to the ground and as he disappeared in the midst of a stabbing and hacking crowd the hullaballoo reached a new crescendo.

Tissee's hand gripped Cameron's arm. Exhibiting no visible signs of emotion at what she too had just witnessed, she said simply, 'Come.'

Pulling him after her, Tissee fled back the way they had come, keeping to the shadow of the trees. At the rock they had so recently deserted, she paused to retrieve the fish she had caught before resuming their flight.

'Where are we going?' James asked the question breathlessly, unused to such strenuous activity.

'We hide.'

'Why have your people attacked us?'

'They are *not* my people. They are Crees. Bad for you, bad for me.'

James thought of the savage scene he had just witnessed and he shuddered. 'What of the others? Some may still be alive.'

'None of the trappers still alive. My man, the others . . . all dead.'

James looked quickly for some sign of anguish on Tissee's face; he saw none.

'Don't you care about what's just happened to them, Tissee? To Urquhart . . . your man?'

Coming to an abrupt halt, Tissee looked up at him defiantly. 'You think I should tear my hair because my man is dead? You want me to make plenty noise and bring Crees to us? Maybe you think they say, "Sorry, Tissee. We not know one trapper your man." No. If I stop to be sad they kill me. Then kill you. We hide, long way from here. Then I have time feel sad in here.'

As Tissee put a hand to her heart, James knew that she had put him firmly in his place for asking such a stupid question. He told himself that the slaughter he had just witnessed must have induced a state of shock in him.

Tissee led the way along the shore for about a mile, wading knee-deep in the water of the lake in order to leave no footprints when they reached a stretch of smooth, unmarked sand. Soon after this they came to a swift-running stream that emptied itself into the lake.

Keeping to the centre of the stream, Tissee led the way inland, sometimes pushing her way through undergrowth so dense they would have made no progress had they left the water. They followed the narrowing stream for about a mile before Tissee stooped beneath the low-hanging branches of a tree and dropped to her hands and knees. Crawling ashore, she led Cameron through the undergrowth until they reached a small gap between two bushes.

'We stay here.'

'For how long?'

Tissee shrugged. 'We sleep now. When we wake, we talk about it.'

'What if the Crees come looking for us? We have no guns.'

'Too much whisky in camp for them to look for us. They drink, sleep, maybe look around for while. Then they go. Take furs to Nor' West Company store.'

'How do you think they knew where to find the furs?'

Tissee shook her head. 'If they see Murray hide furs they would steal and sell. I think maybe Nor' West Company man see and pay them to wait for us to come for them.'

James found it difficult to accept her explanation. 'You mean someone – a *white* man paid the Crees to wait for us to arrive . . . and to *kill* us?'

'You think such things not done by white men? That only *Indians* kill people?' Tissee looked at Cameron scornfully. 'Dan said you know nothing of this land . . . .'

Suddenly Tissee stopped talking and an expression of anguish contorted her face. James realised that the memory of Dan Urquhart's death had come flooding back to her.

'I'm sorry, Tissee . . . .'

'Sleep. Maybe tonight we go back see what Crees are doing.'

James Cameron was convinced that he would not be able to sleep, and the prospect of going back to check on the Crees alarmed him. Yet it was with a sense of guilt that he realised that the sight of his companions being hacked and clubbed to death had neither frightened nor horrified him. There had been almost a *thrill* to it, a sense of great excitement. He was still reliving the details of the massacre when he fell asleep.

James Cameron awoke with a start, convinced he had heard voices. Then he realised that he was listening to the chatter of a bird somewhere nearby in the forest. Sitting up, he looked about him for Tissee but she was nowhere to be seen.

He experienced a moment of panic. What if she had deserted him? Worse, what if Tissee had decided to betray him to the Crees, in exchange for her own safety? Gradually, common sense over-rode the confusion of his sleep-befuddled mind. Tissee could have deserted him when they heard the first shots at the edge of the lake, or later in the forest. She would hardly have gone to such lengths to find a secure hiding-place had she intended handing him over to the Crees, and turning him over to them would be no guarantee of her own safety.

He relaxed. Tissee would not be far away. She had probably gone off to find food – berries or something similar. He hoped so. He was ravenously hungry.

Hunger might be the immediate problem, but James knew that finding a way off the island and making his way back to Murrayton was the most important issue. He had no experience of surviving in such a hostile environment and would need to rely entirely upon Tissee's skill and knowledge.

Tissee did not return to the hiding-place until another hour had elapsed. Her arrival was so silent that she startled him. One moment he was alone, the next he looked up to see Tissee standing before him. In her hands she carried a rifle, a powder-horn and a large leather pouch, attached to which was a rolled blanket.

'You've been back to the camp! Have the Crees gone?'

'No, they are too drunk to leave yet. Most are asleep. They have five canoes. When night comes we take one.'

'What if they have a guard?'

'No guard. Crees think they kill everyone.'

James mulled over her information – and her suggestion that they steal one of the Cree canoes. The thought did not greatly appeal to him.

'We eat now.'

Unrolling the Hudson's Bay Company blanket, Tissee removed a thick wadge of pemmican, the size of a man's clenched fist. The standard food for trappers and other travellers in this part of the world, pemmican was made from buffalo meat which had been shredded, dried and pulverised. To this sadly abused meat was added boiling buffalo fat and Saskatoon berries. The end product gave off an aroma that was inclined to offend a delicate palate, but it was highly nutritious. Once he had overcome his aversion to the rancid smell, James realised that he was actually enjoying the unfamiliar food, and wished they had more.

Fortunately, they now had a rifle and game would be plentiful in the two hundred miles or so of forest that lay between them and Murrayton. The thought of the stockaded trading post reminded James of Vanessa. He wondered how she was enduring life so far from civilisation and, more important, how long it would be before someone at the fort realised that something had happened to the party that had been sent off to collect the furs.

James suspected it would be some weeks before he was missed. If Detroit was all the now-dead Scots trapper had claimed it to be, the American town would be blamed for their late arrival.

'We go now.'

Before setting off, James loaded and primed the rifle, at the same time praying that he would not need to use it. One shot could account for only one Cree Indian and the ensuing fight would be a one-sided battle. Nevertheless, there was something comforting about having a loaded rifle in his hands.

They did not follow the stream all the way to the lake this time. Before it came into view between the high trees, Tissee struck off through the forest, rounding angrily upon James when he trod on a dead twig that snapped noisily between his feet. James tried desperately hard not to make a sound, but it was difficult to see where he was putting his feet. The light was fading fast and the tall trees cast deep shadows on the forest floor.

When he finally caught a glimpse of the lake, Tissee brought him to a halt. Speaking softly, she said, 'Stay here.'

Without waiting for a reply she went off silently, disappearing in the thick undergrowth before she had taken ten paces.

The forest seemed to be filled with strange sounds. Birds settling down for the night, small mammals rustling the rotting leaves on the forest floor, and the continuous and unnerving crackling of fir cones shedding their seeds.

Tissee's reappearance was as sudden and silent as her departure had been.

'The Crees have gone.'

'Gone? Are you sure?' Cameron's response was a conflicting combination of relief and dismay. He had feared his courage might fail him when it came to stealing a canoe from under their very noses but at the same time, he realised that he and Tissee were trapped on the island.

Tissee led him through the trees to the edge of the lake. On the way they passed the camp which had been occupied by the Crees while they waited for the trappers of the Upper Canada Trading Company to return to claim their furs. Emerging from the trees at the lakeside, about a half-mile from where the Upper Canada Trading Company trappers had been massacred, Tissee held up her hand for silence. Immediately James could hear voices as the Crees called from canoe to canoe far out on the lake. An occasional eruption of laughter showed them to be in high spirits, the ambush and murder of the trappers and the theft of their pelts being regarded as a great victory by the Indians.

'What do we do now?'

'We eat and sleep. Tomorrow we think.'

As Tissee led the way towards the deserted camp, James thought again how reliant he was upon this Indian girl. He knew nothing of the country, its resources, or its dangers. In addition, he had only the vaguest idea of the direction they needed to take in order to reach Murrayton.

At the Cree camp Tissee raked over the ashes of three small fires. When she found a tiny red glow deep in the heart of one of them she gathered up a couple of handfuls of twigs, piling them on top of the faintly burning ashes. Crouching down low, she breathed new life into the fire and minutes later flames were consuming the twigs and throwing dancing shadows around the small forest clearing.

Tissee sent James to gather wood and when he returned, the two fish they had caught earlier in the day were spitted on two long, green sticks and sizzling over the fire.

They ate without speaking as the night sounds of the forest closed in around them. The advent of darkness brought with it an awareness of the vastness of the forest. Here they were on an island, yet they might have been anywhere in the hundreds of thousands of square miles of dense vegetation that covered this vast land.

Guiltily, James knew he should search the scene of the massacre in the remote possibility that any of the trappers had survived. He justified his failure to make such a basic check by telling himself he would see nothing in the darkness and a light at the water's edge might bring the Crees back. Besides, Tissee had said no one was alive, and she should know.

Thinking of lights and the Crees, he became alarmed when Tissee rekindled the other two fires to form a triangle of light about them.

She shrugged off his fears. 'The Crees too far away now to see fires so far in forest. Fires keep bears and mosquitoes away.'

'Bears . . . ? But this is an *island*.'

'Bears swim. I see no tracks so maybe no bears, but best we sure.'

The thought of bears prowling around the camp frightened James almost as much as the thought of the Crees. He knew he would not close his eyes all night. Even as his thoughts were turning to sleep Tissee was making up a bed, gathering dry leaves into a heap in the space between the fires. When she was satisfied, she lay down upon them and pulled the blanket over her.

'Where do I sleep?'

Pulling a corner of the blanket back, Tissee replied, 'Here. The night will be cold. Both must use same blanket.'

James knew she was right. The early hours in particular were giving a warning that the short Canadian summer was drawing to a close. Lying beside Tissee, he was acutely aware of her closeness. She lay on her back, unmoving, beside him, but a bare arm was pressed against his and she was so close that he could smell the woodsmoke in her hair.

'What will you do when we return to Murrayton, Tissee?'

'I don't know. Find another man, maybe. Or go back to my people.' She spoke matter-of-factly, as a woman in Britain might have contemplated purchasing a new dress.

'How long were you and Urquhart together?' He knew it was an insensitive conversation, but it seemed equally unnatural *not* to say something about the trapper who lay dead on the shore with the others.

'He bought me three summers ago.'

'*Bought* you? From whom?'

'My father. Dan gave a horse for me. A good horse and a barrel of rum.' Tissee turned her head and he could read nothing of her thoughts in the dark eyes. 'What did you pay for *your* woman?'

James slipped away from her gaze and looked up at the night sky which was pinpricked with stars shrunken by distance. *His woman!* He had given little thought to Vanessa during the past twenty-four hours. He wondered what she would do if she knew her husband was lying beneath a blanket with an Indian girl who had just referred to her as 'his woman'.

'We don't buy our women. That's not the way we do things.' Even as he was uttering the words, James was self-questioning the truth of them. He may not have handed Cuthbert Lansdown a sum of money for his daughter, but Vanessa's extravagance had cost him dearly over the years. Had it not been for her, he would still be living in the great house at Ratagan, still a Cameron of Glenelg.

James's own folly and the years of dissipation and mismanagement were forgotten in that moment of resentment, as he laid the blame for his misfortunes on the head of his wife. He wondered how Vanessa would have behaved had she been confronted with the situation he and Tissee were in today. He doubted whether her first thought would have been to save *him,* as Tissee's had been. Vanessa had never been called upon to make a life-or-death decision, but in any minor emergency she was concerned only with the effect it would have upon *herself.*

The events of today would have proved too much for Vanessa. She would probably have sought escape in a fainting fit. She was renowned for fainting with great effect when confronted with difficult decisions – or when she did not get her own way. He doubted whether such a ploy would have influenced the Crees.

'Tell me about your country. Is it like this? In Murrayton they say you were a great chief in your own land.'

It pleased James Cameron to know that the trappers at Murrayton had spoken of him in such a manner. He had believed them to be scornful of his background. Warmed by Tissee's words, he told her of his lands in Glenelg, of the parties he had held in the house on the hilltop at Ratagan, and of some of the important people who had visited him there. He doubted whether she understood a fraction of what he was saying, but she was a good listener and by talking to her he could forget the dangers of the forest about them.

He had been talking for a long time when she stirred beside him.
'What are you doing?'
'I must put more wood on the fires. They burn low.'

Tissee was right. The fires had burned so low that her face was now hidden in shadows, only her eyes clearly distinguishable.

'Wait . . .'

Reaching up, James drew her face down to his. When he kissed her she neither encouraged him nor offered any resistance, but her mouth was soft and pliant against his. Thoroughly aroused by the feel and smell of her, he pulled her down, at the same time turning so he was lying over her. When he struggled to pull up her buckskin skirt, she helped him by arching her body clear of the leaves on which they lay – but it was the only measure of co-operation he received from her. When he thrust deep inside her body her responses were muscular and not emotional.

Her indifference incited him to physical feats that would have provoked a torrent of protest from Vanessa, but Tissee made no complaint. Eventually, his passion spent, he lay on her, panting like a summer-hot dog.

Later in the night, when Tissee disturbed him to place more wood on the fire, he made love to her once more. Yet again, she did not resist him, but neither did she actively encourage him.

Had Cameron known her better, he would have known that she had raised what the late Dan Urquhart referred to as her 'Indian Barrier'. It was a barrier through which no man might pass unless Tissee willed it so.

It took nine weeks for James Cameron and Tissee to reach Murrayton. In the meantime, a trapper and his Indian woman, heading out to winter in the trapping grounds, had stopped overnight on the island where the two had been marooned. Finding evidence of the massacre, he sent word back to the trading post.

James and Tissee had still been on the island when the trapper landed there but by this time they had moved to the far side, in view of the mainland. Here, by stitching birch bark to a sapling frame with the aid of a patiently made bone needle, and using the roots of a tamarack tree as thread, Tissee had constructed a fragile but serviceable canoe. The small craft carried them safely to the mainland and negotiated long stretches of two rivers before being wrecked on a turbulent stretch of rapids on a waterway that was little more than a stream.

Being unable to take advantage of river travel slowed them down alarmingly, and when temperatures plunged below zero and snow clouds piled up on the horizon, they were fortunate to stumble across the meagre camp of a small family band of impoverished Ojibwe Indians.

Tissee belonged to a Sioux tribe and had the two tribes met whilst out hunting they would have fought. Nevertheless, she and Cameron were taken in and invited to share the Ojibwe's meagre supplies.

For a month all travel was out of the question. As snowstorms raged through the land, each day brought a new battle for survival. During this time a thick white blanket lay over the countryside, obliterating trails and landmarks and turning hollows and thinly iced lakes into deathtraps for the unwary.

Unexpectedly, a brief thaw set in and the head of the family group offered to guide James and Tissee to Murrayton. His motives were not entirely philanthropic. The Scotsman and his Indian woman were consuming valuable winter rations. Even before their arrival the family possessed barely enough to survive the winter. James Cameron was an important man in the Upper Canada Trading Company, and the family head expected to be well rewarded for returning him safely to the trading post. He would be provided with enough stores to bring a degree of unaccustomed comfort to the grinding poverty of the Ojibwe.

James Cameron's return to Murrayton was an experience he would remember with great satisfaction. For the first time in his life, he was hailed as a hero. The trading post even produced a piper from among the trappers to greet him as he, Tissee and the Ojibwe trudged to the trading post gate on their snowshoes.

Outwardly, Cameron accepted the reception as being no more than his due. After all, he had left the trading post inexperienced in the ways of the forest. He had returned the sole survivor of an horrific massacre, had escaped from an island and trekked through two hundred miles of unknown, snow-covered country. Tissee had helped, of course – as he generously admitted to all to whom he told his story – but the Iroquois would undoubtedly have killed her had he not been present to protect her against them.

Cameron's greatest disappointment was that Vanessa was not at Murrayton to welcome him and witness his moment of triumph. Secretly, he also found it something of a relief; he knew Vanessa would have asked a great many embarrassing and awkward questions about the nature of his relationship with the Indian girl during their nine weeks together.

He was not surprised that Vanessa had left Murrayton when she learned what had occurred on the island in Georgian Bay. However, he was puzzled to learn she had left the trading post in the company of Henry Murray and René Lesouris *before* he and the trappers had been reported killed.

'To tell you the truth, Sir James,' said Andrew Farr, unhappily, 'I don't think Lady Cameron enjoyed life here at the post. You mustn't blame her too much. There's times when *I* find it hard to accept the ways of the trappers. A trading post is no place for a woman of breeding. When Henry Murray said you'd be calling at York town before returning here he invited her to go there and wait for you.'

Although James expressed his disappointment at the absence of his wife, it meant that by remaining at Murrayton he could continue his relationship with Tissee. He even managed to convince himself that at least one of the directors should be at the trading post to take care of the company's interests.

He wrote two letters, one to Vanessa, the other to Henry Murray, telling the story of the massacre of the trappers and his own safe arrival at Murrayton. The letters were carried to York by a small band of trappers who had decided to take advantage of the break in the weather to head south and winter in the lakeside town. It was October now, and they would probably be the last men to leave Murrayton until the spring.

By the time Lady Cameron received the letter telling her of her husband's safe arrival at Murrayton, she had already come to terms with titled widowhood. It was a state she might have learned to enjoy had it lasted a little longer. Her title ensured her acceptance in the fast-growing society of York and, as a widow, she enjoyed a freedom she had never known before.

Vanessa had also been enjoying the attentive company of René Lesouris. Away from the forest and the company of trappers,

Lesouris displayed all the charm and gallantry associated with Frenchmen.

He had also been guiding Vanessa on business matters. James Cameron's directorship entitled him to six thousand acres of company land that would belong to Vanessa if he died. The Frenchman's advice to her was to take five thousand heavily forested acres on the shores of Lake Huron. The timber could be cut down and floated across the lake to the growing industries of America, where there was a lucrative market for good timber. This would provide her with a steady income and leave her with cleared land to offer for sale to settlers.

Lesouris suggested that the remaining thousand acres should be taken in the vicinity of Murrayton. This would be a longer-term investment, but René was convinced that a town would one day rise around the trading post, greatly increasing land values. In addition to these vast holdings, Henry Murray had made Vanessa a present of a plot in York on which to build a good-sized house should she decide to remain in Canada.

Only one thing cast a shadow over the future Vanessa envisaged for herself: she was pregnant. She had realised her condition soon after James left on his trip to find Henry Murray. This was the reason she had left Murrayton before the snows of winter made travelling impossible. She had no intention of bringing a baby into the world attended only by a couple of dirty, lice-ridden Indian women.

During the short time she spent at the trading post Vanessa had witnessed a baby being born. Hearing that one of the young Indian women was about to give birth in a communal cabin occupied by trappers, Vanessa felt obliged, as the only white woman on the post, to offer her help.

The few moments she spent in the cabin would be engraved on her mind for ever. The air inside the cabin was thick with the smoke from the pipes of trappers who were there to watch the childbirth and who were not above offering crude advice to the panting mother-to-be.

The Indian girl at the centre of the 'entertainment' squatted in the centre of the single room, her hands tightly gripping a stake driven into the hard earth floor. Naked from the waist down, bleeding heavily and perspiring, she occasionally cried out in agony as she approached the final stages of childbirth.

Two older Indian women kneeled beside the girl, offering encouragement, and as Vanessa watched in shocked horror, their voices rose to a new pitch. For a while the screams of the straining mother-to-be rose above the encouragement of the other women. Suddenly a bloody, blue-tinged shape slid from its mother's body to dangle helplessly at the end of its umbilical cord, before falling to the filth of the dirt floor.

As Vanessa pushed her way from the cabin, leaving the cheers of the drunken trappers behind her, she determined that her child would not be born in Murrayton.

That year Upper Canada experienced one of the hardest winters in living memory. For weeks at a time the residents of Murrayton found it impossible to leave the trading post. Within the stockade much of each morning was spent clearing pathways through the snow from the cabin to the store and the well. Before long the snow on each side of the narrow paths was piled higher than the height of a man.

The consumption of liquor soared to record heights and fights between trappers were frequent. Fortunately, only two resulted in fatalities.

In March, when tensions seemed likely to get completely out of hand, the country experienced an early spring. Overnight the temperature rose fifteen degrees. Melting snow poured like rain from the trees and snow slipped away into streams that grew into torrents and became rivers that flooded the land for miles about their banks.

Less than a week after the thaw began, a messenger reached Murrayton from York town with a letter from Henry Murray. It informed an astonished James Cameron that his wife had given birth to a son two days before the thaw set in. It would be named Charles Cuthbert James, in honour of both grandparents. They were names Vanessa and James had agreed upon years before.

Now that Vanessa had produced an heir to the baronetcy, Henry Murray suggested that James should leave the affairs of the trading post to Andrew Farr, and return to York town as soon as possible. All that day James Cameron pored over the ledgers in the trading post, copying the figures he would take to Henry Murray when he went to York. On many occasions he paused in his work, wondering how he would break the news of his impending departure to Tissee.

It would not be easy. Tissee had looked after him well during the long winter months and the passion that had been lacking in their early love making had gradually found its way into the relationship. Making love to Tissee had become a new and exciting experience every night.

As the day drew to a close and the moment of confrontation drew closer, James fortified himself with numerous glasses of whisky from Henry Murray's personal barrel, kept in the trading post office.

Not until darkness fell did James Cameron weave an unsteady path through the trading post to the cabin he shared with Tissee. At the door he braced himself for the inevitable storm, wishing he had drunk more whisky.

The cabin was in darkness. This in itself was unusual. When he stumbled inside and lit a lamp, James realised that his concern for Tissee and the hangover he would suffer the next morning were unnecessary. Tissee had gone.

Not a single item belonging to the Indian girl remained in the cabin. She had gone from his cabin, from the trading post – and out of his life.

Tissee had released Sir James Cameron in a characteristic manner. He could return to York town and resume life with his wife as though the Indian girl had never existed.

FIVE

Van Dieman's Land 1818

When the transport *Hercules* arrived at Botany Bay, the naval Lieutenant who had brought the ship from Tenerife was summoned to the Governor's office. Word of the problems that had beset the ship had been sent to the Governor in a despatch from the British Admiral at Tenerife. After discussing the situation with his staff, the Governor had decided that the convicts on board the *Hercules* were not welcome in the mainland colony. Declaring every man and woman on board to be 'second offenders', he ordered the Lieutenant to take his convict cargo to the penal colony of Hobart, on the island known as Van Dieman's Land.

Virtually a self-governing adjunct to New South Wales, Van Dieman's Land was first and foremost a gaol. The military here possessed frighteningly wide powers and they enjoyed the status it gave to them. The harsh, military-style administration occasionally spilled over to affect the settlers, yet free settlers came to the island from all over the British Isles, drawn by the attraction of free land and convict labour.

One such settler was Jonathan Sinclair. A displaced tacksman from the Highlands of Scotland, he was sympathetic to his fellow countrymen, accepting the three Scotsmen to work his land in spite of Angus Ross's disability.

Sinclair's wife had found it difficult to settle in the new country. Terrified by the convicts and Aborigines who were dwelling in Van Dieman's Land, she pined for Scotland and the family she had left behind there.

When the two Rosses and Charlie Campbell were allocated to the Sinclairs to work their land Mrs Sinclair improved. As she came

to know them better she realised that the three Scotsmen were unlikely to murder her while she slept, and for two years the three men
worked contentedly, improving the land and troubling no one.

Then, one night the house was attacked by Aborigines. The raid
was in retaliation for an 'Aborigine-hunt' organised by the army,
who seemed determined to exterminate every native in the area.

With the assistance of the three convicts the Aborigines were
beaten off, but all Mrs Sinclair's fears returned. After weeks of
heated argument between them, she presented her husband with an
ultimatum. She would not remain in Van Dieman's Land any longer.
If he would not return to Scotland with her, she would go alone.
Reluctantly, Jonathan Sinclair decided to sell up and return with his
wife to Scotland.

Thanks to the hard work of his three Scots convicts, Sinclair's
small farm had become a showpiece, and he had no problem finding a buyer willing to pay his price. The farm was sold to an army
captain.

Currently serving in New South Wales, the soldier had spent
many years in Van Dieman's Land. He was due to retire soon and
intended making his home on the convict island. He had already
bought up many other properties in the area and the addition of
Sinclair's farm gave him an impressive holding.

Unfortunately, Captain Yelland had not been cast from the
same mould as Jonathan Sinclair. The new owner of the Sinclair
farm had arrived in the settlement as a young ensign with the first
convict transports in 1788. When other officers moved on to find
glory, promotion or death in the wars against Napoleon Bonaparte,
Yelland remained, climbing the slower but less dangerous ladder of
promotion in the convict colonies of Australia.

Anthony Yelland had not joined the army to find glory and he
had no incentive to return to England. Before an uncle had purchased a commission for him, he had been a nobody, destined to
go nowhere in the world. The son of a failed shopkeeper who had
committed suicide rather than face his debts, life had held little
prospect of success. It would be no better there now. Retirement
on half-pay would mean, at best, a frugal and penny-pinching
lifestyle.

Here, in Van Dieman's Land, he was a substantial landowner
and, as an ex-army officer, had considerable influence. Furthermore,

an unpaid labour force, subject to Anthony Yelland's own form of harsh discipline, would one day make him a wealthy man.

Yelland's future neighbours were overjoyed to have him in the community. An army man would know how to deal with the thieving Aborigines who roamed the area. He would also keep the convicts under control. It was said that even the children born to Yelland's convicts arrived in the world bearing lash-marks on their backs.

Anthony Yelland was proud of his reputation as an inveterate flogger of convicts. It was said that he employed a convict for the sole purpose of administering his punishments. He also favoured keeping convicts moving from place to place, splitting up families and friends. He had been quoted as saying that convicts became lazy and prone to temptation if they kept the same company and remained in one place for too long.

'The only hope we have of staying together is to go on the run.'

Murdo Ross made the gloomy observation as he wiped the last vestige of gravy from inside his pewter eating-bowl with a hunk of coarse, black bread.

'You mean, become bolters?' Charlie Campbell viewed the suggestion with alarm. 'We wouldn't last more than a few days out there. All we'd do is set ourselves up for a flogging and a few years at Macquarie Harbour. Governor Sorell's hard on bolters.'

'Can you think of any other way?' The red-haired and red-bearded Murdo growled the question at Charlie Campbell as he set aside his food bowl. Packing his pipe with tobacco, he lit up, using a flaming twig drawn from the fire.

Two years of hard, physical outdoor life had shaped Murdo into a tall and powerfully built young man. 'Jonathan Sinclair's done the decent thing and let us know what's happening here. He's as good as told us that bolting's the only hope we have of staying together.'

'There's no need for you two to put your futures in jeopardy for me.' Angus Ross sat leaning back against the rough timber wall of the hut that was home for the convicts. 'We've had two good years here – better than we had any right to expect when we arrived. Let's take things as they come and allow fate to take its course.'

Murdo rose to his feet and began pacing the small patch of cleared land in front of the cabin. 'We swore when we arrived here that we'd stay together in Van Dieman's Land. That's what we've done up to now. It's not our fault that Jonathan Sinclair is giving up his farm and returning to Scotland. If we hadn't worked so hard for him he wouldn't have been able to afford to go. He didn't *have* to sell to Yelland.'

'Trying to decide who's to blame isn't going to help anyone. The best thing we can do is carry on working and hope this Captain Yelland isn't as bad as people say. Perhaps when he sees how well this farm's been kept up he'll be content to leave things the way they are.'

Angus Ross provided the voice of calm reason and although the others murmured their misgivings, they agreed to do as he suggested and not join the small army of bolters who terrorised certain areas of the island. Angus was still the accepted leader of the trio.

Angus Ross realised he had made a terrible mistake the moment Captain Anthony Yelland arrived to take possession of Jonathan Sinclair's farm. It would have been better had he heeded Murdo's advice.

Riding beside a wagon containing numerous items of furniture, the army officer was tall, thin and unsmiling – but it was his travelling companions who dismayed the three Scotsmen. Eight chained convicts walked wearily and with bowed heads behind the wagon, the leading man secured to the vehicle. Yet Angus hardly noticed them; he had eyes only for the wagon driver, who was also a convict. The man who looked down at him with mutual recognition was – Bill Bloxham!

When he overcame his initial surprise at the unexpected meeting, a smile of anticipation spread across the Londoner's face. With an increasing sense of dismay, Angus realised the rumours about Captain Anthony Yelland were true. Bloxham's sadistic talents had been recognised and he had been given employment flogging the army officer's convicts.

Jonathan Sinclair emerged from his small cabin with his wife to greet the new owner, advancing with hand extended. Ignoring the greeting, Captain Yelland indicated towards the Rosses and

Charlie Campbell. 'Are these the three convicts I am taking on from you? Why are they not chained?'

Taken aback by the other man's attitude, Jonathan Sinclair said, 'They've been with me for more than two years. You'll not find harder workers and I've never needed to put chains on them.'

'There are too many settlers like you, Sinclair. You're far too soft. Such men as these aren't *grateful* for kindness. They're convicts, criminals. If they seem to behave like normal, decent people it's usually because they're getting away with something they shouldn't. These three won't be getting away with a thing in future, I can assure you. They'll be back in chains by morning and everyone around here will sleep more securely in their beds because of it.'

'Begging your pardon, Captain Yelland, but you'd do well to chain 'em tonight. I know these three. Travelled 'ere on the transport with 'em. They're trouble-makers, and no mistake.'

'Damn you for the Devil's man you are, Bloxham!'

Angus Ross put out his hand to restrain his hotheaded son, but Murdo was too angry to heed the warning.

'It's *you* who ought to have swung at the end of a rope for killing my brother. I'll give you trouble . . . .'

'Stop right there, convict! One further pace and you'll join your brother in whatever particular hell he happens to occupy.' Captain Yelland pointed a cocked, large-bore horse-pistol at Murdo's head.

For one sinking moment Angus thought his son would disregard the warning. His shoulders sagged with relief when Murdo remained where he was.

When Yelland realised he was not going to have to shoot, he said to Bill Bloxham, 'There are manacles in the wagon. Fetch them and secure him.'

'There's no need to chain Murdo. He saw Bloxham whip his brother – my son – to death. It was the shock of meeting up with him again that made him say what he did.'

'You'll speak only when you're spoken to. Put manacles on the other one as well, Bloxham. Don't bother with the one-armed man, he'll not be able to do much.'

Bill Bloxham could not find the manacles and Captain Yelland irritably ordered him to wrap chains about the two men's wrists and secure them with padlocks. Murdo and Charlie Campbell submitted to being secured by Bill, although Murdo had difficulty controlling the anger he felt.

When they were both secured, Captain Yelland ordered Murdo to be brought before him. Murdo was not skilled at hiding his true feelings and his expression showed his fury and disdain as the ex-army officer asked his name.

'You need to be taught a lesson, Ross. I'll have no convict talk in my presence as you just did. You've been working too long for a slack master and he's done you no favours. Bloxham, tie this man to the tree over there and give him twenty-five lashes.'

Jonathan Sinclair added his protest to that of Angus Ross, but Captain Yelland rounded on him angrily.

'Such protest ill becomes you, Mister Sinclair. Had you remembered these men were convicts and disciplined them accordingly, a flogging might not have been necessary. I have taken that into account by only awarding him twenty-five lashes. Had I not, it would have been a hundred.'

'You have no right to order him to be flogged. That's for a magistrate.'

'I dispute your argument, Mister Sinclair, but it matters not. Governor Sorell has seen fit to appoint me magistrate for this district. Ross will be flogged now and tomorrow he will be returned to Hobart, with a recommendation that he serve the remainder of his sentence on a chain gang. The other two will be transferred elsewhere too. No doubt they also need reminding that they are felons, sentenced to *punishment*. All right, Bloxham, begin flogging when you're ready.'

Bill Bloxham delivered each stroke of the lash with power and formidable expertise, yet he was unable to draw more than a momentary gasp from Murdo Ross.

By the time Captain Yelland ordered Murdo to be unfastened from the tree, Mrs Sinclair was in tears and only now did Murdo show the effects of the flogging. His legs began to shake and refused to support him. As Murdo sank to his knees, Bill Bloxham attempted to haul him to his feet, using the chain connecting Murdo's wrists.

'Leave him!' Knocking Bloxham to one side, Angus Ross used his one arm to raise Murdo to his feet, doing his best to avoid touching the flayed skin on Murdo's back.

A single look from Angus was sufficient for Bill Bloxham to lose all interest in the man he had just flogged. Without seeking permission from Captain Yelland, Angus led Murdo to the hut they had occupied for the last two years.

Satisfied that he had asserted his authority in a suitable manner, Captain Yelland allowed father and son to go their way while he set Charlie Campbell and his own convicts to work unloading his chattels from the wagon and carrying them inside the house.

Later, when darkness fell, the other convicts joined the Rosses inside the small hut. Only Bill Bloxham had separate quarters, being allocated a space in a lean-to outhouse attached to the cabin recently vacated by the two Sinclairs.

The hut had not been built to accommodate eleven convicts and after a while the two Rosses and Charlie Campbell went outside, where the air was colder, but also a great deal fresher.

Murdo's back had been treated with an ointment sent out to him by Mrs Sinclair before she and her husband departed, but he was unable to lean back against the wall of the hut as did his two companions.

'You were right, Murdo, and I was wrong. We should have bolted before Captain Yelland came here.' There was much bitterness in the voice of Angus Ross.

'It's too late to think of that now,' declared Charlie Campbell.

'I didn't say *that*.'

Charlie Campbell looked at the elder Ross as though he could not have heard him properly. Holding up his manacled hands, he said, 'What about these – and Murdo's back? We can't do it now and after tomorrow none of us will know the whereabouts of the others.'

'That's why it *has* to be tonight. There's a hammer and cold chisel at the back of the hut that will have those chains off in minutes. Murdo's back isn't so bad that we can't put a great many miles between us and Captain Yelland by the time the sun rises tomorrow.'

'You mean . . . we're going? We're bolting?' Murdo's excitement caused him to raise his voice more than was wise.

'Shh! We don't know who's listening. I don't trust any of the new arrivals. They're all far too keen to keep in with Bloxham. But whether we go or not is up to you. You're the one who's been flogged . . . .'

'*Pm* not a sixteen-year-old boy, and I only took twenty-five lashes. God! What our Cathal must have gone through. I'd willingly swing for Bill Bloxham.'

'You'll not swing for anyone — not if we can get clear of this place tonight. If we're all of the same mind I'll go and fetch the hammer and cold chisel. You two make your way to the north-east corner of the wheat field. I'll bring the tools there. Hurry now, before someone gets the idea of coming out here and locking us in the hut with the others.'

Angus found the hammer and cold chisel where he had said they would be and then hurried to where the others were waiting. There was a large rock here and Angus ordered Murdo to lay his hands on the rock in a manner that stretched the chain to its full extent. Charlie would hold the cold chisel, while Angus, more skilled in the use of a hammer, would strike the blows to break the padlock.

The operation was hampered by the lack of light, as the moon had not yet risen and the stars provided Angus with only the feeblest of illumination. It proved noisy too. The clanging of metal against metal was amplified further in the ears of the men by fear of what would happen if the sound carried to the cabin and Captain Yelland. But it was essential that the chains came off here. It was rough country dense with trees beyond the edge of the field. A man would need two free hands to make a successful bid for freedom.

At last the hasp of the padlock securing the chains about Murdo's wrists parted, and as he threw them off, he said, 'Give me the hammer, I'll free Charlie. My back's sore, but it hasn't affected the muscles in my arms.'

It took Murdo a fraction of the time to chisel through the padlock but as it fell away there was a shout from nearby and the great bulk of Bill Bloxham loomed above the three men.

'I thought that's what you was up to. Well, well, well! Captain Yelland's going to enjoy having you three brought back to him. The last men who bolted from him got a thousand lashes apiece. You won't shrug them off, Murdo Ross. Your father neither. *I'll* see to that. If you haven't joined that weak-kneed brother of yours by the time I've finished with you, you'll be wishing you had.'

Bill Bloxham's confidence in dealing with the three men was boosted by the broad-bladed dagger he held in his hand which was clearly visible in the pale starlight, but he was given no opportunity to put it to use.

Murdo came up from the ground swinging the heavy, short-handled hammer in an overarm blow that the other man tried in vain to ward off. The head of the hammer struck Bill Bloxham on the temple with the sound of an egg falling from a height and he fell to the ground without a sound. The sadistic man would never again flog the skin from a fellow convict.

'You've killed him!' Charlie Campbell was aghast. 'They'll be after us for murder now!'

'First they'll need to find him – and then us.' Angus picked up the dead convict's knife and tucked it inside his belt. 'Help Murdo carry him to the river. I'll bring the chains.'

Struggling with the heavy body, the two men followed Angus along the course of a stream that emptied into a river that was deep, slow-moving and well stocked with weed and reeds. When they reached the river Angus weighted the body with chains, stuffed a number of rocks inside the dead man's shirt and then Bill Bloxham was committed to the water.

'By the time they find him – if they ever do, we'll be long gone,' declared Angus with a great deal of satisfaction. 'They might even believe he's bolted with us!'

'I hope so.' The perspiration gathered on Charlie Campbell's forehead was due more to fear than his recent exertions.

'If the worst happens and we're caught you can turn "King's evidence", Charlie. Murdo and me won't hold it against you. Bloxham deserved to die for what he did to Cathal, but there's no reason why you should swing for it.'

Angus let his hand rest on his son's shoulder for a moment. 'We're not going to be caught. I've had this day in mind for some months now. Come on, we need to head towards the Western Tiers. I know someone there who'll help us.'

The three escaping convicts travelled north-eastwards for four days through country that became increasingly forbidding. They saw no signs of pursuit and Angus correctly surmised that Captain Yelland had assumed them to be travelling downriver towards the southern coast.

At dusk, on their first day of freedom, they hid until it was dark before raiding a remote farm from which they stole a lamb. The young animal provided them with meat for the next couple of days.

On the fourth day Angus paused at the foot of a low yet formidable mountain range and studied the scene before him carefully. Finally he pointed up the slope to the space between two of the highest peaks, saying, 'We'll go that way.'

His navigation was faultless. Two hours later they were challenged by a black-bearded man who pointed a cocked musket in their direction. Noises on either side of the newcomers suggested that the bearded man was not alone up here in the mountains.

Suddenly the armed man peered more closely at Angus. 'Angus! It *is* you . . . ? Of course it is! There can't be two red-bearded, one-armed men in Van Dieman's Land!'

Putting up the rifle the stranger advanced to clasp Angus in his arms. 'So you've finally made up your mind to become a bushranger. You should have done it a year ago.'

'It's been forced on us. The farm was sold to an army man – a Captain Yelland. He brought along his own flogger – as my son Murdo will testify. His back's in need of treatment.'

'We've someone here who's had plenty of practice treating flayed backs – you'll find no one better in the land. She's an Abo woman and as ugly as a gaoler's dog, but I don't need to look at her face under a blanket in the dark, and she makes herself useful around the camp during the day. Come on in and meet her and the others.'

Angus Ross introduced the armed man to the others as Johnny Galleon.

'Johnny Galleon, the *famous* bushranger?' There was awe and respect in Charlie Campbell's voice. Johnny Galleon was the most renowned of the island's many bushrangers. Galleon had succeeded in escaping from every category of penal servitude devised by the authorities in New South Wales and on Van Dieman's Land. He had been hunted by soldiers, Aborigine trackers and fellow convicts. Yet, despite a price of a hundred pounds on his head, he remained at liberty.

'How do you two know each other?' Murdo was as curious as Charlie Campbell.

'Has your pa never told you? I always knew he was a man to trust!' Johnny thumped Angus so hard on the back that he staggered and almost fell on the rough ground. 'It was about a year back when I came close to being caught. I'd been shot in an ambush by Governor Sorell's men. My mates were killed and I was wounded, but I managed to get clear. Your pa found me down by the river on the farm where you worked. He fed me and kept my wound clean until I was able to make it back here for "Beauty" to fix me up properly.'

The story came as a complete surprise to Murdo and Charlie. Angus had kept his secret well.

As they toiled higher up the slope other men came out from hiding to walk with them, and by the time they reached the hidden camp they must have been accompanied by at least twenty men. Every one of the escaped convicts was well armed and looked as though they knew how to use their weapons.

At the camp Johnny unceremoniously jabbed the toe of his boot in the ribs of a near-naked Aborigine woman who was squatting by a fire, smoking a clay pipe. When she turned around to remonstrate with the bushranger leader Angus found himself looking at the ugliest woman he had ever seen.

'Stir yourself, Beauty. We've got company. Throw a hunk or two of woolly-back in the pot then come and tend to this young man. He's had a flogging. Come on, move yourself, you lazy, good-for-nothing cow. Get up on your feet!'

This time the kick that accompanied Johnny's words was considerably harder than before, but the woman merely grunted and rose from the ground unhurriedly.

'She'll fix you up directly. Come and have a drink of good whisky while you wait. I took it from the home of the local magistrate up at York town. You'll not have tasted anything like it since you left Scotland . . . .'

As Johnny talked, Angus was looking around the camp. It was spread about the entrance to a small cave and was dirty and untidy. There were three other Aborigine women in addition to Beauty. Two of the three appeared to be in drunken stupors, lying sprawled on the ground in a state of total nudity. The other woman sat by a fire, breastfeeding a young baby that was as black as she was, yet sported a head of reddish hair.

The whisky was as good as Johnny had promised. As the new-comers sat around drinking with the bushrangers, their leader asked Angus if he intended remaining at the camp and throwing in his lot with the gang. Angus felt mellowed by the excellent whisky. It brought back memories of happier days – drinking Highland-distilled whisky on the heather-clad slopes of Eskaig while the young girls played about him and Ailsa waited at home in the small cott – days that had gone for ever.

Angus pulled his thoughts back to the realities of the present.

'I've seen one son die from a flogging. I'll not watch another's life choked from him on a gallows tree. I'm going north, Johnny. Across Bass Strait to the mainland, and then far enough inland to forget about convicts and gaolers. We talked about it one night when you were wounded, do you remember?'

Johnny nodded, but said nothing.

'Come with us, Johnny. If you stay here you'll be caught one day, you know you will. Come with us and begin a new life away from here.'

Johnny shook his head, but there was a note of wistfulness in his voice when he said, 'I can't, Angus. Not now. Two years ago – even a year, maybe. But now I'm the *famous* Johnny Galleon, the success-ful bushranger. The leader of a gang that strikes fear into informers and floggers and those settlers who'd rather beat the hide off their convicts than kick a dog. I've become a *somebody*. Do you know the Governor even offered me an amnesty a while back? Invited me to his "residence" to discuss it. Can you imagine that? Why, he'd have crossed the road to avoid getting a whiff of me if we'd met back in England! Oh, yes, I know they'll take me, sooner or later – but I'll give 'em a run for their money first and then they'll need to shoot me dead. I won't be chief guest at no neck-stretching party. They'll make up stories about me, Angus. Stories to give hope to a man when he's chained hand-and-foot in some dark hole because he's looked at a gaoler when he shouldn't. I'll still be remembered when the world's forgotten the name of the superintendent of the prison at Hobart and the judge who had me sent out here.'

'I wish you'd give the matter some thought, Johnny. We need a man with us who knows how to live off the country. It could be a good life for all of us – in a place where there are no gaolers . . . no soldiers.'

'*This* is a good life. If I want anything I go out and take it. If I'm feeling lazy I send someone else to get it for me. We take only from those who can afford to lose a few sheep, in the main. That way we keep the small settlers happy and they remain on our side. We've got women here . . . of a sort. If we want more, we go out and take 'em from the Abos. When I go into a settlement folk *know* me. I see respect in their eyes. How many convicts have *ever* known the meaning of respect? How many ever will? No, Angus, I'll stay here and do what I'm doing now. I accept I'll not live to be an old man, but, by God, I'll enjoy the years I have!'

The bushranger poured half a mug of good whisky down his throat and promptly refilled the mug. 'But you'll need a guide to take you to the coast and I've just the man for you. Skinny . . . ? Skinny Harris, where are you?'

It was quite dark now, the flames from the fire casting dancing shadows around the small clearing outside the shallow cave.

'Skinny'll be off in the bushes with that young Abo girl. We only captured her last week and he can't leave it alone. If he works any more weight off on her we won't be able to see him at all. Skinny? Come here . . . I want you.'

A tall, gaunt man came from the bushes to one side of the clearing, pushing a young Aborigine girl ahead of him. The girl was one of those who had been lying on the ground in a drunken stupor and it was clear that the effects of the alcohol had not worn off. Bleary-eyed and rubbery-legged, she sank to the ground on the spot she had previously occupied and curled up to resume her sleep.

'What do you want?' Skinny Harris scowled down at the seated bushranger leader.

'I've a job for you. I want you to take my three friends up to Bass Strait and find a boat to take them off Van Dieman's Land.'

Skinny Harris looked at each of the three men in turn before speaking to Johnny again. 'Where are they going? Getting one man on a boat bound for England's bad enough. Three's well-nigh impossible. They smoke out every ship with sulphur before it leaves Hobart — *and* hand out heavy fines to the crew if anyone's found . . . .'

'We want to reach the mainland of New South Wales — and we'd prefer to be landed somewhere quiet.'

'Then you'll need to find a whaler, an American whaler, and they demand money. The days are gone when an American would help a convict just to cock a snook at British justice.'

This posed a problem. The three runaway convicts had no money and little prospect of obtaining any.

'How much money?' The question came from Johnny and brought immediate protests from his fellow bushrangers.

'Angus Ross saved my life. All the gold in Van Dieman's Land couldn't repay him for that.' Johnny scowled at the men around him and when the protests ceased, he turned back to the tall, thin member of his gang. 'How much do you think the Americans will want?'

'Fifty guineas . . . in gold.'

Skinny Harris's reply was quick. Far too quick.

'Taking away what you've added on for yourself that makes about twenty-five pounds. I'll give Angus the money. You'll do your part for nothing, Skinny — because I say you will. Just in case you get any more of the ideas that had you sent to Van Dieman's Land in the first place, I'll be arming the three of 'em; rifles for hunting and pistols for protection. Honest men with money in their pockets can't walk in safety in this country.'

Johnny's humour brought dutiful laughter from his companions.

'I'm obliged to you, Johnny. If you ever change your mind about leaving Van Dieman's Land you'll know you have friends on the mainland.'

The three Scotsmen, guided by Skinny Harris, set off from the mountain hideout of Johnny Galleon and his bushrangers two days later. Harris was in a sulky mood. He had wanted to bring the young Aborigine girl along but his leader refused to allow her to go. He believed her presence would attract unwelcome attention from any of her people they might meet along the way. A bitter enmity had grown up between white men, settlers and convicts, and the Aborigines, but the original occupiers of the land tended to stay clear of the newcomers, unless they had a very good reason for launching an attack. The presence of one of their women with a party of runaway convicts would provide such a reason.

Skinny Harris was a taciturn man and the Scotsmen soon gave up trying to make conversation with him. He led the way and they followed, but Angus kept a careful check on the route they were taking and when they made camp for that night he suggested to their guide that their present course would take them dangerously close to Launceston, the penal colony where they had first landed on Van Dieman's Land.

Harris's reaction was one of immediate anger. 'If you think you know better than me where to go, then I'll be happy to go back and leave you to it. I never asked to come on this jaunt, I was quite happy to stay in the mountains.'

'We're grateful to you for guiding us to the coast,' said Angus in placatory tones, 'it's just that I don't want to run the risk of meeting up with any soldiers from Launceston.'

'I have more to lose than you if they take us,' replied their guide. 'I killed one soldier in making my escape and I've shot two more since. All you'll get if you're taken is a taste of the lash and a couple of years on a chain gang. It'll be the gallows for me. Just you remember *that* when you start worrying about which way I'm taking you.'

Harris's reply satisfied Angus, but his concern returned once more the following day when they encountered reasonably kept roads and cultivated fields and began to sight flocks of sheep, guarded by convict shepherds, grazing on the hillsides. Angus brought the party to a halt and asked Harris point-blank what he was doing. It should have been possible to reach their destination in the far northeast corner of Van Dieman's Land without passing through settled territory. Unrepentant, Skinny Harris growled that he had 'private business' to attend to before they reached their destination.

'What sort of private business? You're supposed to be guiding us to the coast and putting us in touch with American whalers, not carrying out some plan of your own.'

'I used to work on a farm not far from here. I've unfinished business there.'

'You'll not risk our chances of escape because you have a grudge to pay off. Settle your differences on your return – when we're safely on a boat to New South Wales.'

'I don't intend coming back. I'm going to the mainland too – but there's someone I want to take with me.'

'A woman?'

'What if it is?'

Angus hesitated. He did not trust this man, but reaching New South Wales was likely to prove very difficult without him.

'All right – but if anything goes wrong you won't have to worry about ending your life at the end of a rope. I'll end it for you – with this.'

Angus Ross brandished his rifle in the other man's face before turning back to the others.

The farm to which Skinny Harris led the Scotsmen was situated in a pretty valley on the far edge of the settlements. They reached the spot in mid-afternoon but did not approach the cabin immediately. The guide assured the others that no one would try to cause trouble against four armed men, but Angus preferred to wait in the trees at the edge of the cleared land until he learned how many men were inside.

Their hiding-place was a considerable distance from the cabin, but by the time dusk fell, Angus was satisfied that there were only two women and two men, one seemingly a convict farm-labourer.

'All right, we'll go down now,' declared Angus to Harris. 'While you go in and sort out your "business", we'll make sure their convict doesn't run off and warn anyone that we're here.'

The arrangement seemed to suit Harris and he led the way towards the cabin.

The three Scotsmen surprised the convict farm-labourer, a middle-aged man, in the act of washing in a lean-to beside the small barn some distance behind the cabin.

'Don't make a sound,' Angus warned the startled man. 'We'll be here no more than a few minutes and if nobody does anything silly nobody will be hurt. You understand?'

The convict nodded, far too terrified of the gun being pointed at him to attempt to speak.

After they had waited in silence for more than ten minutes, Angus growled, 'What's keeping Harris? What can he be doing in there?'

'Shall I go and find out?' Murdo asked the question.

'No, give him a few more minutes. The girl might have some things to pack.'

'Is your friend . . . the tall one who's gone inside . . . is he Skinny Harris?'

'Yes. Do you know him?' Angus was surprised Harris had not said anything about knowing the man they were holding at gunpoint.

'No.' The middle-aged convict licked his lips nervously, yet he seemed less frightened than he had been a few minutes before. 'But I've heard all about him from Mr Kennedy – and from Amy too. They've always feared he'd come back one day.'

'What do you mean *feared* he'd come back? Why should the girl fear him? He's come back for her.'

'She's the reason he ran off in the first place. She didn't want anything to do with him and one day he attacked her. Mr Kennedy took him in to the magistrate at gunpoint and Harris was on his way to gaol when he escaped with half-a-dozen others. Amy *hates* him. She'd never go off anywhere with *him* . . . .'

The sound of a shot came from inside the cabin. It was followed by a woman's sustained screaming. Moments later Skinny Harris hurried towards the lean-to, propelling a young girl before him.

A gasp of recognition came from Murdo when he saw the girl, but his father had eyes only for the tall bushranger.

'What happened in there?'

'The farmer attacked me. Wanted to arrest me.'

'He's lying!' The girl shouted the accusation. 'He couldn't do anything. He was tied up when Skinny shot him.'

Harris released the girl only to knock her to the ground with his fist. When he leaned over her to pick her up, Angus ordered, 'Leave her.'

He too had recognised the girl. It was Amy MacDonald, the girl from the transport *Hercules* – Cathal's girl.

'Murdo . . . Charlie. Keep Harris here until I come back. Shoot him if need be. You, girl. Come with me.'

Inside the cabin it took Angus only a few minutes to discover the truth of what had happened. Clothes and belongings were strewn all about the floor and rough-wood cupboard doors were hanging wide open. The cabin had been thoroughly searched.

On the floor, still bound to a chair that lay on its side, was the body of a man, his face a mask of blood. He had been shot in the head. By the man's side kneeled a weeping woman, wringing her hands in despair.

'Do what you can for the woman.' Angus was beside himself with anger. He should have trusted his instincts and not allowed Harris to enter the cabin alone. His irresponsible and callous actions had put the whole escape in jeopardy.

Outside, Harris watched Angus's approach defiantly and while the Scotsman was still trying to control his anger sufficiently to speak coherently, the tall bushranger said, 'There's money hidden in the cabin somewhere. He wouldn't tell me where it is. Anyway, he'd have sent to the magistrate and had us all tracked down if I hadn't shot him. You'd best shoot their convict . . . the woman too. No one will find them for weeks. We'll be long gone by then.'

The report from Angus's gun startled everyone in the lean-to as Skinny Harris died with a surprised expression on his face and a bullet in his heart. The sound of the shot brought Amy to the door of the cabin and she saw in an instant what had happened.

'Go back inside and look after the woman,' said Angus. 'I'm taking the convict off with us for a way but he'll be released unharmed when I think we're too far off to be caught.'

'Leave him here, he won't tell anyone. It was Skinny who killed Mr Kennedy, not you. I'm coming with *you*.'

'We have troubles enough without having a woman along with us.'

'If you don't take me I'll follow you anyway. Mrs Kennedy won't stay on the farm alone now that this has happened and I'll be sent somewhere else. I put up with more than my share of grief before coming here. I'll not go through all that again.'

'Let her come, Pa . . . for Cathal's sake.'

As Angus tried to weigh up Murdo's words, Charlie Campbell said unexpectedly, 'It's what Cathal would have wished, Angus.' Angus suddenly remembered how Cathal had looked when he first saw Amy MacDonald climbing the gangway to the transport at Woolwich reach.

'All right. Get anything you need to bring, we're leaving right now.'

As Amy hurried away, Angus turned to the convict employed on the farm. 'If I leave you here with the woman, will you give us until morning to get away?'

'I'll give you longer than that. So will Mrs Kennedy, I don't doubt. It wasn't you who killed her husband – and you made Harris pay for it. She's in your debt and she's a woman who puts great store by such things.'

'I'm only sorry I couldn't prevent it from happening. But give us as much time as you can.'

Amy MacDonald came from the house stowing a few items of clothing inside a faded shawl as she ran towards them. She seemed desperately afraid that they might leave without her.

Leaving the body of Skinny Harris behind on his victim's farm, the two Rosses, Charlie Campbell and Amy MacDonald put as many miles between them and possible pursuit as was possible before the next dawn.

It was not easy going. The logical course for them to take was northwards, skirting the settlements. For this very reason Angus headed eastwards, into wilder, more mountainous country. Darkness made it doubly hazardous. When dawn came they found they could still see the settlements which seemed dangerously close.

It was now that Amy was able to make a worthwhile contribution to the party's progress. Without going into any great detail, she confessed that before going to work for the Kennedys she had been with a party of surveyors and prospectors who had explored much of the area into which they were now heading. Although she had little knowledge of geography or navigation, she would be able to save them from making time-consuming errors on their journey to the lonely north-eastern coast.

Even with Amy's help, the journey of about eighty miles took them ten days, five of which were spent in the mountains, and two hiding among rocks after fighting off a small band of hostile Aborigines.

For the final two days the weary party caught tantalising views of the sea whenever they topped a rise, only to find their way blocked by a river. They spent many hours travelling along the overgrown riverbank, only to find that it joined with another, larger river and they were forced to retrace their steps.

Their condition by now was becoming desperate. The prison-issue uniforms of the three men had long ago been replaced by the settler with whom they had been employed, but the clothes had been old and cheap and had disintegrated. Footwear was in an even worse condition, and no longer protected their feet from rocks and thorns.

Then, when they were almost ready to believe the sea was no more than a figment of their imagination, they emerged from a patch of dense, skin-clawing scrub onto a wide beach.

As the three men let out wild yells of glee, Amy ran down to the water's edge. Wading into the water until she was knee-deep she began scooping up the salt water and throwing it over her face and hair. For a few minutes, Amy forgot all her cares. Forgot that she was a convicted felon, on the run from the authorities. Instead she was a young woman, enjoying the sunshine and the feel of the sea.

Then Amy looked up and the carefree moment was gone. In throwing sea water over herself, she had soaked her thin linen dress and it clung tightly to her, accentuating instead of hiding the lines of her body. Murdo was looking at her with an expression she had seen on men's faces too many times before. For a while she had almost forgotten . . . .

Turning away from Murdo, her foot touched something that moved away. Looking down, she plunged her hand beneath the water and it emerged clutching a huge crab. She threw it high up the beach, calling for the men to capture it before it returned to the sea, then she searched about her and before long had caught three more.

That evening, when they had a fire going, Amy baked the crabs in mud and Angus declared he had tasted nothing to equal the meal since leaving Scotland.

Scotland seemed a lifetime ago: no more than an unreal dream. Yet he had left a wife and family behind there, to fend for them-selves . . . . There was nothing more he could have done to help them then or since, yet the thought of them filled him with a guilt he would never lose.

It was warm and still that night, and the lapping of the waves on the beach generated a soothing, soporific feeling among the four fugitives. Yet something woke Angus far into the night. Opening his eyes he looked up to see the branches of the trees above him bathed in moonlight, but he knew it was not this that had woken him.

He heard a faint sound and turning his head he saw Amy walking slowly down the beach towards the sea, her attitude that of someone lost in thought.

Angus was debating with himself whether or not to go after her and discover whether anything was wrong, when there was another movement, closer at hand. His hand felt for the rifle lying at his side, and then stopped. Murdo was sitting up on the ground, looking down the beach to where Amy walked. Moments later, he rose and set off after her.

Angus relaxed. It seemed that Cathal was not the only one of his sons to find Amy attractive. Had Cathal lived, he would have spent his first couple of years in Van Dieman's Land pining for her. Now, it seemed, Murdo was following the example set by his brother. On the other hand, Murdo's interest in the girl might be far less complicated . . . .

If such was the case, Angus believed Amy had had enough experience of life to deal with Murdo in whichever way she wanted. Angus thought of what the future might hold if Murdo *was* smitten with the girl. Amy was not the type of wife he would have chosen for his son had they still been in Scotland, but here . . . ? Angus believed his son would not find anyone better.

Standing at the water's edge, gazing out along a path of silver moonlight that stretched all the way to the far horizon of the sea, Amy knew Murdo had followed her, even though his feet made hardly any sound on the soft sand.

'Are you all right?'

He spoke after standing silently and uncertainly behind her for some minutes.

'Is there any reason why I shouldn't be?'

'No . . . I just wondered. I saw you get up and walk down here . . . .'

'So?'

'So I thought I'd come down here too, and keep you company.'

Murdo became more sure of himself. He remembered that Amy was a convict, like himself. She had shared a cabin on board the *Hercules* with an 'uncle'; had accompanied a survey party through much of this part of Van Dieman's Land; and he remembered how

148

she had looked standing in the sea in a wet, clinging dress earlier in the day.

Amy began walking along the edge of the sea, not bothering to change her course when the water swirled up the beach and around her ankles. She walked without talking and Murdo walked along beside her, feeling angrily uncertain of himself again. He could hold his own in the company of convicts or free men. He basically believed himself to be as good as *any* man, whatever their station in life. He told himself there was no reason at all why he should suddenly be doubting himself in the company of a woman . . . a fellow *convict*.

A large crab rose from the sand almost beneath Amy's feet and brushed her toe as it scuttled sideways towards the sea. Momentarily startled, she came to an abrupt halt, one of her hands reaching out and clutching Murdo's arm.

It was all the encouragement he needed. Pulling her to him he kissed her. As the kiss became more demanding, Murdo dropped a hand to the small of Amy's back and forced his body against hers.

Suddenly, she moved her head to one side and refused to cooperate when he tried to kiss her again.

'Come on . . . don't try that game with me, I'm not Gathal . . . .'

She broke away from him, but he would not allow her to go beyond arm's length.

'No, you're not Cathal.'

Even in his aroused state, Murdo recognised the sorrow in her voice.

'I think I was hoping that because you're a Ross, you might be just a little bit like him.'

'What do you mean by that?' Murdo felt the uncertainty once more.

'I mean that we were both wanting the other to be something we're not.'

'I still don't understand.'

Murdo was confused. Somehow she had made him feel that he was the failure. That *he* was the one who had not done all that had been expected of him.

'I really don't believe you do, Murdo. But don't worry about it. It's my fault, not yours.' She shrugged, unhappily.

'You're not telling me you've never been with a man before . . . ? I wouldn't believe it. I *know* it isn't true. On the *Hercules* . . .'

'I don't want to talk about anything that happened on the *Hercules* or that's happened since . . . .'

Amy lapsed into an abrupt silence that lasted a full minute. When she looked up at him he saw there were tears on her face.

'Yes, there've been other men, Murdo. Men who did what *they* wanted to do with me, not what *I* wanted them to do. The only one I really cared for was Cathal – and he died for something he never did. I thought I could see in you some of the things I loved in Cathal. I was wrong.'

She stood facing him and suddenly her hands dropped to her side and she looked tired and defeated. 'All right, if you want to do it to me, you can. God knows, you've had little in your life that you really want – but don't expect me to enjoy what you're doing. You'll be no different than any other man I've known and I'll go my own way as soon as I get the chance. But that won't matter to you, you'll have had what you want. Where shall we go . . . up there, among the trees? Or right here, on the beach?'

Amy's reaction to Murdo's clumsy and unsubtle attempt to seduce her took him by surprise and her words troubled him far more than he wanted to admit. His shoulders sagged and he raised and dropped his hands in a gesture acknowledging defeat.

'I'm sorry, Amy.' Murdo was thoroughly contrite. 'Are you coming back with me to the others, or would you rather stay out here for a while?'

'You mean . . . you don't want to do it?'

'I'm not saying that, at all. But you're right, it should mean something . . . to both of us. It would have done to Cathal.'

He started walking back to where the others lay beneath the trees and she came with him, trying hard to keep up with his rapid pace.

They had almost reached the place where the others were, when Murdo suddenly stopped and turned to speak to her. 'I thought Cathal was foolish for the way he thought about you, Amy. I was wrong – as I was wrong just now. You're a very special girl.'

He had taken perhaps a dozen more paces when Amy's soft call brought him to a halt once more. When he turned, she walked up to him and he saw tears on her face. 'That's the nicest, kindest thing anyone's ever said to me, Murdo, and I'll never forget it. Thank you.'

Lying on the ground in the shadow of the trees, Angus heard Amy's call to Murdo. Although he could not hear what was being said, he saw them standing very close to each other on the sand. Turning over, he closed his eyes and enjoyed a rare moment of satisfaction. Given only half a chance in life, he believed Murdo and Amy might find great happiness together, and it was his intention that they should be given such a chance.

Early the next morning Murdo shot a brush kangaroo which foolishly wandered close to their camp. This lucky chance ensured they would not go hungry for a couple of days, while the animal's tough hide renewed their primitive footwear, this time fashioned by Charlie Campbell in the style of crude sandals.

As they sat at the edge of the sandy beach, revelling in the warm sunshine while kangaroo meat cooked on a spit over the fire, Charlie said, 'This is the life, Angus. I'd sooner be tasting 'roo meat than Captain Yelland's whip.'

'We're not safe from Yelland yet,' said Angus grimly, 'and it won't be the whip, but the noose. Having a beach to ourselves is pleasant enough – but we came here to find someone who'd take us off Van Dieman's Land. Unless we get to the mainland we'll never be free men. We'll rest up here today then set off eastwards along the coast. Skinny Harris could have saved us a lot of time, but if there are sealers or whalers along this coast we'll find 'em for ourselves.'

After two days of fruitless searching, it began to seem that Angus's optimism had been misplaced. Not only was there an absence of human beings, but the country itself had become more inhospitable. Great rocky cliffs reared from the sea along the coast and the few beaches they found were rarely accessible unless they scrambled down steep, rocky slopes, risking life and limb.

Just when Angus had begun to believe their attempt to escape from Van Dieman's Land was doomed to failure, Amy excitedly cried out that she could see smoke drifting above the cliff from a spot far below.

At first the others thought it no more than a wisp of distant cloud, but as they drew closer they could all smell the distinctive aroma of woodsmoke and there was great excitement as they sought to see who was below.

Eventually, Charlie located a spot almost a quarter of a mile away from where they obtained a view of a long, shallow-sloping beach. A seagoing vessel rested high and dry on the pebbles, leaning over at an acute angle. A number of men were at work caulking the hull of the ship, while others relaxed on the long, low-lying strip of beach.

Evidence of the men's trade was strewn along the beach for as far as the eye could see: sealskins were heaped in great piles above the high-water mark, while the abandoned carcasses lay wherever the unfortunate creatures had been clubbed to death and skinned.

There were hundreds of such carcasses and as many more waiting to be dealt with. Only a short distance away, on a portion of beach not yet visited by the sealers, other seals, seemingly oblivious of the fate that awaited them, lay on low rocks, or disputed an area of beach with younger cubs. Here and there a number of baby seals, conspicuous by their pale fur, crawled among the carcasses, seeking a mother they would never recognise again.

Rising from the scene of carnage was a smell of rotting flesh that Angus was surprised they had not smelled from miles away. Yet the stench was unimportant. They had found what they were seeking. A steep path led down to the beach, proof that the men below them were not the first sealers to land here.

Before beginning their descent along the cliff path, Angus ordered Murdo and Charlie to conceal pistols in their clothing, together with a small quantity of shot and powder.

He had counted eighteen men on the beach, and they had two Aborigine women with them. Sealers were tough men and they led a hard, but rarely celibate life. They had probably kidnapped the Aborigine women from their tribe, killing the women's menfolk in the process.

Runaway convicts had no more rights than Aborigines – especially when an attractive young girl was among their number, which was why Angus ensured that each man's rifle was loaded and primed before the small party took to the cliff path.

They were no more than halfway down when the sealers saw them and set up a hullaballoo that echoed from end to end of the cliff-fringed beach. By the time Angus and his party reached the sand of the shore, every sealer had stopped working and advanced to meet them, standing together in a loose-knit group. All eyes were on Amy, and Angus knew he had been wise to take precautions.

Last to join the group was an overweight, black-bearded man whose nose bore unmistakable signs of having been broken more than once. He appeared to be the Captain of the sealing vessel and his eyes took in Amy from head to toe before seeking out Angus.

'Who are you – and what are you doing here?' The accent was not American, but Welsh.

'We're seeking a passage to the mainland . . . .'

Before Angus could say more, the Captain spat on the pebbles at his feet and said, '*Convicts!* I've half my crew afraid to show their faces above deck whenever we put into port. I don't need any more on board. As for helping you to escape, why should I risk my future for someone I don't know – and who was probably lucky not to have been hung in the first place? You tell me that, if you can.'

'We're willing to pay you.'

'Pay me? How would a convict come by passage-money, unless it was stolen?'

'It's not been stolen – at least, not by anyone here.'

The bearded Captain looked at Angus suspiciously, but Angus thought he detected a greedy look in the Captain's eyes. The Captain's next words confirmed his belief.

'How much are you willing to pay?'

'Fifteen guineas – in gold.'

'Risk my freedom for fifteen guineas? Do you take me for a fool? Thirty, or nothing.'

'A friend gave me twenty and said I'd find someone to take me for that – or possibly less. It's all we have.'

'Tell 'em to throw in the girl and we'll take 'em for ten, Cap'n.'

The suggestion came from one of the crew and the others voiced their noisy agreement.

'Shut up!' The sealing Captain barked the order over his shoulder, but it was not heeded. Turning back to Angus he said, 'All right, I'll take you for twenty guineas, but I'll see the colour of your money first – and you'll hand over those guns.'

'You can have the guns when we're safely on board — and the money will be yours when we reach the mainland. When can we sail?'

'Early tomorrow morning if I can stop this lazy lot from gawping at your woman and get them back to work. Come on, all of you, get this boat seaworthy. The woman's sailing with us so you'll see all you want of her – but only if we catch tomorrow morning's high tide.'

As the men began drifting away, the bearded Captain said, 'I'm Captain Abraham Adams. I don't want to know your names, the less I know about you the better it will be for everyone. Now, seeing as you don't intend giving me those guns of yours just yet, why don't you go off and shoot a kangaroo or two for meat? We haven't had anything but fish for weeks. Leave the girl with me, if you like. I'll take good care of her.'

'We'll go hunting for you,' said Murdo. 'But Amy comes with us.'

Murdo did not trust Captain Adams any more than he did the sealer's crew but, as Angus told his son, they had no alternative but to take passage in the seal hunters' ship. However, Angus emphasised his own concern by giving Amy a vicious-looking knife the others were not aware he possessed. He also arranged for himself and the other two men to operate a watch system to guard against any surprise move by the sealers.

The three Scotsmen brought two kangaroos to the men on the beach, and the sealers called for a celebration. Wisely, neither the Scotsmen nor Amy joined in the drinking orgy that followed. During the night the three men needed to use rifle-butts to beat off four sealers who approached Amy's sleeping-place with amorous intentions.

The sealers were forced to seek their pleasures elsewhere and when the sun rose, one of the Aborigine women was found spread-eagled on the pebbles. She had been choked to death by one of the drunken seamen. Whilst making love to her he had put all his weight on the forearm resting across her throat, mistaking her death throes for appreciation of his crude lovemaking.

When the tide came in it floated the sealing vessel off the beach, but for a while it looked as though they would never get out to sea. The cliffs shut off the wind needed to fill the small ship's sails and not until Captain Adams put ten men in a longboat to tow the boat clear of the cliffs did they finally get underway.

It became apparent from the first that the crew had not forgotten their designs on Amy, and Murdo was forced to lay one man out when he tried to fondle her. Angus asked Captain Adams how long it would take to reach the mainland, but the Captain was alarmingly vague. 'Who knows? Unless this wind picks up we could be out here for a week. It wouldn't be the first time. What's the hurry? The longer we're out here, the more chance you have of being forgotten by the authorities.'

Angus was no sailor, but he felt that they should have had more sails raised. If the Welsh sea Captain was serious about taking his passengers to their destination, he would want to get them there as quickly as possible in order to resume sealing. There was also a great deal of drinking taking place on board the vessel and Angus became increasingly anxious.

Late that afternoon land was sighted on the horizon and Captain Adams called Angus on deck. 'There you are, that's your destination. Your promised land. Australia.'

'I thought it would take much longer than this.'

'That's because you're not a seaman. You know nothing about tides or wind. I'll put you ashore tonight, when no one can see you. Have your money ready before you step into the longboat.'

Conferring with the others, Angus passed on the Captain's information. He also expressed his own deep misgivings.

Charlie Campbell agreed with him. 'I know nothing about sailing – but I *do* know men. The sealers are sharing some joke and I've an uneasy feeling that we're at the wrong end of it.'

'It's the way they look at Amy that worries me,' declared Murdo. 'But there are too many of them for us to beat them off, even with our pistols. What can we do?'

'I'm not sure yet,' said Angus, 'but when I do move I'll need you to follow my lead. One thing is certain, we're not being put ashore tonight and Amy, stay close to Murdo. Don't let any of the crew come between the two of you.'

'Do you think things are that serious?'

'Not yet, but anything's likely to happen after they've been drinking for a few more hours.'

At dusk, Captain Adams brought his ship close inshore and dropped anchor. Beaming amiably at Angus he said, 'Here we are. Australia. It's a good safe shore so when you've paid me what you owe we'll lower the boat and you can go on your way.'

Angus looked up at the sky. The sun was dipping beneath the horizon. In a few more minutes it would be nightfall. 'I don't fancy going ashore in the dark. We'll wait until morning.'

Captain Adams scowled. 'I'm Captain on board my own ship – and I have other business to attend to. You'll go ashore tonight.'

'We're fare-paying passengers. I say we don't leave until morning.'

Captain Adams gave an almost imperceptible nod and one of the crewmen standing nearby disappeared down the ladder that led to the captain's cabin. He was gone for only a moment before he returned carrying one of the muskets handed over by the three Scotsmen. Angus knew he had been right all along. The Captain had anticipated that there would be objections to the plans he had for his passengers.

'I don't take orders on my own ship – least of all from *convicts*,' Captain Adams smiled, 'but I'm not an unreasonable man. I'll allow the three men to go ashore – but the girl stays.'

As the seaman raised the gun, Angus quietly told Charlie to move in front of him – but Captain Adams was too quick for him.

'Stay where you are. *Exactly* where you are.'

The musket swung to cover Angus and he froze. The three men stood in a line and had no chance of taking out one of the pistols without being seen. However, Amy was partially concealed behind Murdo and he suddenly felt her hand slide beneath his jacket from behind and gently ease free the small pocket pistol that was tucked in his belt.

Murdo held his breath as the pistol came free. He wondered whether Amy knew how to handle a pistol. It was in the half-cock position for safety's sake, and would not fire unless it was fully cocked . . . but he could say nothing.

When the pistol came free nothing happened for what seemed an interminable time. Murdo wanted to turn around, but dared not as Captain Adams gave his crewman instructions concerning the fate of the convicts.

The report of the pistol being fired made Murdo jump. The crewman dropped the musket and let out a scream of pain as the pistol-ball burned its way into his upper arm, and as Angus scooped up the gun, Charlie drew his pistol.

'Quick! Grab the Captain and get down to his cabin.' Ignoring the wounded seaman and pushing the Captain ahead of them, the three men and Amy tumbled down the ladder and crowded inside the cabin as Angus slipped the bolt on the door behind them.

Their muskets had been placed in readiness on a table and there were half-a-dozen more weapons chained in a rack against the wall. It was only a thin chain compared with those the escaping convicts had once worn and it was the work of a moment to snap it, using the butt of one of the rifles.

'Load the guns and place them in readiness on the table, Charlie – and deal with the Captain. Ships' masters usually carry manacles in readiness for trouble. See if you can find some.'

Those in the cabin heard the sound of feet clattering on the ladder outside and someone tried the door.

'Stand away!' Angus's voice was loud enough to carry to anyone standing outside. 'If anyone tries to open the door again I'll shoot through the woodwork.'

There were hurried movements in the space outside the cabin and Angus called again, 'Go back to your quarters and we'll talk again in the morning.'

'You might as well let me go and give up now, you're not going anywhere. If my crew weigh anchor you'll be in the hands of the authorities by morning.'

'No, Captain. You have convicts in your crew who haven't served out their time. They'll do nothing to risk capture. Pass those manacles around that stanchion before you secure them, Charlie. I don't want Captain Adams to have the slightest opportunity of escape. He's not a man to be trusted.'

When grey light showed through the small, brass-encircled porthole, Angus banged on the inside of the Captain's door, at the same time calling out, 'If there's anyone out there you'd better go up on deck. We're coming out, but before we do I'm putting two shots through the door and panelling.'

There was the sound of voices from outside followed by the clatter of at least two men clambering hastily up the ladder to the deck. Flinging open the door, Angus saw that the space outside was empty. Motioning to the others he said, 'Get on deck and take the guns with you. Muster around the wheel.'

The wheel was only a few feet aft from the hatchway and Angus's speed was justified when, a few moments after the four had gathered there, the crew spewed from their quarters, armed with a variety of knives, axes and marline spikes.

'Don't come any closer!'

For a moment it seemed Angus's shouted warning might be ignored but a pistol shot aimed above their heads brought them to a halt.

Angus dropped the weapon to the ground and picked up a rifle. 'That's better. Remember we've weapons enough here to kill the lot of you if you try anything stupid. You . . .' Angus spoke to the coxswain who had been steering the ship for much of the previous day, '. . . what's down there?' He indicated a large hatch cover in the centre of the deck.

'Sealskins, that's all.'

'Murdo, take off the hatch cover and check. See if there are any doors leading from the hold.' To the sealers he ordered, 'Throw all your weapons over the side.'

There was a murmur of anger from the sealers but it ceased abruptly when Angus brought his gun to bear on one of them. The man promptly threw the knife he carried into the sea. Rather more reluctantly, his companions followed suit.

Climbing back to the deck, Murdo confirmed that there were no doors leading from the hold.

'Good!' Using his gun as a pointer, Angus said to the crew, 'Get down in the hold, all except you . . . and you . . . and you.'

Those told to remain were the seaman who had been so anxious to be rid of his knife and two of the older men. The other sealers protested at the order to enter the hold but when four guns were brought to bear on them, they climbed down inside, albeit reluctantly.

'Now put the hatch cover back on and secure it with ropes. Be sure and do it well, I'll inspect it when you're done.'

The crewmen remaining on deck obeyed Angus's orders. When it was done, he ordered the seamen to weigh anchor and unfurl the sails while the coxswain took the wheel.

'*Is* this the mainland?' Angus pointed to the nearby land.

The coxswain nodded, but he had hesitated a little too long.

'I hope so, for your sake. I intend trying to sail around it. If it turns out to be an island I'll shoot you and heave your body over the side for the sharks.'

The sun was not yet high enough to give off any heat, but the coxswain began to perspire profusely. After two unintelligible attempts to speak, he blurted out, 'I . . . I've got this place mixed up with somewhere else. This *is* an island.'

'I thought as much. Are there any charts on board?'

The frightened coxswain nodded vigorously, still not certain of what Angus would do.

'Charlie, go with him and fetch them. Murdo will take the wheel while you're gone.'

When Charlie and the seaman returned, the charts were spread out on the deck and Angus asked the coxswain where they were.

The coxswain pointed to a spot off a fairly large island and this time Angus believed him to be telling the truth.

'How long will it take us to reach the mainland?'

'We could be there by nightfall, but . . .' the seaman fell silent.

'What were you going to say? Let's hear it.'

'If you go ashore at the nearest landfall you'll starve. There's nothing between the sea and the mountains beyond – and no way out.'

'What's the alternative?'

'If we travelled north for a few days you could put ashore close to Sydney and make your way over the Blue Mountains – there's a road through there now, I believe. Once on the other side you'll have the whole country in front of you. A man could disappear there — and survive, so I've heard.'

'Or be turned in by you and the others as soon as you're rid of us.'

The seaman shook his head emphatically. 'No, listen to me. Cast the Captain and all the men except three of us adrift in the longboat tonight. Take the sails out of the boat and give them only two oars. They'll reach the mainland – eventually, but by that time we'll be long gone.'

'What of the other two?'

'We'll take two bolters. They wouldn't dare try to tell anyone. Instead, they'll most likely try to sail the ship back to pick up the others.'

'And what about you? What will you do?'

'Ah! Now this is the clever part — for you too. Six or seven of the crew are ex-convicts who've served out their sentences and have papers to prove it. Take their papers and we're all free men.'

The coxswain's manner was far too intense for him to be lying, but Angus asked, 'What will you do when you become a free man?'

'That depends on you. If you think I've helped enough for you to pay me the money you were going to give to Captain Adams I'll buy a passage back to England on the first ship that's leaving.'

Angus was silent for a few minutes, then he extended his hand to the other man. 'Get us safely ashore and the money is yours. We'll all begin new lives – and they can't be worse than the old.'

Three weeks after being landed on the shores of the Australian mainland, Angus and Murdo Ross, Amy MacDonald and Charlie Campbell were heading inland. Mounted on stout horses, and leading others heavily laden with provisions and stores, they drove a sizeable flock of sheep ahead of them. What was more, both sheep and horses had been purchased honestly – with gold coin.

Searching the cabin of Captain Adams after he and his crew had been cast adrift from their ship, Charlie had found the money locked away in a stout, wooden chest. The rich find ensured the success of their bold venture. Mounted and with receipts for the stock they were driving, they were not once called upon to produce the stolen proof that they were free men and woman.

The possession of horses and stock made them respectable in the eyes of those in authority, but no member of the small party felt able to relax until they were well clear of the penal setdements and the last convict-worked property was far behind them. Until this time there was always a danger that a convict would recognise one of the bolters and shatter the fragile shell of respectability they had built around themselves.

Their troubles were not over, even now. The acquisition of possessions brought its own problems, as the small party discovered when they were threading their way through the Blue Mountains. They followed a route that had been discovered less than ten years before, yet it had already become well-worn by many men and women heading inland, seeking a new life away from the penal settlements.

The path had also been trodden by those with lesser ambitions: men who sought nothing new, desiring only to continue a way of life that would have been cut short on the gallows tree had it not been for the absolution of transportation. Angus saw three such men lounging at the side of the track when he and his party were still a half-mile away from them and immediately recognised the trio for what they were.

'Clear your rifles from their scabbards – and check they're primed and ready to fire. Amy, take my pistol. Use it if you have to. In the meantime stay close to Murdo.'

'Who do you think they are, soldiers?'

'We'd have no trouble with soldiers . . . spread out now. Murdo, Charlie, don't take your eyes off 'em for more than the blink of an eyelid.'

As the four escapees drew closer, driving the sheep before them, the three men beside the track stood up. They were accompanied by an Aborigine woman and a boy of about six. She alone remained sitting beside the track, a dejected, emaciated figure, holding the boy to her. About her ankle was a fetter and chain of the type used to secure convicts. Attached to the chain was a heavy log of wood.

One of the three men moved on to the track, a musket cradled in the crook of his arm. Holding up his free hand, palm forward, he gave the semblance of a smile, the gap in his heavy black beard parting to reveal an irregular set of very bad teeth.

'Hello, friends. There hasn't been anyone along this road for nigh on a week. It's good to have company. Where're you heading?'

The man's first and last glances were directed towards Angus. For the remainder of the time he stared at Amy.

'Inland.'

Angus's single-word reply was civil enough, if hardly conversational. The fact that the gun resting on the saddle in front of him was pointing squarely at the other man might have been no more than coincidence.

When it became evident that Angus intended saying no more, the black-bearded man shrugged and produced his version of a smile once more. 'A man's entitled to keep his business to himself. Are you a settler or a freed man?'

'Are you a freed man — or a bolter?'

The black-bearded man's eyebrows rose and this time the smile was genuine.

'They call us bushrangers, here on the mainland. Bolters are what we'd be if we were in Van Dieman's Land. Now I ain't never heard of any freed men finding their way here from Van Dieman's Land – no more than one or two bolters, neither. I think you and me talk the same language, friend. Why don't you and your friends . . . and the lady, set down and talk with us a while. We've a pot on the fire and can offer you a jug of tea.'

'I thank you kindly, but it's my intention to cover a few more miles before sundown.'

There was no smile from the bushrangers' spokesman now. 'Well then, we'll have one of those woolly-backs from you. You can take the Abo woman in exchange.'

'They're not for sale – or exchange. There's few enough to start a sheep farm as it is. We need every one.'

'Well if that ain't downright unfriendly . . . !'

There was menace in the man's voice now but, although he had moved, Angus's gun had moved too. It still pointed at the leader of the bushrangers. The black-bearded man looked about him at his companions, as though expecting them to take an initiative. But they had made the same discovery as their leader. No matter how often they shifted their position, they too were covered by the guns of Murdo and Charlie.

'I'm much obliged for your offer of hospitality, but as I can't see my way to accepting it, I'd like to see you and your friends comfortably settled by your own fire before we move off.'

Angus's voice was quiet, his manner mild, but something told the black-bearded bushranger that he would be a dead man if he failed to follow the one-armed Scotsman's suggestion.

'I won't forget this.' The black-bearded man moved slowly backwards, his eyes on no one but Angus now.

'I trust not. I certainly won't.' Angus motioned for the other two bushrangers to make their way back to the fire and they did so with more alacrity than their leader.

Not until all three men were seated did Angus give a signal for Murdo to take the sheep on.

'You backed them into their hole right enough, Angus.' Charlie was jubilant. 'They'll think twice before they tackle another Scotsman.'

'I wish I believed you were right,' declared Angus grimly, 'but those are hungry men. There was no food cooking at their fire – and we've hurt their pride. We'll need to guard the sheep and horses well for the next few nights.'

'I'd better teach Amy something about shooting,' said Murdo. 'If she ever has to fire at one of the men we've just left it'll take more than a hole in his arm to stop him doing what he's intending. She'll need to kill him.'

That night they made camp in a small, blind valley and were able to cut down enough small trees to form a satisfactory barricade that would be easy to guard. Angus decided they would mount guard in pairs, nominating himself and Amy for the first half of the night.

Angus smiled to himself when he saw the expression of disappointment that crossed Murdo's face. His son was beginning to take more than a passing interest in the girl and Angus approved. Amy had shown a great deal of character both before and after the incident on board the sealer. She would make a good wife for Murdo, and would also provide a living reminder of Cathal.

There were no incidents that night. Low cloud settled over the shallow valley, bringing with it a penetrating drizzle that leaked inside the neck of dress and shirt. It would also serve to keep the bushrangers shivering in whatever shelter they had been able to find.

The next night found the sheep-herding quartet on lower and more open ground. There was more grass for the sheep here, but making any kind of pen was more difficult, there being no more than low scrub and a few saplings in the immediate vicinity. It was almost dark by the time the task was completed and after a hurriedly prepared meal Angus and Charlie took the first guard duty.

Some time close to midnight, Murdo was shaken into wakefulness by Angus. He woke with a start and reached out for his gun, but relaxed when told everything was quiet. It was time for him and Amy to assume the task of guarding the camp and their livestock.

Amy was placing green twigs on the low-burning fire by the time Murdo had tied on his boots and gathered up his gun. It was chilly enough to make him shiver, but when he crouched beside the fire and held out his hands towards the warmth of the glowing wood, Amy rounded on him.

163

'What do you think you're doing?'

'Warming my hands. Why?'

'I didn't build up the fire for you to sit beside it all night. We're meant to be guarding the animals. I'll take the north and east sides, which includes the fire. That way I'll know for certain it's kept going. You take the south and west.'

'I don't think it'll be necessary to wander too far, Amy. I thought we'd spend our time here by the fire – going out and checking every so often, of course . . . .'

'I know very well what you were thinking, Murdo Ross – but you can think again. We're protecting the camp and the animals against those bushrangers we left along the road. *You* may not take the task seriously, but *I* do. If you're so fond of my company you can make certain you meet up with me here about every half an hour. That way we'll each know the other is all right.' With this final directive, Amy turned and was swallowed up by the night, leaving a decidedly ruffled Murdo behind her. As she walked away into the darkness, she smiled. She had become very fond of Murdo during the weeks they had spent in each other's company, but she knew better than to expose her feelings for him too quickly.

When Murdo returned to the fire for their second meeting of the night he found Amy waiting for him with a mug of coffee ready.

'I was about to come looking for you,' she said. 'I thought you might have need of this.'

The night had become colder and Murdo took the mug gratefully.

'I don't think we'll see anything of any bushrangers tonight,' Murdo said hopefully, 'we'd hear their teeth chattering from a mile away.'

'They none of 'em struck me as men who'd let a little cold weather put 'em off doing what they wanted. We can't afford to take any chances, so don't take all night with that coffee.'

'You seem to know a whole lot about men and their ways, Amy.'

'What's that supposed to mean?' She rounded on him instantly.

'Nothing.' It had been an unthinking remark and Murdo wished he had never made it.

'Yes, I know a lot about men. I came here on a convict ship, remember? Then I was handed around like a beggar's hat before I went to the Kennedys' farm. Yes, Murdo, I know just about all there is to know about men.'

There was just the hint of a break in Amy's voice, but she spoke defiantly. Her experiences since leaving England were the last thing she wished Murdo to know, but it was better perhaps that he should learn now, from her.

'I'm sorry, Amy. It can't have been easy for you. I shouldn't have reminded you.'

There was an awkward silence between them for a few moments, before Murdo asked, 'How do you see the future, Amy – *your* future?'

'I dunno.' Amy wished it had been a suggestion rather than a question. 'That depends a lot on you . . . and your pa.'

'Does that mean you want to stay with us?'

As Amy drew in her breath to answer, they both heard a sudden flurry of sound from the sheep on the far edge of the makeshift paddock, in the area Amy had been guarding.

'What's that?'

'Shh!'

Sheep were bleating now and milling around. Suddenly Murdo heard what sounded like a muffled curse.

'Wake up Pa and Charlie, I think we've got company. I'll go and see what's happening.'

Before Murdo was halfway to the spot where the sheep had been sleeping he heard the pounding of their hooves and frightened bleating and he knew he was too late. Something, someone, had frightened the sheep badly and they were running panic-stricken into the night.

It was no use charging unseeing into the darkness and Murdo dropped to one knee, hoping that he might see something silhouetted against the skyline, but it was too dark. The moon and stars were hidden behind a high blanket of cloud.

There were sounds behind him and Murdo called softly, 'That you, Pa?'

'Yes, and Charlie. What's happening?'

'Someone's just run off the sheep, but they won't be able to catch any of 'em before morning any more than we will.'

'Damn! We should have had it out with those bushrangers when we met up with them. I guessed something like this would happen.'

At that moment a man shouted from the direction of the camp where the two men had been sleeping.

'The horses . . . !'

The words had hardly left Murdo's mouth when a shot echoed in the night and the three men sprinted to the camp. For a few moments all was pandemonium. In the darkness a brief flash of light lit up the night and a musket ball scattered the hot ashes of the fire not two paces from where Murdo crouched. He fired in the direction the shot had come from, but there was nothing to indicate whether he had hit anyone.

'The horses are safe. Stay with them. If the bushrangers hang around they'll try for the horses.'

'Where's Amy?'

'I thought she came after you?'

'I'll go back and see if she's there.'

Murdo slipped away quietly and made his way to where the sheep had been. He called softly, in case the bushrangers had doubled back, but the only sound was from a variety of insects and a fast-running stream that had its source in the mountains behind them.

Back at the camp, Murdo rummaged through his things in the faint, flickering light from the bullet-aroused fire until he found his pistol. Slipping it in his pocket he picked up his rifle.

'Where are you going?' Angus put the question to his son.

'To find Amy.'

'Wait until morning. There's nothing you can do before it's light . . . .'

'If the bushrangers have her there's a lot *they* can do before then. You and Charlie stay with the horses. I'll find you here.'

Murdo had no plan in mind, only a burning determination to find the bushrangers and rescue Amy – for he was convinced that they had her. He had no idea of the direction they would take, but guessed they would head back the way they had come, to the safety of the wooded mountains. No doubt they would know a route across country while he would be forced to find and follow the road – but it was the only course open to him. He had to take it.

It took Murdo an hour to find the uncertain track in the darkness and then he made what speed he could, pausing every half-mile or so to listen.

Dawn was not far away, the trees vague shapes in the greyness when he heard a sound that told him he was travelling in the right direction – yet it was the one sound he would rather not have heard. A musket shot – two musket shots. They must have come from almost a mile ahead of him. Murdo broke into a jog, slowing only when he knew that he could not be far away from the source of the shots. To continue running now would be foolish in the extreme.

Leaving the road, Murdo began to search but it was futile until morning arrived and he was able to see for some distance about him. Then far ahead, where the road rose to climb into the mountains, Murdo saw his quarry — but there were only two of them now: two men.

Murdo redoubled his efforts. The shots had come from the vicinity where he was now. If Amy had been killed by the bush-rangers, her body would be here somewhere. If she was not dead, there was still one bushranger unaccounted for. Murdo had been searching for no more than ten minutes when he saw a still form sprawled in the shadow cast by a rocky outcrop no more than fifty paces away.

Resisting the urge to call out, he broke into a run. Halfway to the body he slowed to a halt. It was not Amy, but the third bushranger. The discovery meant that the possibility of being taken by surprise by one of the bushrangers had gone – but there had been *two* shots.

Approaching the body, it was immediately apparent that he had been shot in the back, and at very close range. The jacket around the wound was badly charred. The dead man had suffered another wound too, in the leg. Judging by the amount of blood staining the man's trousers this was an earlier wound, probably incurred during the raid on the Ross camp.

Straightening up, Murdo suddenly saw another body, but he could see immediately that this too was not Amy. It was the Aborig-ine woman. She too had been shot at close range, this time between the eyes. As Murdo looked down at the remains of the dead woman's face he knew that he had solved the riddle of the two shots – but where was Amy?

Suddenly, from the corner of his eye, Murdo caught a movement among the rocks nearby and he brought his gun up immediately. The movement was not repeated but, crouching low, he ran to the shelter of a rock to one side of the place from which the movement had come. From here he worked his way closer, without exposing himself to possible danger.

Murdo was behind the other's hiding-place now and by shifting his position slightly he viewed his quarry along the barrel of his musket – and immediately lowered the weapon. He was looking at the small Aborigine boy he had last seen being held close by the dead woman.

Murdo called to the boy and at the sound the young Aborigine jumped as though he had been shot. He began to run away but Murdo went after him, catching the boy as he tried to scramble over a boulder as high as himself. The boy struggled and fought with him, all the time squealing in terror.

'Take it easy . . . easy, boy. I'm not going to hurt you. I'd say you've suffered quite enough for one young lifetime.'

Murdo realised that the boy probably did not understand a single word he was saying, but eventually the calm, soothing tone of his voice got through and the boy stopped his struggling.

'That's better.' Crouching down in front of the child, Murdo could see that he had been crying. His nose had been running too, probably as a result of his recent exertions.

'Well, you're not exactly what I expected to be taking back to camp with me, but I can't leave you out here on your own.'

The two bushrangers were much farther away now, and travelling fast. They posed no threat to the boy, but he was no more than six or seven. He could not be left out here to fend for himself. He would have to be taken back to the camp – and then the three men would begin their search for Amy.

Murdo saw Amy when he was still a long way from the camp – and she saw him. Running to meet him, she paused, momentarily taken aback at the sight of the small Aborigine boy, but then she hugged Murdo with a warmth he would not have believed possible only twelve hours before.

'Murdo . . . ! You don't know what a relief it is to see you. We thought we heard a couple of shots earlier this morning. We feared . . . . What happened – and what are you doing with the boy?'

Murdo told his story as briefly as possible, adding, 'He's got no one else now – and *you* know what that's like. I think we'll have to keep him . . . but what happened to you? We all thought the bushrangers had taken you off.'

'No – but I almost had *them*. It might have been me who wounded the bushranger you found. When I woke your pa and Charlie, they ran off to help you and it suddenly came to me that chasing off the sheep was a ruse. What the bushrangers really wanted were the horses. I waited up here by the camp, and sure enough this was where they came. I shot at them and they ran off. Then when you came back there was a lot of shooting and we all seemed to be going in different directions. I ran back down to where the sheep had been because I thought you'd gone that way. I didn't find you, but I did hear some of the sheep. I knew if they got away we might never find them again, so I stayed close to them until it was daylight. Then I brought them back.'

Amy made it all sound simple, but Murdo knew she must have been terrified all alone in the darkness. It would have required great courage to stay within hearing of the sheep, never absolutely certain whether she would be able to find her way back to the camp again. The fact that she had brought them back safely confirmed what he had come to accept in recent weeks: Amy was a very special girl, and he had no intention of losing her again.

To Amy's surprise and the delight of Angus and Charlie, Murdo took her in his arms and kissed her as she had never been kissed before. When he was forced to break away in order to breathe, he said, 'Amy MacDonald, don't you ever run off like that again. It aged me all of ten years. It's going to take you a lifetime to make it up to me.'

Murdo Ross and Amy were married a month later by a missionary minister in the vicinity of the small community of Bathurst. The occasion marked the beginning of a very successful marriage, but not the end of their journeying.

Three times they settled down to farm, and three times an unwelcome civilisation caught up with them. Not until they had journeyed far to the north, to a place where no others would come for almost twenty-five years, did they at last find the peace they sought, and here they set up home and raised their family.

SIX

Missouri 1820

'Goddammit! That's the fourth wagon we've seen this week.' Sam Chisholm buried the blade of his axe deep in the huge tree stump. He and Robert MacCrimmon had been working for a full morning to clear the stump from newly-won pastureland. All about them were a depressingly large number of similar such obstacles to farming progress. Flexing his aching fingers he spat on the ground before turning his back on the object of his displeasure, ignoring the waving hands of the occupants.

'Where they all coming from? Afore you know it folk'll be thicker on the ground around here than fleas on a Pawnee dog. It's making me feel uncomfortable, Bob. Damned uncomfortable. It won't be long before they begin crowding us – and I don't like being crowded.'

Returning the greetings of the passing family, Robert leaned on his own axe and grinned wryly at his companion. 'Folk have been moving in since soon after we arrived in the Ozarks, Sam. Is it really them bothering you so much – or is it that you're here clearing land – your own land, while Gil's out there somewhere in the mountains at one of the rendezvous you've talked so much about?'

'Hell, no . . . .'

Sam Chisholm dropped his gaze to the two great hands, calloused from months of hard axe-work, and shrugged his shoulders sheepishly. 'I guess you're right, Bob. I wasn't cut out to be no farmer. I start to swing an axe and before it's struck I'm thinking of the mountains . . . wondering how many of the trappers me and Gil knew are alive to keep the rendezvous this year. I look up at the skyline – and I'm seeing for a thousand miles, to a valley filled with mountain men, Indians, traders, mules, horses and furs. For a week or two there's no place like it on the whole of God's earth. Men trade furs, stories . . . and wives too. There are men who've seen sights that no one would believe who hasn't been in the mountains for himself. There's others who risk their lives for weeks on end to bring in a few furs that'll keep 'em drunk for maybe a fortnight. When they sober up they go right back and do it all again. But most of all there's the country – miles and miles of mountains and emptiness. Just the way the Good Lord made it . . . .'

'Annie's going to miss you, Sam.' Robert spoke softly, almost wistfully.

'I didn't say I was leaving . . . !'

'You don't need to, your eyes are saying it for you. I wish I could come too.'

Sam was about to suggest they go together, but left it unsaid. Hugh MacCrimmon needed his son here to help carve a farm from the forest of the Ozarks. Hugh had a new family to support . . . and Annie.

'Annie's no more than a child.' Sam's argument was no more than a weak, defensive statement, and both men were aware of its frailty.

'Annie's turned fifteen, Sam. She's a young woman – and she thinks the world of you. The least you can do is tell her what you have in mind. If you were to slip away during the night without saying goodbye you'd feel bad about coming back again – and we'd all regret that.'

Sam Chisholm broke the news of his proposed departure to Hugh MacCrimmon when he rode to his fellow Scot's cabin that same evening. Hugh tried to persuade the big frontiersman to stay, but when he realised Sam had made up his mind, he echoed Robert's words.

'We'll all be sorry to see you go, Sam. The MacCrimmon family owe you a debt that we'll never be able to repay, but we all know where your heart is. We knew when Gil left us that it was only a question of time before you set off too. Robert and I will see that your land is kept cleared and we'll take care of your stock. But, talking of hearts, I'd be obliged if you'd make a special point of telling our Annie what you intend doing. That girl's more than a mite fond of you.'

'I wouldn't dream of leaving without speaking to her, Hugh . . . and telling her I'll be back one day.'

'Good!' Hugh extended his hand. 'You'll find Annie down at the new barn, feeding the calf we're weaning. All that remains is for me to wish you good fortune and tell you we'll include you in our prayers.'

Sam found Annie MacCrimmon on her knees in the barn, her arms about the neck of a spindly-legged calf. She was trying to coax the reluctant young creature to drink milk from a wooden bucket, a feat which seemed beyond its comprehension. Annie never looked up when Sam entered the barn, even though the evening sun shining through the open doorway threw his long shadow across her and the calf. After standing in the doorway in silence for longer than a minute, Sam cleared his throat noisily, causing the calf to throw up his head in fright, almost upsetting the bucket.

'If you've come to say goodbye, then say it and get it over with, Sam Chisholm. I'm trying to feed this calf and I don't want to be all night about it.'

Annie spoke without raising her head and she never saw the frontiersman's expression of agonised uncertainty.

'How — how'd you know I'd come to say goodbye?'

'You're not dressed for clearing land, Sam . . . .' This was true, he was wearing soft-buckskin trousers and coat. 'Besides, I saw you ride up to the house leading a spare pony loaded with your things.'

'Oh!' Sam was often tongue-tied in Annie's presence, but it had never been worse than it was today. 'I . . . I wanted to see you before I went. Wanted to see you . . . especially, to say I'll be back some day. That I hope . . . you'll still be here too.'

Sam Chisholm, frontiersman, mountain man, man of action, was in an agony of indecision. Unable to marshal his thoughts into any orderly sequence, he could not have put them into words had they fallen into place.

When he could endure the silence no longer, he turned and walked away, his tread already that of a man whose life might depend upon making no sound.

'Sam! Sam Chisholm!'

He turned to see Annie standing in the barn doorway. The sun shone upon what might have been tears, but he was too far from her to see.

'I'll be here when you come back – but don't you make it too long, you hear?'

Sam nodded. 'I hear you, Annie.'

The land to which Sam Chisholm had guided the MacCrimmon family did not remain beyond the frontiers of civilisation for very long. On August 10th, 1821, Missouri was admitted into the Union as the twenty-fourth State, by which time much of the public lands had been sold and the trappings of government were already functioning.

Carving a home and a livelihood from virgin forest was gruelling work for every member of Hugh MacCrimmon's family, but by the time Missouri achieved statehood he was self-sufficient. So much so that when a depression gripped Missouri he was able to buy land from less fortunate farmers and become one of the larger landholders in the new State, whilst continuing to manage the lands belonging to Sam Chisholm.

For three years Robert helped Hugh to establish his new family in their home in the Ozark region of Missouri. Meanwhile, others moved in around them, their numbers always greater than those who moved out, and improvements were made. Roads were built, churches raised and a school opened.

News of Sam Chisholm occasionally filtered back to the Ozarks. He had been seen up north, close to the Canadian border . . . westwards in lands that did not yet have a name – in the Rocky Mountains . . . .

Each report left Robert feeling more and more unsettled. There was an understanding between himself and Morna Ross that they would one day marry. It was something his father had always desired . . . but Robert was not ready yet. They had come to a vast new country and there was so much to see, so much to be done. The day came when Robert could contain his feelings no longer. He told a hushed family – and Morna – that he had decided to ride westwards, following the path taken by Sam Chisholm.

Later, Robert gave Morna a solemn promise that he would one day return and marry her and she, as had Annie, promised in her turn that she would wait for her man. Nevertheless, as she watched Robert ride away she wondered whether she would ever see him again.

Hugh had similar misgivings, but he had made no attempt to dissuade his son from leaving. America was a great country, an exciting country — and its future was dependent upon young men like Robert who made themselves familiar with the land in which they lived.

Over the next few years Robert MacCrimmon became a wanderer, a frontiersman, like the man he so admired. News of him found its way to the Missouri farm occasionally. He was fur-trapping in the Rocky Mountains, trading in Santa Fe, hunting with the Indians on the great Plains, acting as a guide for troops fighting Indians in the north . . . .

For two years he accompanied Sam Chisholm and Gil Sherborne on their travels through the Rocky Mountains. He was with the two close friends when Indians attacked their camp and Gil was treacherously killed whilst attempting to parley with them. Gil's death wrought a great change in Sam Chisholm. He remained on the frontier for only another listless year before returning to Missouri to marry Annie MacCrimmon and finally settling down to farm the land he owned there.

For many years afterwards, the Chisholm farm was a stopping-place for old friends returning from the west and most had some news of Robert. He had acquired a set of bagpipes from somewhere and had livened up more than one rendezvous in the mountains.

Seven years after leaving the MacCrimmons' Ozark home, Robert returned and for a while it seemed his roaming was done. He married the patient Morna Ross, bought land of his own, and worked hard. Then a businessman from St Louis asked him to guide a large wagon train along the Santa Fe trail. He offered Robert an opportunity to stock a couple of wagons with trade goods, ensuring him a healthy profit on the venture. It was an offer too good to be turned down.

When Robert returned to Missouri seven months later he had a baby son – but no wife. Morna had died giving birth to the child of the man for whom she had waited so many long years. She was twenty-seven years old.

Before she died, Morna had named the baby Andy, in memory of the brother she had left in Scotland. The child was still only weeks old when Robert left him in the care of Rose, the youngest daughter of Molly Brooks, and rode westward once more.

For ten tempestuous years Robert MacCrimmon was a member of a veritable army of footloose men who roamed beyond the frontiers of their expanding country, leading adventurous lives.

After spending a year inside a Mexican prison for daring to plead the cause of a group of Americans who had settled in Mexican-owned Texas, Robert escaped and fought for the independence of Texas as a Captain in the army of Sam Houston. When General Santa Anna and the Mexican army were defeated and Texan independence was assured, Robert headed north once more, the wanderlust finally worked free from his system. He was returning to Missouri to see the father he had not seen for ten years and a son he did not know – but it would be a while yet before he rode among the hills of the Ozarks.

Travelling through an area of gently undulating hills, Robert Mac-Crimmon left the newly independent Republic of Texas behind him and entered the State of Arkansas, travelling north-westwards now. He was on his way home, but first he intended visiting Ben Calloni, the frontiersman he had first met twenty years before when the Macrimmons were on their way west with Sam Chisholm.

Calloni had also fought for Texan independence and had been wounded at the battle of San Jacinto, when Sam Houston and a small force routed the Mexican army and captured Santa Anna. Calloni had been taken to an army hospital on the western border of Arkansas and Robert hoped to find him fully recovered.

The hospital was located in a small community huddled around an army fort and there was far more activity here than Robert had expected. It seemed that half the United States army was in the vicinity – and Ben Calloni was so far recovered that he was on horseback among them.

When the now ageing frontiersman recognised Robert, he let out a yell that reminded Robert of the rendezvous in the north-western mountains where each new arrival was greeted in a similar exuberant manner. The cavalry horses were not used to the sound and for a few minutes there was chaos among the frightened animals.

'Well, if you ain't a sight for sore eyes, Bob, boy. What you doing up this way? I'd have thought Sam Houston would have the sense to make you a minister of something-or-another in that new country of his.'

'Sam's up north somewhere, getting treatment for an ankle wound . . . but it's good to find you sitting a horse again. I last saw you being carried away bleeding enough for two men.'

'I'd have bled enough for *three* if I hadn't threatened to shoot the damn-fool surgeon who treated me. It wasn't until I was able to get my hands on some whisky to top me up again that I began to get better.'

'You look fit enough now,' commented Robert. 'But what's going on here? There are enough soldiers around to take Mexico.'

Ben Calloni spat contemptuously into the dust beside the front hooves of his horse. 'That'd be too much like fighting, Bob, boy – and a man can get hurt that way. No, this lot are off on a jaunt that's much more to their liking: it's *Indian* duties. They're going east to Tennessee and Georgia with orders to escort Cherokee Indians to Indian territory. There's fifteen or sixteen thousand to be moved, so they're saying – yet there's not a single one of these soldier-boys knows the sign language for anything that ain't connected with laying a squaw on her back with her legs apart.'

'Surely they're not going to try to move that many Indians at this end of the year? Winter will catch up with 'em almost before the tail end has left Georgia.'

'*You* know this, and *I* know it. No doubt some of the soldier-boys know it too – though, God knows, they don't know much else. But their orders come from some General sitting in a warm office in Washington. This army ain't like Sam Houston's army, Bob, boy. If Sam gave an order that didn't make no sense there was always someone ready to jump up and tell him so. In *this* army a man's scared of passing water unless he's got permission.'

Robert was only half-listening to the contemptuous frontiersman. 'But, there won't only be Indian men in these parties going west. There'll be women — children too.'

'That's right, Bob, boy – and if these soldier-boys don't have a few of us along who have some savvy about Indians – and the country they'll be travelling through, they're going to lose half of 'em.'

Ben Calloni spat into the dust once more, this time in disgust. 'I'm not sure the government in Washington wouldn't be relieved if they lost the *lot*. I'm no Indian-lover, as well you know, but I'm no Indian-*hater* neither, and I'm damned if I'll let 'em all be led off to their deaths when I can do something to stop it.'

'You really think you'll be able to prevent it happening?'

'I wouldn't be wasting my time on such a damn-fool journey unless I believed it, Bob, boy. You could come with me if you'd a mind to.'

Now Robert realised how easily he had walked into the trap the frontiersman had laid for him. 'Perhaps the army doesn't want men like us to go along with them.'

'That wouldn't matter one single duck's feather to me, Bob, boy – nor to you neither, unless I don't know you as well as I think I do. All these officers aren't bad, in spite of what I've said. They know they've a problem on their hands and they don't want to have women and kids dying all along the way. Far as I know I'm the only man travelling with 'em who can talk to the Indians, but I won't be able to go along with all of 'em. They'll likely be stretched along a couple of hundred miles of trail.'

While the two men were talking the soldiers had formed up into some semblance of a column and now one of the officers called to Ben.

Acknowledging the shout with a wave of his hand, Ben made one last appeal to Robert. 'I know you'll be anxious to get home to see that son of yours, Bob, boy, but back in Georgia and Tennessee there are folk with kids, too. I know the Cherokees. They're good people – as Sam Houston would tell you. They took care of him when he was as far down as any man could have been. When they'd got him back on his feet they sent him out into the world again, to fight for Texas. They've done the same for me, too. I'm not likely to do any more fighting – but I'll not see Cherokees die while I have any breath left in my body.'

Ben's horse seemed to want to follow after the soldiers who had begun to move off. The animal turned a full circle before the frontiersman brought it under control.

'What's it to be, Bob, boy? Will you come along with me and do what you can for the Cherokees?'

Robert MacCrimmon rode with Ben Calloni as far as the town of Calhoun, in the Appalachian Mountains of Tennessee. Here, some thirteen thousand Cherokee Indians were being held in pens, as though they were cattle. The facilities for them were totally inadequate and boded ill for the long journey ahead.

The military men in charge blamed their tardiness in setting off for Indian territory on the chiefs of the tribe. Most were in Washington, desperately trying to have the tribal removal order set aside. Their argument, and it was a strong one, was that they were a settled nation with houses, farms and a great deal of property in the land they claimed for their own.

Unlike most other Indian tribes, the Cherokees had long ago adapted themselves to the white man's way of life. Indeed, many of their men, and women, were married to white Americans.

Unfortunately, the Cherokees were the victims of one of the most ruthless 'land-grabs' in the history of the young United States of America, and their removal was all part of the lifelong ambition of the country's still-powerful ex-President, Andrew Jackson. The Indian delegation in Washington was doomed to fail in its objective.

Although Robert found conditions at the camp appalling, worse was to come. He had left Ben Calloni and was riding around the various 'pens' when a dishevelled party of Indians arrived on foot. They were being driven before a troop of mounted volunteers who seemed in high spirits.

All the Indian men in the party had their hands bound, and some had ugly wounds about the face and head. Robert noticed that some of the women too were bloody and dishevelled and one in particular caught his attention. Tall, she had a dignity that bare, dust-stained feet and a badly bruised face could not take from her.

When Robert made to approach the arriving party, one of the volunteer Sergeants blocked his way, saying, 'Where do you think you're going?'

'To have a talk to these Indians. Some of them seem to be in need of a doctor.'

'That's none of your business. They were runaways, hiding out in the Smoky Mountains. We've had a hell of a job to find and bring 'em in. The Captain says they're to speak to no one. They're trouble.'

Some of the Sergeant's fellow volunteers were gathering about Robert, and they were no longer laughing. His years in the mountains had taught Robert to calculate odds carefully and they were weighted far too heavily against him at the moment.

Shrugging his shoulders, he said, 'I guess they're *your* trouble, not mine.' All the same, as he rode away, apparently indifferent to the fate of the Cherokee prisoners, he carefully noted the group to which they were eventually allocated.

The thirteen thousand Cherokees being held at Calhoun were divided into thirteen separate groups, the whole guarded by more than half their number of soldiers.

Later that evening, Robert was still haunted by the memory of the Indian prisoners who had been brought in by the Tennessee volunteers. One face in particular remained in his mind – the girl with the badly bruised face. Making up his mind to discover what had happened to them, he made his way to the group where he had seen the prisoners taken. To his surprise he found a Cherokee preacher with them. The preacher was taking a prayer meeting and Robert waited for the final 'Amen!' before asking in halting Cherokee whether all was well with the Indians who had joined the group that day.

'What business is it of yours?' countered the preacher in excellent English.

'I came up with Ben Calloni to act as an interpreter – although it seems I'm probably not needed,' explained Robert. 'I saw the soldiers bring a number of prisoners in, but they were no more communicative than you when I asked about them.'

'I am sorry.' The preacher seemed suddenly to sag. Extending his hand, he introduced himself. 'Elijah Brown. I was the minister of a Baptist church in Echota until the government of Andrew Jackson decided to move us westwards. Had I known you were a friend of Ben Calloni I would have been more polite. He is a good friend of my people.'

The preacher rubbed a hand about his face. 'For too long now I have felt angrier than any man of God should ever feel. Today my anger is fuelled by bitterness and directed against the Tennessee volunteers who brought our people in from the Smoky Mountains.'

'They were bringing in Cherokees who were determined not to be moved. It couldn't have been easy for 'em.'

'The volunteers didn't have to go into the mountains. They captured three young men who they accused of waging war against the settlers and threatened to hang them if the others didn't come in peacefully. It was a large family group so they gave themselves up to save their men – but the volunteers hanged them anyway. By the time the young women reached here they were wishing they'd been hung too. Yet these are the men who are supposed to take care of our people for a journey of almost a thousand miles. How many of us will reach this new land alive?'

Robert did not doubt the truth of what the preacher told him. He had suspected something was wrong when the Tennessee volunteer Sergeant prevented him from talking to the Cherokees.

'Who's the army officer in charge of the removal?'

'Major General Scott, but he's at Gunter's Landing, watching over the first of the Cherokees to go by river.'

Gunter's Landing was on the Tennessee River, about a hundred miles away, over a tortuous and mountainous road.

'Can I talk to some of the people who've just been brought in from the Smoky Mountains?'

'What do you hope to achieve? What's done is done . . . .' 'There are a lot of miles between here and Indian territory, and time for this sort of thing to become a habit unless someone puts a stop to it – now. But before I decide to do anything about it I want to hear first-hand what's happened.'

'Why should you become involved? The volunteers are *your* people. We are just – *Indians.*'

For a few moments Robert MacCrimmon asked himself the same question. He wondered whether it was no more than the sight of the pretty young Cherokee girl with the bruised face. Then other memories flooded back to him with astonishing clarity.

'Minister, I'm not a Tennesseean. I was born in a land called Scotland, thousands of miles from here. Many years ago another country claimed the right to rule Scotland and as a boy I talked to those who had fought and lost the last battle against those people. They told me of men and women who had suffered as the Chero- kees are suffering now. Then, when I was a young man, my family and many others like us were told we had to go elsewhere because our land was needed to graze sheep. Many didn't want to go, but they were forced to leave – same as your people. Some, including a number of those in my wife's family, died as a result. A great number were forced to leave our country. This is why I am in America now.'

Robert was not used to talking at such length, or to searching so deeply into his emotions.

'That may or may not explain to you why I'm involving myself in your affairs, Minister Brown – I'm not sure myself – but I do know

I don't like to see folk being pushed around in such a way. All the same, I've made it a habit to check my ammunition before I get into a fight.'

'I understand.' Minister Elijah Brown laid a sympathetic hand on Robert's arm. 'But I think I can introduce you to someone unfortunate enough to be able to answer all your doubts.'

The soldiers guarding the Cherokees had orders not to allow any of the Indians to leave their prison pens, but no one attempted to prevent the Cherokee minister and Robert entering.

The group Robert had seen being brought to the camp was here, and when the minister called for 'Nancy', the girl with the bruised face raised her head in response.

'Nancy, this is Robert MacCrimmon. He wants to help us, but first he needs to know first-hand what happened when you and the others came in and surrendered to the volunteers.'

'It's a very simple story . . . but we are a very simple people, who for far too long have believed what every white man tells us. We were told that unless we gave ourselves up, the volunteers would have my brother and two cousins hanged. We gave ourselves up – but the Sergeant still hanged them. He said there were more of us in the hills, and it would show them he "meant business". Then the Sergeant too said he wanted to "help" me.'

Nancy turned the side of her face towards Robert and put the tip of a finger gingerly to the bruising. 'This is what happened when I told him I did not want his "help". He said I was too "uppity" for an Indian girl. When I bit him he got two of his men to hold me down while he "helped" me. Then he held me down while the others "helped" me too. So you will excuse me if I am not overjoyed by *your* offer of "help".'

Robert felt a deep sense of revulsion and the feeling took him by surprise. Nancy was not the first woman on the frontier to suffer rape. Indeed, many frontiersmen took it for granted that if they encountered a small group of hostile Indians they would kill the men and rape their women. Many Indians would do the same to white women – but listening to this obviously well-educated Cherokee girl talk of her experience at the hands of the Tennessee volunteers brought it home to Robert in a way it never had before. Muttering some totally inadequate remarks, he made his escape. On the way back from the prison compound the Indian minister caught up with him.

'I see you believed Nancy's story?'

'I guessed the truth when I saw her being brought in with the others. Where did she learn to speak such good English?'

'At a boarding school in the east. Nancy's father is one of the chiefs who is in Washington, trying to have the removal order cancelled. He owned considerable lands among the Smoky Mountains.'

'It's a pity he didn't take her with him – and his son, the one who was killed.'

'I fear death will be a familiar companion on the road to the new lands if winter overtakes us along the way. What will you do now?'

'I'm going to speak to Ben, then I'll go and find this Major General Scott. If he's like all the other officers I've known he'll do damn-all to help your people – but I'll make certain he can never slide out of all responsibility by pleading ignorance.'

Major General Winfield Scott was *not* like every other army officer Robert had ever known. A giant of six feet, four inches, the General had a personality to match his size. A veteran of the 1812 war between the United States and England, he had won some notable battles in the vicinity of Niagara Falls. He was credited with having prevented the English from crossing the weakly held border and occupying America's northernmost States.

More recently, General Scott had been back on the Canadian border preventing ill-organised volunteers from crossing into Canada to support a confused 'uprising' there. This task was not yet complete and the General could have done without the added responsibility for the removal of the Cherokees to Indian territory.

Ben Calloni had been a scout for the General during the war of 1812, and his name was the magic key that gained Robert an interview. In truth, the General greatly admired men like Robert and Ben who ranged far beyond the borders of the United States relying entirely upon their own ingenuity and resourcefulness for survival. After a few questions, Robert was invited to join the General for dinner that evening.

Much to Robert's surprise, dinner was not in an officers' mess accompanied by members of the General's staff, but in a cabin close to the river, attended only by a couple of slaves, loaned to the General by a local landowner.

'I thought it would be better this way,' explained the giant soldier, 'not all my staff agree with the way I'm organising this removal. Word's been getting back to Washington that I'm too soft with the Cherokees. Besides, I'm Virginia-born and-raised. I'm more comfortable in a cabin.'

'Your critics wouldn't think you're being too soft if they saw some of the Cherokees being brought in to the prison pens . . . .' Robert told Winfield Scott the story recounted to him by Nancy.

'Damn those volunteers!' The Major General choked on his food. 'How the hell am I and my officers supposed to maintain discipline when we're given soldiers who can't even spell the word, much less take any notice of it.'

Rising from the table the General rummaged through a file of papers, tore one free and slapped it down alongside Robert's plate with such force that the plate jumped in the air.

'Here, is this plain enough, or isn't it? I issued this order four months ago. I would have thought even the damnedest fool would understand what it has to say.'

Dated May 17th, 1838, the order read:

The Cherokees, by the advances they have made in Christianity and civilization, are by far the most interesting tribe of Indians in the territorial limits of the United States. Of the 13,000 of those people who are now to be removed (and the time within which a voluntary emigration was stipulated will expire on the 23rd inst.) it is understood that about four-fifths are opposed, or have become averse to, distant emigration; and troops will probably be obliged to cover the whole country they inhabit in order to take prisoners and to march or transport prisoners, by families, either to this place, or to Ross's Landing or Gunter's Landing, where they are to be delivered to the Superintendent of Cherokee Emigration.

Considering the number and temper of the mass to be removed it will readily occur that simple indiscretions – acts of harshness and of cruelty on the part of our troops – may lead to a general war and carnage – a result, in the case of these particular Indians, utterly abhorrent to the generous sympathies of the whole American people. Every possible kindness must therefore be shown by the troops and, if in the ranks a despicable individual should be found, capable of inflicting a wanton injury or insult on any Cherokee, man, woman or child, it is hereby made the special duty of the nearest good officer or man, instantly to interpose, and to seize and consign the guilty wretch to the severest penalty of the laws.

The letter was signed, Winfield Scott, Major General. When Robert looked up at Scott, the General said, 'That was the beginning of the Washington "Scott's-gone-soft-on-the-Indians" campaign by Senators who've never been within sniffing distance of an Indian and who wouldn't know a Cherokee from an Apache.'

'Did you mean what you put in this order?'

'I don't issue orders just because I enjoy seeing my name at the bottom of a sheet of paper.'

'Are you going to punish these Tennesseean volunteers?'

'I can't do what I'd *like* to do, that much is certain. They're "Old Hickory's" boys. He may no longer be President, but the administration is still packed with his men. If I were to charge a Tennessee volunteer with killing an Indian, or even have him arrested, I'd have the rest of the volunteers packing their bags and going home and the howl from Washington would be heard clear to the Canadian border.'

'So what *will* you do about what's happened?'

'I'm going to do what the government should have done before they threw me into the middle of this mess – talk to the Cherokee leaders. They're in Washington pleading their people's case. I'll go there and see them. In the meantime, I'll send a Captain I can trust back to Calhoun with you. Point out the Sergeant and his men to him and let him know the details and they'll be sent home with orders to stand down. There'll be no fuss, but the other men will know why it's being done. All right, before you say any more *I know* it's not enough, but although there's a lot of sympathy for the Cherokees, it hasn't yet reached the stage where the country will stand for a United States citizen being convicted of a crime against them. They're still Indians. All it would succeed in doing is lose support for them – and I need every scrap of that I can get.'

Robert knew that the Major General was right, but he rode back with the regular army Captain the next day feeling he had failed in his self-imposed mission.

Elijah Brown did not agree with Robert's gloomy verdict on his trip. The Cherokee minister was a realist. He was aware of the difficulties faced by Major General Scott. The Sergeant and the men who had brought in Nancy and her party were sent home and would take no further part in the removal of the Cherokees to Indian territory. It was a very small victory – but it was a victory nonetheless.

However, a much more important concession to the Cherokees resulted from General Scott's meeting with the Cherokee leaders in Washington. So impressed was the army officer with their integrity and leadership that he delegated to them the task of superintending the removal of their own people. At the same time he agreed to an increase in their scale of rations, in the hope that it would see them safely through the impending winter.

By taking such a course of action, General Scott incurred the anger of ex-President Andrew Jackson. Angry letters passed between the Hermitage, Jackson's Tennessee home, and Washington, but Scott stood firm. The Cherokee leaders would take their people to the new lands – escorted by the army, of course.

With the departure of the Tennessee Sergeant and his men, things should have improved for the Cherokees, but two far more formidable enemies were forming an alliance against them: time and the weather.

In Washington, the Cherokee leaders had been hoping to make time an ally while national sympathy was building up in their favour. By delaying the departure of their people for as long as possible, it was hoped that winter would set in, making the removal impossible before spring. By then they might have excited public opinion to the point where the removal could have been halted. It was not to be. Official policy hardened and time became an enemy instead of a potential friend.

It was September, but still the Cherokees were not ready to move. Many were ill and there was a serious drought throughout the land. Food and fodder could not be provided.

Not until October did the first of thirteen groups begin its journey: a thousand Cherokees, bidding farewell to the land that had given birth to the Cherokee nation, the home of countless generations of their forefathers. They moved off in silence, only the children turning to look back.

Nancy and her family were in the seventh party to move off. Minister Elijah Brown had been put in charge of this group and he asked Robert to accompany them, hoping that Robert would be able to hunt for them and supplement rations already diminished by their extended stay to the east of the Tennessee River. But Robert refused. He had come this far with Ben Calloni only because he thought his services would be required as an interpreter. It seemed they were not, so he intended going home, to Missouri.

Yet the thought of leaving this mess behind and seeing his family once more no longer carried the thrill of anticipation it should. He longed to see his son, yes. He should have returned to him many years before . . . . At the same time he could not shake off the feeling that he was deserting a people who needed all the help they could get.

Robert sat beside the river, smoking a thin, brown *cigarillo*. The last of the Cherokees moving off that day were halfway across the river on the flat platform-ferry. Those who had crossed earlier formed part of a long line of Indians, wagons, oxen, mules and soldiers, snaking slowly away to the west. Robert felt he was witnessing the passing of a whole nation.

All along the riverbank thousands of Cherokees sat in silence watching their departing kinsmen, knowing that their turn would soon come. Many of the older Cherokees had blankets draped about their shoulders. The weather was turning colder, even here.

There was a movement near-at-hand but Robert took no notice until a voice said quietly, 'Will you be sitting here watching when we move off, Mister MacCrimmon?'

Robert looked up and saw Nancy, the Cherokee girl, standing beside him. It was the first time she had spoken to him since the day of her arrival, although he had occasionally seen her about the prison camp. The bruises on her face had healed and he thought she was probably one of the most attractive women he had ever seen.

'Minister Brown says you will not be accompanying us to our new land. It must be very nice to be able to choose what you will do, and where you will go.'

'Your people can get along without me. I'll go where I was heading before Ben Calloni persuaded me to come here with him.'

'And where is that?' Nancy squatted on her heels beside him and plucked a parched blade of grass, twirling it between her fingers.

'Missouri — the Ozarks.'

'Didn't I hear my father say we would be passing close to the Ozarks?'

'Probably. There are a couple of routes you might take, but I'll move a bit faster than you will. I want to be home before winter sets in. There's a ten-year-old son waiting for me there. When I last saw him he was no more than a babe-in-arms. I'd like to spend the winter months getting to know him.'

'Oh! Then you must go, of course.' Nancy threw the blade of grass from her. It landed in the river and was caught in a small eddy that brought it back to the bank against the flow of the tide. 'Has your wife also waited ten years for you?'

'She died giving birth to the boy. He's been brought up by my pa, helped by my stepmother and her daughters.'

'A boy needs his father. You have been away too long, but my people will miss you too. We have not known you long, but in that time you have been a good friend to the Cherokees. I have never thanked you for what you did for me and my family.'

'You have little reason to be grateful to anyone. The volunteers should have been put on trial and hanged for what they did.' Just remembering made Robert angry.

'Gaining revenge would change nothing. What mattered was that someone — you and General Scott — cared enough to *want* to do something about it.'

'Ben cares too. He'll take care of you along the way.'

Ben Calloni would never take care of anyone again. Robert had his saddle-bags packed, ready to ride away the next morning, when word reached him of the frontiersman's death.

Ben had left with one of the early parties, ten days before. It was his intention to ride back and forth along the route, checking that each group of Cherokees was making satisfactory progress.

Unfortunately, the early cold weather he encountered along the way seriously affected the lung damaged by a Mexican musket ball at San Jacinto. The frontiersman developed pneumonia, and forty-eight hours later he was dead.

Respected by Indians and soldiers alike, Ben was buried beside the trail and each passing party of Cherokees would pause at the graveside to say a prayer for him.

Minister Elijah Brown, accompanied by Nancy, brought the news to Robert. It left him stunned for a while, and then he began to realise what Ben's death would mean to the Cherokees.

'With Ben gone your parties will have no one to hunt for them – and no one to take their part against the army, if the need arises.'

'There will be little left to hunt by the time the last of us leave. As for the army – we'll all be too busy fighting the weather to make trouble for each other.' Elijah Brown was as philosophical as ever. 'Ben will be sadly missed by all of us, but no one man can protect our nation against the rest of the world.'

Robert thought that Minister Brown was probably right. Nevertheless, the knowledge that Ben was a friend of Major General Winfield Scott had been sufficient to curb the excesses of the few unremitting Indian-haters serving with the escorts. Robert also knew that *he* was believed to have the ear of the Major General.

After being absent from home for so long, the urge to return to the Ozarks and the son he did not know had grown steadily stronger in recent months. But a few more weeks would make very little difference to anyone – except the Cherokees.

Robert was convinced that the exodus of the Cherokee nation would have tragic consequences for all those concerned. If he was brutally honest with himself, he had been hoping to be well away before it occurred. He would have excused his desertion of the Cherokees by telling himself that if Ben could do nothing to prevent a tragedy from happening, he could have done no better. Such an evasion of responsibility was no longer open to him.

'I'll saddle up in the morning and go on ahead to find out what's happening to the other parties. But first I'll need to check with the chief; he made the arrangements for stores to be available along the way. Someone will need to make certain they're waiting.'

'You are going to stay with us, until we reach Indian territory?' The question came from Nancy.

As he walked away to find the Cherokee leader, Robert thought that the brief expression of joy he had seen on Nancy's face when he confirmed that he intended staying on with the Cherokees almost made his own sacrifice worthwhile.

The weather steadily deteriorated from the day the last of the thirteen Cherokee parties crossed the Tennessee River, heading northwestwards. The progress of the Cherokees was far slower than had been anticipated and icy rain and snow slowed the pace even more. To add to their problems, an unprecedented series of epidemics struck the evicted tribe. Dysentery, measles and whooping cough took a heavy toll and later parties followed a trail marked by the graves of those who had succumbed.

By mid-December, five thousand Cherokees were marooned in a no-man's-land between the icy Ohio and Mississippi rivers, pinned down by a bone-chilling northerly wind that cut through their too-thin clothes. Many others were encamped on the east bank of the Ohio. All were short of food and desperately in need of blankets and warm clothing.

To make matters worse, the wife of the indomitable Cherokee chief became so ill that he felt obliged to abandon the slow-moving columns and transfer her to a boat on the Ohio River. Travelling via the Mississippi and Arkansas rivers, the weather finally brought the trip to a halt close to Little Rock, on the Arkansas River. Here, camped on a bluff overlooking the river, the chiefs frail wife gave her blanket to a sick child. As a result of her selflessness she developed pneumonia, the illness that had killed Ben Calloni, and she too died.

There was little opportunity for the remainder of the Cherokee nation to go into mourning. They were fighting a desperate battle against unrelenting death every hour of the day and night.

In sheer desperation, Robert took some of the remaining chiefs up the Mississippi River to St Louis. Here, by borrowing money, they were able to obtain sufficient supplies to make the difference between life and death for at least some of the freezing Cherokees.

*

Upon his return from St Louis, Robert found Nancy waiting for him at the small tent he shared with Minister Elijah Brown. In spite of the many demands made upon him during the nightmare journey, he had managed to spend some time with the Cherokee girl and had become very fond of her.

Elijah was away conducting a service for one of the other parties and as Nancy served Robert up some hot food, she said, 'I went to visit one of the other groups yesterday and met a woman I think you should speak to.'

Robert nodded, his mouth full of hot food. When it had gone, he said, 'What's her problem?'

'That is something you will need to ask her. She is known by the others as "the Sioux woman", but I think she is white.'

Robert frowned. 'Is she married to one of your people?'

'No. I believe her husband was killed by the Kiowas and she was made a captive. She was sold to my people as a slave and then set free.'

'You must be mistaken, Nancy. If she were white she'd have told someone long before this. Why should *anyone* put up with these conditions if they didn't have to?'

'I don't know, but I think you should speak to her.'

'All right, you can take me to her later this evening. Just now, I'd like some more of whatever that was I just ate. I need thawing out from the core.'

Robert was convinced that Nancy must be mistaken, but he went along with her because it gave him an opportunity to enjoy her company for a while.

Christmas had come and gone while Robert was in St Louis. There had seemed something indecent about the shops bulging with food, happy children in the streets and the general air of festivity that was abroad in the city while thousands of Cherokees were dying of disease and exposure less than a hundred miles away.

Making his way through the thronged streets of St Louis, Robert had paused at a gunsmith's. In the window was a lightweight Sharp's hunting-rifle. It would be ideal for a boy. He had no idea of his son's interests, but any boy would be delighted with such a present. Buying the gun gave him a great deal of pleasure. Whilst still in this mood of benevolence and acting upon a sudden impulse, he had purchased a silver chain and crucifix for Nancy. There had been little joy in her life during the brief time he had known her and he thought it might please her.

Robert gave the crucifix to Nancy when they were walking to the camp where she had seen 'the Sioux woman'. He was totally unprepared for the Cherokee girl's reaction. Her initial disbelief that he had bought a present for *her* was followed almost immediately by tears – and then Nancy was hugging him, declaring it was the most marvellous present anyone had ever bought for her. She made him fasten it about her neck and as they walked along she smiled happily at him whenever he looked in her direction.

When they reached the camp, it was some time before Nancy found 'the Sioux woman'. She was seated alone in a grass-and-twig-frame shelter propped against a tree that had been stripped of all foliage and minor branches.

As they approached, Robert was more convinced than ever that Nancy was mistaken. 'The Sioux woman' looked like any other Indian woman, perhaps more slightly built than many, but most Cherokee women had lost all their excess weight during the two months of the long march.

When the woman looked up and saw them approaching an unexpected expression crossed her face. It could almost have been fear, but there was something else .... The face was vaguely familiar to Robert, although he could not think why it should be. He had a good memory for faces and was almost certain he had never seen this woman before, and yet ...

The woman lowered her gaze before they reached her. With her chin resting on her chest she stared down at the frayed blanket on which she squatted. It was as though she was willing them to pass her by.

'Sioux Woman,' Nancy spoke quietly, 'I have brought someone to speak to you.'

The woman said nothing, nor did she raise her glance from the blanket.

'I've brought someone to speak to you. I would like you to tell him about yourself.'

'There is nothing to tell.' The woman spoke English with difficulty, as though it were a language with which she was not familiar, and yet there was something about her that concerned Robert.

191

Crouching down before the woman he reached out and put his hand beneath her chin. Lifting her head, he forced her to look at him. Nancy was right. The Sioux woman's eyes were too light to be those of a true Indian. A half-breed, perhaps . . . . Then a sudden surge of excitement went through him: he had suddenly realised why her face was familiar. Yet he needed to be certain. 'Tell me about yourself. The Cherokees call you "Sioux woman", yet you are not a Sioux.'

'The Sioux are my people.'

'No, the Sioux are *not* your people. Before them it was the Shawnee — and before the Shawnee . . . ? Look at me!'

The Sioux woman was desperately trying to look away from Robert, but he would not let her.

'Before that, it was *Scotland* — and a ship to America. A river trip with a man named Ferris — and the murder of your father. You are a Brooks girl, daughter of Molly Brooks. Which one are you, Eileen, or Helen? You can tell me, because if you put your mind to it you'll remember me too — Robert MacCrimmon, son of the piper who entertained you on the ship during the crossing of the Atlantic . . . .'

The wail that rose from the woman was more animal than human and it turned every head in the camp. On her blanket the woman began rocking backwards and forwards, continuing to wail in a way that made the hairs rise on the back of Robert's neck.

Nancy dropped to her knees beside the Sioux woman. Cradling her close, she began to rock with her. Looking up at Robert, she said, 'Go. Leave us for a while. She will be all right soon.'

It was late evening before Nancy returned to the camp, an arm about the Sioux woman. Smiling somewhat wearily at Robert, Nancy said, 'She will talk now. You were right. Her name *is* Brooks. Helen Brooks. She has a horrific story to tell — but I think perhaps she would rather tell it to you herself, in her own way.'

'Come and sit in the tent. I'll light a candle . . . .'

'I will talk to you outside. It will be easier for me if there is little light.' Once again the woman spoke as though English was a language with which she was not familiar and during the narrative that followed she occasionally lapsed into the Sioux tongue, although she was quick to recover.

She told the story simply and starkly, but it was none the less horrific. Taken by Ferris and his men, she was sold to the Shawnee chief Stone Cutter, but he did not keep her for very long before selling her to a Hunkpapa Sioux. Although her status was no more than that of a slave, her new owner treated her as one of his lesser wives. The other wives did not treat her quite so well, but Helen passed over twenty unhappy years by saying simply, 'Times were not always bad, especially when my daughter was born. I was lucky, had it been a son they would have taken him from me. A daughter could be mine – for most of the time. Even when my man died and I was passed on to a Cherokee, they let me bring her with me, but she was a young woman by now and had plans of her own. She was not happy away from the Sioux.'

'Where is she now?'

'Gone. Before we had been four days with the Cherokees she had run off. There was a young warrior, a man who will one day be a great war-chief – even though he had a white father.' Helen Brooks choked on her words, as she said, 'I will never see her again, she is dead to me . . . .'

Helen Brooks began to wail like an Indian woman once more, but this time she did it more quietly than she had earlier in the day.

'If she's still alive there's always hope,' said Robert firmly, in a bid to bring her wailing to a halt. 'Your mother never gave up hope of finding you and Eileen again and I and some of our friends have enquired after you whenever we've met up with Northern Indians. Of course, it would have helped had we known you'd been passed on to the Sioux.'

'My mother is still alive? She escaped from Ferris?'

'You mean you never knew? All these years and you didn't know whether she was alive or dead?'

It was twenty years since Ferris and his men had murdered Helen's father and taken the two daughters away. 'She was alive last time I heard from home. She married my pa. They and your three remaining sisters are living with them not too far from here, in Missouri.'

Helen was crying normally now, almost as though just talking about her white family had helped her revert to her origins. 'They'll all be overjoyed to have you with them. If only Eileen could be found too.'

'Eileen's dead,' declared Helen fiercely, 'she tried to run away at every chance she got, and eventually they shot her. There are times when I wish they'd shot me too. This is one of them. I can never go back to the family. *Never*, not after all that's happened to me.'

'Nothing that's happened to you was any of your doing,' replied Robert, 'and I'd say there's a whole lot of life owed to you.'

'Leave her with me,' said Nancy, unexpectedly. 'Helen needs to be with a family for a while. She can stay with us and we'll have time to talk along the trail.'

Nancy admitted to Robert that persuading Helen Brooks to change her mind about returning to her family was hard work. Sometimes, Helen would behave like the woman she was supposed to be, and Nancy would think she was winning. The next morning when Helen awoke she had reverted to being the Sioux woman.

The weather had improved a little and the Cherokee nation was on the move once more. They had crossed the Mississippi and were pursuing a route through Missouri that had taken them even closer to the Ozarks than Robert had anticipated.

'Perhaps she'll feel differently about things when she actually sees her ma again,' said Robert, hopefully. 'That's if she doesn't run out on me along the way.'

'Your son will be pleased to see you. You *will* be seeing him?' Nancy asked the question almost casually, but they both knew a great deal hinged on his reply. They had grown very close during the weeks they had been travelling together. They both realised that it was so – as did every one of the Cherokees in their particular party – and it was a romance that had brought a small breath of pleasure into the lives of the still-suffering Cherokees.

'I haven't made up my mind yet,' said Robert.

'You must, Robert. He is your son, you have been away from him for too long. You must go to him.'

'I want to,' said Robert truthfully. 'But I feel I can't desert you and your people. Not now. The bad weather isn't over yet, and there's still a long way to go. I can take Helen home once we've got you to Indian territory.'

Robert hesitated, there was more to be said, but he wondered whether this was the right moment. 'There's something else – you and me.'

'That will wait, Robert. Go and find your son first. Get to know him . . . . If you still feel you want to come and see me I will not be hard to find.'

'You'll wait for me?'

'If that is what you really want. But I am Cherokee – an Indian. That is why you must go home first. Stay with your own people for a while before you make up your mind.'

'I don't need to do that before I make up my mind, Nancy. It's already made up – but I would like to tell the boy first.'

'Of course . . . I am happy you think this way.'

The severe weather returned with a vengeance when they were no more than forty or fifty miles from the MacCrimmon home. For nine days they sheltered while an icy northerly wind brought snow piling up against the flimsy tents and makeshift shelters of the Cherokees. By the time the weather improved they had eaten every scrap of food and had gone hungry for a full twenty-four hours.

The question of whether or not Robert would go home before the Cherokees arrived in Indian territory had been decided for him. He would take Helen with him, find his father and organise food supplies for the Cherokees.

To Robert's surprise, Helen put up no more than a token resistance when he told her he was going to take her to meet her mother and the remainder of her family. The weather and their present predicament played a large part in her acceptance of his decision. Life had become a fight for survival. Without help there would be a great many losers and Helen had not yet reached the stage where she would deliberately throw away a chance to live.

With Helen riding a Cherokee horse beside him, Robert rode hard through the hills of the Ozarks. There were still many deep pockets of snow to be carefully avoided, and partly frozen streams constituted a dangerous hazard. Nevertheless, they were able to reach the cleared lands that belonged to Hugh MacCrimmon that same day – and as they approached the house Robert heard the unmistakable sound of the bagpipe music.

When they rounded a turn in the track Robert saw a diminutive figure, bagpipes tucked beneath his arm, marching towards the Mac-Crimmon cabin – now much larger than when Robert was last here. Robert knew that he was looking at Andy, the son he had last seen when he was a tiny baby, newly taken from his dead mother's arms. For a moment Helen was forgotten and as Robert rode towards his son she reined in her horse, knowing this was not *her* moment.

Pulling his horse in beside the boy, Robert looked down at his son; he was a fine-looking boy, straight and tall for his age. Robert fancied that he favoured himself, yet there was also a hint of his mother in the sensitive features.

The boy removed the blowpipe from his mouth and as the bagpipes wailed a final melancholy note before lapsing into silence, he looked up at the rider in surprise. The noise of the pipes had prevented him from hearing the approaching horses.

'You play the pipes like a MacCrimmon, boy.'

'That's because my grandpa makes me play them every day on the way to visit him. He's a MacCrimmon – and was the finest piper in the whole of Scotland, or so folk say.'

'They're not lying. He's the finest piper anywhere.' Robert's voice was husky with emotion. *This was his son.*

Andy MacCrimmon looked at Robert with a slightly puzzled expression. 'Do *you* play the pipes?'

Swinging down from his horse, Robert took the pipes. Tucking the bag beneath his arm, he breathed air into the bag and began to play. The tune was a jig, composed by Hugh MacCrimmon on the ship that had brought them to America from Scotland, to help while away the long, boring days.

As the tune progressed the boy looked at Robert increasingly wide-eyed. When it droned to a halt, he said, 'You . . . you're my pa!'

Not trusting himself to speak, Robert nodded and held out his arms and his son flung himself at him. Behind them, Helen Brooks sat her horse with tears streaming down her face. It was not only the reunion of father and son that had affected her. She remembered the tune Robert had played. It reminded her of long ago, when she had been travelling with a happy family to begin a new life in a new land.

There was much joy in the MacCrimmon home that evening. Not one, but *two* of the family had returned, one of whom had been given up for dead by everyone except Molly Brooks. There were a few tears shed too, for the other daughter who would never return.

But lengthy celebration parties needed to be put off for another time. When Robert explained the desperate plight of the Cherokees, messengers were sent throughout the Ozarks to gather every scrap of food that could be found for the starving Indians.

Hugh himself donated a hundred sheep and twenty steers, and more animals were added to the flocks and herds as they began driving them southwards through the Ozarks the following day. Other men went ahead with the carcasses of slaughtered animals slung across the saddles of their horses. More carcasses were despatched on wagons, driven at breakneck speed along barely discernible tracks.

There were many Scots among these hills who had been driven from their homes and who had experienced the bitter pangs of hunger. But it was not only the Scots who gave aid. Others had moved into these hills and founded their own communities. Germans, Scandinavians, Cornish and Americans from the east who had moved west in search of a better life for their families. Missouri had not experienced the Indian troubles of many other States and their sympathies were with the deposed people who had put up a desperate, yet peaceful fight to keep their homeland.

Even the few who were against any Indians, regardless of their tribe, were eager to sell food to the Cherokees when Robert guaranteed payment.

Robert remained in the Ozark settlements for three days, ensuring that the flow of food did not dry up. During this time, Andy did not leave his side. It was as though the boy was fearful that after so many years his father would once more ride out of his life.

When Robert felt it was necessary to return to the Cherokees, Andy's fear was so evident that Robert said his son could come along with him. Hugh, too, insisted that he was not too old to go along, and so three generations of MacCrimmons rode southwards to the trail being followed by the dispossessed Cherokees.

Robert had already told his father about Nancy, and the elder MacCrimmon assured his son that a Cherokee woman would be welcome into the household. Hugh had many secret doubts about her acceptance into the steadily increasing social life of the expanding communities now crowding around their extensive land-holdings, but he kept such thoughts to himself.

Robert had given Andy the rifle he had bought for him in St Louis and along the way the boy delighted himself and everyone else by shooting a turkey. Although Robert felt he had said very little about Nancy in his son's presence, Andy proudly announced that he was going to give the turkey as a present to 'the Cherokee girl who was Pa's special friend'.

When they reached the site of the camp, Nancy's party had moved on and another group of Cherokees were camped on the spot where they had been. When Robert expressed surprise to the Captain in charge of this group's escort, he was told that orders had come from Washington to complete the removal to Indian territory as quickly as possible. Politicians who knew nothing of the appalling conditions along the trail were angry with the time the operation was taking, and upset by the spiralling cost of the food being purchased along the way. Human life meant little to the men who managed the country's finances in Washington – nothing at all if those lives were Indian.

Food was coming into the camps in increasing quantities now and Robert knew there would be no more shortages. With his father and son he set off westwards to overtake Minister Elijah Brown's party.

They had covered ten miles when they encountered Indians who should have been on the march encamped alongside the trail. A few miles further westwards the congestion grew worse, and when they met an army rider coming towards them they stopped him and asked what was happening.

'The ferry boat taking Cherokees across the river capsized and broke up. It was overcrowded and the river was swollen . . . . I've got to go back along the trail and halt the parties coming along. If I don't there'll be standing room only down at the riverbank.'

As the soldier dug his heels into his horse's belly, Robert called, 'Which party was on the boat?'

'The one being looked after by that Cherokee preacher, Elijah Brown. He was one of those who drowned . . . .'

The three MacCrimmons rode through the throngs of waiting Cherokees at a reckless pace, but the speed at which they reached the river's edge would change nothing.

The ferry had been grossly overloaded, but had there not been a general impatience on the part of the army to ford the river and keep the Cherokee columns moving, such a crossing of the swollen river would not have been attempted.

After searching frantically among the survivors of the party, Robert began the grim task of checking among the dead. When he failed to find Nancy's body among the many laid out beside the riverbank, his hopes rose. Then, as the search extended farther downstream, he found her lying with the bodies of two other women. Their bodies had been dragged from the river more than a mile from the scene of the accident. Around her neck she still wore the crucifix Robert had brought for her from St Louis.

Robert stood beside her until his father placed a hand on his shoulder and said, 'She was a beautiful girl, son. One who would not have been out of place in any gathering.'

Robert nodded in silence, then, with his arm about the shoulders of his son he walked away from the tragic scene, and away from the Cherokees with whom he had spent the past few bitter months.

Helen Brooks remained with her family for only two months. Her immediate family and the MacCrimmons showed her every possible kindness and did their best to prove to her that all the unhappiness she had suffered was in the past – but the last twenty years had instilled too much Indian in the long-lost daughter. She could not get used to living in a house again, and whenever friends came visiting she was convinced that they had come only out of curiosity to stare at her, and she would disappear into the woods.

At first she would go for only an hour or two, but then her absences became longer, occasionally lasting all day and all night. Then came the day when she failed to return to the MacCrimmon home at all. Every man from the nearby farms joined in the search, but Helen had disappeared from her true family once again. Reports came back that she had been sighted in a number of places, all of them to the north-west, in the direction of the Sioux country, but not even trackers with the experience of Sam Chisholm and Robert could find her.

Two years after his return, Robert married Rose, the youngest of the Brooks girls. She had looked after Andy since the death of his mother, and that day the growing young MacCrimmon thought himself the happiest boy in the whole State of Missouri. Not long after

Robert's marriage, the county in which they farmed was named after one of its pioneer residents and it became 'MacCrimmon County'.

In view of the family's association with the area, and Robert's background, he was asked if he would serve as the county's first sheriff. It was a popular appointment, one that was acceptable to men of all political leanings.

Meanwhile, the Cherokees were building towns, schools and well-ordered communities in Indian territory. They had come to terms with their new land and would set a standard for those who came after.

But they would never forget the terrible trek from their home-lands in Georgia and Tennessee; the removal in which one in four of the nation died. It would forever more be referred to as their 'Trail of Tears'.

SEVEN

Canada 1840

For a while, Sir James Cameron was one of Upper Canada's most successful and wealthy men. Upon the death of his partner, two years after the Indian attack on the Lakes, Cameron inherited the whole of the Upper Canada Trading Company. A year later he sold it to the Hudson's Bay Company, the trading giant which was battling for sole control of large-scale commercial activities in the vast northern continent.

Although he sold the company, James Cameron retained most of the lands it had once owned. As a result, when a town grew up around the trading fort at Murrayton, he prospered accordingly.

Public honours also came his way. The chairman of numerous subcommittees and judicial boards, he was eventually appointed a Judge of the High Court of Upper Canada, a post that brought him all the pomp and dignity of high office.

Despite his standing in the community, and having a son and heir upon whom he doted, James Cameron was not a happy man. The main cause of his unhappiness was Lady Cameron. He was an extremely wealthy man, but her extravagance was legendary throughout both Canadas – and so too were her indiscretions. For many years she carried on an association with René Lesouris that was open secret in Upper Canada. It teetered on the verge of an outright scandal when she travelled to Europe on the same ship as the aristocratic French trapper, leaving her husband behind in Canada.

However, with the passing of the years Vanessa began to be seen in the company of men only a little older than her own son, and amusement replaced scandal. Yet public opinion stopped short of open ridicule, and it was far less damaging to Sir James. Meanwhile, the baronet himself was not above censure.

It was strongly rumoured that Sir James had developed an appetite for Indian women during his first winter in the forest. His critics pointed to the preponderance of attractive young Indian girls among the ranks of his many servants, a number of whom were said to have left his employment with considerably expanded girths.

More recently, James Cameron had become increasingly concerned for his son. Charles Cuthbert James Cameron was a wild, spoiled, rich young man whose sole purpose in life seemed to be a determination to outdo the escapades of other wealthy young men.

When James remonstrated with him, Charles suggested there was nothing else for him to do about the city of Toronto – the name given to York some four years before. The recriminations took place in the hall of the large mansion built by James Cameron on the land granted to his wife by Henry Murray, many years before.

James Cameron, a glass of whisky in hand, had intercepted his son as he was about to leave the house to join his friends in another evening of carousing.

'Why don't you find something profitable to occupy your time? A business? I'll advance you any money you require . . . .'

'Do you have something special in mind? Perhaps you'd like me to learn a *trade?*' Sarcasm had always been a strong suit with Charles.

'There's no reason to talk to me like that, Charles. I can buy you a directorship of any company you'd like to join . . . .'

'A *company*? That's only one step up from being a *shopkeeper*. I'd never be able to face my friends again.'

Charles Cameron made for the door and had opened it before he paused and turned back. 'If you *really* want to do something useful you might arrange a commission for me in the militia. Two of our crowd have tried for commissions and been turned down. I'd like to succeed where they failed – and rounding up rebels might turn out to be fun.'

As usual, Sir James carried out his son's wishes, but, only three weeks after being granted his commission, Charles learned there was more to being a militiaman than wearing an attractive uniform.

General Sir Hector Bligh, KB, was Commander of the militia. An ex-regular army general who had fought in the war against America twenty-six years before, he resented those men who had made a fortune in Canada without raising a hand in her defence. He put Sir James Cameron foremost on his list of such people. The baronet's son had been granted a militia commission despite objections from the commanding officer of the part-time force, and the anger of the notoriously irascible military man had been quietly smouldering ever since.

For more than a year there had been armed incursions across the border separating Canada from America. Those responsible were followers of William Lyon Mackenzie, a native of Dundee who had emigrated to Canada in 1820. He founded a newspaper which he used to castigate the government and vilify the pillars of Canadian society. Eventually his outspoken campaign forced Mackenzie to flee the country, but he found men sympathetic to his cause in the northern States of America. For many years they made largely futile raids across the border, retiring at the first sign of any opposition.

When another such raid was reported to the authorities in Toronto, General Sir Hector Bligh ordered Charles Cameron to take a company of militiamen and drive the rebels back across the border. There was unlikely to be any danger attached to the assignment, but the choleric General knew there was a possibility it might cause embarrassment to Sir James Cameron.

The area where the incursion had occurred was far to the west, on the shores of Lake Superior. It was an area claimed by the immensely powerful Hudson's Bay Company and the administrators of Upper Canada, both of whom were vague about the extent of the country's western borders.

Delicate negotiations were currently in progress with a view to merging both Upper and Lower Canada into one country. Many of the colony's politicians and officials hoped that self-government would follow unification. The considerable power wielded by the Hudson's Bay Company with its vast resources would be a crucial factor in the negotiations. Those with most to gain by the merger of the two Canadas were anxious that nothing should cast a doubt in the mind of the British Prime Minister about Canada's ability to manage its own affairs.

General Sir Hector Bligh had enjoyed an illustrious past and harboured no ambitions for the future. Indeed, he had antagonised so many of those who might one day hold high office in the country, he would prefer Canada to remain a colony, administered from London.

By sending the hot-headed son of Toronto's most influential judge into disputed Hudson's Bay Company territory, there was a very real likelihood of so much trouble being stirred up that the English government would refuse to relinquish control of its vast North American colony.

The militiamen and their horses were carried for most of their long journey to the north-west by paddle steamer, but they had to disembark and ride the last few miles.

Riding at the head of seventy mounted militiamen, Charles Cuthbert James Cameron savoured the sense of importance it gave him. The waves and cheers from settlers in the villages and small communities as the small party rode through fuelled his self-importance. Charles Cameron hoped that the rebels had not all returned across the border before the militia arrived. This, at least, was a sentiment he shared with his men. Having ridden so hard and far they did not want to return to Toronto without having fired a shot.

However, the militiamen from Toronto were dealing with an 'enemy' who had no intention of standing and fighting. After crossing the unguarded border the rebels fired a couple of cabins and retired, the ex-newspaper owner claiming another 'victory' in his long-running war with the Canadian authorities.

Disappointed, Charles led his men in futile and much belated pursuit towards the border – and met up with a dozen heavily armed men riding from America. Convinced he had intercepted another of Mackenzie's raiding-parties, Charles Cameron ordered his men to prime their ready-loaded rifles and form a line to oppose the oncoming men.

For their part, the Americans seemed genuinely puzzled to have met up with the uniformed party in such a remote area.

'Halt where you are, or we'll open fire,' called Charles, as the Americans rode slowly towards the militiamen. The Americans slowed their horses to a walk, but one man cantered on towards the Canadian militiamen. 'What the hell do you think you're doing sticking *us* up – and where d'you find those uniforms? When I saw you I thought I'd brought my men the wrong way and crossed the *Mexican* border. Have you killed the Indians?'

Now it was Charles Cameron's turn to be puzzled. 'What Indians?'

'Sioux Indians. They attacked a party of settlers on their way to Oregon country, then headed this way. We had our own soldier-boys with us until we got to the river, then their Captain said it was part of the border and he couldn't come any further. That wasn't good enough for us. You let an Indian get away with anything and he'll do it again. We aim to make sure they don't.'

The American was aware he was dealing with a young and inexperienced militia officer, and he relaxed. 'But if you're not after Indians, what are you doing out here?'

'We were searching for a party of rebels who came over the border and burned a couple of cabins.'

'Oh, *tikem!*' The American's manner was contemptuous. 'We heard about 'em. They gave themselves up on the American side of the border and the soldiers took their guns away. You'll have no more problems from them – but you'll have big trouble from the Indians unless we catch up with 'em fast.'

'Are you certain they came this way?' Charles allowed his uncertainty to show. He had been sent out after Canadian rebels and their unwillingness to stand in serious battle was well known. Indians – *armed* Indians, were an entirely different matter.

'Does it get dark when the sun goes down?' countered the American. 'We've got "Old Grizzly" Palmer scouting for us. An Indian couldn't shake him off by floating ten foot high over solid rock. They came this way, right enough – and they're not too far ahead of us now. You and your men coming to help us find 'em?'

Charles thought it was time he asserted the authority that was invested in his militia commission.

'You and your men are on Canadian soil now. Catching up with the Indians is our business, but you're welcome to come along and help us.'

The American looked at Charles speculatively and shrugged. 'I thought this was Hudson's Bay Company territory, but it's all the same to me. The more of us there are, the better our chance of catching up with 'em and making sure they don't kill any more settlers.'

Charles Cameron felt he had satisfactorily established who was in charge of the party and he sensed that his own men approved of the manner in which he had asserted his authority over the Americans.

'Old Grizzly' Palmer's nickname might have had to do with the bear-skin hat he wore, or the state of the ancient, lined and weather-beaten face visible above a bushy beard – but he was an excellent tracker.

Sent to range ahead of the main party, he found the Indians less than twenty-four hours after the meeting of Americans and Toronto militia. He reported a band of seven males, four women and three children camped on the bank of a river about six miles away.

It hardly seemed to be a group of sufficient strength to have attacked a whole party of armed wagoners, but the leader of the Americans explained this away by suggesting that the Indians must have split up after the attack. He insisted that the Indians they had been following *were* responsible for waylaying the small wagon train.

'We'll find out soon enough,' declared Charles Cameron. 'Let's go and see what they have to say about it.'

'*Say?* Hell, Mister, I'm not risking the lives of my men by going in and trying to talk to no Indians. We'll wait 'til dark, then attack 'em. If any of 'em survive we'll consider talking, but I don't guarantee it.'

'There are women and children in the party. If we attack in the dark they might get hurt too.'

There was a guffaw of laughter from one of the Americans and their spokesman pushed back his hat and assumed an air of incredulity. 'I can see you've never been around Indians, boy. Their women are worse than the men. When a white man's taken prisoner the Indian women cut bits off him that decent women don't even know about. As for the kids, unless something's done to stop them, they'll grow up and do exactly the same.'

Charles Cameron realised there was a huge gulf between the American and Canadian thinking on Indians. Whether the Indians of the two countries *were* different, or behaved differently because of the attitude of the white men they encountered, would always be a matter for heated debate. What the young militia Lieutenant *did* know was that he objected strongly to being called 'boy'. It was a word he had heard used by Americans when speaking to their 'niggers'.

'How you deal with Indians in your country is your business. In Canada they're entitled to the benefits of the law, the same as anyone else. We'll take them prisoner to Toronto and you can come there and give evidence against them in the courts.'

There was an angry murmur from the Americans, but Charles Cameron felt he had the backing of his militiamen who were closing in on either side of him.

'You're making a bad mistake, boy. That ain't the way to deal with Indians. You can't take a wolf out of a pack and put him in a pen to guard your sheep. He's just naturally wild, same as an Indian. You take my word for it.'

The 'boy' was there again and it riled Charles Cameron as much as before. 'If you don't like the way we treat Indians on this side of the border I suggest you go back to America and find the rest of the Indians who attacked your wagon train. We believe in law and order in Canada. I'll arrest the Indians on your say-so but only if you agree to come to court and give evidence against them. If you won't then I have no evidence they've broken any laws here. I'll talk to them, of course, but I'll have no reason to take them into custody.'

'Goddammit! The boy talks like a lawyer. I reckon we must have killed off all the soldiers in the war of 1812.'

As Charles flushed angrily, one of the Canadian militiamen said, 'His pa's a judge – but what he says is right. Indians on this side of the border are mostly peaceable. We don't need you to come here stirring 'em up.'

'A judge's boy, eh?' The leader of the Americans looked at Charles scornfully. 'I knew for sure he weren't no Indian fighter – nor any other sort of fighter, neither.'

'I've given you your choices. Agree to give evidence against the Indians and I'll arrest them. If not, I must ask you to return across the border to your own country.'

The American glared at Charles angrily for some moments, then spat noisily on the ground. 'You've got numbers on your side right now, boy . . . but don't you ever cross the border to America when you're chasing these rebels of yours. You'll find you're as welcome as a free nigger in Missouri.'

Wheeling his horse, the American called on his fellow countrymen to follow him, sharply silencing the men who protested that by leaving they had wasted all the time they had spent in pursuit of the small band of Sioux Indians.

Accepting the praise of his militiamen for the manner in which he had handled the Americans, Charles tried not to let them see how pleased he was. It was not due to any modesty. The Americans had accepted the situation far too easily: he was not at all sure they had seen the last of them. He would speak to the Indians first, and then ride southwards to satisfy himself that the Americans had returned to the United States.

The Indians were in camp at the river's edge, as Old Grizzly Palmer had said, but there were only five men here, all of them armed.

The arrival of the Toronto militia caused a momentary panic, but it quickly subsided when Charles Cameron ordered his men to remain at a discreet distance from the camp, and advanced accompanied only by a Sergeant who claimed to have a knowledge of Indian languages.

The Sergeant spoke a few, halting phrases to the Indians, but when one of them responded in a guttural language, he turned to Charles perplexed.

'I'm sorry, sir. I'm damned if I can make head nor tail of what he's saying. It's no Indian language I've heard before.'

With only the merest trace of a smile, the Indian said, 'I speak the language of my people. I am Spotted Pony of the Hunkpapa tribe of the Sioux nation.'

'Your English is better than my Sergeant's Sioux,' said Charles, greatly relieved. The life he had led had brought him into little contact with Indians. He had imagined them to be far less civilised than the tall, dignified young man of about his own age who now stood before him.

'You come with many soldiers,' said Spotted Pony. 'You are at war with someone?'

Charles Cameron was impressed with the bearing of this Indian, but he had no intention of explaining Toronto militia business to him.

'We heard you were here so came to see what you were doing. We met some Americans who seemed to think you'd been involved in a fight with some of their people heading west in wagons.'

'The men who fought those in the wagons were Oglala Sioux,' said Spotted Pony. 'We rode on the same trail for a while, on the American side of the border.'

Charles nodded non-committally. The chances were that the Indian was telling the truth. The tracks of one Indian pony would look very similar to the tracks of another, especially if they travelled the same path for some distance.

'They also said we would find seven men here.'

'We are seven,' agreed Spotted Pony. 'Two are hunting. We have women and children to feed.' Even as he spoke the two men in question came along the riverbank, a small deer slung on a pole between them.

Two of the children had come to stand close to Spotted Pony and were gazing up at Charles and the Sergeant with undisguised curiosity.

For a few moments, Charles could think of nothing more to say to the man standing in front of him. He had done nothing against the laws of Canada to justify arresting him and had given a satisfactory explanation about the raid.

Charles had made up his mind to ride away and leave the Indians to their own devices, when suddenly a volley of shots rang out from the forest farther along the bank, beyond the Indian encampment. Two Indian women and four men dropped to the ground and there was consternation among the remainder. As Spotted Pony ran back to join his companions, two of the surviving Indians fired upon the militiamen.

'Don't shoot . . . . Go and find out who fired those shots!' As Charles shouted his orders there was another shot from the Indians. The Sergeant beside him groaned, and slipped to the ground from his horse. Looking behind him, Charles saw Spotted Pony with his rifle to his shoulder, gunpowder smoke seeping from his gun and drifting away on the wind.

'Arrest those Indians! Quickly.'

Militiamen and horses were going in all directions now, as some men rode towards the forest edge, others rode at the Indians and a few fired at both forest and Indian encampment. It was many minutes before order was restored on the riverbank, by which time four Indian men lay dead. Two of the women had also been killed and another wounded.

The militia had also suffered casualties in the brief and unexpected skirmish. The Sergeant and two militiamen were dead, and three militiamen were wounded. Two of the wounds had been inflicted by knife-wielding Indian women and Charles was reminded of what the leader of the Americans had said to him.

When Charles Cameron passed close to Spotted Pony, the Indian gave him a look of naked hatred. 'Are there not enough of you to attack us openly? Are you so afraid of us that you needed to trick us?' The Indian spat out the words.

'The shooting was none of our doing. It was probably the same Americans who'd tracked you from the scene of the attack on the wagon train. I'd ordered them back to the border, but it seems they were determined to have revenge before they went.'

One of the militiamen had tied Spotted Pony's hands in front of him and the Indian held them up to Charles. 'Will you now go after the Americans and bring them back tied like this for killing us?'

'I'll send men after them, yes, and if they're caught they'll face the same judge as you. But whether we catch them or not won't alter the fact that you fired on my men and killed my Sergeant. You and the others will stand trial for murder.'

As he spoke, Charles needed to make a conscious effort to stop his limbs from shaking. The Sergeant had been no more than an arm's length away when he was killed. The bullet might easily have ended his life and not the other man's.

There was never any chance of catching the Americans. After firing a volley at the Indians, they had ridden hard for the border, no more than ten miles away. Charles returned to Toronto with his prisoners – although the only unwounded woman managed to escape along the way.

The surviving Sioux Indian warriors were charged in Toronto with the murders of two militiamen. The hearing at the lower court was well reported and much anger was generated when three were set free. The defence lawyer successfully argued that the men had believed their families to be threatened when the volley came from the forest. Only Spotted Pony had been seen to shoot the Sergeant. For all that could be proved, the other militiamen might have been killed by the Americans who had so recklessly put the lives of the Canadian part-time soldiers at risk.

Since the skirmish with the Indians there had been another cross-border raid into Canada. This time the rebels were believed to have been supported by Americans of Irish origin. Blaming the Americans for what had happened to the Toronto militiamen was not unpopular.

The furore in the press soon died down. Spotted Pony was patently guilty of murder. When he appeared at the High Court Judge Cameron would bring the full process of law to bear on the man his son had captured. The hanging of Spotted Pony would satisfy the public demand for vengeance, if not justice. Meanwhile, the public had many other things to occupy their minds.

It now seemed certain that the two provinces of Canada would be united, but rumblings from London indicated that self-government was not likely to be achieved for many years to come. Opinion throughout Upper Canada was equally divided between those who favoured self-government, and those who wished to remain a colony. Both sides were stating their cases vociferously. The certain fate of a Sioux Indian meant nothing to anyone – unless it was the women in his life, and few people in Toronto cared anything about them.

Working late in his chambers at the High Court, Judge Cameron looked up irritably when a knock came at the door and the duty clerk entered.

'What is it, man? I told you I was busy and not to be disturbed . . . .'

'I'm sorry, your Honour, but there are two Sioux women outside. I believe they're relatives of the man who comes up before you next week on a charge of murdering the militiaman. They want to speak to you.'

'I can't speak to them, they might be called to give evidence at the trial. Besides, I've already told you, I'm far too busy to see anyone right now.'

'That's what I told them, in no uncertain terms, but one woman in particular said she must see you. She asked me to give you this, Sir James. I told her you weren't allowed to accept gifts, not a man in your position, but she insisted. Not that it could be termed a gift, it's just a cheap trinket . . . .'

James Cameron had stopped listening. In his hand the clerk had placed a cheap tin trinket, a pin in the shape of a thistle-head. It was the sort of thing a Highland girl might purchase at a local fair. But as he looked at the trinket, Judge Cameron's thoughts went back twenty years to the weeks he had spent in the forests between the island on Georgian Bay, and Murrayton – and to the girl who had shared the hardships and dangers of those weeks with him. The girl to whom he had made a gift of the brooch he now held in his hand – to Tissee.

'Shall I call a constable to put them out, Sir James?'

'Eh? Oh . . . no. Send them in. I'll have a word with them.'

'Is that wise, Sir James? They haven't been searched . . . .'

'I'll decide what's wise, man. I said send them in.'

The irascibility of Sir James Cameron was well known. Hastily closing the door behind him, the clerk went off to escort the two Indian women to the chambers of Toronto's Chief Justice.

Two women preceded the clerk into Cameron's chambers. The first was young, slim, and pale-skinned for an Indian girl. She had a bold manner that bordered on arrogance. The other was an overweight, prematurely aged woman who showed none of the beauty she had once possessed. For a moment he thought there must be some mistake. This could not be Tissee. She had been more like the girl . . . . Then the Indian woman looked directly at him and he recognised the eyes. They, at least, had not changed. This *was* Tissee.

'All right, you can go.' James dismissed the clerk, who hovered in the doorway, uncertain whether or not he should remain.

When the door closed, James crossed the room, intending to take Tissee's hand, but she was looking down at the floor once more.

'This is a most unexpected surprise, Tissee. I never thought I would see you again. Here, this is yours.'

Tissee took the brooch he proffered to her, but still said nothing.

'Well, why have you come here? The clerk said it had something to do with the young Sioux who is being brought before me next week on a charge of murder. If you're here to plead on his behalf I am afraid I can do nothing to help you . . . .'

'You *must!*' The sudden outburst came from the girl and James was not displeased to turn his attention to her.

'Must I indeed, my dear. Perhaps you'll tell me who you are and why I *must* help this young man.'

'You could not speak my Hunkpapa name, but sometimes I am called Katie. I am the wife of Spotted Pony. I come to ask your help because he has done nothing for which he should die. We came here, to Canada, to leave behind those who wish to fight.'

'It's for the court to decide whether or not he's guilty, Katie – but from what I understand he was actually seen to shoot one of our militia Sergeants. That's hardly the act of a peaceable man.'

'He shot because white men were shooting at us. They killed our people first.'

'I regret I can't go into the details of a case I'll be trying, my dear – much as I would like to help you.'

Tissee said something in the Sioux language and after a brief exchange between the two women, Katie left the room with obvious reluctance.

When she had gone, Tissee said, 'You will save Spotted Pony.' It was not a question but a statement of fact and James felt a flicker of irritation.

'You heard what I just told Katie. The verdict of the court is made on the evidence put before it. From all I've heard, I'd say there's overwhelming evidence that this Indian is guilty.'

'It is for you to decide whether Spotted Pony shall live or die?'

'Yes, but if he's guilty of murder he'll die – and my own son saw him shoot the militia Sergeant.'

'You will tell your son not to speak against Spotted Pony.'

'I can't do that, Tissee. Anyway, why should I? This Spotted Pony shot a man. The law says . . . .'

'Does the law say a brother should speak against his brother? Does it tell a father he must order the death of his own son?'

Tissee was looking at James boldly now, her eyes meeting his, as those of Katie had.

James looked at her disbelievingly. 'What are you trying to say to me, Tissee . . . ? Spotted Pony is a Sioux, an Indian.'

'I am his mother. I am Sioux. You are his father. Spotted Pony is *our* son.'

'I, I don't believe it. This is a trick to save his life! It won't work . . . .'

Tissee shook her head. 'No trick. Go to see him. Look at him. Look at him closely. You will see.'

James was aghast. Suddenly it felt as though the whole foundation on which he had built his life was crumbling away.

'Why . . . why didn't you tell me about this before?'

Tissee shrugged. 'You had other son. You not care about this one – but you *must* care now. I will come to see you again. Remind you.'

'No!'

It was too emphatic and Tissee gave him a direct look once more.

'What I mean is, not here. You mustn't come to see me here. I've a fishing lodge up on the west bank of Lake Scugog. I'm leaving for there tomorrow morning – that's why I'm working so late tonight. Come and see me there, if you must.'

Through the window of his chambers James watched the two Indian women walk away from the High Court building. Then he went to his desk and, opening a drawer, pulled out a bottle of whisky. Half filling a tumbler, he drank most of it in one deep draught and sat back to think. He had a problem on his hands, but he had scraped through worse ones in his time.

James Cameron had been at his fishing lodge for two days when he returned one evening to see an Indian girl wrapped in a blanket huddled on the front porch. His heart sank at the thought of having to face Tissee once again, with nothing resolved, but when the sound of his footsteps carried to the Indian she looked up, and he saw it was not Tissee, but Katie.

The greeting he gave to the Indian girl was much warmer than the one that Tissee would have received, and as he ushered her inside the cabin, he said, 'What are *you* doing here? I was expecting Tissee.'

'I told her I would come instead. I thought I might be better able to convince you how much it means to us to have Spotted Pony freed.'

'Oh? And how do you propose to do that?' James was impressed with this girl's command of English. There was also a familiar and exciting emotion stirring inside him when he looked at her. She really was a very attractive Indian girl . . . .

'In every way I can – I would like one of those.'

Katie pointed to the drink James was pouring for himself.

'Of course.' James smiled at her as he poured her a full tumbler of whisky. It had been a long time since an Indian girl excited him as much as Katie did. Perhaps not since Tissee . . . .

The night before the trial Sir James had a meeting with his son, his *legitimate* son. Charles Cameron was filled with his own self-importance. Tomorrow he was due to give evidence that would send a man – albeit an *Indian,* to the gallows. Already it had raised his prestige among his circle of friends and acquaintances – especially with the young women.

Father and son met in James Cameron's study and after chatting about nothing in particular, James said, 'I've been doing a great deal of thinking about this case tomorrow.'

'It seems that everyone in Toronto is thinking about nothing else. I don't know why, I'm sure.' Charles added with assumed modesty, 'I was only doing my duty, after all.'

'And you did it extremely well,' agreed his father. 'I'm as proud of you as any man could be of his son . . . but I 've been thinking about this unfortunate Indian . . . Spotted Pony? All he was doing – no, all he *thought* he was doing, was protecting his wife, and the wives and children of his people. It wasn't a deliberate murder, not like some of those I've had before my court in the past few years.'

'How do you know? You weren't there. I was. It was murder, I tell you. Deliberate, cold-blooded murder. Why, the Sergeant had his *back* to the Indian.'

'I know all that, but . . . think about it. The sudden onslaught on his people from the Americans hiding in the forest. Don't you think it possible he reacted in a way that many people – white as well as Indian – might have done? In the mistaken belief that he was defending his family, his people?'

'No, I don't! It was murder – straightforward, cold-blooded murder!' Charles downed his drink and banged the glass down heavily on the table. 'Anyway, I'm not at all sure we should be talking about the case like this. We should leave it all until tomorrow when the evidence is put to you. You'll see then whether it was murder – or just a mistake.'

Halfway to the door, Charles Cameron stopped and turned back to face his father.

'I'll just say one thing, Father. If you let this Indian off, you'll never see me in this house again – no, nor in this town. It will make me a laughing stock. Not only because it will mean my arrest of the Indians was a fiasco, but because it will seem that my own father doesn't believe my evidence.'

Charles paused, before delivering his parting shot. 'I'll tell you something else. You let that Indian off and *you're* finished in Toronto, too, certainly as far as public office is concerned. All those rumours about you and your love of Indians – especially their women – will be trotted out again – rumours I had to live with as a boy, rumours I'm still living down. You think about *that* when you're trying to think up excuses for the Indian who's shot dead a Toronto militiaman.'

The courtroom was crowded for the trial and James was discomfited to see Tissee and Katie among a group of Indians sitting near the front of the spectators.

When Spotted Pony entered the courtroom, there was a chorus of sound from the Indian spectators and as ushers and police quietened them, Judge Cameron looked for the first time upon the man Tissee claimed was his son.

Spotted Pony bore little resemblance to his alleged father. Sir James had almost decided that the two Indian women had used the story as a ruse to have the accused Indian acquitted – but then the Indian turned and looked upon the crowded court.

His look of sheer arrogance was an expression James Cameron had seen very many times on the face of his legitimate son, Charles. The likeness was so apparent in that revealing moment that he needed to cast a quick look at the court officials to learn who else had seen the resemblance. No one had, but from that moment the trial became a nightmare for the Judge, who was afraid that his guilty secret was going to be revealed at any moment.

Fortunately for Sir James, the case was mercifully swift. In deference to his father's position as Chief Justice, Charles was not called to give evidence. Four other militiamen had also seen the Indian fire the shot that had killed their Sergeant and their evidence was conclusive.

The defence could only plead mitigation: Spotted Pony had believed his wife and companions to be in mortal danger. His defence counsel assured the court that his client bitterly regretted the death of the Toronto Sergeant.

To counter this, the prosecution suggested that Spotted Pony should have expected retribution after launching a savage attack on an American wagon train, in which numerous men, women and children were killed.

The defence objected to such evidence being placed before the court. The objection was sustained by Judge Cameron and he issued a stern warning about the dangers of hearsay evidence, but the damage had been done. Any thought the jury might have entertained of dealing leniently with the defendant had gone. They now believed that Spotted Pony had not only murdered a respected Toronto militiaman, but had also raided a wagon train across the border.

The verdict was never in doubt, and the jury reached their decision without even bothering to leave the court: Spotted Pony was guilty of murder.

Few people in the crowded courtroom either heard or understood the words uttered by Judge Cameron prior to his passing sentence on the convicted Indian. His almost incoherent mumbling left them bewildered. Judge Cameron was not famed for the wisdom of his judgements, but the confident manner in which they were delivered had always been able to fool many of his listeners.

Suddenly his words became less garbled and they could be heard and understood by his audience. '... You will be taken from here to a place of execution, and there you will be hung by the neck until you are dead.'

There was a moment of deathly hush in the courtroom. Then it erupted in pandemonium as the Indians shrieked in fury and disbelief.

James rose from his seat to leave the courtroom, not looking in the direction of where the Indians were seated. A woman hurled herself across the courtroom towards him and he saw the dull glint of a knife in her hand. A court official intercepted Tissee, and was stabbed in the stomach for his pains. She slashed another before being shot dead by an armed constable when she was close enough to James for him to read the hatred in her eyes.

Judge Cameron was the target of other Indians and as they swarmed over the wooden benches in his direction he was bundled from the courtroom. He never saw Katie struck down by a policeman's truncheon, but was told later that she was among the six Indians and five court officials and constables who were hurt in the fracas.

Katie lingered between life and death for seven days, breathing her last in the same hour that Spotted Pony paid for the murder of the Toronto militia Sergeant.

Judge Cameron publicly expressed his shock and outrage at the scenes in his courtroom. Secretly he was a very relieved man, the deaths of both Tissee and Katie being more than he could have dared hope for. He had braced himself for a scandal that had been unexpectedly averted. Indeed, the standing of the Cameron family had never been higher in the Upper Canada community.

Nevertheless, James felt the need to get away from it all. He went to his fishing lodge on the shores of Lake Scugog, apparently insensitive to any memories it might hold for him. Unfortunately for Sir James, his fishing lodge held more than memories. When he did not return to Toronto to attend a conference attended by all the judges of Upper Canada, his son set out to check whether all was well. He found Sir James lying on the floor of the cabin, the rough planking floor stained with the blood that had poured from the fatal knife wound in his throat.

Enquiries were carried out extending all the way to the United States border, but the murderer was never found. It was hardly surprising. The only clue they ever had was that for a couple of days before the murder a middle-aged Indian woman was seen in the vicinity of the cabin. Most described her as a Sioux woman, although a Metis woman who spoke to her thought she might have had white blood in her veins. The woman also spoke of having recently lost her daughter, and of having travelled with the Cherokees of the eastern States of America when they set out on their 'Trail of Tears'.

EIGHT

Queensland 1856

The hot Australian sun painted distant horizons yellow and set them to dancing while most land animals sought the shade. Only a high-gliding, wedge-tailed eagle, circling high on the warm air currents, and those animals unfortunate enough to be owned by man, and man himself, were abroad.

'The first sheep to set foot this side of the creek bed will be shot. The same applies to cattle. Try to drive them over here *and you'll* be shot. All the land on this side of the creek for as far as you can see is Ross land.'

Flanked by three grown sons, each armed with a hunting rifle, Murdo Ross issued the ultimatum to a grey, grim-faced man sitting a bony horse on the far side of the waterless river bed.

'I'm not looking for trouble, friend. All I want is water for my stock and we'll be on our way.'

'On your way to where?'

'To a new life . . . . Same thing that brought you so far from anywhere, I've no doubt.'

Behind the man a wagon headed slowly towards the dried-up water course, followed by eight cows, each one as scrawny as the horse the man sat. A wheel of the wagon was in sore need of grease and its screech of complaint was enough to set a man's teeth to aching.

Suddenly one of the sheep bounded down to the three-feet deep creek bed and hobbled across to the side where the four men stood in line. As the other sheep prepared to follow, Murdo Ross's gun came up. There was a sudden, startlingly loud shot and the leading sheep fell dead.

Three guns were brought to bear on the mounted man, but he seemed more hurt than angry.

'There was no need to do that. We've lost more than our share of animals on the way here without having someone shoot the poor foolish creatures when we've almost reached our destination.'

'You're a way from your destination, wherever it may be. All the land on this side of the river for as far as you can see belongs to the Rosses.'

'I'm not after your land. All I ask is water for my animals and I'll be on my way. You can stand here and wait for the next settler, and the next, and the one after him. You'll kill a whole lot of sheep by the time you're through, Mister Ross – if that's your name – but you won't stop people coming through. They'll be here in droves one day, seeking cheap land, somewhere to raise their kids and earn a living.'

Murdo Ross swung around and raised an arm, pointing to a nearby hillside where there was a small plot of land enclosed by a stout picket fence. Within the fence were a number of wooden crosses.

'You see up there? Those are the graves of my pa, his partner, my two sons, a daughter and my wife. Two were killed by Aborigines almost twenty-five years ago, one was bitten by a snake, and my wife died last year, worn out after a lifetime spent fighting the country and making a home for us. It took us eight years to find this place and I buried three more children along the way. You call this *cheap* land? No, mister, I and my sons have paid dearly for what we've got, and made it a damn sight safer for those of you who are coming out here now. We've paid for it — and we're going to hang on to it.'

At that moment a wiry pony ridden by what at first sight appeared to be a young boy came into view from behind the wagon, and headed for the man sitting his horse on the riverbank.

'I heard a shot . . . .' The new arrival saw the sheep lying dead in the creek bed.

Kneeing the horse forward, the rider slid it down the crumbling bank to where the sheep lay on its side. When Murdo Ross's rifle rose to cover the rider his nearest son reached out and pushed the barrel down until it pointed to the ground.

'What d'you think you're doing?' Murdo snapped angrily at his son. 'He may only be a boy, but if he tries to come over this side I'll shoot his horse.'

'It's not a boy, but a girl,' said Tristram Ross, and Murdo's head snapped up in surprise. Now he looked more closely he could see the rider was indeed a girl, but his mistake was hardly surprising. Skinny rather than slim, the girl wore boy's clothing and the fair hair above the heavily freckled face was cut as short as any young man's.

Releasing his hold on the barrel of his father's rifle, Tristram dropped to the cracked, dry bed of the creek and made his way over the parched mud to where the girl had dismounted and was kneeling on the ground beside the dead animal.

'Who shot her – and why?'

'It was necessary, she was leading the others to our side of the river. We've a lot of sheep and can't risk sheep scab coming in.'

'There's nothing wrong with our sheep, or the cattle. You didn't have to kill her.'

'I'll replace it with one of ours. You can have this one for meat. You look as though you could all do with a good meal.'

Murdo had listened to the exchange and now he spoke to his son angrily. 'Are you running the Ross lands now?'

Tristram inclined his head in the direction of the wagon. 'If you look back there, Pa, you'll see a woman with a young baby. She looks sick. The whole family could do with some help. Had they come a year ago Ma would still have been with us. What do you think she would want us to do?'

After a few moments' silence, Murdo said quietly, 'It's a good thing for all of us you're not my *oldest* son. You'd give away all we've worked for when I'm dead and gone.'

'Tristram's right this time, Pa. We've plenty of sheep and these folks are only doing what you and Grandpa did years ago.' Tristram received support from Donald, his oldest brother.

For a few moments it seemed as though Murdo would argue with both sons. Instead, he let out his breath in an explosive sound and walked away without another word.

'You go back with Pa and Rory, Donald. I'll take these folk to the waterhole at Bushman's Creek. There's enough water there for all their animals, and it's far enough away from our stock.'

Donald nodded his agreement and followed his father away from the creek bank.

'Being able to offer another sheep in exchange doesn't give you the right to shoot one of our animals.' The short-haired young girl was still bristling with indignation.

'Do you want me to show you where you can find water, or would you prefer to stay here and have an argument with my pa?'

The girl rounded upon Tristram immediately. 'Is everyone out here as arrogant as you and your family?'

'There *is* no one out here but me and my family.' Turning his back on the girl, Tristram nodded to the man on the horse.

'We never got around to introductions. My name's Tristram Ross.'

The rider swung down from his horse and shook Tristram's hand warmly as he introduced himself. 'John Carr – and the girl who might have given you an impression of ingratitude is my daughter Sadie. If you can lead us to water my family will be deeply indebted to you, Tristram Ross. It isn't only my animals who are suffering from thirst.'

'That's what I thought. I'll help you load the dead ewe on the wagon, then I'll go ahead and bring some water back. Keep moving towards that odd-shaped hill to the north-west and I'll find you.'

'I'll come with you,' said Sadie. Observing the surprise her announcement caused, she thought it necessary to add, 'Two of us can carry twice as much water. We'll be able to bring back enough to quench the horses' thirst, at least.'

Tristram's horse was tethered in a gully on the Ross side of the river and as he walked towards it, Sadie rode alongside him. The other Ross men could still be seen, skirting the hill on which stood the small, lonely cemetery.

'Does all this country really belong to your family?' There was something akin to awe in Sadie's voice as they topped a small rise and the extent of the Ross lands became apparent.

'Like Pa said, it's ours for as far as you can see. The run's split between my two brothers and me, but Donald is the official owner of all the waterholes.'

Outright ownership of all available waterholes was a legal ploy used by a great many of the country's sheep-and cattle-men to ensure no one else would move in on the vast expanses of country on which their stock grazed. Few squatters could afford to pay the official government land prices and purchase runs outright.

Sadie had an empty leather water-bottle slung over the pommel of her saddle. Tristram's was half-full. Before setting off he emptied the contents into a bucket produced by John Carr and it was carried eagerly back to the small family waiting patiently in the wagon. In addition to the baby there was a girl of about seven, and a boy of nine or ten, just old enough to sit on the wagon seat and guide the horses.

When Tristram suggested to Sadie she should bring a gun with her, Sadie shook her head. 'We have a gun but Father uses it only when it's necessary to hunt. He doesn't approve of guns.'

Tristram looked sharply at Sadie, thinking she was joking. When he saw she was serious, he asked, 'What happens when you meet up with hostile Aborigines?'

'We pray.'

Once again Tristram needed to check whether Sadie was making a joke at his expense, but she forestalled another question by explaining, 'Father is an ordained minister of the Church of Scotland.'

'You're Scots? So are we.'

'You don't *talk* like a Scot.'

'Well, no, we boys were born here — but Pa was born in Scotland, in the Highlands. He says once a Scot, always a Scot. But what's a minister doing in the bush? There aren't many souls to save here. Any he'll find won't be worth saving anyway.'

'Father's given up preaching. He became disillusioned. Soon after I was born the Church of Scotland split in two: half remained under the protection of the English government and the landowners, the rest formed a "Free Church". Father opted for the Free Church. Some of the ministers were lucky. When they left the established Church they took their congregations with them and had a lot of support. Father didn't. He was the only Free Church minister in the area. He was deserted by the congregation, the landlord threw us out of our house and he was given no help by the new church. When he preached in the open air he was arrested and after this happened a few times he'd had enough. He said it was time he thought of his family and decided to bring us to a new life in Australia. Since we came here we've moved from one place to another. I'd hoped this would be our final move, but I doubt if it will be now.'

Sadie turned to Tristram. 'What brought your father here?' When he remained quiet, she asked, 'Was he a convict? What did he do?'

'Nothing. After he and his pa were put off their land in the Highlands they took the remains of a lamb from an eagle to feed their starving family. The sheriff's men said they'd stolen it and they were transported.'

'Father says there was a lot of that went on. He says the Highlands lost its best men because of the greed of the landlords.' After a few moments' silence, she added, 'I would have thought it would make him more sympathetic to those who come out here seeking a place of their own.'

'All that was a long time ago. Since then Pa's had to fight to take and keep everything he wanted. He's a good man, really. Everyone who knows him says so.' In a bid to change the subject, Tristram asked, 'Does your pa have any experience of working land?'

'No, but I'm sure he'll manage well enough. He's a very clever man, and he's got all of us to help him now.'

Tristram gave Sadie a sidelong glance and thought there was hardly enough of her to put in a full day's hard work on the land, but he kept his thoughts to himself. Instead he said, 'This is a hard country for those of us who were born here and know it well. It can be cruel to strangers.'

'If you say that to my father he'll tell you it just means praying a bit harder, that's all.'

'Prayer won't raise a house or build a fence. Not out here.'

'Perhaps not, but last night when we knew we were almost out of water and didn't know where we were, Father made us all go down on our knees and pray for help – and today we found you!'

Tristram thought there had to be a suitable reply to such ill-founded logic, but he could not think of one, and he did not try too hard. Sadie was a very easy girl to talk to and the miles to the waterhole passed quickly. It would be very pleasant to have her and her family as neighbours. He did not know how hard they had been praying for a piece of land on which to build their future, and he was not so presumptuous as to believe God would use him as his instrument, but Tristram knew a wonderful section of land, only twenty miles from the Ross holding . . . .

For more than three years the Reverend John Carr struggled to eke out an existence on the land to which Tristram Ross led him. It was good land, but the disillusioned minister was no farming man, and luck and his God seemingly had higher priorities elsewhere.

Every member of the Ross family gave much time and labour to helping the new settlers, and Ross livestock was given freely in a bid to build up the Carr flocks and herds. Yet, as an exasperated Murdo Ross was once heard to say, 'You pull John Carr one step forward, but as soon as you leave him to walk alone he falls two steps back.'

The weather did not help. Now incorporated in the newly formed State of Queensland, the region suffered two years of severe drought. Grass dried back to the cracked and parched earth and sheep and cattle were fed on the foliage of the Mulga tree – but this source was not unending.

Soon, even the wild birds and animals deserted the parched area to seek more equable regions. This meant the loss of an important source of food for the settlers, and removed an excuse for Sadie and her younger brother, Ronald, to go out hunting with Tristram. Neither of the young Carrs shared their father's distaste for guns. Sadie, in particular, was an excellent shot. In better times she would have been capable of keeping her family in meat.

The Aborigines were an additional source of trouble for the Carr family. Reverend Carr had provided them with a regular supply of food when he first settled on his land and they had come to look upon his gift as a right. When things became difficult and the supply dried up, the Aborigines turned sullen and aggressive and sheep began to disappear.

The stealing of stock by Aborigines in times of need was something that had happened to the Rosses on more than one occasion. A remonstration was usually enough to cut down the losses until nature brought the problem to an end, but things were far more serious this time. Although clouds had been building up over the hills many miles to the east and lightning had illuminated the horizon for a couple of nights, rain seemed as far away as ever.

Tristram was repairing fence posts with the help of Tommy, an Aborigine who had worked for the family for twenty years, when the wizened little man suddenly said, 'New fella over-that-way go soon?'

Tommy waved a hand in the direction of the Reverend Carr's homestead.

'No. I don't think he's any plans for leaving.' Tristram spoke past a half-dozen nails held between his lips to leave his hands free as he worked. Nails were a new innovation on the Ross holding. They had been purchased on his last cattle drive to Bourke, almost five hundred miles distant.

'New fella go soon,' Tommy repeated, but this time it was not a question.

Taking the nails from his mouth, Tristram set down his hammer and turned to face the Aborigine.

'What are you trying to tell me, Tommy?'

Tommy would not meet his eyes. 'He go soon.'

'Who says he's going? What have you heard?' Tristram had been brought up in the company of the Aborigine. He knew him as well as he knew his own brothers. 'I want to know, Tommy. If anything happens to the Carr family because you haven't told me, you're finished here – all your people too.'

'Guji say new fella come, rain stop. He go, rain come more quick.'

Guji was the leader of a large band of Aborigines who had arrived in the area only a short while before the Carrs.

'That's nonsense. I know it, and so do you. The Carrs weren't here when we had the last drought. Neither, for that matter, was Guji.'

'You, me, know pretty damn good, boss, but Guji say fella go.'

Handing the hammer and nails to the Aborigine, Tristram said, 'Put these away, then get the horses. You and me are going to pay Guji a visit.'

To a casual onlooker, Tristram's visit to Guji's camp with the gift of a newly killed ewe was the visit of a friendly, generous landowner to the camp of a less fortunate neighbour. Only the most observant would have detected the nervousness of Tommy, and the sullen attitude of the large family group led by Guji, who accepted the gift without thanks.

Tristram sat with the men of the tribe, sharing out his tobacco and ignoring the unprecedented fact that many of the men seated at what was supposed to be a friendly gathering were carrying spears.

'I hope Mister Carr is looking after you,' said Tristram, conversationally, 'he's a very important man.'

'How he important?' Guji sounded singularly unimpressed.

'He talks to God quite a lot. White man's God. Yes, him and God have quite a bit to say to one another.'

Tristram had Guji's interest now, but he went on almost casually, 'I wouldn't be surprised at all if God hadn't sent Mister Carr here with something special in mind.'

'Why your big God send this fella here? Why not send rain?'

'You know, I've been thinking about that. It's my opinion God hasn't enough rain to go around right now. He's sent Mister Carr down here to see just how long we can hang on without rain. As soon as Mister Carr reckons we can't go on any longer he'll pass the word to God and down it'll come.'

'Rain need come pretty damn quick.'

Tristram nodded seriously. 'I think you're right, Guji. I'll take a ride over to see Mister Carr right now and suggest he tells God it's time He sent us some rain. In the meantime, you and your people enjoy that meat – and keep away from Mister Carr's place. If Mister Carr's to persuade God to send it to us instead of some other place he'll need to put up a pretty good argument. He won't want any distractions from you.'

The Reverend John Carr refused point-blank to leave his home. Not wishing to alarm him, Tristram at first explained that the prolonged drought had made the Aborigines uncertain neighbours. When this failed to move him, Tristram told him of the warning Tommy had given of an impending attack by Guji and his men.

'Nonsense!' exclaimed John Carr. 'They are my friends. They would no more think of harming me than I would of leaving them to face this drought alone.'

'If you won't do anything to save yourself then at least think of your family.' One daughter had died soon after they settled, but the girl who had been a baby when the Carrs arrived was now a three-year-old, and another girl had been born a year before. 'Let them come to stay with us for a few weeks.'

Having Sadie living beneath the same roof had a strong appeal for Tristram. He had been trying for a long time to find a way to ask her to marry him, and if she were living in the Ross house the opportunity would surely present itself.

'In times of trouble families should draw together, not allow themselves to be divided. Drought is our enemy, not the Aborigines – and we'll face it together. But I thank you for your concern, Tristram. It warms me to know we have such caring neighbours.'

Later, as Sadie walked with Tristram to his horse, she asked, 'Do you really think we're in danger, Tristram?'

It was difficult to know what to say to Sadie without alarming her too much. The best he could think of was, 'I don't know for certain, but it's best not to take any chances. Keep a loaded gun handy – and don't allow Guji or any of his men to come too close to the house. I'd feel happier if you came to our place for a while.'

'I'd like that too, Tristram.'

There was something in the way Sadie made the statement that sent Tristram on his way determined that she should be brought beneath the roof of the Ross house before very long. Tristram's hopes would be fulfilled sooner than he expected. In the meantime, God solved John Carr's problems in His own fashion.

That evening the hills to the east were shrouded in heavy black cloud and during the night thunder and lightning combined in an awesome display that allowed little sleep to the Queensland settlers.

No rain fell on the lands of the Ross and Carr families during the night, but when Murdo left the house in the morning, he let out a yell that brought his three bleary-eyed sons running from their beds.

'Look at that!' There was no need for his pointing finger. The roar of rushing water in the creek, dry for many months, turned every head in that direction and a yell of glee went up from three throats.

Water was thundering along the creek, overflowing banks and spreading out in a damp stain that outpaced the parched land's ability to soak it up. The dark clouds that had brought a deluge to the hills during the night were now billowing out over the land to extend to their dominion a curtain of torrential rain, linking earth and sky, creeping out to envelop the plain.

'Wake the boys – get out and drive all the sheep and cattle to the pens around the house – but don't let the rain catch up with you. Unless I'm mistaken, this is going to be a storm like none we've ever known before.'

Even as he was speaking Murdo Ross's three sons were pulling on trousers and shirts and shouting for the Aborigines to get up and help bring in the stock.

The wall of black cloud seemed all the more ominous because of its agonisingly slow progress. It was as though the storm had been meticulously planned with the intention of saturating every square inch of bush-land before moving on to the next.

It gave time to the Ross family to move their stock to the high ground about the house, but many times Tristram's anxious glance went to the creek. The pounding water had torn away the crumbling banks now and water was spreading over the land for as far as could be seen.

Tristram was concerned for the Carr family. Their house was also on a rise, but it was lower than the one on which the Ross house stood. It would have been clear of any flood previously experienced by the Rosses – but no man living had known such a storm as this.

When the black, rain-bloated bank of cloud reached the Ross house, day was immediately changed to night, and as the last of the men stumbled inside the door the holocaust struck with an awesome fury. The whole building shook and for some moments those inside believed it would collapse about them, but the home had been solidly constructed from wood. Some of the trees that went into its making had been cut miles away and brought to the site. It held, although a number of mud outhouses were washed away.

Throughout the great storm, as the Ross men sat in the darkness of the cabin passing around a jug of whisky and cracking jokes to maintain their courage, Tristram worried about the Carr family – and Sadie in particular. Theirs was a mud cabin, with only a skeleton framework of wood. It was doubtful whether it could survive the storm. If the flood rose high enough the house was likely to collapse about their ears.

*

The Reverend John Carr had been slower to react to the slowly advancing storm than the Rosses. He heard the unfamiliar sound of water coursing along the nearby creek bed, and it was a sound that brought him to his knees murmuring a prayer of thanks to God. He did not become aware of flooding until the small rise on which his mud-walled, two-roomed house stood had become an island.

By this time, cattle and sheep had sought refuge around the house from the advancing waters. He had no pens or barns in which to put them, but John Carr was confident that they would remain safe during the coming deluge.

The storm struck the house with the force of a giant hammer. A howling wind drove smoke before it down the chimney and the cooking-fire hissed in futile protest as heavy raindrops followed in the wind's wake.

'I don't like this, John. I don't like this one little bit.'

Not wanting to frighten the children, Rachel, John Carr's uncomplaining wife, tried hard not to allow the terror she felt to show itself in her voice. She only partially succeeded.

'It's all right, my dear.' John Carr spoke confidently. 'We were told to expect floods when the drought broke. Once the water recedes there'll be grass and greenery such as we've never known before. You'll see. Now, I'll tell you what we'll do. We'll sing hymns. You choose the first one . . . .'

Inside the small cabin, while the storm played a violent and discordant accompaniment all about them, John Carr kept his family singing hymns even when the water about them rose so high it washed over the stone-slab step and seeped beneath the door, flooding the earth floor of the cabin and converting it to a glue-like morass.

Through the ill-fitting shutters of the small window on the sheltered west side of the house the family could hear the increasing terror of the animals as they huddled closer together in the lee of the west wall of the house.

Still the waters continued to rise and when it became impossible to ignore it any longer, the two youngest Carrs, Kirsty, now three years old, and Mary, the baby, were bedded down on a high bunk affixed to the west wall and four feet above the floor. The remaining four members of the family, John and Rachel, with Sadie and

Ronald, sat on the table and as water swirled about their feet they resumed their hymn-singing.

The storm was at its height now, thunder rolling all around and lightning visible through the many cracks around warped shutters and door as the wind buffeted the small home with a frightening power. Suddenly, lightning struck very close to the house, its awesome power discharged with a sound resembling the sizzling of fat in a giant frying-pan. For a moment the storm seemed to hold its breath, and then thunder broke over the small, insignificant cabin with a crack that split the skies asunder.

The animals outside went crazy with terror. Cattle stumbled over sheep and they all blundered about frantically in the darkness. As they pressed closer to the house their combined weight put an unendurable pressure upon the mud wall, already weakened by rain and flood water.

The wall collapsed suddenly, the noise from it lost in the tumult of the storm. Rachel Carr was seated facing the wall and she screamed a split second before half the roof followed the wall to the ground. Wind, rain and portions of roof beat in upon the unfortunate Carr family, and the surviving sheep and cattle trampled over the wreckage in search of refuge from the holocaust.

The first thought of everyone inside the house was for the two youngest children who had been on the bunk built against the fallen wall. In the uncertain light from the flickering lightning, Ronald thought he saw a small figure tumble down in the water where it was trampled beneath the feet of the cattle before being swept away by the flood waters.

In the din it was impossible to communicate with anyone else and as the others dug desperately in the debris of the eastern portion of the house, Ronald fought his way outside to try to find his young sister.

It was eight days before the river and the swirling flood waters subsided sufficiently to allow Tristram to ride to the Carr household and check on the well-being of Sadie and her family.

He found Sadie and her mother huddled in the remains of their cabin, surrounded by a landscape that was still more mud and water than dry land. Looking about him in dismay, Tristram said, 'God, what a mess! I've been worried about you all, but I never dreamed you'd be in such a state as this. Where are the others — your pa, Ronald and the babies?'

Sadie turned red-rimmed eyes upon him and looking at her gaunt face, Tristram rightly guessed that she had slept very little since the day and night of the great storm.

'The baby's dead. Kirsty and Ronald have been missing since the storm. Father's still out there somewhere, searching for them. We were with him until this morning, but Ma couldn't take any more. I had to bring her back here.'

Rachel Carr began to weep softly as Sadie was speaking and Tristram said, 'I'm sorry about Ronald and the others . . . .' He knew that words were not enough — would never be enough.

'I'll bring Pa and the others here with some of our boys. What do you have to eat?' Both Sadie and her mother looked as though they had not eaten since the storm.

'The Aborigines – Guji, brought us some fruit. We've had nothing else. We can't even light a fire, there's not a piece of dry wood for miles.'

'I've some salt beef here – and a flask of water. I'll leave it here and my horse too. When you've eaten take the horse — you and your ma put together don't weigh much more than a large man. Ride to our place – use the lower ford, not the top one. You'll find Donald at the cabin, tell him what's happened. He'll know what to do. I'll go out and try to find your pa and the others.'

Tristram, his two brothers and Murdo Ross, together with all the Aborigines from their farm, searched until dusk without result. Long before the end of the day, Tommy, the oldest and most knowledgeable of the Aborigines, told Tristram that the search was hopeless. The bodies of the missing Carr children, were, he said, 'Gone-along the river, longaways.'

Tristram knew that Tommy was right, as did the others, but in deference to John Carr they continued the search until it was too dark to search any longer.

The land and everything upon it might have been soaked, but the Aborigines knew how to make a fire and as the men sat around it that night, Murdo told John Carr that he and his three sons would help to rebuild the ruined cabin.

Squatting on the ground outside the remains of his ruined home, John Carr was grey with fatigue and grief. Looking up at the man who had spoken to him, he shook his head wearily. 'We won't need any help. I don't intend rebuilding.'

'You don't have to make up your mind just yet. This isn't the time. I shouldn't have mentioned it.'

'It had to be said sooner or later. I made a mistake coming out here, a tragic mistake. I'm no farmer, or stockman. I should have admitted it to myself long ago and not played games with the lives of my family. I'm not even a countryman. I belong in a town, where there are people around to stop me putting the lives of others at risk. This is God's way of telling me I've taken the wrong path.'

Murdo knew that much of what John Carr was saying was true and he was not hypocritical enough to argue with him. It was left to Tristram to ask, 'What about Sadie? What will she do?'

'She'll come with us. She's all the family Rachel and I have now. I know how you feel about her, Tristram, and I'd hoped you and she would marry one day, but I can't allow Rachel to lose *all* her family at once. You'll always be a welcome visitor in our new home and given time things may change, who knows?'

'Where will you go?' Tristram found it hard to hide the dismay he felt.

'I don't know. Somewhere far from here. I haven't thought beyond that just yet.'

Unexpectedly, Donald Ross came up with a suggestion. 'They've built a new chapel at Springfield. I saw it when I was on my way back from the last cattle drive. It's a Presbyterian chapel, I think they said. When they started building it they had a minister to preach there, but he ran off with someone's wife. I doubt if they've found anyone else to take his place just yet.'

Springfield was no more than a hundred and fifty miles away. Visiting Sadie would pose many problems, but in a land of such vast proportions it was relatively close.

Tristram took up the suggestion eagerly. 'Ifyou like I'll go there and find out what's happening, tell them you'd like to become their preacher.' He remembered Sadie telling him that her father was by inclination a Presbyterian. He could see no problem standing in John Carr's way.

'I haven't preached for a very long time. When I left the Church I was a sadly disillusioned man. I don't know if I could take on such an exacting task. Not after what's happened here . . . .'

233

'You've just said God is telling you that you've taken the wrong path. Couldn't this be His way of showing you the *right* one again?'

'I – I must think about it and discuss the matter with Rachel.'

Further search for the missing children would be futile. John Carr was eventually forced to admit this tragic fact to himself. The searchers rode back to the Ross home that night guided by a full, plump moon that was meant to inspire poets and lovers. Instead, it lit the way for searchers who had failed in their unhappy task.

Tristram rode in total silence and eventually his father brought his horse alongside that of his youngest son.

'Something's bothering you, boy. Is it the girl?'

'Yes. If she goes off to Springfield I'm likely to see her only when we drive sheep or cattle that way. Perhaps once a year. I can't expect a girl like Sadie to wait for me for ever. Besides, once she gets used to life away from the bush she'll not want to come back.'

'What are you trying to say? If it's to be a choice between a girl and our life here, there's no one can make up your mind but you.'

'I know that.'

'I think you've already made up your mind, boy. What's it to be?'

The wide-brimmed hat worn by Tristram cast a shadow over most of his face and his father did not see his expression of near-agony as he said, 'I've got to go where Sadie is, Pa. I've got to.'

Murdo nodded, hoping his face was as shadowed as his son's. 'You're as much of a man as you're ever going to be, boy. You must do what you feel is best for you. I can't say I'll be pleased to see you go, but I won't hold you back if that's what you've decided. I can't give you a whole lot of money to take, but if you wait until we make the next drive half the money made on the sheep and cattle will be yours. That will be all you'll ever have from me. The land and everything here will go to those who stay.'

'I understand that, Pa. I wasn't expecting anything at all.'

'I'm going to miss you, boy – but I miss your ma, and I could do nothing about losing her, either.'

Murdo pulled his horse about roughly and cantered towards the others who had drawn farther ahead. Tristram watched him go with a lump in his throat that threatened to choke him. His father's words

came as close to a display of affection as he had ever shown to any
of his sons.

'It's high time we sold off some of the stock, Pa. We've more sheep
than we can comfortably manage yet we haven't had a drive for
almost three years. As for supplies . . . we've never been so desperate. In another month or two we won't have enough powder left to
fire a gun.'

'You've been telling me that for months, Rory — and the answer's
still the same. There are so many sheep in New South Wales right
now they're spilling out over the border. We'd need to nigh give 'em
away – and think ourselves lucky to find someone willing to take
stock off our hands.'

'So what do we do? Stay here until we're reduced to wearing
sheepskins and hope that no rogue Abos come along because we've
no powder or ammo to fight with?'

There was both petulance and exasperation in Rory Ross's voice.
Since Tristram had left the farm two years before, the middle Ross
son had become increasingly restless and impatient with everyone
and everything about him. Murdo knew it was time to do something
if he was not to lose another son from the farm.

'No.' Murdo weighed his words carefully. He had thought long
and hard about the problems, yet he was reluctant to voice the conclusion he had reached. 'How many horses do we have running out
there now?'

'I don't know. There might be as many as two hundred, why?'

Years before Murdo had returned from one of his stock-drives
with a number of half-broken horses and turned them loose in the
nearby hills. Their numbers had increased over the years and it
would be difficult to say with any certainty exactly how many the
Rosses now owned. Whenever they needed new saddle-horses they
captured only as many as needed to be broken in.

'You and Donald round up as many as you can – and tell Tommy
and the boys to bring in the sheep.'

'We're having a drive? But you said . . .'

'I know what I said, but we'll not be taking this lot down Sydney way. We're going to Adelaide.'

'Adelaide?' Both sons chorused the word and Rory added, 'Ain't that somewhere on the coast in South Australia?'

'That's right, come and look at this.'

Reaching on top of a rough-wood dresser that held the assortment of family crockery accumulated during the years Amy Ross had been alive, Murdo pulled down a large, rolled-up piece of paper. Spreading it out on the kitchen table, he weighted it down on one side with a half-filled water bottle, on the other with a pistol taken from his belt.

'That's a map.' The observation was made by Rory.

Murdo looked at his middle son with an expression of mock-admiration. 'You know, boy, if your ma and me had been able to give you some school learning instead of what she was able to teach you right here, you might have grown up half-smart.'

The sarcasm was lost on Rory. 'How'd you come by a map, Pa - and what's it going to tell you? Ain't no map going to show us how to get to this Adelaide you're talking about.'

'That's where you're wrong, boy. You remember that explorer who came through here a month or two back?'

'The Englishman?'

'That's the one. Well, *he'd* come up from Adelaide. He had a couple of newspapers in his saddle-bags and he left one here. It's got the latest stock prices in Adelaide – they're a sight higher than those in Sydney. He left something else too – a map. He copied it for me from the one he'd drawn on the way up country.'

'Why would he have done that – unless you intended all along to make a drive to Adelaide?'

'I had it drawn for me in case we ever needed to go that way. I didn't want to make use of it because he said we'd be travelling through some harsh country. It's not too bad for horses, they can move faster, but for sheep . . . ? Still, as you keep telling me, we've too many sheep right now. There won't be enough feed for 'em next year, so we've no alternative. But just in case they don't make it, I thought we'd take horses too. There'll always be a sale for them.'

'This is great news, Pa!' All the ill humour had left Rory. 'When do we leave?'

'As soon as you bring in the horses and get Tommy and his boys to bring in the sheep.'

Four days after Murdo announced his decision, he and Rory were heading westwards with two hundred horses and more than a thousand sheep. With them they took nine Aborigine herdsmen, all mounted on Ross horses. Donald remained behind at the farm.

Despite his earlier pessimism, Murdo believed that they had a good chance of reaching Adelaide with the majority of the sheep and horses. More rain had fallen in recent months than he could ever remember. If it had been the same in South Australia they would succeed.

For a month they headed westward, the horses having first choice of the grazing, the sheep razing to the ground what remained. No difficulties were encountered on this part of the long journey. The Ross men and the Aborigines had travelled most of this country in search of food or more land, and between them they knew the most comfortable routes and well-filled waterholes.

For four days they skirted an arid desert where even the very air seemed to be holding its overheated breath. Just when the sheep were beginning to show real signs of distress they reached a creek that carried adequate water for their needs. Their direction became southerly now, as they headed in a straight line for their destination — but the worst part of the journey was yet to come. Before they had travelled another forty miles, the bed of the creek they were following became a mosaic of cracked and dried mud, relieved occasionally by a rapidly evaporating pool of stagnant water.

The Aborigine horse-herders and shepherds scoured the river bed and surrounding area for water, but they had entered a dry area where there was nothing to be seen but sand dunes.

'Now what do we do, Pa?' Rory asked the question anxiously as he wiped dust and perspiration from his face. Ahead the course of the cracked riverbed was lost in a shimmering haze that set sky and land dancing together to the indistinct horizon. 'If we go on there's no telling where we'll find the next water.'

'We'll be no better off if we turn back,' replied Murdo grimly. 'What little water we've left back there will have dried up by now and the sheep have grazed out everything that was worth eating. We've no alternative but to go on. What do you say, Tommy?'

This last question was directed at the Aborigine head-herdsman who sat his horse nearby, listening to what they were saying, but offering no advice.

'I say maybe blackfella know, boss.'

'Black fellow? What black fellow?' This had always been Tommy's way of referring to his fellow Aborigines, but Murdo had seen no sign of native Australians apart from his own men.

'They be following two, maybe three days.' Tommy held up three fingers to emphasise his statement.

'Why haven't you told me this before? If they live in this region, they'll likely know where we can find water.'

'These maybe not good blackfellas, boss. Best we leave 'em 'lone. Maybe go 'way.'

'We need to talk to them. Go and find them, Tommy. Ask them to come in and talk to us. Tell them we'll give them a fat sheep for their pot.'

It occurred to Murdo that if the unseen Aborigines allowed the sheep to die of thirst they would have all the meat they wanted. However, curiosity might be enough to bring them in.

'Better I take gun, boss.' Tommy was clearly reluctant to go off and speak to his fellow Aborigines.

'No gun. Kill one of the sheep and take that to them – and remember, Tommy, *we need their help.*'

Tommy had serious misgivings about his mission, but he had worked for Murdo for very many years. He would do as he was told.

Tommy was absent for more than three hours; when he returned he had five Aborigines with him. Most Aborigines who had met up with white men sported at least one item of European clothing. These men were almost naked and each carried a wooden spear.

Murdo did his best to make them welcome but the men appeared to be ill at ease. It was noticeable too that the herdsmen from the Ross farm made no attempt to speak to the newcomers. This was unusual in itself, since the Aborigines were a gregarious people and loved to exchange news and gossip.

'Have you asked them about water, Tommy?' Murdo put the question to his head-herdsman.

Tommy nodded. 'They say they show you water, boss – but you give 'em three more sheep.'

'Three sheep between five men. That's a bit greedy.'

'More blackfellas over that way, boss.' Tommy waved his arm vaguely in the direction from which he and the Aborigine men had come. 'Plenty women, children.'

For the first time, Murdo accepted that Tommy's suspicions were well founded. Aborigines who lived in the heart of Australia, subjected to nature's uncertain whims, teetered constantly on the brink of starvation. They were unlikely to forego the opportunity of a feast such as a white man driving a flock of sheep would offer.

But the Aborigines offered the only chance they had of finding water. 'Tell them we'll give them their three sheep – but only when they've led us to water.'

Tommy passed on Murdo's proposition, and it met with the immediate approval of the newcomers. Indeed, there seemed to be a relieved eagerness among them.

'There's something wrong here, Rory. Keep a close watch on them.'

'Right – but I think you're being overcautious, Pa. They probably haven't seen a white man before. They're just nervous of us, that's all.'

'Perhaps, but don't turn your back on them.'

Heading in the direction indicated by the Aborigines, Murdo kept the sheep ahead of the horses, telling the herders to keep them under as close a control as possible. The animals were thirsty and if they stampeded when the smell of water reached them there would be many injuries among them.

The Aborigines guided the Rosses and their animals across an apparently featureless area of sand dunes until they were confronted by a creek, seemingly a tributary of the one they had been following from the north. For almost half an hour they followed this channel although it seemed as dry as the one they had just left. Suddenly the pace of the leading animals increased, and the others followed.

'Hold them back . . . they've smelled water. Slow them down.'

For a few minutes Murdo's shouted order was obeyed, then a column of sheep snaked past the line of mounted Aborigines trying to hold them back. The line broke as men pursued sheep – and all became chaos. The sheep pounded forward, spilling up over the shallow banks of the creek, urged on by a craving for water. The horses would have gone too, but Murdo and Rory with the remaining herdsmen managed to keep them back.

Tommy had gone ahead with the other Aborigines and suddenly he let out an agonised cry.

'Boss! Boss! Turn 'em sheep. Quick-quick! Water bad . . . .'

'Hell . . . !'

Murdo and Rory raced to the front of the flock and plunged in among them. Neither man knew how Tommy had discovered the water was 'bad', but they had known him for too long to doubt what he said.

They were too late to prevent the front ranks of the flock from drinking but, as the bulk of the flock slowed, the two men and their drovers formed a line and began to beat the sheep back, first shouting, and then firing off their guns, bringing down the front sheep where necessary. Eventually their tactics met with success and as the sheep began milling about in confusion the drovers forced them back along the dried-up creek.

'How do you know the creek-water's bad?' Murdo shouted the question across the backs of the sheep to where Tommy was ensuring none of the horses broke through the thin cordon of men to drink.

By way of reply Tommy pointed to where the bodies of a few small mammals and birds lay close to the edge of the water. Even as he pointed out the evidence one of the sheep fell to the ground in a spasm of agony.

'Is it bad water – or poison?' Murdo looked about him, rising in the saddle to peer high over the rim of the creek. 'Where have the Abos gone? The ones who brought us here?'

'Gone, boss. Far away now.'

'Do you think they poisoned the water deliberately?' Rory, his face streaming with perspiration as a result of their efforts in turning the animals, rode close and put the question.

'Either that, or they knew it was poisoned and deliberately led us here.'

'Why? We were happy to give them enough sheep to keep them fat and happy for a month.'

'Who knows?' Murdo shrugged despondently. 'Perhaps they've met up with white men before. It's not unknown for our people to feed Abos with poisoned meat to clear them from good grazing land. We're lucky not to have lost more than a few animals – but we still need to find water. Send Tommy further along this creek. This water's no good, but there might be more.'

The Ross stock-drive ended some miles short of Adelaide. By the time they reached the township of Kapunda they were travelling through settled country. Word had gone ahead of the sheep and horses they were bringing in and they found buyers waiting for them.

Drought and desert, followed by storm and flood, had reduced the numbers of the sheep by almost half, but not one of the horses had been lost and the sale of the animals gave the two Ross men a handsome reward for three months of toil and danger.

Tommy and the other Aborigines were accommodated on a farm outside Kapunda until it was time to return to Queensland. With a cheque for two and a half thousand pounds safely tucked in a shirt pocket, Murdo rode on to Adelaide with Rory.

The reason for going on was threefold. Rory had earned himself a week or two of relaxation in a large town, and there were supplies to be purchased to take back to Queensland. The third reason was one Murdo kept hidden from his son.

Only three days before their arrival at Kapunda, Murdo had been bitten on the arm by a snake which had crawled under his blanket during the night. The whole thing had happened so quickly he never knew what variety of snake it was – although it was most certainly poisonous. Murdo had cut the arm open himself with his knife and Tommy had applied the juice of certain plants to the wound. Unfortunately, because they were so far away from familiar surroundings, Tommy was unable to find all the plants he needed.

The crude treatment undoubtedly saved Murdo's life, but the wound was reluctant to heal. It had become infected and was more painful with each passing day. Even more worrying, three times during the last twenty-four hours Murdo had felt the countryside suddenly spin around him. On each occasion only by clinging desperately to the pommel of his saddle had he avoided falling to the ground.

Fortunately, Rory appeared not to have noticed and Murdo resolved to consult an Adelaide doctor at the earliest opportunity.

When Colonel William Light was South Australia's Surveyor-General, he laid out Adelaide in the manner of a chessboard. The blocks of buildings were still in neat squares, but in the saloons and hotels that had sprung up along the river front, frequented by seamen, drovers and other travellers, chess was not one of the diversions offered by the bar-girls of the area.

Murdo and Rory found a room in one of the more modern of the area's hotels, but here their paths diverged. Rory expressed a craving for a cold beer, whilst Murdo thought he 'might look around for a while and work up an appetite before going to bed'. In fact, he had seen a doctor's shingle above a door between the saloons on the street outside.

The Rosses had been fortunate to find a market for their sheep at Kapunda instead of needing to drive them on to Adelaide. Two farmers driving stock from New South Wales had battled the elements – and each other – in a bid to be first to reach the Adelaide market.

Despite the fierce and occasionally violent competition between the two farmers, they had reached Adelaide within hours of each other. Now, the drive over, the rival farmers and their stockmen were the best of friends, buying each other drinks and swapping yarns of the journey.

Rory entered the hotel occupied by the New South Wales stockmen and stood self-consciously at the bar, patiently waiting his turn to be served. He was not used to such crowds. Had it not been for the thought of a cold beer, he would have left and found himself a quieter bar.

'Yes, mate. What'll you have?' The barman eventually noticed him.

'I'll have a cold beer – no, make it *two*, it'll save me fighting my way to the bar again in a few minutes.'

'You come in with these sheep-herders from New South Wales?'

'No, Pa and me brought horses and sheep down from our place in Queensland.'

'You've come all the way from *Queensland*?'

The awed question was put to Rory by a small, dark-haired, dark-eyed girl. Her red satin dress provided a colourful contrast to the drab clothes of the drovers. She ducked beneath his arm as he reached out for his two beers, and picked them up for him. Taking a sip without asking from one of the glasses, she smiled up at him and said, 'My name's Lily. I'll find you a table, then you can buy me a drink and tell me all about your journey.'

Carrying the two beers, Lily elbowed her way through the men standing at the bar counter and Rory followed her with the unfamiliar smell of cheap perfume in his nostrils, bemused at being singled out for this girl's attentions.

Lily's drink turned out to be a splash of brightly coloured liquid in a small glass and it cost four times what Rory had paid for his two beers – but the cost was not important. He would have paid much more for the company of this girl who looked at him with an expression he had never seen before.

Rory knew little about women. Apart from Aborigine women, the only ones he had met before today were his mother and the Carr women. He knew nothing of girls who were employed in bars frequented by sailors and drovers. Neither was he used to drinking. Whenever stores were brought home after a stock-drive a small keg of rum was included, but it was sparingly drunk and only when a special occasion warranted it.

Here, in Adelaide, Rory had the company of a girl unlike any he had ever met, and before long he was being treated to beers by the New South Wales drovers. Each of them was aware of the dangers of a drive along a *recognised* stock route, and they gathered about the table to listen to the story of the epic Ross drive through unknown country with a thousand sheep and two hundred horses.

The drinks were still coming when Rory's chin sank slowly to his chest and his body fell slowly forward until his forehead was resting upon the table. He knew what was happening but could do nothing to prevent it. Neither did he really care if it helped bring to an end the conflict between his senses and the gyrating room. His only concern was that Lily might leave him. Lily . . . Lily . . . .

'It looks like your admirer's bought you all the drinks he's going to tonight, Lily.' The bartender was one of a four-man syndicate who owned the hotel. He came from behind the bar wiping his hands dry on a grubby apron. 'I'll put him out on the street. If he's going to be ill it's better there than in here.'

'Just help me get him on his feet, Charlie. I'll take him upstairs to my room.'

'On a busy night like this? I pay you to persuade men to drink. What you do afterwards is your business, but I'll not have you taking 'em away in my time . . . .'

'Stash it, Charlie. You pay me damn-all. I get commission on the drinks I'm bought, as well you know – and this bloke's bought enough tonight to make anyone but you happy. You've got enough girls in here to keep this lot happy. If you don't like it, fire me. I'll take my talents – and the customers – elsewhere. Now, you going to help me, or shall I let him be sick all over your floor?'

Rory returned to consciousness with a feeling that the whole world was shaking about him. He reached out a hand to steady himself – and touched a bare arm. Opening his eyes painfully, he saw Lily standing above him. Her hand was on his shoulder and she was shaking him violently.

'Don't, don't do that. My head . . .'

'Open your eyes. Come on, wake up. Rory – is your other name Ross?'

Opening his eyes, he winced and closed them again, but not before he saw that Lily was dressed only in a slip, a loose, silk garment that revealed much of what it was intended to hide.

'That's right.' He squinted up at her. 'Have we . . . ? Did I . . . ?'

'If you're asking whether you screwed me, the answer's no – and it was no fault of mine. But there are more important matters for you to worry about right now. The owner of your hotel's just been here looking for you, he had some bad news. I said I'd tell you. It's – it's your pa, Rory.'

Rory struggled to a sitting position. The room swung about him again, but it was not entirely due to the drink he had consumed.

'What's happened to Pa? Has there been an accident?'

Lily put both her hands on his shoulders. 'He's dead, Rory. The chambermaid found him this morning when she went to his room.'

By the time Rory went up to the room he should have shared with his father, he knew more of what had happened. The doctor who certified death had been the one to whom Murdo had gone for advice about the poisoned arm. The doctor had lanced the snakebite and bled him extensively, but the poison had already done its work in weakening Murdo's heart – the Queensland farmer had died of a heart seizure during the night. The doctor added that Rory could console himself with the knowledge that there was nothing he or anyone else could have done.

Murdo was buried that same afternoon in the Adelaide church-yard. A storm was about to break over the South Australia town, and the preacher hurried the graveside service to the point of indecency. Not that it mattered to the two mourners. Rory was too filled with grief to take notice of what was happening, and Lily O'Rafferty had no experience of funeral services – or any other form of church service.

As the first heavy drops of rain fell, the preacher shook Rory by the hand and inclined his head to Lily before hurrying away. When the aged gravedigger began shovelling earth on the coffin that held Murdo's body, Rory remained uncertainly at the graveside, reluctant to go. It seemed disloyal to leave his father here in this strange place.

'You'd better come back with me for a while.' Lily took Rory's arm and led him away, heading for the bar where they had first met.

The town was quieter that evening. One of the New South Wales farmers had set out on his return journey and most of his drovers had returned with him. The others were in the bar, but Rory was spending money as fast as any of them and the establishment's owner raised no objection to Lily keeping him company.

For the next five mornings Rory awoke in Lily's bed, with no recollection of how he had got there. Each day Lily urged him to face up to the future. Her manner was gentle at first, but as the days passed she became more firm and occasionally angry. It made no difference. Rory told her there was plenty of time to think about the future – and each day he began drinking earlier.

On the sixth day Rory woke late but when he reached out for Lily she was not there. Opening his eyes, he saw her seated at the dressing table, dusting rouge on her cheeks. Hanging over the chair beside her was the red silk dress she had been wearing the first time they met.

'What you doing up so early, Lily – and why have you got that dress out? Where we going today?'

'I'm going to work in the bar. What you do is up to you – but you'll need to be out of this room tonight.'

'Hell, Lil, what you talking about! You don't need to go to work. You said yourself that I spend enough in the bar to keep Old Man Willard happy.'

'I don't give a damn about Willard – it's *me* I'm thinking about. I don't intend working in a bar until I'm so old that sober men shy away from me and I have to put up with drunken men slobbering over me. I intend earning enough money to get away from here – and I can't do it in a bar. I need my room.'

Rory winced at Lily's blunt words. She had never pretended to him about her way of life, but neither had she spelled it out before.

'I thought you and me was getting along fine, Lil. That you'd given up – all that other business. I'll make up your money, if that's how you want things to be.'

Lily sat down on the edge of the bed and looked at Rory with a sorrowful expression. 'Things will never be how I *want* them, Rory. What will we do when your money runs out – as it will damned quick at the rate you're spending it.'

'You don't need to stay here, Lil. You can come back to the farm, up in Queensland.'

Lily stood up abruptly. 'Farming's a dirty word with me, Rory Ross. Unlike you, I've never had any ma or pa to grieve for. All I can remember of life as a kid is being passed from one family who didn't want me, to another who wanted me even less. I ended up on a farm where *she* didn't want me, but he did – and he had me every opportunity he got. She suspected what was going on and she gave me tasks you wouldn't give to a Chinaman. Oh no, you'll never get me back on a farm. Any farm. I've got plans for my life – but I can't get working on them until I have my room back. I'll expect you to be out when I come back here tonight, Rory.'

Lily looked down at him, bright-eyed and with chin held high. A little too high.

'I thought you was fond of me, Lil. I really did.'

Lily closed her eyes momentarily before saying, 'I *am* fond of you, Rory. If I weren't I'd let you stay around until you'd spent all your money on me. As it is I'm sending you home, back where you belong. Go today, Rory and – take care.'

*

When Rory entered the bar-room Lily was seated at a table with a man who looked and smelled like a teamster. She saw him come in but continued talking to her companion.

'I want to speak to you, Lil.'

When her companion protested that he had bought Lily's time with a drink, Rory said, 'What are you drinking, friend?'

The teamster looked down at his empty glass. 'Whisky, but . . .'

At the bar counter, Rory impatiently ordered a full bottle of whisky and carried it back to the table. Banging the bottle down with a force that turned heads at nearby tables, he said to the startled teamster,

'Here, it's a present from me – but go and drink it at another table. Lily and I have something to discuss.'

The teamster weighed Lily's charms against the whisky for only a couple of moments. Grabbing the bottle he scuttled off to a table in a corner of the bar-room.

'What's this all about, Rory? What do you think you're doing?'

'This plan you have for the future, what is it?'

'Why . . . ?' Until she met his eyes, Lily intended telling Rory it was none of his business. 'I want to go to the gold-diggings up near Ballarat and open a bar like this one.'

Rory exhaled his breath in an explosive sound. 'Whew! No one could accuse you of lacking ambition, Lil. How long d'you think it's going to take you?'

'Too long. News has just come in of another rich strike. If I could get up there now I'd make a small fortune. As it is . . . .' She shrugged. 'By the time I've saved enough money the get-rich-quick miners will have gone somewhere else and the companies moved in.'

'How much more do you need?'

'Another thousand pounds – two if I'm to do things properly.'

From a pocket, Rory pulled out a piece of paper. Carefully smoothing it out he laid it on the table in front of her.

When she saw the amount written on the cheque, Lily's eyes opened wide. Looking up at Rory, she said, 'Where did you get this much money?'

'From the sale of the stock we brought down from Queensland.' Rory did not add that his father had reminded Rory that half of the money had been promised to Tristram before he left the farm.

'But is it all yours?'

'I'll need to buy a wagonload of stores to send back to the farm – and deed my share of the land over to Donald, but he won't mind. He's a better farmer than I'll ever be. He'll be happy for the chance to do things his way without having to convince me first.'

Lily suddenly shook her head. 'I couldn't take such money from you, Rory. I just couldn't.'

'I'm not offering to give it to you, Lil.' Rory smiled at her puzzlement and tried to dismiss the image of Tristram from his mind. 'I'm suggesting you and I get married and make this business idea of yours a partnership. What do you say?'

Tristram met up with Ezra Hanrahan, founder and self-elected leader of the Miners' Protection Fund before he set foot in Jeremiah Williams's coal mine. Hanrahan and three of his committee were waiting for Tristram outside the entrance to the mine when he arrived for his first day at work.

'You Tristram Ross?' Hanrahan put the question while his three companions spread themselves across the path in such a way that Tristram would have had to push one or more aside in order to continue on his way.

'That's the tag that was put on me twenty-two years ago. What can I do for you?'

Tristram's reply was light-hearted, but he eyed the squat Hanrahan and his companions warily. This was no welcoming party waiting to greet him on his first day at work.

'My name's Hanrahan, Ezra Hanrahan. It's more a matter of what *I* can do for *you*, Ross. Rumour has it you're a personal friend of Mister Williams. It's being said he appointed you himself. Friends of the owner aren't welcome underground in this mine, Ross.'

So that was it! Tristram wondered who had passed on such information to this man.

'Then rumour, as is so often the case, is wrong. Jeremiah Williams is a member of my father-in-law's congregation. He heard I was desperate for work and offered me a job in his mine. I'll be digging coal for a living, same as everyone else here. If I don't dig enough I'll get the sack, same as anyone else.'

'You're saying you're *not* a friend of the owner?'

'He's spoken to me once. How many times have you spoken to him?'

Ezra Hanrahan took a good look at Tristram. He saw a power-fully built young man with a tanned skin that no coal miner would ever acquire, and an unexpected air of self-assurance. The Protection Fund's leader blinked his eyes rapidly; it was a habit that occurred when he was angry, or uncertain.

'This is my first morning at work and I don't want to be late, so if you gentlemen will kindly stand aside . . .'

'If you're not an owner's man then you'll be wanting to join our Fund – the Miners' Protection Fund. For only two pounds a month we take care of your family if anything happens to you while you're working.'

The last thing Tristram would want if anything happened to him was to have any of these men 'take care' of Sadie. 'I'll need to think about it. Two pounds is a big chunk from what I'll be getting.'

'Don't think about it for too long. Accidents are liable to happen when you're least expecting 'em. Especially when you're an inexpe-rienced miner.'

Leaving the men of the Miners' Protection Fund behind, Tris-tram made his way to the pithead. He thought he would need to take a great deal of care if he decided against joining Hanrahan's Fund. All the same, two pounds *was* a lot to pay out. Especially with Sadie expecting their first baby within the month.

News of the death of their father had been brought to Springfield by Donald as 1861 was drawing to a close. The tragedy had been the final, cruel blow in what had been a disastrous year for Tristram. Only the love and support of Sadie had prevented him from going under, as so many others in the area had.

Soon after his arrival in Springfield from the farm, Tristram had found employment with a local blacksmith. He had shown such an aptitude for the work that the smith readily agreed that they should go into partnership when Tristram's share of the money promised to him by his father was forthcoming.

The money failed to arrive, but a serious slump in Queensland's economy did. A great many farmers deserted their land, leaving more debts than regrets behind them. Instead of the hoped-for partnership, Tristram was told there was no longer work in the smithy for two men and he and the blacksmith parted company.

The news of his father's death hit Tristram very hard. Not until much later was sorrow replaced by bitterness. Rory had taken more than Tristram's inheritance when he went off with an Adelaide bar-girl; he had taken away Tristram's hopes of an early marriage with Sadie.

The following year, the Reverend John Carr was invited to become the minister of a new church in Brisbane, the rapidly expanding capital of Queensland. He accepted the exciting new post, but Sadie refused to accompany her parents unless her father agreed that she and Tristram could be married before the move.

Deeply in love with Tristram, Sadie felt they had both waited long enough – and she was a very determined girl. John Carr's last duty before leaving Springfield was to marry his daughter to Tristram. Then the whole family set off for Brisbane where Tristram felt certain he would find work.

The complex of underground tunnels was far removed from work on a farm, but Tristram found it a fascinating new world. Following his future workmates he was one minute crawling along narrow, low-roofed burrows, the next walking tall through a tunnel with the lofty dimensions of a cathedral.

'Have you met up with Ezra Hanrahan yet?' The question was put to Tristram by Tom Hardy, the senior miner who had been given the task of teaching him all he needed to know about winning coal from the depths of the earth.

'Yes.'

Hardy was a big, tough man of about fifty. Tristram had taken an instant liking to him, but he had not known the other man long enough to want to amplify his single-word reply.

'Did you agree to join his Miners' Protection Fund?'

'I told him I'd think about it. Have you joined?'

'I wouldn't join a line of men at St. Peter's Gate if Ezra Hanrahan was leading it. Mind you, there aren't more than four or five of us on the mine who *haven't* joined — and unexplained "accidents" have been known to happen to a new miner who's slow to make up his mind.'

'Hanrahan said as much. Why hasn't anything happened to you?'

Tom Hardy's laugh was short and without mirth. 'Ezra knows that if he arranged any accident for me he'd need to kill me. If he didn't, I'd kill him sure enough – if someone else doesn't do it first. Ezra was a flogger on Norfolk Island and he enjoyed his work. One day he's going to meet up with one of his victims and the Miners' Protection Fund will be looking for a new leader.'

Tristram remembered the scars on his father's back, the cause of which had always been referred to as a 'minor' flogging. Others had suffered far more, and ex-convicts carried long memories. He knew he would never get on with Ezra Hanrahan.

That night as Tristram sat in a wooden bath in front of a fire in the kitchen of their small rented house while Sadie helped wash coal dust from his hair and body, he told her of his meeting with Hanrahan.

Pausing to straighten up and placing a hand to her aching back, Sadie said, 'You'd better join this Protection Fund. We can use every penny you bring home – but I need you more.'

Looking down at her husband, Sadie asked, 'You *will* join?'

'I haven't made up my mind yet. I don't like to be bullied into something I'm not sure of.'

Sadie gave birth to a son two days before Tristram's first pay day on the mine. It was a difficult birth and Tristram's happiness was marred by his concern for Sadie. A doctor was called in and his bill was high. When Ezra Hanrahan and his men called on Tristram for his first month's dues for the Miners' Protection Fund, Tristram was able to say with complete honesty that he could not afford to pay two pounds. Tristram still owed money to the doctor the next month – and this time his refusal to join the Fund was met with a scarcely veiled threat.

A fortnight later, Tristram was at work shoring up the roof of a narrow tunnel. Tom Hardy had traced a seam of coal along here and declared it would be worth working when they had dug it a little further. The only problem was that the roof of the tunnel was in a dangerous condition. Tristram was given the task of shoring it up while the other members of his team worked on the main coalface in another tunnel.

It was hot in the small tunnel and the candle-lamp by which he worked cast an uncertain light on the rough-wood lined walls and roof. He had been working for almost two hours when he thought he heard a sound from the tunnel behind him.

'Is that you, Tom?' Tristram listened for a reply. When none came he thought he must have been mistaken. Sound sometimes played tricks underground.

Suddenly he heard another sound – and this time there could be no mistake. It was the sound of falling timbers. A moment later there was a roar accompanied by a rush of air that extinguished the candle in the lantern.

Tristram threw himself down alongside the stack of roof timbers as a cloud of choking dust filled the air and the rumbling reached terrifying proportions. He had not been working in the mine long, but he did not need to be told what was happening: the roof was collapsing in a run that was bringing timbers down with it.

He had been holding his breath but now he was forced to breathe. He began choking as dust entered his mouth, nose, throat and lungs. He coughed until he thought he would choke. It was not until the lengthy coughing bout ended that he realised the rumbling sound had ceased. The roof fall had not run the length of the tunnel. He was alive.

He felt around him for the lamp, but it had gone. Where it had been was a heap of shingle and stones that rose in a steep slope towards the roof of the tunnel. The run had halted no more than six feet from where he had been lying. He groped upwards in the darkness, hoping there would be some space between the fall and the roof – but there was none. He was entombed in a space no more than twenty feet long by six feet wide and high.

In a moment of panic, Tristram began digging frantically with bare hands at the shingle, then common sense came to the fore and he stopped.

There was air in here at the moment, but it would not last for ever. He needed to lie still and hope help would come before the air ran out. There was a sudden trickle of earth and stones from the roof to the floor and he knew it was not going to be easy.

For a while Tristram tried to count the seconds in a minute, then the minutes in an hour, but concentration became increasingly difficult and it was uncomfortably hot now.

A great deal of time passed and Tristram had an overpowering urge to sleep. He tried hard to remain awake but eventually realised that he had not been conscious all of the time. He wished there was some way of knowing how quickly time was passing. He could not trust his own reckoning. He might have been in the tunnel for hours, or days. His lips and throat were dry and he would have given a month's pay for a drink of cold beer.

He wondered about Sadie. How would she cope without him? Sadie and their son, Sidney . . . .

Tristram opened his eyes and tried to breathe normally but it was impossible now. It felt as though he had a great weight on his chest and his breathing was rapid and shallow. He thought he heard a sound, as though men were digging towards him, but he had heard such a sound many times before in the darkness and he lay back weakly.

The Reverend John Carr would take care of Sadie . . . and Sidney . . . . Tristram heard the noise again – and then the sound of metal against stone. This time there was no mistake, help was coming. Men were digging through the shingle towards him. He tried to sit up, to shout. The exertion caused his head to swim and no sound came from his dry mouth. He lay back, panting. He would hold on. He *would* live.

Tristram must have lost consciousness again, but suddenly it was as though a great wind blew through the tunnel. The weight lifted from his chest – but his ears hurt with a pain so intense that he cried out.

'He's here – and he's alive!'

Tristram heard the cry and as he forced his features into the semblance of a smile the light from a lantern showed him timbers that had withstood the fall. He saw too the mass of shingle, roof-to-floor, that had almost engulfed him. Then the weary voice of Tom Hardy was saying, 'I'm glad you didn't make me out a liar, boy. I told your missus we'd have you back with her fit and well to have that boy of yours christened this Sunday, and it's not even Saturday midnight yet.'

Tristram hoped God was able to hear the prayer of thanksgiving he mumbled through dust-dry lips. The roof had caved in on Thursday.

*

Ezra Hanrahan lived in a large, solidly built house about half a mile from the Williams's mine, which had a garden that sloped down to the riverbank. Shutting the door behind him, Hanrahan looked to where the early morning mist followed the river towards the sea beyond the trees. It was an impressive house for a miner to own, but he considered himself to be no ordinary miner. He was the leader of the Miners' Protection Fund. As soon as he succeeded in having the Fund recognised he could give up his work underground and take an office in town. He would extend his activities to the new mines opening up along the river, take on more men to collect the Fund dues. Yes, all was going well for the one-time Norfolk Island flogger.

'I want to talk to you, Hanrahan.' A figure broke free of the shadows of the trees beside the roadway and the Fund leader recognised the speaker as Tristram Ross.

'If you want to join the Fund speak to me at the mine. I'm on my way to work . . . .'

Before Hanrahan had finished talking, Tristram grabbed his arm and heaved him from the path to the trees where he tripped and fell to the ground.

'Why, you . . .'

Once again Tristram cut the other man's reply short, this time with a fist that caught Hanrahan in the mouth and sat him back on the ground as he was rising to his feet.

'It's Fund business I'm taking up with you, Hanrahan – in particular, your recruiting methods.'

Hanrahan came up from the ground at Tristram, but he was ready, and his knee sent the other man back to the ground.

'You damned near killed me, Hanrahan. How many others have you done the same to – and succeeded? How many "accidents" have happened to others who didn't join your Fund?'

Hanrahan tried to rise to his feet but Tristram's fist, a smithy-hardened fist, put him down yet again. Hanrahan was sweating now, with the sweat of fear he had seen on the face of many men when they were lashed to a flogging frame.

'Your accident had nothing to do with me, Ross. Roof falls are unpredictable. You've not been in mines long enough to . . .'

Tristram's fist swung again, then once more.

'Roof supports don't *pull* themselves down. Your men should have removed the ropes before Tom Hardy found them.'

Ezra Hanrahan was a powerful man, but he was no match for the strength and cold anger of Tristram. He was left lying on the ground beneath the trees and did not appear at the mine for work for three days.

Tristram did not expect the Fund leader to allow the incident to pass without attempting retribution. However, when some of the men who helped him collect the Miners' Protection Fund dues thought they had Tristram trapped in one of the underground tunnels, they suddenly found themselves surrounded by silent miners wielding pickaxe handles. The warning was passed on to Hanrahan that if any harm came to Tristram, the same men would attack the Fund leader's home and see to it that he never worked at a mine again.

Ironically, eighteen months later Tristram Ross was instrumental in founding the first genuine Miners' Union at the Williams's mine. He was underground when there was a horrific explosion on one of the coalfaces close to the surface. Seventeen miners were killed in the accident, one of them Ezra Hanrahan.

This was the latest in a series of accidents that had occurred in the colliery, and the miners walked out, refusing to go underground again until satisfactory safety measures had been introduced. They also demanded that money be given to the dependants of the dead miners, to tide them over until they were able to make some provision for their futures.

Jeremiah Williams refused to talk to the men unless they returned to work and the stalemate went on for three weeks before Tom Hardy came to Tristram's home with a request from the men that Tristram approach the mine owner on their behalf. Tristram agreed reluctantly but he did not think the mine owner would agree to a meeting, far less enter into any agreement with the striking miners.

As luck had it, the two men met at Reverend John Carr's house after the Sunday morning service. Tristram and Sadie were there, together with Sidney and their newborn baby, shortly to be christened Mary. Jeremiah Williams was accompanied by his wife Jenny, and their daughter Stella.

255

Tristram and Jeremiah Williams discussed the mine's problems and the mine owner reiterated his demand that the men return to work before they negotiated *anything*.

'That's just it.' Tristram spoke quietly and reasonably. 'The men are fearful of going back down the mine. There have been far too many accidents there.'

'Then I'll need to recruit miners from Newcastle. They're ex-government men — convicts for the most part — men this area can well do without, but I'm left with no alternative.'

'Accidents will continue to happen, Mister Williams. All you'll be doing is doubling the number of men with a grievance. The miners *aren't* being unreasonable. They're men like Tom Hardy and me, family men. Men who're not scared of working underground, but who are concerned about what will happen to their families if they're killed or maimed.'

'I thought there was a fund for such exigencies. What's it called, the Miners' Protection Fund, or some such?'

'The Protection Fund died with Ezra Hanrahan – and the monies banked in the Fund's name totalled one hundred and forty-three pounds. Hardly enough to give each dead man a decent burial.'

The baby began to cry. It was a weak, uneven sound that brought every woman in the room gathering round, making their own particular comforting sound.

'Billy Conrad and Albert Penfold both had babies no older than Mary.' Tristram's voice was even quieter than before, but not a word was missed by the occupants of the room. 'They were all to be christened together, here in this church.'

'And we were hoping you'd be Mary's godfather,' Sadie added.

Every eye in the room was upon Jeremiah Williams, including those of baby Mary.

The mine owner felt his anger seeping away, but he clung to his dignity. 'I won't be held to ransom by my workers, but I'm not an unfeeling man, Tristram. I'll see you, Tom Hardy and any other two men the miners choose in the mine office tomorrow. But if it seems we're likely to reach any sort of agreement I'll expect the men to be back at work the following day.'

Forty-eight hours later, the Williams colliery was back in production with all the safety measures demanded by the miners being implemented. In addition, every widow of a miner killed in the accident had been given twenty-five pounds, with an additional five pounds for each child in the family. It was not a huge amount, but it was better than nothing.

Seven months later Tristram came home from work to find two men waiting at home for him. They had travelled all the way from Sydney and they brought news that was to change his life. A National Union of Miners was being formed and meetings were currently taking place in Sydney to thrash out its constitution and elect full-time officials.

Word of Tristram's successful negotiations in the dispute at the Williams mine had reached Sydney and lost nothing in the intervening miles. The two men had travelled to Brisbane to ask Tristram if he would represent Queensland in the proposed organisation. The appointment had the backing of the new Governor of Queensland and if Tristram accepted, the Governor would like to meet him before he sailed to Sydney.

Tristram Ross was to light a torch that would one day be handed on to the eleventh and last child born to Sadie. His name would be Henry; Henry Murdo Ross.

NINE

America 1862

Captain Andy MacCrimmon of the Union army rose early. Pushing back the flap of his tent he ducked outside and stood looking about him for some minutes. There were only a few tents pitched among the trees but for almost as far as the eye could see men slept wrapped in blankets, exhausted after three days of fierce battle. Undulating pillars of smoke rising almost lazily into the morning sky from cooking-fires were a sign that others were also awake.

Making his way to one of these fires, Andy MacCrimmon grunted a wordless greeting to the cook before dipping into a steaming cooking pot suspended over the fire, helping himself to a cup of hot and acrid coffee.

Cup in hand, Andy MacCrimmon made his way to the crest of the ridge, no more than sixty paces away. From here he gazed down upon a narrow, hump-backed bridge that spanned a creek – the Antietam Creek.

Suddenly, he shivered. It had nothing to do with the cool air of the September morning. It was the thought of the bloody battle that would rage when the indifferent sun rose in the hazy, Maryland sky. The Antietam bridge was to be the objective for the Union army corps to which his regiment was attached.

It was 1862 and the war between the Southern Confederate States and the Northern 'Union' army had entered its second bitter year. A great many battles had already been fought between men who spoke the same language and who, in many cases, had been neighbours before some donned the grey uniform of the Southern army, while others chose the Union blue.

Although he had taken part in a number of those battles, Andy had witnessed nothing in that time to compare with the slaughter of the past three days – and he knew that today would be no different.

Andy was not a career soldier. He did not find excitement in fighting. He had been a lawyer in the Missouri town of Sedalia when the gulf between the northern and southern states widened so much that neither side could prevent itself sliding in to war.

Even then, he would probably not have joined the army had his father not been asked by the Gommander-in-Chief of the Union army, his old friend General Winfield Scott, to take the rank of Colonel and lead a Missouri regiment to war. Robert MacCrimmon was now a Brigadier, and Andy was a Captain in one of the Pennsylvanian regiments under his father's command.

Somewhere along the Union lines a bugle sounded 'reveille' and the strident summons was taken up in camps all across the hillside. Andy MacCrimmon poured the bitter dregs of the coffee to the ground and made his way to where the men of his own regiment were remaining beneath their blankets until the last possible moment, reluctant to face the new day.

For two-and-a-half hours Union troops had flung themselves at the narrow bridge across the creek only to be forced back by a ferocious storm of bullets, leaving a third of their number lying on the ground behind them. The bridge was only wide enough to allow five men to cross shoulder-to-shoulder and it seemed to the attackers that every rifle and every field gun in the Confederate army was focused on this twelve-feet-wide space.

The bridge was essential to the Union commander's plans and his increasing irritation showed in the number of couriers riding furiously between his headquarters a mile behind the lines, and the officer who had been handed the unenviable responsibility for taking the bridge.

Finally, the commander of Andy's regiment was ordered in no uncertain terms to move up and to take the bridge, 'regardless of the cost'.

Accompanied by a regiment from New York, the Pennsylvanians fought their way forward, suffering heavy casualties once they came within range of the devastating fire from the enemy guns on the far side of the creek.

Suddenly and inexplicably, there was a lull in the Confederate fire and with a yell that could be heard at the headquarters tent, the men of the Pennsylvania regiment rose with bayonets fixed and hurled themselves at the bridge with a fury that would not be stayed – and the bridge was theirs! Before them the Southerners were in full flight, and it could be seen how few men had held the army of the Union at bay for the whole morning.

The infantrymen of the Confederate army had left the scene of the battle for the moment, but their artillerymen were still full of fight. Even as Andy turned to raise a cheer for the men of his regiment, a shell landed no more than ten paces away and the explosion cut the legs from under him. He tried to rise and had almost succeeded when he fell back again. Only then did he realise he had been wounded.

Even now, Andy MacCrimmon protested when the medical orderlies came to carry him away. There were men more seriously wounded than he – his regiment needed him . . . .

Back in the hospital area the surgeon removed five pieces of shrapnel from Andy's legs. The operation was far more painful than the original wounding. Seemingly disappointed that an amputation would not be necessary, the surgeon left it to an orderly to attempt to staunch the considerable bleeding he had caused, and moved on to his next patient.

From the direction of the battle-front the big guns of both armies fired virtually non-stop, the noise made by the opposing guns as alike as the men of each side who fired them.

Andy felt weary now, but he found sleep impossible. All around him were the cries and moans of wounded and dying men, and the screams of soldiers as their limbs were being amputated by surgeons who used the techniques of master butchers. As more and more wounded men arrived at the improvised hospital it became evident that the facilities available to the surgeons and their helpers were being overwhelmed.

Andy felt guilty. So many of the men about him were far more seriously wounded than he. Rising from his blanket with more difficulty than he had anticipated, he called to one of the overworked orderlies. Minutes later, with an improvised crutch tucked beneath one arm, the Missouri Captain was limping among the wounded, giving out water to thirsty soldiers, appalled at their great numbers.

While he was carrying out this self-imposed task there was a sudden flurry of activity at the edge of the hospital area. A blue-coated officer wearing the insignia of a Colonel and clutching a badly mangled arm was hurried through the waiting soldiers to a surgeon. With a sense of shock, Andy recognised the Colonel as a senior member of his father's corps headquarters staff.

Hobbling after the hurrying soldiers, Andy caught up with them as the surgeon began cutting the improvised bandage from the bloody arm. One of the officers with the Colonel tried to prevent Andy from coming any closer, but, in spite of the handicap of the crutch, he brushed the officer aside and spoke to the Colonel, who was now gasping in pain as the bandage was removed.

'Colonel Smart, it's me, Captain MacCrimmon. My father, Brigadier MacCrimmon – is he all right?'

The Colonel's pain was so great it was doubtful whether he heard the words, and suddenly the Lieutenant who had been brushed aside took Andy's arm. 'Please, come with me. I am also with the corps headquarters.'

Andy allowed himself to be led away a few painful paces. When he stopped it needed only a single look at the Lieutenant's face to tell him as much as the words that followed.

'I'm very sorry to be the one to inform you, sir. Your father was killed by the same shell that wounded Colonel Smart.'

The news rocked Andy MacCrimmon. The two men had become very close in recent years. When he felt he had sufficient control of his feelings, he asked, 'How did it happen?'

'The corps was fully committed in fierce fighting with some Confederate light infantry and a couple of Reb' guns were giving our men a lot of trouble. We had no reserves to send against the guns, so Brigadier MacCrimmon said the headquarters staff would have to go and do the job ourselves. We did it, but it cost your father his life and, I suspect, Colonel Smart his arm. I'm sorry, Captain. Your father was a brave man and a brilliant soldier. We will all miss him.'

Andy nodded numbly. 'Where is his – where is he now?'

'On a gun limber, on the far side of the bridge. The Commander-in-Chief says his body should go east for burial.'

Andy shook his head. 'Tell General Winfield Scott I'm taking my father home. He'll be buried in MacCrimmon County, where he belongs. Where we both belong.'

Brigadier Robert MacCrimmon w.as buried alongside his second wife, Rose, in the family grave in Hughsville, county seat of Mac-Crimmon County. Both places had been named in honour of Andy's grandfather, the man who had pioneered settlement in this part of the Ozarks. At the funeral Andy played a lament on the bagpipes that had been brought from Scotland by Hugh MacCrimmon, and there was not a dry eye in the vast assembly of mourners.

The funeral marked the end of Andy's career as a soldier. His heart had never been in soldiering and a leg wound that would leave him with a permanent limp provided him with all the excuse he needed to remain in Missouri and resume his career as a lawyer.

The resumption of his career was to be short-lived. Among the many distinguished guests at Robert MacCrimmon's funeral had been Hamilton R Gamble. In 1861 Gamble had been appointed to take on the task of governing Missouri when the elected Governor, Claiborne Fox Jackson, fled south. There, Jackson tried in vain to persuade his southern neighbours to take Missouri into the Confederacy by force of arms.

Hamilton Gamble had taken on many daunting problems with the governorship. Not least were the bands of Confederate irregulars who roved the State almost at will, terrorising the populace and pillaging and looting whole townships.

Equalling the Confederate irregulars with their ruthless, often mindless violence were the 'Jayhawkers'. Based in Kansas, they terrorised the communities of the States west of the Missouri, who were believed to be sympathetic towards the Southerners' cause.

After one particular raid, in which a rebel guerrilla force swept through the heart of Missouri burning and looting a whole town, the clamour grew for Gamble to take steps to protect them against such raids. The army stepped up patrols throughout the State, but if they had brought in any more men to combat the guerrilla menace, the Southern irregulars would have succeeded in their purpose and drawn soldiers away from the main battle areas.

*

Andy MacCrimmon was poring over a land deed in his small office in Hughsville when the door opened. Looking up, he was startled to see Governor Gamble standing in the doorway.

'Governor Gamble!'

'Don't get up, Andy, you need to rest that leg.' Looking weary, the Missouri Governor sank down in a cushioned, half-wheelchair. Taking a handkerchief from his pocket he looked about the room as he mopped his brow. 'All this takes me back to my young days when I started off in law practice. I had an office just like this. They were good days, Andy, carefree days. Where did they go?'

Governor Gamble sighed. 'But there's no going back in life. We have to face up to our problems – and I've got more than any one man's share.'

'Pa reckoned there was no one else more capable of taking on the governorship when you did. I doubt he'd have supported any other man.'

Andy poured two glasses of whisky and handed one to his visitor. He wondered why Governor Gamble had come to see him. It was not a social visit, of that he was certain.

'Your father was a good man. His death is a great loss to the State – and to me personally. He helped me out of more than one scrape, Andy, and I'm hoping you will do the same.'

The Governor of Missouri had not taken long coming to the point of his visit. Andy took a sip of his drink and waited.

'You've heard of the troubles I'm having in the western border counties?'

Andy nodded. The troubles on Missouri's border with Kansas were older than the Civil War. Southern sympathies were strong there. They had led to cross-border clashes with the Kansas men who held strong feelings about the Union long before the rest of America went to war. More recently, raids on both sides of the border by Confederate irregulars had cost many lives. These men were mostly outlaws, given a tattered cloak of respectability by the Confederate flag they claimed to support.

As a result of the guerrilla activities there had been a resurgence of Unionist zeal. Originating from the Kansas side of the border it was aimed at those in the Missouri border counties who held Southern sympathies.

'I have to put an end to what's going on there, Andy. If I can't, this State will still be fighting the war when the rest of America's reading about it in their history books.'

'I thought you'd just appointed General Ewing to sort out that problem.'

Governor Gamble looked at Andy sharply. 'I *approved* Tom Ewing's appointment because General Schofield said he was the best man for the job. Do you know him?'

'We've met. He's a good soldier, but I always believed he fought his battles with an eye to entering politics one day.'

'He's certainly got influence right up to the top in Washington.' Governor Hamilton Gamble gave Andy another searching look. 'It makes the offer I have to make even more important. I need a circuit attorney in Westport. It's not going to be an easy post – but I think *you* can do it, Andy.'

'*Me?* Governor, I've only just come back to the law after a couple of years in the army. Right now I probably know more about weaponry and battle tactics than I do about the law.'

Hamilton Gamble smiled. 'As I said, I think you're the right man for the job. It wouldn't suit a bookish man, or a legal theorist. The last man was run out of town by the relatives of a Southern sympathiser he was prosecuting. The attorney before that was killed by Quantrill's men.'

'It sounds a hell of an appointment, Governor. Should I be pleased that you thought of me?'

'No, Andy – and I can't even dangle an appointment as a judge at the end of it. I'm a sick man, I doubt if I'll be around long enough to reward those who serve me well. All I can promise is that Missouri will one day be grateful to those men who've tried to uphold the rule of law during these difficult days. It's something your father and I often talked about.'

'Bringing my father into this isn't playing fair, Governor.'

'Your father died fighting for what he believed to be right. Anyway, I never said I play by the rules to do what needs to be done, Andy. Missouri's future is at stake – and my time is running short. Will you accept the office – for the sake of your father's memory, if not for Missouri?'

'I'll do it, Governor, but I've a feeling I'll regret it.'

*

The situation in Kansas City was no more comfortable than Andy MacCrimmon had expected it to be and he did not enjoy living in a town – any town. Kansas City was a bustling, expanding riverside community. Wide, dirt roads retreated from the junction of the Missouri and Kansas rivers. Muddied by fall storms the roads had been rendered almost impassable by wagon wheels and the hooves of a continuous cavalcade of horsemen.

Beyond the boardwalks on either side of each muddy thorough-fare modern brick-built buildings vied with false-fronted shacks. Festooned with shingles and billboards they advertised everything from gunsmiths to comfortable hotels. 'Saloon with dancing girls' rubbed shoulders with 'Baptist chapel, Jesus *lives* here'.

There were many blue uniforms to be seen in Kansas City. Cavalrymen, artillerymen, engineers and infantrymen. They walked in twos and tens, and rode in their hundreds. Yet Andy saw little of the jauntiness or pride he expected from men who wore the uniform of their country and walked on home ground. Some of the soldiers exhibited a wariness he had seen in men newly returned from battle. All moved like men who occupied enemy territory.

These were Andy's first impressions, but they were confirmed on his first evening in Kansas City when he mentioned them to Sheriff Conrad Phelpmann, chief lawman of the border city.

'It's hardly surprising. Outside of the city they are often in hostile country. There are plenty of Southern sympathisers in these parts. It's well known that if Bill Quantrill enters the county with fifty men behind him, there'll be a hundred and fifty riding with him when he carries out his first raid.'

Bill Quantrill was a man whose destiny had been shaped by civil war. An Ohio schoolteacher, he had moved to Kansas to try his hand at farming. When this failed he returned to teaching, but soon turned to less peaceful pursuits on the wrong side of the law. Branded an outlaw by the Unionists, he was given the rank of Captain by the Confederate army, who also gave their official blessing to his outlaw troop. The gang made Missouri and Kansas their personal battle-ground and roved a wide area, pillaging, burning and killing.

'There'll be times out in the county when you'll feel as much of an outsider as the soldiers. We opted for the Union, Andy, but it was a damn close thing and folks around here are still a long way from accepting Abe Lincoln as *their* President.'

The Kansas City sheriff stretched his six-feet-four frame in the armchair and grinned up at Andy. 'You'll learn what frustration is all about when you've got a man up in the dock who you know damn well has murdered a whole family, but all your witnesses have suddenly "lost" their memories because he's a good old Southern boy, and you're a damned Yankee.'

Sheriff Conrad Phelpmann, like Andy, had been appointed to office by the Governor of Missouri. One had only to speak to the man for a few minutes to understand the reason for the governor's choice. Conrad Phelpmann was a big man in every way.

'But you don't need me to tell you what goes on, with a name like MacCrimmon you must know all about this "clan" system. Don't they have the same thing in Scotland?'

'Something similar. I was bom right here in Missouri, but Pa used to tell me how he and his father were driven out of Scotland by their clan chief. That's why he always felt so strongly about the slavery issue. He said no one has the right to own another man or woman, body and soul. All the same, he was proud of being a Scot and I'm proud of being the son of a Scot. No doubt the Southerners are the same.'

'You'd better believe it, Andy. Remember it, too. It will help explain things when nothing else seems to be making any sense.'

It so happened that Andy's very first case involved a slave. Although slavery was a major difference between the North and South, slavery was still legal in Missouri and the laws governing the practice still pertained. Owned by a man suspected of having strong Southern sympathies, this particular slave had run away and joined the Union army. Instead of being sent out of Missouri to join one of the Negro regiments, as was usual, the slave, known only by the name of 'Billy', was drafted into a Negro regiment currently serving in Missouri.

Billy had been unlucky enough to be taking an off-duty stroll through a small town fifty miles from his old home when he was recognised by two friends of his former owner. They promptly whisked him away and returned him to their friend.

One of Billy's friends had witnessed this and tried to help him escape. Negroes, whether free men or slaves, did not fight with white men and the friend was badly beaten about the face for the loyalty he had shown to his fellow soldier. When he walked in to the sheriff's office and complained to Conrad Phelpmann, the big sheriff promptly arrested the two white men for assault. He also took Billy into protective custody until it was established whether or not he had become a free man by virtue of his enlistment in the Union army.

The two cases came before Judge Roper, a circuit judge whom Andy had never before met. Neither case called for a jury and it was not expected they would last for very long. As it happened, the cases ended far more quickly than he had anticipated. Both men involved in the assault case pleaded 'Not guilty' and Andy had hardly begun to outline the case against the two men before Judge Roper intervened.

'Is the assaulted Negro a free man?'

Andy was startled. 'He's a soldier in the Union army, Judge. They're all presumed to be free men . . .'

'My court isn't run on "presumptions", Mister MacCrimmon. Do you have a certificate to say the Negro these men are alleged to have assaulted was a free man?'

'I have certified copies of his enlistment papers . . .'

'That isn't what I'm asking for, Mister MacCrimmon, as well you know. I'll ask you once more, for the record. Do you have a certificate to say this man has been freed by a court of law?'

'No . . .'

'Then I have no alternative but to dismiss the charges against these two men.'

Nodding in the direction of the two defendants, Judge Roper said, 'The case against you is dismissed. You may go.'

Raising his voice to make himself heard above the cheers and catcalls of friends of the two acquitted men, Judge Roper looked coldly in Andy's direction. 'Now, Mister MacCrimmon, what's next on the list?'

There was only one more case on the list and Andy was aware that the Judge knew exactly what it was. He also realised that the question of whether or not Billy was a free man or a slave had been prejudged by the man presiding over the court.

'I move that the next business be adjourned, Judge.'

'You'll learn I don't adjourn cases on my circuit, Mister Mac-Crimmon. If a matter needs judging there's no sense keeping folk waiting. What's the case?'

'The case of Jedediah Armstrong versus Billy. Armstrong claims Billy is his slave, Billy claims he's gained his freedom by joining the army – but, with all due respect, you've prejudged the case by virtue of your last verdict. I must move for an adjournment.'

'I've told you there'll be no adjourning in *my* court. However, I'm a fair-minded man, Mister MacCrimmon. I wouldn't want it said that I never gave a fair hearing to a circuit attorney on his first time in my court. Present your case, Mister MacCrimmon.'

Andy thought that the scales of justice had already tilted so far they would never again recover an even balance, but when he glanced in the direction of Sheriff Conrad Phelpmann, the big man gave him an almost imperceptible nod.

'Thank you, Judge. I'll try to keep the case as brief as I can. I'd like to call Jedediah Armstrong.'

Once in the witness box, Jedediah Armstrong affirmed that he would tell the court the whole truth and looked down at Andy almost cockily.

'Mister Armstrong, you are claiming that Billy is your slave?'

'I ain't laying claim to nothing. Billy *is* my slave. I've got a legal receipt for him.'

'That's as may be. Will you swear to this court that your allegiance is to the State of Missouri and to the Union?'

Jedediah Armstrong seemed momentarily nonplussed and his eyes flicked to the Judge.

'What's that to do with this case, Mister MacCrimmon?'

Judge Roper's intervention put his partisanship beyond any doubt, and Andy realised that nothing he said would make any difference to the outcome of the case. Judge Roper's sympathies lay with the South. Anyone with differing views stood no chance of achieving justice in his court.

Nevertheless, Andy was the State's attorney. It was his duty to attempt to uphold the laws of the State in which he served.

'Governor Gamble issued a directive that if the slave of a loyalist joins the army, his owner will receive three hundred dollars as compensation. If the owner is a Southern sympathiser, he receives nothing and the slave's freedom is confirmed . . .'

Judge Roper's gavel came down with a force that stopped Andy's explanation and cut short the angry murmur rising from the public benches.

268

'That's enough, Mister MacCrimmon! Talk of freeing slaves has caused great suffering and distress to the people of this land – and in particular this part of Missouri. Renegades from across the Kansas border use it as an excuse to spread death and destruction in our county and I'll not hear talk in my court of freeing slaves.'

'The order has come from the Governor, Judge.'

'This is *my* court, Mister MacCrimmon, and you'll do well to remember it in the future. A slave is a man's property. Whether property is stolen by an individual or by the State, it's still stealing. I'll not condone that in this court. The slave, Billy, is Mister Armstrong's property. He holds receipts to confirm the ownership. The slave will be returned to him – and that's an end to the matter. Now, if there's no more business, I declare this court adjourned.'

Andy MacCrimmon's protests were drowned by whoops of glee from the public section of the court, but it seemed Judge Roper had decided court was over for the day anyway. Gathering up his papers he left the courtroom through a door behind the judge's bench.

Standing in the rapidly emptying courtroom, swept by the laughter of Jedediah Armstrong's supporters, Andy felt frustrated and angry as he watched Billy being manacled and pushed roughly from the court. When he was joined by Sheriff Conrad Phelpmann, Andy said fiercely, 'Is this Kansas City justice? Are all the judges here the same as Judge Roper?'

Sheriff Phelpmann shook his head. 'He's the last of his sort. He'd have gone too if it hadn't been for a relative with a lot of influence in the Justice Department. Don't worry too much about it, Andy. I'm used to Judge Roper's ways and there's more than one sort of justice.'

'What does that mean?'

'Come and see for yourself.'

Wondering what the big man could possibly do to help Billy now, Andy followed the sheriff from the courtroom.

Outside the building, the men who had cheered the Judge's decision had been herded into a sullen, angry group some yards along the boardwalk. Guarding them were a dozen soldiers – Negro soldiers. Forming a half-circle about the front of the courthouse were seventy or eighty more. All were mounted, and each held a carbine at the ready.

Billy was sitting on a horse among the soldiers, buttoning on a dark-blue cavalry jacket. He grinned at Sheriff Phelpmann and Andy.

A few minutes later, as the soldiers were cantering out of town, an angry crowd surrounded Andy and the sheriff.

'What are you going to do about this, Sheriff? You were there when Judge Roper ordered Billy returned to me. Those nigger soldiers just stole him from me. You going to let them get away with it?' Jedediah Armstrong confronted Conrad Phelpmann.

'Now, Jed. You know very well that anything they get up to is army business. I ain't got no jurisdiction with them fellas. Tell you what, you come in to my office tomorrow and swear out a formal complaint. I'll see that it's forwarded to their Provost Marshal.'

There was a howl of angry derision from the crowd about them and Jedediah Armstrong said, 'You don't really give a damn, do you, Sheriff? Just so long as their uniform was blue you wouldn't care if a whole regiment of nigger soldiers came into town and took everything we've worked for all our lives.'

'Well now, Jed, I could take issue with that and say that you've never done a full day's work in your life. In fact your daddy had to spend a whole lot of *his* hard-earned money bailing you out of gaol when you'd been on one of your drinking sprees. But none of that don't matter to me. I'm here to see that folks obey the law – same as Judge Roper.'

The sheriff smiled benignly at Jedediah Armstrong. 'You should have listened to Attorney MacCrimmon, Jed. You might have been three hundred dollars richer right now.'

As Jedediah Armstrong and his friends walked away along the street, talking and gesticulating angrily, Andy said, 'Justice was done according to my book, Conrad – but I don't fancy your chances when election day comes around.'

'The day I'm voted into office by men like Jedediah Armstrong is the day I retire. I was appointed by the Governor, same as you. I reckon he knew what he was doing, but it ain't going to be easy for either of us, and there's a few things I might be able to teach you.'

Andy MacCrimmon quickly became familiar with the routine duties of a circuit attorney in Kansas City and the surrounding Jackson County. Unlike Judge Roper, most of the judges on the circuit did their best to dispense justice even-handedly, in spite of many difficulties. The men who lived along Missouri's western border were more familiar with the dispensation of 'frontier justice' than with the formalities of statutes. Far swifter than the due processes of law, 'frontier justice' usually had fatal consequences for the recipient. It was neither impartial, nor renowned for its accuracy, yet it suited those who had lived by its rules for much of their life.

Unfortunately, there were those who took advantage of the war between the States to extend the principles of 'frontier justice' to include whole communities. Raids and counter-raids continued with increasing ferocity on both sides of the Missouri-Kansas border, despite all the efforts of Major General Thomas Ewing.

Ewing commanded a Union military district that included many of the troublesome border counties – and he was an unfortunate choice for the post. Not the most diplomatic of men, Thomas Ewing had very strong political views and was contemptuous of those who did not share them. This included every man Ewing suspected of possessing a modicum of sympathy with those who fought on the side of the Southern States.

Because Missouri was a border State that might as easily have been fighting for the South as for the North, Ewing mistrusted the Missouri militia and recruited the bulk of his men from Kansas. The Missourians complained that many of his Kansan soldiers had themselves been involved in cross-border raids from Kansas, and were greatly aggravating what was already a very difficult and sensitive situation.

When these men were brought in to round up the wives, sisters, mothers and daughters of men suspected of guerrilla activities, the mood along the border became increasingly ugly. Rumours began to spread that Ewing intended removing every man, woman and child from the rural areas of the border counties. Those able to prove unswerving loyalty to the Union would be permitted to live in the vicinity of one of the border region's many military posts, the remainder would be moved away altogether.

Andy was in Sheriff Phelpmann's office one afternoon discussing the legal implications of Major General Ewing's latest moves, when there was a sudden rumbling that shook the office building for some twenty seconds.

'What the hell's that – an earthquake!' Sheriff Phelpmann pushed himself up from the wooden armchair behind his desk.

'It sounded more as though a building fell down, is there any demolition work going on?' Andy spoke as he limped towards the door.

'If there is, no one's told me about it.'

The street outside was almost deserted, but a pall of dust rose above the buildings across the road and as they stood looking at it uncertainly, a portly figure in a soiled apron ran into the street from a hardware shop.

'What is it, Ben? What's happened?' Sheriff Phelpmann called to the man.

'It's the old gaol, Sheriff. The one General Ewing put the women in. It's collapsed.'

Andy and Conrad Phelpmann looked at each other in horror. The gaol was an old, three-storey building – and Ewing had crammed it almost to overflowing with the women his men had rounded up.

Both men started running at the same time, and Andy's wounded leg did not prevent him from reaching the scene of the tragedy only seconds behind the tall sheriff.

Two tall walls of the gaol and part of a third remained standing. The other, together with much of the roof and every one of the floors had collapsed, and the sound of women screaming came from inside. Outside, on the rubble-strewn boardwalk, two young soldiers used their muskets to try to force panic-stricken women back against one of the walls, and Andy turned upon one of them angrily.

'What are you doing, soldier?'

'Stopping these women from running away, sir. They're prisoners.'

'God Almighty! You've a major tragedy on your hands and all you can think about is stopping some women from running away? Go and find your Commanding Officer. Get every available man down here – with shovels and picks – and fetch a doctor too. You,' Andy pointed to the other man, 'get inside, help clear the rubble and get the rest of the women out.'

'Yes, sir.' Both soldiers seemed relieved to have someone with an air of authority to give them specific orders.

'Thank the Lord there's someone in this town with a scrap of sense.' The accent was that of the South, the speaker a dust-covered girl of no more than eighteen. Andy had seen her arguing with one of the young soldiers as he approached the shattered prison. 'Can you get some of these men standing around to help us dig? There are at least forty women beneath the rubble.'

Sheriff Phelpmann and a number of women were already digging at the rubble with their bare hands, and as Andy followed the girl inside the shattered building an injured woman was lifted from the rubble.

She was the first of many. Thirty minutes after the collapse of the building five bodies were laid out beneath blankets on the sidewalk. Among the rescue workers a great deal of anger was directed against the Major General who had ordered the arrest and incarceration of the women.

As the men worked, Andy saw the young woman who had spoken to him earlier leave the scene holding the hand of an older woman who was being carried away from the collapsed building.

Andy toiled with the other men for some hours before all the rubble was cleared and it became obvious that no more women were trapped beneath the rubble.

On the way back to his cabin near the edge of town, Andy had to pass Kansas City's hospital. On an impulse he turned in at the door – and immediately encountered a scene of near-chaos. Kansas City was still a small community and the hospital had not been equipped to deal with the number of casualties brought in from the collapsed house.

Although Andy told himself he was concerned for *all* the women who had been imprisoned in the old gaol, he stopped looking around the hospital when he found the young girl who had helped him dig out the other women. She and the woman who had been removed from the gaol on a stretcher were in a corridor. The older woman lay on a blanket, moaning in agony while the Kansas City doctor bound a splint on her leg as it was being pulled taut by an assistant.

'Is there anything I can do to help?' Andy volunteered.

The young woman's expression was one of surprise when she looked up and saw Andy, but it was not unpleasant surprise.

The doctor also looked up. 'Hello, MacCrimmon. No, we're no shortage of helpers. We're a bit tight on space, but after the way things were in the gaol-house I haven't heard any complaints. That man Ewing ought to be horsewhipped.'

'So he would be if we were murderers or horse-thieves, but we're not, we're *Southerners*. We've got no rights – not even the right to protest in court that we've done nothing wrong.'

'If you've something to say about the shortcomings of the law then you're talking to the right man, young lady.' His task completed, the doctor stood up. 'Mister MacCrimmon is the circuit attorney, appointed personally by the Governor. I'm just a doctor with too many patients and not enough time.'

When the doctor had gone, Andy turned to the girl. 'The doctor told you my name, Andy MacCrimmon. I don't know yours.'

'Is there any reason why you should?'

There was an antagonism in her voice that had not been there before. Andy suspected it was because the doctor had told her he was an attorney.

'Hush now, child. Is that the way to speak to a gentleman who's kind enough to come to see how we're faring – and it looks as though you've been digging at the gaol-house too. I thank you for your interest and your compassion, Mister MacCrimmon. I'm Amy Houston and this is my daughter, Hetty.'

The woman spoke with an unmistakable Southern accent, but she had the voice of an educated woman and there was a distinct air of breeding about her.

'You are from Scotland, Mister MacCrimmon?'

'No, ma'am. Missouri born and bred – but my father came from Scotland. Glenelg. You know it?'

'I'm from Virginia, as was my father. But my grandfather and my husband's grandfather were both Scots, from the Highlands.'

'Your husband . . . . He's still alive?'

'What you're really saying is . . . is he riding with the guerrillas? The answer is No! Yes, we're from the South, and yes, we have a great deal of sympathy with those who are fighting for her. But I, too, was born in Missouri; we've never owned slaves, and Pa is *not* riding with Quantrill, Anderson, or any of the others they say he's with.' The heated reply came from Hetty.

Amy Houston nodded. 'That's the truth, Mister MacCrimmon. My husband disagrees with what the South is fighting for, so he wouldn't join them. Neither would he fight against his friends, although right now he's on his way to St Louis with a herd of cattle that will probably go to feed Federal soldiers.'

Andy was puzzled. 'Then why were you arrested and put in gaol, here in Kansas City?'

'You'll need to ask General Ewing the answer to that question, young man.'

'No you won't, *I'll* tell you why. We were arrested because General Ewing is a great friend of Senator Jim Lane. Not only does Lane lead a gang of jayhawkers from Kansas – and they're far worse than any Southern guerrillas – but he tried to buy our place a year or two back.'

Andy looked from Hetty Houston to her mother, his disbelief plain to see. Hetty snorted and turned her back on him, but her mother said, 'That's the truth, young man. You ask any of the women arrested with us, they'll tell you. So will my husband when he returns — but not if he goes back to our place first. He'll no doubt find Lane's men there and one more murder isn't likely to weigh on the conscience of any one of them.'

Had Andy not prosecuted in the court of Judge Roper that day, he might have been far more sceptical of the story told to him by Hetty Houston. As it was he was impressed by both women, especially young Hetty. Grimed though she was with the dust of the collapsed gaol, Andy had never in his twenty-nine years met a girl to whom he had been more instantly attracted.

'What plans do you folk have now?'

'Plans?' Hetty spoke derisively. 'Ma might have a broken leg, but we're still General Ewing's prisoners.'

'You leave that to me. Even General Ewing is not above the law. President Lincoln has suspended the writ of *habeas corpus,* but there are other laws and there's more than one man in Washington who owes the MacCrimmons a favour. Do you think you're fit enough to move, ma'am, if I find a couple of strong men to stretcher you to my cabin? It's not palatial, but I guarantee you'll enjoy it more than you did the old gaol-house.'

'Why should you be so anxious to help us?' Hetty queried.

'Anxious?' Andy thought Hetty looked terribly vulnerable as she stood before him, her face streaked with dirt, her hair untidy and her body held in taut defiance. 'I'm an attorney, Hetty. My interest is – in justice.'

Major General Thomas Ewing never took any action to have the two Houston women returned to army custody. It was possible that he never even knew of their release and soon he had other, more serious, matters to deal with.

Word of the tragedy in Kansas City sped around the mid-west States, losing nothing with each telling. When the story reached William Quantrill and his large guerrilla band they did not doubt that the tragedy had been a deliberate act, planned by the Union General.

One week later, the guerrillas fell like a biblical plague on the Kansas town of Lawrence. In a few bloody hours they shot every man and boy old enough to handle a gun, and then set fire to the town. When they galloped back to their hiding-place they left behind a hundred and fifty bodies and almost two hundred burning houses. Southern 'honour' had been satisfied.

On August 25th, 1863, General Ewing issued General Order Number Eleven. It confirmed the rumour that had been circulating for weeks: every man, woman and child who lived more than a mile from a Union military post was ordered to leave their homes – and Kansas soldiers were sent out to ensure that the order was obeyed. Within a matter of days the border region lay in ruins, the work of generations gone for naught, homes and crops burned to the ground.

After settling the Houston mother and daughter in to his cabin, Andy moved in with Sheriff Phelpmann and his wife. The sheriff's wife took it upon herself to help the two displaced women. It was an arrangement that worked well, but it meant that Andy saw far less of Hetty than he would have liked.

On the occasions when he did call at his cabin, Hetty had very little to say to him and it was left to her mother to express the gratitude she insisted they *both* felt for his generosity.

It therefore came as a surprise to Andy when the door of his office opened one day and he looked up from his desk to see Hetty standing before him.

'Hetty! This is a very pleasant surprise . . . .' His expression suddenly changed. 'Is something wrong? General Ewing . . . ?'

'No, there's nothing especially wrong . . . .'

Hetty seemed to find it difficult to say what she had come for and Andy prompted her. 'If it's something I can help with I'd enjoy doing it, Hetty.'

'Why?'

For a moment she was her old, defiant, rebellious self and Andy only just succeeded in repressing a smile. Instead, he offered a serious reply to her question.

'Because this war is now two years old, and I've seen more of it than any man should. I've been left with a limp that will be with me for life and I've taken the body of my father home from a battlefield. I'd almost forgotten there was still beauty in the world until I saw you standing outside the ruins of Ewing's gaol.'

Andy was amazed at what he had just said to Hetty. His words expressed sentiments he had never felt before – and they were true.

Hetty's glance went to Andy's leg, stretched out in a vain bid to find a comfortable position. 'I'm sorry. Sheriff Phelpmann's wife told me you'd been wounded, but I didn't know the rest.'

She looked up at him and met his gaze. 'Perhaps what you've suffered will help you to understand my fears. My father must be on his way back from St Louis right now. I'm terrified he'll return to our farm and be picked up by Ewing's men. His Southern accent will give them all the reason they need to hang him from the nearest tree.'

'Then we'll need to stop him going home and make sure he comes here, to Kansas City. Let's go and see Sheriff Phelpmann. It might be possible to telegraph the sheriffs' offices along the route he'll take and get a message to him.'

The war had brought very few benefits in its wake, but one was a rapid expansion of telegraph communications throughout the country. It meant they were able to locate William Houston and bring him safely to Kansas City.

The safe arrival of her father marked a turning point in Hetty Houston's relationship with Andy. She no longer treated him as an enemy and even let him know she enjoyed the compliments he paid her – but on the occasions when he felt bold enough to tease her he learned that she had a hot temper that was more in keeping with an Irish background than with a Scots ancestry.

Andy got on very well with Hetty's father. William Houston was an honest and straightforward man – but he showed flashes of temperament that left Andy in no doubt of the source of Hetty's temper. Occasionally William Houston's frustration with the situation in which he found himself boiled over in anger. It happened on more than one occasion when the dispossessed farmer was talking to those who agreed with the policies of General Ewing.

Andy was worried that William Houston would either get himself arrested by Ewing, or would become so despairing of his awkward predicament that he would decide against all advice to return to his borderland farm.

Hetty's mother was convalescing now, and Andy hit on an idea that he hoped would ensure the safety of the whole Houston family. He took them to the MacCrimmon farm in the Ozarks. It was a huge land-holding and the neighbours here were sympathetic towards the dispossessed farmer and his family. Andy did not find it difficult to persuade William to take on the task of managing the farm until the war ended and he was able to return to his own land.

The plan suited Andy well, and he was soon finding reasons for returning home from Kansas City far more often than he had when the farm held only memories of his dead father. The arrangement worked well for the Houstons, too. William Houston was a hard-working and instinctive farmer and he made many improvements to the MacCrimmon land.

In January 1864 Governor Gamble died; with his passing, the politics of the State of Missouri slid into turmoil and early in 1865, in the dying months of the Civil War, Andy left Kansas City behind and returned home to the Ozarks. An 'Ousting Ordinance' had been passed by the State, declaring the offices of all judges, county clerks, circuit attorneys, sheriffs and county recorders to be vacant.

Soon after his return, Andy took Hetty riding through the hills at the heart of MacCrimmon land and, gazing out over the huge farm that had been carved from the wilderness by his father and grandfather, he proposed to her and was accepted.

The couple were married in the church at Hughsville on September 14th, 1866. The country was no longer at war, and the valleys and hills of the Ozarks echoed to the music that had been played by generations of MacCrimmons in the glens and mountains of Glenelg.

TEN

Canada 1869

After Charles Cameron inherited the baronetcy from his murdered father, the passing years played many tricks with the family fortunes. Rich in shares and land – it was land that no one seemed to want to buy, and as his inheritance brought with it very little cash, it was necessary for him to find employment.

Among the shares Charles Cameron now owned were a sizeable number in the Hudson's Bay Company, and some in a local bank. Coupled with his mother's romantic affairs with men in influential places, these shares ensured that he obtained paid directorships that were neither onerous nor time-consuming. For a great many years he enjoyed a life little changed from the one he had always known.

When Sir Charles Cameron began courting the daughter of one of the big political families in Toronto, it seemed that he was assured of a career in politics, with all the privileges it would bring.

Then suddenly Toronto buzzed with the news that Sir Charles Cameron had been jilted. Few who knew him were surprised; his liaisons in the disreputable waterfront area were well known. When he left Toronto abruptly, the small-town colonial society nodded its approval. He had taken the accepted and only honourable course open to him. It was many months before the whereabouts of Sir Charles Cameron became known, by which time the headlines had been captured by the activities of a small group of Irish dissidents known as 'the Fenians'.

The disclosure of his whereabouts warranted only a few lines informing an indifferent public that Sir Charles Cameron, until recently Toronto man-about-town, was now a Hudson's Bay Company factor at one of the company's trading posts on the shores of Lake of

the Woods, a thousand travelling miles away. He would never again
be seen in Toronto.

Strangely, life at the remote outpost on the fringe of the vast, nation-
sized Red River settlement was enjoyed by Sir Charles Cameron.
He had a house built on a gentle, wooded slope facing the lake,
surrounded by gardens that were superb by any standards and for
many years he enjoyed a series of 'country wives'. The 'wives' were
women who performed all the duties of a wife, including giving
birth to his children, without the benefit of a clergyman's blessing.
It became a settlement joke that if someone stood at a doorway in
the lakeside community and called 'Cameron!' more than half the
children within hearing would cease their play and come running.

Then, fate took a hand in the affairs of Sir Charles Cameron
yet again. While America was in the throes of a bitter civil war just
across the Canadian border, a determined attempt to wrest land and
power from the Hudson's Bay Company took place.

Alarmed by events across the border, the British government
realised that Canada needed to progress from being a few loosely
united provinces dominated by an aggressive and massively over-
privileged company, to a proper country capable of running its own
affairs. More importantly, from Britain's viewpoint, Canada needed
to be capable of defending its own ill-defined borders.

One of the problems associated with such a bold design was that
of communications. So, when a newly formed company requested it
be given a ten-mile-wide strip of land stretching from the Atlantic
to the Pacific in order to erect a telegraph line, construct a road, and
survey a railway, the British government gave it unqualified support.

The only thing standing in its way was the Hudson's Bay Company. Such a problem was of short duration. With the backing of a
number of eager city bankers a bid was made for the Hudson's Bay
Company and, much to the surprise of everyone, was accepted.

It was a very good deal indeed for the company's shareholders.
For every hundred-pound share held, the new company offered
three hundred. Overnight, Sir Charles became a rich man. It helped
soften the blow when the company closed down the small trading
post on the shore of Lake of the Woods and he lost his position as
Chief Trader.

Had Sir Charles Cameron invested his money wisely, he might have spent an early and very comfortable retirement. But wisdom had never been a serious contender for a place in the make-up of the Camerons of Glenelg, and when Sir Charles caught his first glimpse of Lucy Franchere, any last grain of sense disappeared entirely. For possibly the first time in his life, Sir Charles fell in love – hopelessly and foolishly in love.

Charles first saw Lucy Franchere when he visited the home of Louis Riel. He had gone there to discuss the formation of a company the baronet hoped to set up, to trade in skins of the many buffalo killed each year by the Metis and their friends, the Cree Indians.

Lucy Franchere was a Metis girl. The offspring of unions between Indians and trappers, especially those trappers of French descent, the Metis were now numerous enough to be accepted as a distinct ethnic group, and one that had pride in its origins.

Lucy was no prim, young angel. Twenty-eight years of age, she had already been a 'country wife' to two senior officials of the Hudson's Bay Company at nearby Fort Garry. Tall, with long dark hair, she had a skin that hinted of her Indian blood and a natural elegance that had been honed during the years she had shared the luxuries enjoyed by senior 'company' men.

The second of her 'husbands' had left the company and returned to Scotland when ownership passed from the hands of the select few and the new company reduced the number of trading posts in order to cut costs and attract new investors.

On the fateful day, Lucy walked up the path to the house where the two men were talking. Following Sir Charles's glance, Louis Riel smiled. 'I see you have an eye for more than a good buffalo hide, Sir Charles.'

'I'm sorry . . . .' Charles Cameron offered his apology without entirely allowing the woman out of his gaze. 'It's just — I can't remember when I saw a more attractive woman.'

'Cousin Lucy is indeed a very striking woman. Please allow me to introduce her to you – Lucy! There is someone here I would like you to meet. Sir Charles Cameron is here to discuss business with me . . . .'

Charles Cameron could never remember what Lucy Franchere said to him at that first meeting. Standing in front of him, she was even more beautiful than she had appeared from a distance. He was approaching fifty now and Lucy was little more than half his age, yet he knew he would never be entirely content again until he possessed this woman.

The business with Louis Riel was soon concluded and Sir Charles knew he had been less than businesslike, but it did not matter – he had met Lucy Franchere.

'The English nobleman was very taken with you, Lucy.'

'I think you'll find he's a Scot. They do not like being called "English".'

'English or Scot, what does it matter?' Louis Riel's voice was tinged with irritation. His attractive cousin had spent too much time with weak Englishmen. She had forgotten how a woman should behave. 'He is neither Metis, nor French – but he *is* a rich and influential man.'

'I suppose that means you think he can help your cause?'

'Not *my* cause, Lucy. The cause of our people.'

'Oh! And just who *are* "our people"? The Frenchmen who left their women and families behind when they returned to France? Or the Indians who refused to take back their cast-off women and their hordes of bastard children?'

'All that happened generations ago, Lucy. The Metis are a people to be reckoned with now, in our own right.'

'Then we don't need the help of men like Sir Charles Cameron.'

Louis Riel tried to keep his rising anger under control. 'We need help from everyone who has something we want. There's been word that surveyors are tramping over the lands of our people who farm along the Red River, as though we didn't exist. Unless we stand up for our rights we'll disappear in an avalanche of English-speaking people who'll stamp out everything we've built up over decades. Our homes, way of life — even our religion.'

Lucy was a devout Catholic and Louis Riel hoped that if she thought her religion was under threat she might be more inclined to help the cause he espoused.

'Does Father Claude agree with you?' Father Claude was the priest of the small church on the edge of Lake of the Woods. He had been responsible for the religious well-being of the Metis community for more than thirty years. He was also responsible for an area that would have required the services of a bishop or two had it been in Europe.

'Why don't you ask him?' Louis Riel knew he was on safe ground. Father Claude had expressed his own concern to Louis only a few days before.

Father Claude watched Lucy from the back of the church for many minutes before making his presence known. She was on her knees in prayer and he left her in peace for as long as was possible – she probably had need of communion with God.

Father Claude had been a priest among the Metis for far too long to condemn her way of life. It had always been traditional for Metis women – the attractive ones – to find a man among the employees of the great fur companies trading in the north. The more attractive a girl was, the more chance she had of finding a man of importance. Some of the liaisons became permanent and a number lasted for a great many years. Quite often the children of these unblessed unions would be schooled in the great cities of the east – some even went to Britain or France. Almost all of them embraced Catholicism.

When Lucy rose to her feet, Father Claude made his way from the rear of the church. She turned and saw him and her face lit up with pleasure.

'Lucy, my dear, I heard you were back with us. I wondered how long it would be before you came to see me.'

He embraced her, then held her at arm's length. 'You are more beautiful than ever – but I see sadness in your face too. Will you be with us for long?'

Lucy shrugged. 'I don't know. I'm staying at my aunt's house. Cousin Louis is there too.'

'Ah yes, Cousin Louis. The saviour of the Metis people – or so many believe.'

'You don't?'

Father Claude had forgotten how disconcertingly honest and straightforward Lucy could be. He was pleased that this, at least, had not changed.

'He holds the respect of your people, and I know of no one else who could take on the leadership at such a time, but he worries me sometimes. He has control of the Metis, but not of himself.'

'Are times any more difficult for the Metis than they have always been?'

'I fear so, Lucy. Canada is expanding. Soon it will become a nation, a strong nation stretching from the Atlantic to the Pacific. In order to do this it will need to absorb all its peoples into one. One day the Metis will need to choose whether they are going to be part of such a nation, or outsiders – like the Indians in America.'

'Is there no way we can become a part of Canada and still keep our identity as Metis, Father?'

Father Claude shook his head. 'I doubt it. The Metis would need very many powerful friends. Friends who would be listened to in government circles in Ottawa. Such men are usually far too involved with their own careers to risk unpopularity by taking up a minority cause. After all, what reason could such a man have for wishing to help the Metis?'

Sir Charles Cameron found the service in the Red River Settlement Catholic Church difficult to follow; those parts of the service not conducted in Latin were in French, and he was familiar with neither language. He would not have attended at all, but the invitation from Louis Riel had explained that it was to celebrate the end of a successful year's hunting for buffalo. He hinted that the baronet's presence would guarantee him first choice of the buffalo hides the following year.

After the service, there was a large reception on the lawn at the rear of the church. The noisy and exuberant Metis were not the type of companions Charles enjoyed and he had decided to leave at the earliest opportunity when a voice alongside him said, 'I had no idea you were a Catholic, Sir Charles.'

Turning towards the speaker, Charles found himself looking into the pale-green eyes of Lucy Franchere. She was as beautiful as he remembered her. Not until she began to smile did he realise that he had not replied to her observation.

'I'm not. I suppose I'm here under false pretences, really; because I've bought most of this year's buffalo robes Louis must have thought I ought to join in the celebrations. I'm glad he did.'

Lucy inclined her head in acknowledgement of his implied compliment. 'What is your religion?'

'I'm rather ashamed to confess there's been little room for religion in my life.'

'How sad for you. I really don't know how I would have survived had it not been for my faith. But I was brought up here. Father Claude and this church are among my earliest memories. In fact, my grandfather helped build it.'

'It must make you very proud.' Looking at this woman, Charles felt familiar stirrings in his body, and less familiar was the realisation that he enjoyed *talking* to her.

'It should – but it also makes me very sad. I've listened to my cousin and Father Claude talking and it seems that our way of life is threatened by the events taking place about us.'

'You mean the fact that Canada is now a Dominion, with our own government? It shouldn't change things here very much. At least, I hope it won't. I live nearby, remember?'

'You are not a Metis . . . .'

At that moment Father Claude advanced towards them. His smile embraced them both, but Lucy knew the ageing priest well enough to recognise the warning in the glance he gave her and she smiled. Father Claude was a caring priest who was unable to accept that she no longer needed protecting against men like Sir Charles Cameron. In fact, Lucy had the situation comfortably in hand.

'I'm pleased to see you two getting along so well,' the priest lied. 'I wasn't aware that you knew each other.'

'I saw Mademoiselle Franchere when I was visiting her cousin, some weeks ago,' explained Charles. 'But we were able to spend far too little time chatting to each other then.'

'Sir Charles Cameron is a great man for flattery.'

The smile Lucy Franchere gave the smitten baronet made him feel years younger.

Father Claude's geniality successfully hid his misgivings, as he said, 'I came to speak to Lucy about the arrangements for our Saint's Day festivities in a couple of weeks' time. You'll not have attended them, Sir Charles? No, of course you won't. You haven't been in this part of Canada for long and you live too far away from this particular church.'

'It's no more than a day's ride away and I would be delighted to attend.' The priest had given Charles Cameron an opportunity to meet Lucy once more.

'You must invite Sir Charles, Father,' said Lucy. 'I was just telling him of the comfort I have had from my faith in times of trouble. I had the impression he'd like to know more.'

This time the warmth of the priest's smile was genuine. 'You'll be a most welcome guest, Sir Charles, and I'd like you to feel that my church, here or at Lake of the Woods, is open to you at any time of the day or night.'

The day of the celebrations for the Metis church's patron saint was a momentous occasion for Sir Charles Cameron. After the festivities ended, Lucy Franchere rode to the baronet's impressive house at Lake of the Woods – and never returned home.

There was no sense of outrage in the communities of the Red River settlement. Such domestic arrangements, although falling somewhat out of favour in the urban areas of late, had long been an accepted part of life in Upper Canada for Metis women. Besides, Lucy Franchere soon made it clear that her influence upon Sir Charles extended far beyond the confines of his bedroom. They travelled everywhere together, even to the extent of visiting the local Catholic church on Sunday. It was apparent to everyone that the baronet was besotted with the Metis girl.

However, the Red River settlements to the south and west of Lake of the Woods soon had far more serious matters to occupy their thoughts. Anger with the surveyors who trampled over their lands without even bothering to seek permission reached a head, and the Metis, led by Louis Riel, ran them off the settlement.

Even as the evicted surveyors were making their way back to the capital of the new Dominion, the authorities in Ottawa appointed a Governor for the Red River region – and once again it was done with a total disregard for the wishes of the settlers.

By now the Metis people were in a thoroughly aggressive mood and, late one evening, Father Claude came to Charles Cameron's house with startling news. He had hurried from his church and, still puffing from his exertions, he was shown into the room where Charles and Lucy sat eating dinner.

'Have you heard the news? No, if you had you would have no appetite now . . . .'

Taking the glass of wine that was offered to him, he drank it down in one long swallow, before declaring, 'Louis has turned back the Governor sent from Ottawa and declared the Red River settlement a republic – with him as its President!'

'What!' Charles sprang up from his chair so hurriedly that he sent a half-full wine glass crashing to the ground, but he seemed not to notice. 'Has he gone mad? He'll have the troops sent here and all we've been working for will be lost!'

Charles looked accusingly at Lucy. 'Did you know that he was planning this?'

'Of course not. Had I any idea, I would have told you.'

'Of course you would – I'm sorry.'

Turning back to Father Claude, Charles Cameron asked, 'Where is Louis now?'

'Riding on Fort Garry,' came the alarming reply. 'He intends taking it and making it his headquarters.'

Charles groaned and sat down again suddenly. Looking up at the priest, he said, 'I've risked my reputation by going into business with a lunatic! Is there anything you haven't yet told me?'

'The trouble we are in is bad enough. But what can we do? What can anyone do?'

'I can go to Fort Garry and try to end this madness.'

'I'll come with you.' Lucy rose hurriedly from the table. When she saw Charles's expression, she said, 'Louis is my cousin. I know him better than anyone else. If you can't make him see sense, perhaps I can.'

'All right. While you get ready, I'll arrange for horses and an escort.'

Fort Garry was close to a hundred miles from Sir Charles Cameron's lakeside house and though he and Lucy rode hard with their escort, by the time they reached Fort Garry it had already been taken by Louis Riel.

Fortunately, although a number of European protesters were locked up, there had been no bloodshed and the riders from Lake of the Woods found the self-proclaimed Red River 'President' in a jubilant mood.

'Sir Charles . . . Lucy! You've come to share in my victory! Welcome! Where would you like to stay while you are here? Choose a house and it shall be yours . . . .'

'Victory? Louis, what the hell do you think you're doing? You've taken Fort Garry because they weren't expecting an attack. When word of what you've done gets back to Ottawa they'll send the army out after you.'

'Let them! I too have an army. An army of Metis warriors who are a match for any English-speaking army.'

'All guns speak the same language, Louis – and there's no answering *them* back.'

Louis Riel seemed to be struggling to find an answer. Finally, he said, 'If you're frightened then go back to Lake of the Woods. No one asked you to come here. I've captured Fort Garry and I'll hold it against any army that's sent against me.' With this declaration of defiance, Louis Riel turned on his heel and walked away, ignoring Lucy when she called after him.

For five days Sir Charles Cameron remained in Fort Garry trying to speak to Louis Riel again, but he and Lucy were kept from him by the guards with which he surrounded himself. On the sixth day when they tried yet again they were told he had left Fort Garry with a party of his 'soldiers', and was not expected to return for some days.

There was no sense remaining at the fort any longer and Charles returned to Lake of the Woods with Lucy to inform Father Claude and the other settlers what was happening.

A few weeks later, the weather had turned bitterly cold when a senior Hudson's Bay Company official arrived on the border of the Red River settlement.

Donald Smith was a tall, bearded man with a high forehead that lost itself in his balding head. The Chief Commissioner for Montreal and Labrador, he had spent more than half his lifetime in the service of the company. He understood the country – and the Metis. Travelling with Donald Smith was his 'wife'. Like Lucy, she too was a Metis and related to many of those who lived in the Red River settlement.

Donald Smith wasted no time in seeking out Sir Charles Cameron. The day was cold and blustery and curtained with billowing grey clouds that threatened snow, when the Hudson's Bay Chief Commissioner rode up to the baronet's house.

Cutting short the other man's welcome, Smith swung down off his horse and slid the cape from his shoulders. 'I'm not here on a social visit, Cameron. I've come to put an end to this rebellion and I want to know where you stand.'

Taken aback by such bluntness, Charles tried to gain time by blustering.

'You don't believe *I* have anything to do with all that's been happening? I think the same as you. It's foolishness.'

'I didn't say it was foolishness. The Canadian government should have behaved with far more sensitivity than they have. The Metis have a strong moral case – but we're not living in a moral world. Neither am I interested in what you *think*. I want to know which side you're supporting. There's too much at stake for playing games. I'm here to bring some sense to the present situation – and that's what I'll do. It would help if people like yourself were on my side. Not *essential*, I'll succeed in doing what needs to be done, anyway, but it will be done a sight quicker if those with some authority help me. Well, where do you stand?'

It was a moment for decision. Prevarication would not work with this man. Donald Smith was a man used to getting to the heart of matters and reaching immediate decisions. He expected others to be the same. They were qualities that would one day bring him a barony, and make him one of the wealthiest men of his age.

Sir Charles had always given his support to Louis Riel, but the Metis leader was not here and Donald Smith was. Besides, he had not expected Louis to declare a republic and capture Fort Garry.

'I'm with you, of course.' Charles Cameron was aware of Lucy's scornful expression, but he refused to meet her eyes.

'I'm with you. You and the government – as are all sensible people. We need to bring this uprising to a swift end.'

When Donald Smith had left the house, Lucy rounded on Charles. 'Why did you agree to help that man against Louis?'

'Because "that man" is the most important official in the Hudson's Bay Company – probably one of the most influential men in the country — and as you've said yourself, Louis has gone too far. By taking over Fort Garry and refusing to let the new Governor assume his duties, he's committed treason. He could hang for that – and so could everyone who helps him.'

'All the more reason to try to stop him before he goes any further. He's always supported you. If he hadn't, no one would ever have sold buffalo robes to you when you first came here.'

'I haven't *deserted* Louis. I shall send word to him that Donald Smith is here and advise him to make peace with him. If he doesn't, he's finished – as I will be if Smith thinks I'm in league with Louis.'

'I think you're just looking for an excuse to break with Louis. He's too much of a man for you.' Lucy spoke scornfully. 'There's no question of you being accused of siding with the rebellion. You even rode to Fort Garry to try to persuade Louis to bring things to an end. You're just frightened of upsetting this Donald Smith because he's a Hudson's Bay Company man. You're no longer with them and yet you're still terrified of upsetting them. Why?'

'They wield an awful lot of power in this country and I'm trying to build up a business. Nobody who hopes to earn a good living in Canada can afford to make an enemy of the Hudson's Bay Company.'

'I hope they'll show their appreciation for your "loyalty" – but I doubt it very much. Meanwhile, everyone is ganging up against Louis. He, at least, is fighting for an *honest* cause!'

Donald Smith was a man with boundless energy. He ranged far and wide throughout the Red River settlement and beyond, mustering support for his efforts to bring the rebellion to an end. Those who relied upon the Hudson's Bay Company for any part of their livelihood were reminded of their obligation to 'the Company'. They were also left in no doubt of the consequences they would suffer if they failed to come out against the rebellion.

In the meantime, Donald Smith's wife, Isabella, was calling upon those with whom she could claim even the remotest common ancestry, seeking assurances that their loyalty was with 'the Company', the government, and Donald Smith.

Winter had set in and on most days temperatures were many degrees below freezing, but this did not deter the indomitable Company man. One day he called upon Sir Charles and asked the baronet to accompany him on a journey to Fort Garry. Donald Smith wished to call a meeting of the settlers, with Louis Riel in attendance. He felt strong enough now to challenge the leader of the rebellious settlement.

It was quite a large party that set out for Fort Garry. In addition to the Smiths, Charles took Lucy and Father Claude came too. The outcome of the meeting would directly affect his 'flock'. He would try to persuade Riel to agree to a meeting if the Metis leader proved difficult. The bitter civil war in neighbouring America was still a vivid, recent memory. The Catholic priest did not want to witness another such conflict involving the community he served.

The priest's intervention was not needed. Confident of his own position, Louis agreed to meet Donald and Cameron and address a meeting of the Red River settlers. The meeting took place in the open air on a day so cold that a man's breath settled as frost on his beard, but there was heat enough in the arguments put forward by both sides.

Donald Smith had been in contact with the Ottawa authorities and he was able to offer the settlers a fair hearing by the new Canadian government. The only stipulation was that they lay down their arms, study the proposals put forward by the government, and send a delegation to Ottawa to discuss the needs of the settlers.

Louis Riel was against the proposal. The settlers had opted for independence and *he* was their leader. No further discussion was necessary. The government must recognise their legality immediately. If they failed – well, there were always the Americans . . . .

Louis Riel's fiery rhetoric failed however to win over the settlers. The English-speaking settlers and most of the older Metis preferred the reasoned arguments put forward by Donald Smith. He offered a stable future ruled over by a British-backed government. There was also a very strong hint that the Canadian government might be willing to offer the settlement provincial status.

By the time the meeting broke up, Donald Smith had won the day and forty representatives had been chosen to examine the offer made by the Canadian government and to put the settlers' case in Ottawa.

Donald was not a man to show emotion. He shook hands gravely with all those who had supported him in his campaign to bring sense to Red River settlement – and he included Sir Charles Cameron among these. When his farewells were over, the Hudson's Bay Commissioner returned to Ottawa, carrying with him the gratitude of the colony. He told no one of his intention to recommend that troops be sent in to evict Louis Riel from Fort Garry.

Charles Cameron was one of the forty men chosen to study the proposals made by the Canadian government. They were generous. The rebellion of Louis Riel had jolted the consciences of government ministers and they had done their best to make amends. Among the many important concessions they agreed to make were provisions that ensured that the children of the French-speaking Metis would continue to speak their own language and worship in the Catholic faith.

On the return journey to his home on the banks of the Lake of the Woods, Charles was in a jubilant mood. He had successfully extricated himself from the difficult situation created by his association with Louis Riel. What was more, he had been accepted by the most influential man in the land as one of the more important residents of the province that would soon be known as Manitoba. It could lead to a successful future for the baronet.

Charles's smugness was shared by neither Father Claude nor Lucy. The Catholic priest expressed his misgivings as they rode through the heavily wooded country between Fort Garry and Lake of the Woods.

'I fear Louis has taken Smith's success very badly.'

'Why?' Charles was determined that concern for Louis would not lessen his own achievement. 'He should be very pleased with himself. Had it not been for him we would never have been given our own province. The colony should be grateful to him – I am. I should get a seat in the legislature and in a year or two might stand for election to the Federal Parliament.'

'Oh? What will happen to me then? Will you take me to Ottawa, or cast me aside as an embarrassment – as you have Louis?'

'Why, I'll take you with me. If Donald Smith can do it, so can I.'

'You're not Donald Smith,' said Lucy bluntly before turning to Father Claude. 'What do you think Louis will do now?'

'I wish I knew, but I fear only the Good Lord – or the Devil – knows what goes on inside Louis Riel's mind. There are times when I'm very concerned for him.'

The Catholic priest's concern was well founded. Charles had been home for only a few days when a mounted Metis messenger pounded up to the door of the lakeside house. His news caused dismay in the household.

In a bid to reassert his flagging authority, Louis had arrested a young English-speaking Canadian who had been persistently outspoken in his opposition to the leader of the rebellion. To the dismay of the more moderate of his followers, Riel had staged a 'trial' before a hastily convened – and totally illegal – 'court martial'. Convicted on vague and flimsy charges, the man had been executed with indecent haste.

After this example of Metis 'justice', the arrival of government soldiers at Fort Garry was greeted with relief by the jittery population and Louis fled the country. He came to see Sir Charles shortly before making his way to the United States, but Charles made sure that he was away from home until the now discredited Metis leader moved on.

Shortly afterwards, Charles entered the bedroom he shared with Lucy and found her stuffing her clothes into a chest.

'What are you doing?' The baronet was genuinely dismayed. He was more fond of Lucy than of any other woman he had ever known, and he had thought their relationship had settled down well since their return from Fort Garry.

'I'm leaving you.'

'Why? I've done nothing to upset you. We've been very happy these last few months.'

'I know. *Too* happy. I don't want to lull myself into feeling settled, only to have you turn me out because I no longer fit in with your ambitions.'

Now Charles knew the reason for her actions. 'It's Louis, isn't it? Whenever that man passes through our lives he manages to unsettle you.'

'It's not *him* who unsettles me. It's *you*. As I've said before, he did much to establish you in this settlement — enough to expect help from you when he needed it. Instead, you've thrown him to the wolves. If it suits you I've no doubt that one day you'll join them in hunting him down. It doesn't make *me* feel very secure. I'm leaving before I find I love you too much to be able to leave.'

'Don't let Louis do this to us, Lucy. Yes, I've kept him at arm's length ever since Donald Smith paid his visit to the settlement, but it was necessary – and Louis's recent conduct hasn't been that of a rational man.'

'I've heard it said that the conduct of a woman who loves a man isn't rational. I don't think I can afford to take the chance.'

'Lucy, what if I made it so that I could never send you away – even if I wanted to?'

'What do you mean?'

'What if we were married – if you became *Lady* Cameron?'

Ever since Lucy had come to live with Charles the jibe had been thrown at her that she would never become 'Lady Cameron'. Even Isabella, the wife of Donald Smith, had said so.

'Do you mean that, Charles? Would you really marry me?'

At this moment the thought of losing Lucy mattered more than anything else to Charles Cameron. He would have promised her anything.

'Yes.'

Lucy hesitated for only a moment. 'All right, Charles, I'll stay.'

Sir Charles and Lucy were married by Father Claude in the church at Lake of the Woods, but the Camerons seemed doomed to find unhappiness with their women. When Donald Smith was nominated and decisively elected to the Federal Parliament, Charles blamed his own failure to secure nomination on his marriage to Lucy. Father Claude pointed out that Donald Smith was also 'married' to a Metis woman, but Charles declared bitterly that the Hudson's Bay executive had sufficient money to overcome such a handicap. He, Charles Cameron, had not. Soon after this the ageing baronet resumed his former way of life, spending time away from home with Indian and Metis girls.

Meanwhile, life became ever more complicated for Louis Riel. Dividing his time between exile and representation of his people, he spent a while in a mental institution in America and, shortly after his release, became an American citizen.

In 1884 the Metis asked Louis Riel to return to Canada to represent their interests in respect of their new lands in Saskatchewan. Riel promptly instigated another rebellion. This time he was backed by the Cree Indians and far more blood was shed than in the earlier insurrection.

There was to be no forgiveness on this occasion. Captured by government forces sent to put down the rebellion, Riel was placed on trial. Although his insanity was evident to everyone, he was found guilty of treason – and hanged.

Lady Cameron, although heavily pregnant, was prominent among those who campaigned for Riel's acquittal. Her efforts did not cease until the hangman's rope silenced the arguments of all who sought to have him set free.

Baby Louis, heir to the fading Cameron fortunes, was born in January 1886, two months after Louis Riel was executed. His father died only five months later. Sir Charles Cameron was drowned, when the sledge in which the philandering baronet and a Cree Indian girl were travelling fell through thin ice on Rainy Lake.

The baronet never saw his son and he passed on little but the title. Some time before a court had ruled that children born of 'country marriages' could claim upon the estate of their natural father when he died.

A number of claimants came forward to demand a share of the estate of the late Sir Charles Cameron, and many of their claims were upheld. Among those to benefit was a Metis serving with the United States cavalry. The claim was filed on his behalf by a lawyer named Andy MacCrimmon, practising law in Jefferson City, in the State of Missouri.

ELEVEN

Australia 1914

More than three hundred men packed the small, iron-roofed Union hall in the Australian mining town of Garbis. Many had come direct from a shift underground and the hot air was rank with the smell of tobacco, beer and perspiration. It was powerful enough to cause Henry Ross to catch his breath as he opened the door and stepped from the sunshine of a Queensland evening into the hubbub of the crowded building.

His arrival did not pass unnoticed. A loud cheer went up from the assembled men, mingled with only a few boos. As Henry made his way through the packed hall men called his name and a number reached out to pat him on the back as he passed.

At the far end of the hall was a small stage. Henry took the five steps leading to it in two athletic strides. At a table on the stage five wooden chairs were set in a line, facing the audience in the hall. The centre chair was empty and four men stood up to greet the new arrival. After shaking hands, Henry Ross took his place on the vacant seat.

One of the men remained standing and, holding his hand aloft, called for silence. He needed to repeat his appeal three times before the volume of sound decreased to the point where a loud laugh at the rear of the hall brought a hiss of censorship.

'Thank you, mates.' The speaker looked out across the expanse of pebble-faces, all turned in his direction. 'I know you've all been looking forward to meeting our speaker tonight.' A single peal of derisive laughter caused all heads to turn and brought a frown to the face of the man making the announcement.

'Like I said, we've all been looking forward to this visit from Henry Ross, and if there's anyone here who don't want to listen he can bloody well get out now and leave more room for those of us who do!'

This blunt suggestion earned the speaker a round of applause. Heads turned towards the platform once more, but there was no derisive laughter this time.

'Good! Like I said, it ain't often the State Organiser of our Union gets around to paying us a call. He's here fresh from a visit with our Prime Minister, Billy Hughes – and he's brought a message to us from Billy himself. Mates, I give you – Henry Ross!'

Amidst the applause and stamping of feet a voice shouted something that might have been, 'You can keep him!' but it was difficult to be certain.

Henry stood up and looked out over the men. He was tall and red-haired, with a tan that had not been acquired below grass in a mine. One of the growing band of professional Union men, more at home cultivating politicians than among the men they represented, Henry, at least, knew how to appeal to miners.

'My throat's as dry as old Randy Markham's powder store; anyone down there spare me a beer before I start talking?'

A dozen tankards were offered up and Henry chose one that was no more than half-full. Downing it to the applause of the miners, he smacked his lips noisily before handing back the tankard.

'That's what I needed. One good pint's worth an encyclopedia when it comes to finding words to say.'

Henry looked out over the men again, and there was not a man in the crowd who was not convinced that the Union organiser had singled *him* out for special attention.

'Not that I'm going to have trouble finding words today.' Henry Ross suddenly became serious. 'Mates – and I believe I'm entitled to call you that. Unlike some Union men – even those in our own Union – I know what it's like to work underground.'

His words were applauded loudly. The miners in his audience knew that Henry Ross had spent only twelve months below ground, but it was more than most senior Union men could claim.

'Mates, I've spent the last few days with Billy Hughes, in Canberra. He sends you his good wishes. He'd rather be here, speaking to you, than running the government back there, I can tell you. But what I have to say to you today is what Billy himself would have said had he been able to come.'

298

Henry paused. His expression grave, he looked out over the men crowding the small, hot hall. 'The whole world is in turmoil and Great Britain's in trouble. This means that Australia – *our* country – is in trouble too. One hell of a hard war is being fought out in Europe. It may be many thousands of miles away, but it affects us as though it were happening right here on our doorstep and a lot of Australians have already died . . .'

There was an interruption from the back of the hall as a voice called, 'Too many . . . .' The speaker would have said more had he not been shouted into silence by those about him.

'That's all right.' Henry was magnanimous. 'He's only proving the point of what I'm saying. We're fighting for the right to say our piece, to express our views – but, believe me, if Germany wins we'll none of us dare to stand up and speak. All I ask is that I be allowed to finish what *I'm* saying, then I 'll be glad to listen to any other points of view.'

There was fresh applause and, when it had run its course, Henry continued, 'Great Britain has asked Australia to send more men to help fight the war. Billy Hughes has agreed, but – but . . .' Waiting until the noisy dissension from a section of his audience had died down, Henry Ross pleaded, 'Hear me out, will you? I know some of you don't agree with me or Billy Hughes, but you'll have a chance to say what you think. Let me say my piece first.'

This time the interruption came in the form of applause and it responded to a wave of Henry Ross's hand. 'Thank you. Now, as I was saying, Billy Hughes has told Britain that Australia will send more troops to help in the war and he wants to bring in conscription . . .'

This time the roar of disapproval erupted in many parts of the hall and could not be silenced for several minutes.

Henry Ross waited patiently until his officials succeeded in bringing a simmering silence to the hall.

'I know you feel strongly about this, and so does Billy Hughes. Wait . . .' Henry succeeded in stemming the rising hubbub. 'Because of this he's going to hold a referendum, to see what everyone thinks of the idea.'

'Where do *you* stand . . . ?' The question came from one of the men standing close to the platform and the noise in the hall subsided as the men waited for Henry Ross's reply.

'I'm behind Billy Hughes. We have to send soldiers to war and I'm for conscription.'

Later that evening, in the quiet of a house close to the mine, Henry Ross repeated his commitment. His host was Ben Taggart, a tough Scots miner in his fifties. He had been working in mines since the age of nine and had coal dust engrained in the skin in his elbows and the pores of his forehead. He had been on the platform when Henry delivered his rowdily received speech, and was a founder member of the Australian Miners' Union.

'I think you might have backed a loser this time, Henry. You know miners, especially Australian miners. They'll join up and fight all right, but they don't like being told they *have* to join up.'

'Unfortunately we're not just talking about the miners this time, Ben. There are many Australians who don't want to fight and conscription will be for everyone.'

'Let everyone else fight their own battles, Henry. You're our Union boss and we need you. If Billy Hughes doesn't get the right answer in his referendum it leaves you out on a limb.'

Henry Ross shrugged. At thirty-three years of age he was young to hold an important Union post, but he was old enough to have learned that life could be tough. 'I'm the youngest of eleven children, Ben. I needed to fight for an identity every day of my life. I'm used to it out there on that limb.'

Ben Taggart shook his head disapprovingly. 'What does your pa think about it?'

Henry Ross's expression softened. 'You know Pa from his days in this Union, Ben. He's seventy-six now, but if he had his way he'd be in Europe fighting with the rest of 'em.'

'Tristram always did feel strongly about things, no matter what it was. It took a special man to turn his back on all that land for the love of a woman – but then your ma was a special woman, too. Is he getting over losing her?'

Henry shook his head. 'He never will, but he's a fighter. Says it's the Scots in him. You know his father – my grandpa – came to Australia as a convict?'

Ben Taggart nodded. 'Sent here for nothing more serious than trying to feed his family, I believe. There were many men like him, Henry. It's one of the reasons we've such a strong Union here. Most of us have heard first-hand accounts of injustice and exploitation. That's why I say the men won't agree to conscription. The Australian is beginning to develop his own character, Henry. Use the right words and you can lead him anywhere. Try to push and he won't budge any more than old Ayer's Rock might. You remember that. You're Tristram Ross's son all right, and there's nothing wrong with that at all – but you're also the leader of our Union, and we have need of you. Don't back yourself into a corner on the issue of conscription.'

TWELVE

Flanders 1916

'Fighting for a few extra shillings in the pocket of a coal miner is a very different matter to fighting the Hun, Ross. What makes you think you'll make a good army officer?'

The British Colonel asking the question sported a heavy, grey moustache. High on his cheekbones small, purple veins combined with his pale skin to produce a marbled effect.

'I don't. I joined the army because there's a war on and I happen to believe we Australians should be involved in it. I don't suppose it matters very much to a German soldier whether the bullet that kills him comes from an officer or a private soldier. It was one of your Captains at the recruiting station thought I ought to be put forward for a commission.'

An angry flush creeping up the Colonel's face caused the marbled effect to disappear. Colonel Hetherington-Stanford was not used to being spoken to in such a casual fashion, especially by a man wearing the ill-fitting uniform of a newly recruited private soldier.

'It's not only *German* soldiers who have to face bullets, Ross. How do you think *you* might behave under fire?'

'I won't know the answer to that until someone actually fires at me, but a lot of my mates were in the Gallipoli shambles. It seems they behaved pretty much the way they should have done. No doubt I'll do the same if it's ever necessary.'

The Colonel's angry flush deepened. He had been a member of the staff committee that had planned the operation Henry Ross had referred to as a 'shambles'. He had not landed himself, of course. With other members of the general staff he had remained on board a warship off the Turkish coast while tens of thousands of soldiers were ferried ashore to their deaths. Nevertheless, he had been uncomfortably close to the bloody battlefield for much of the time.

'You may leave us, Private Ross. You will be notified of our decision in due course.' The Colonel had heard enough.

When Henry left the room, the Colonel expelled his breath noisily. 'I don't think we need spend too much time discussing *that* application, gentlemen. The man might have been a senior trade union official, but he's certainly not officer material.'

'I disagree.'

The selection board was made up of five officers, three Australian and two British, with the Colonel presiding. The speaker was one of two Australian Captains. 'Ross is very well respected in his Union and he knows how to handle men. I think he'd make a good officer.'

'He would certainly command the respect of Australian soldiers,' agreed the second Australian Captain, ignoring the British Colonel's derisive snort.

'I'll go along with that.' The senior Australian officer, a Major, sported the ribbon of the Military Cross.

The Colonel was outvoted and he knew it, the fiery colour of his cheeks an indication of his inner fury. As the three Australian officers began to discuss the merits of Henry Ross, the Colonel's fellow Englishman, a Major, leaned towards him and said softly, 'He'll be a *colonial* officer, Colonel, leading Australian troops. They have an extremely high casualty rate.'

The Colonel's scowl lasted until his compatriot's words had gone home, then he shrugged and addressed the board at large. 'If you want Ross as one of your officers, then I must accept your decision. Now, let's have the next man in. I'm feeling damned peckish and at this rate we'll run on into good drinking time.'

On the once lush, flat fields of Flanders, a couple of miles short of the small Belgian village of Passchendaele, Captain Henry Ross eased himself up from the relative comfort of an ammunition-box seat and straightened out his aching legs. Lowering his feet to the mud and water that rose above his ankles, he stood up stiffly and peered over the edge of the trench.

There was a faint tinge of pink in the grey sky to the east. Soon it would be dawn, the clean colours of the morning sky in sharp contrast to the horrors of the European battlefield.

'Pass the order to stand-to.'

All along the length of the mud-filled trench soldiers repeated the order into the darkness. Reluctantly, men set aside the unreal, half-dreamworld in which there were loved ones, a degree of comfort and people whose role in life was not to kill or be killed. Stretching battle-weary limbs, they reached out for rifles and prepared to face the grim and stark realities of the approaching day.

There was only a faint sunrise to give a false promise to this day. Low cloud was moving in and as the morning advanced one shade of grey took the place of another, shedding a sombre light over the battlefield. There were few distinguishing features to be seen here, unless one mud-filled, raised-rimmed crater could be said to differ from another. Houses had been shelled into oblivion, the outlines of their foundations buried beneath the mud thrown up by constant shellfire. In place of bushes and trees human limbs protruded from the mud. Not stark and signpost-like, but wearily, as if in apology for the bodies that lay buried beneath the mud. Every inch of this land had been ploughed by the shells of both sides and the bullets of machine-gunners had scoured the land like swarms of angry, lethal bees, seeking the flowers of each combatant's youth.

Many more bodies lay hidden beneath the mud. Thousands — tens of thousands. Whether they had died by bullet or shell no one would ever know — and any who cared were many miles from here. Lost loved ones were mourned in homes in England, Canada, Germany, France and Australia. Not here, in Europe's charnel-house.

Looking out over the scene of carnage, Henry wondered, not for the first time, why so many men had been sent out to die in such a place. He could not believe it was of vital importance whether Germans or Allies held these few square miles. There must be places for which a man felt he *should* fight, more pleasant places in which to die . . . .

'Suicide squad going out, poor bastards.'

One of the soldiers close to Henry broke into his thoughts with the laconic comment.

'All right, stand by to give covering fire.'

All along the lines of trenches rifles were slid over low parapets. Another day of war was about to begin, with the daily sacrificial ritual. The early-morning patrol was setting out.

Henry Ross counted twenty men going out into no-man's-land. They crouched low, as though by so doing they might not be seen. It was absurd. At least twenty thousand pairs of eyes from both sides of the line were watching and waiting.

From the German lines a sharpshooter's rifle barked and one of the patrol dropped to the ground and lay still. His companions began to run, still crouching, but now a machine-gun began to stutter its obscene death-chant and more of the patrol dropped to the ground.

'Open fire! See if you can silence that machine-gun.'

Henry shouted the order and all along the British lines guns opened up upon the enemy. It was a one-sided battle here. The Germans had prepared their defences well. The machine-gun was being fired from a concrete pill box sunk low in the ground, and not even a direct hit from a shell would put it out of action. The only hope was that a stray bullet would enter the narrow slit from which the machine-gun protruded and put one of the gunners out of action.

'Why the hell don't they come back?' Even as Henry uttered the question, as much to himself as anyone else, the surviving half-dozen soldiers turned back towards the lines.

The daily early-morning patrol, in common with much in this section of the battle line, was a costly farce. The men were sent out to 'test the enemy lines', perhaps in the vain hope that the Germans had quit their defences during the night, cold and rain having succeeded where bullets and shells had failed.

The survivors of the patrol were heading for Henry Ross's section of the line now, scrambling and slipping through mud that in the firmest areas rose no higher than their knees.

Three more men were shot down before the others, urged on by the shouts of the soldiers in the trenches, could reach safety. Two men, their faces showing the terror they felt, tumbled into the trench not five paces from Henry, oblivious to the welcoming cheers of the whole Allied lines. Two returning alive from the dawn patrol was better than usual. Henry had seen the third soldier fall and thought he had been shot down, like so many of his companions, but suddenly the soldier began to call for help. He had not been hit. Instead, he had fallen into one of the many ooze-filled shell-holes.

'Help! Help me, please.'

The voice was that of a young man, hardly more than a boy. Henry raised his head as far as he dared above the trench parapet and the move attracted the attention of a sniper, the bullet taking a fragment from a piece of stone embedded in the parapet not an arm's length from Henry's head.

'Are you hurt?' Henry called out the question when he should have known better. Now he was involved with the unseen soldier; the battlefield anonymity on which sanity and survival so often depended was gone.

'No, I'm stuck. The mud's up to my waist – and I'm still sinking. Help me!'

Henry had heard a similar plea many years before, during his year below ground in the Queensland mines. A young lad had been trapped in the heart of a roof-fall. By the time they reached him he was dead.

'Cover me with everything you've got.'

Henry scrambled over the parapet and crouching low he skid-ded and slid his way to the shell-hole. From the trench it had seemed no more than twenty-five or thirty yards distant. Now, with his life at stake, it seemed at least four times as far.

The German machine-gun swung in his direction and as he dropped to the ground at the edge of the crater it chattered into life and he actually heard the bullets slicing through the air only inches above his head. Not daring to rise, he burrowed through the mud rim of the crater in the fashion of a mole, pulling himself forward as the rim crumbled away.

Suddenly he saw the frightened young soldier. Fair-haired and tanned, he did not look old enough to be in the army – and he prob-ably was not. Many young Australian men had given a false age to the recruiting officer, determined to get to Europe and join in the 'fun'.

In front of Henry the earth had been clawed away in the young soldier's vain efforts to pull himself from the clinging mud. Wrig-gling forward, Henry stretched out a hand and the soldier did the same. Their fingertips just touched, but that was all. Henry wriggled forward a few more inches. He dared go no further or he too would have slipped into the evil-smelling morass. But now he could reach the other man's hand and clasp it as he would have done a child's.

When he tugged hard, Henry's hand slipped from the grip of the other. Both were wet with mud.

'Damn!'

As Henry voiced his frustration, the young soldier's face showed fear as he slipped backwards, sinking inches deeper into the mud of the shell-hole.

Unclasping the buckle of his belt, Henry had to slip the attached cross-belt from his shoulder before it was free. Unfastening his revolver and holster, he threw one end of the belt to the trapped man.

'Here, wrap it around your wrist if you can and I'll try to pull you out – ' As Henry Ross spoke the bullets from a German machine-gun scattered wet earth from the crater's rim over both men.

The soldier entangled his hand in the 'Sam Brown' belt and harness, and Henry heaved as hard as he could. Veins stood out on the young soldier's forehead as he too pulled with all his might, but it was futile. He was in mud almost to his chest and the angle from which Henry was attempting to pull him clear was too acute. He did not budge.

Twice more Henry Ross heaved on the belt without success.

'It's no good, you can't do it.' The young soldier was close to tears at the failure of the rescue attempt.

'We're not giving up now . . . .'

An irrational stubbornness had come over Henry. He should abandon the young soldier and make his way back to the trench. That would be the sensible thing to do. He had tried – and failed-but to admit defeat was not in Henry's nature, as many of his Union adversaries knew only too well.

Henry scrambled to his feet – and the sheer audaciousness of his action seemed to take both lines of trenches by surprise. All firing ceased momentarily and in the unexpected lull, Henry called, 'Hold tight now, you're coming out . . . .'

Leaning back, he put all his weight plus that of a silent prayer behind the pull. Agonisingly slowly, it seemed, the soldier slid from the mud of the crater.

As his legs came free, Henry fell backwards off the edge of the crater and the soldier came with him.

'Get to the trench, *quick!*'

Even as he shouted the last word, all hell broke loose along the lines. It was as though the honour of both armies was at stake. Shooting from both sides broke out with renewed intensity and from the Allied trenches the cheers and encouragement of the Australian and British troops added to the tumult.

With bullets flying thick and fast all about them, Henry and the young soldier sprinted for the safety of the Australian lines. Falling in a heap at the bottom of the trench, both men grinned at each other in foolish relief as hands reached out to thump both officer and soldier in triumphant welcome.

The final word on the incident was given to Henry Ross by his Colonel later that morning.

'That was the most bloody stupid thing I've seen since we took up our position here, Ross. It was also the first thing our men have had to cheer about for weeks. I'm recommending you for the Military Cross. If you don't get it, I'll change sides and join the Hun.'

Three days after the incident with the dawn patrol, the Australians were informed they would be handing their trenches over to soldiers of the Canadian Corps that night and retiring from the battle front for a brief period of well-earned rest.

Before Henry Ross was swept along in the general air of relief and anticipation, he was sent for by the Colonel commanding the regiment.

Colonel Ignatius Granville, a veteran of the Boer War, was one of the few Australian career officers serving with the army. He was content to share all the dangers of the front line with his troops, but personal comfort came high on his list of priorities, and he had learned how to obtain it. When it became evident that the regiment would be in the front line trenches for some time, he had his men dig out a hole deep beneath the ground. Lined with the sides of ammunition boxes, it possessed a bed and table manufactured from the same source. The Colonel also ensured he had a regular supply of good French brandy.

When Henry entered the Colonel's underground quarters, which also doubled as the regiment's headquarters, he was immediately offered a glass filled with an extremely generous measure of brandy.

'Take a seat, Henry. I've some news for you, part-good, part-bad. You'd better take a good swig of brandy and enjoy it before it goes sour on you.'

After savouring half the contents of his glass, Henry said, 'Give me a few more of those and you can tell me what you like. I'd almost forgotten what good brandy – or any brandy – tasted like. Perhaps by this time tomorrow I'll be doing a lot more remembering, but I doubt if I'll find any of this quality.'

Colonel Granville reached out and topped up Henry Ross's glass. 'I'm afraid you'll have to wait a while longer before you return to civilisation, Henry. That's the bad news I have to tell you. The Canadians are being brought up here to mount an offensive. Rumour has it that it's a big one – although you and I have heard that before. Be that as it may, I've been ordered to leave an officer behind to pinpoint the Germans' concrete gun emplacements in this area for the Canadians.'

The Australian trenches faced a gap between two low ridges and the Germans had filled this gap with concrete pillboxes. Manned by machine-gunners they formed a formidable and virtually indestructible defensive line.

'I'd intended giving the task to Major Kenratty. Unfortunately, he put his head too far out of a trench today and a sniper shot him. The chances are he'll live, but he'll never see again. Now that he's gone, I think you probably know more about the German pillboxes than any other officer in the regiment, so it has to be you, I'm afraid.'

Henry looked at his Colonel in dismay. He was appalled at the thought of remaining in the fighting line while the rest of the regiment was resting in a town somewhere, relaxing.

'I know how you must feel, Henry. Believe me, I wouldn't do this to you if I had any alternative. But it seems the Canadian Colonel is going to need all the help we can give him. He has damn-all experience of commanding a regiment, let alone leading it into battle. He's a pen-pusher, thrust into command because the regular Colonel's been invalided home suffering from consumption.'

Colonel Granville looked at Henry sympathetically. 'If it's any consolation to you, you'll be going to the Canadians as an acting Major. By the time you return to the regiment, the rank should be confirmed and you'll take Kenratty's place.'

It was probably the effects of the brandy, but at that moment Henry would have accepted demotion to Private if it meant leaving the horrors of the front line behind and returning with the others to where people behaved and thought like human beings.

'I'm sorry, Henry.'

Colonel Granville's sympathy was genuine. No man who had survived a full tour of duty at the front should be asked to do more without a spell of leave. By the end of his tour a man had seen far too many of his comrades die. He began to fear his luck could not last for very much longer. At this point superstition took the place of common sense and a man's thinking was liable to become scrambled . . . .

'Here . . .' Colonel Granville thrust the half-full bottle of brandy at Henry Ross. 'Take the bloody bottle back with you. If you drink it all before the Canadians get here, nobody's going to blame you. Good luck, Henry — and don't do anything foolish.'

Halfway out of the Colonel's dug-out headquarters, Henry Ross paused and looked back. 'You said you had some good news as well as the bad?'

'Oh yes. I thought you'd like to know that the General has endorsed my recommendation that you be awarded the Military Cross. Congratulations.'

The changeover of troops took place in the early hours of the morning. The jubilant Australian soldiers made so much noise leaving their trenches that Henry expected the Germans to light up the area with flares and lay down a barrage in the belief that an attack was taking place.

The troops who moved in to take the place of the Australians were kilted Canadian Highlanders, men with Scots Highland backgrounds, and all were veterans of the three-year-old war. They took up their positions quickly and efficiently, keeping their grumbling low-voiced when the light drizzle that had fallen for much of the night became steady rain.

A Major brought the men to the front line trenches and when Henry showed him to the dug-out vacated by Colonel Granville, the Major gazed about him in the dim lamplight and shrugged indifferently. 'I've been in worse places. I'd say your Colonel was a professional soldier.'

Extending a hand, he said, 'I'm Ian Fowler, born in Oban, but proud to have been a Canadian since the age of seven. You too have a Scots name, Major Ross.'

'My mother was born in Scotland, so too were both grandfathers. The Rosses are from Glenelg, I believe.'

'Now there's a coincidence. Our new Colonel is from a Glenelg family. He's a Cameron. *Sir* Louis Cameron.'

Henry Ross frowned. 'I've heard my father say it was a Cameron who drove out the Rosses from Glenelg, together with most of the other families who lived there – but where is this Colonel of yours? I was told to report to him.'

'He'll no doubt be here tomorrow, weather and Hun permitting.'

Henry looked at his companion in surprise: it was most unusual for a regiment's second-in-command to talk of his Colonel in such a fashion.

Major Fowler correctly interpreted the look and he shrugged apologetically. 'I know, I shouldn't speak ill of my CO, loyalty and all that, but I've learned there are two types of soldiers in this army: fighters — and the others. Sir Louis is probably first class at planning battles and deciding upon strategy, but he's at the pointed end of the bayonet now – and this is the end that hurts. I'm not altogether convinced he's ready for such an experience.'

Ian Fowler chose his words very carefully, but it was clear that the Canadian Major had serious misgivings about the leadership qualities possessed by his Commanding Officer.

'I've said for a long time they ought to prise some of the strategists loose from their office chairs and send them up here. If more of them came and saw it first-hand they might realise the futility of fighting for a bit of swamp-land that no sane man would want anyway. Here, I've half a bottle of brandy tucked away somewhere. It was left by *my* Colonel to console me for being left behind. While we sink it I'll go over the maps with you and tell you what I know. We'll look over the ground tomorrow, but one patch of churned-up mud is pretty much like another and we won't be able to spend too much time looking at it. The German snipers seem to know exactly where an officer's going to raise his head and they rarely miss.'

'It seems some things in a soldier's life never change,' Ian Fowler sighed. 'Now, did I hear you say something about a bottle?'

Colonel Sir Louis Cameron joined his regiment at ten o'clock the next morning. He made his way to the dug-out headquarters through the maze of communication trenches, complaining bitterly about their muddy state.

Arriving at the dug-out headquarters, he directed his anger at Henry Ross. 'These trenches are *disgusting*. They may be all right for Australians, they are certainly not good enough for Canadians. Major Fowler, detail some men to dig out the mud and try to remove some of the water.'

'With due respect, sir, that's not wise. Any sign of activity in the trenches is likely to bring down a barrage from the German guns.'

Sir Louis Cameron thought about Henry Ross's words for only a few moments. 'Nonsense! It will be perfectly clear what we're doing. They must have to do the same in their own trenches – although I can't imagine the Germans allowing them to get into such a state as this.'

Looking about him, he viewed the dug-out with an expression of distaste. 'We'll need to do something about this, too . . . . Where's my batman?'

Outside the dug-out, Henry spoke urgently to Major Fowler. 'I wasn't exaggerating. If they see your men working they're liable to think you're digging tunnels to lay mines. If you have them start clearing trenches I suggest you do it in an area away from the bulk of your men – and make sure there's nothing that matters within fifty yards of the work.'

Everything went exactly as Henry had forecast. He was explaining the map of the area to Colonel Cameron when the Germans fired their first shell. It landed perhaps two hundred yards from the dug-out, but when the Colonel turned to Henry Ross all the blood had left his face.

'What was that?'

'A German shell, sir. That was just a single shot to get the range. They'll fire one or two more and then the bombardment will begin.'

The two men left the dug-out in time to see the second shell fall behind the lines some two hundred yards away. It was immediately behind a place where wet mud glistened on the parapet of a trench, thrown there by a Canadian working party.

As they watched another shell landed, closer to the trench this time – then suddenly shell after shell was pumped into the area as the barrage began in earnest.

In the front line trenches the order was given for all men to stand-to. The Canadian officers and NCOs had more experience of front-line fighting than their Commanding Officer. A German barrage often presaged an attack, and they had no intention of being taken by surprise.

British artillery opened fire in response to the German barrage and stretcher bearers began hurrying along the trench, heading for the bombarded area.

'I trust the men up there appreciate that our noble Colonel only wanted to ensure they died with dry feet.' Ian Fowler hissed the words in Henry's ear. 'Being new to the front line is one thing, refusing to listen to those who know it is another.'

Henry shrugged. 'The Germans would probably have shelled us anyway at about this time. There'll be three or four more barrages before the day's out.'

Farther along the trench, Colonel Cameron said suddenly, 'I'm going to the dug-out to study the maps now. I'll need your help, Major Ross.'

'You'd learn more up here, Colonel. With all this shelling going on, right now's a good time to look out over the German positions.'

'There will be plenty of time for that. I prefer to study a map and have the area firmly fixed in my mind before checking to see what the enemy might have done with it.'

With these words, Colonel Cameron turned away and hurried along the trench to duck in through the low doorway of the dug-out. Behind his Colonel's back, Ian Fowler spread his hands wide, palms up in a gesture of resignation.

Henry hoped that the Canadian Major had a broad back. He would need to provide the effective leadership for the regiment, at the same time carrying his Colonel along with him.

*

The Canadian attack commenced at dawn, three days after they took over the front-line position from the Australians. Henry Ross had expected to be sent back to his own regiment before the assault began, but the expected order never came and Colonel Cameron made it clear that he wanted the Australian Major to remain with him. Henry had annotated the enemy's concrete strong points on a map, but only *he* could point them out in the landscape of mud where constant shelling had changed even the contours of the land.

The attack began, as large-scale British operations always did, with a massive bombardment. Henry believed these bombardments to be foolish – and especially today. The German defences hinged upon their concrete pillboxes, from which shells simply bounced off. All the bombardment served to do was warn of an imminent attack, allowing the Germans to make adequate preparations to meet it.

Even so, the Canadian artillery's support of its own men was superior to anything Henry had witnessed before. A belt of lethal precipitation from the Canadian guns rained death on the German trenches, the bombardment remaining fifty yards ahead of the advancing infantry.

The Canadians fell upon the first German trench and used bayonets to winkle out the dazed defenders, leaving no survivors behind them. But they soon learned they had overrun little more than an advance picquet, sacrificed by the Germans, their purpose being to delay rather than stem the Canadian advance.

Beyond the first German trench the infantry entered the field of fire which came from the near-indestructible concrete gunpositions, sunk into the earth by the Germans. Protruding no more than a couple of feet from the ground and bespatterd with mud, they were almost invisible – yet the fire-power from machine-guns, barely visible through narrow slits in the concrete, was devastating.

Colonel Cameron was not an officer who *led* his men into battle – and in this he could be said to be following the orders of the army's Commander-in-Chief. In the early years of the war, senior officers, continuing the custom of centuries, set an example for their men to follow. Unfortunately, with the armament of modern warfare they were invariably the first to fall. The Allied armies became desperately short of officers who had both rank and experience. As a result General

Haig decreed that they should lead from the rear. Many, especially the colonial officers, ignored this directive. Colonel Cameron did not.

Only when the first German trench had been cleared did the Canadian officer move forward to join his men. From here he waved on the first line of Canadian troops, urging them forward to the next objective.

Before they reached the second trench, the Canadians came within range of the machine-guns of a German pillbox – and the result was appalling slaughter. Henry watched in horror as a whole line of advancing troops fell as though it were corn scythed to the ground by a grim and merciless reaper. Within minutes, not a man remained on his feet. When Colonel Cameron signalled for a second wave of men to leave the trench and make a charge which could only prove equally disastrous, Henry protested.

'Colonel, you're sending those men out to certain death! At least call for smoke to be laid – or, better still, move the attack to our left. There's a very slight rise there that's sufficient to shield your men from the main concentration of machine-guns. With any luck you'll be able to take the German trenches from the flank – or even cut them off.'

For a few moments Colonel Cameron hesitated and seemed about to concede to Henry's suggestion, when he suddenly shook his head. 'My orders are to advance my battalion in line with the other regiments and clear the Germans as we go. The General laid stress particularly on the importance of leaving no strong pocket of Germans in our rear.'

Turning to his second-in-command, he said, 'Major Fowler, if the second line doesn't achieve its object send a third – and a fourth, if necessary.'

Colonel Cameron turned away from Henry as the second line of Canadian troops scrambled over the parapet of the trench and advanced obediently to certain death.

'Colonel, I *beg* you. Go *around* the pillboxes. Look! Knock out just the *one* pillbox – the one on the extreme left. It will leave a gap for the troops to go through . . . .'

Through his binoculars, Colonel Cameron watched the second wave of Canadian troops suffer the same fate as the first. He looked and behaved as though he were completely cool and composed, but this was his first experience of battle, and the first time he had seen men die on such a scale.

Sir Louis Cameron was not frightened. In fact, there was an indefinable thrill in the knowledge that he had the power to send men out to certain death, or allow them to live. It was simply that with the din of gunfire all around him he could not concentrate – could not reach a reasoned decision. The only thing fixed firmly in his mind was the order given to the regimental commanders at their briefing by the General. The Canadians would advance in a line, holding their formation as firmly as possible and sweeping the Germans before them. Maintaining a steady and even advance was of paramount importance to the whole attack.

Sir Louis had gained his rank in a Canadian militia unit in the peacetime army. He had joined because it was what gentlemen of rank were expected to do. Because of his Metis mother and despite his baronetcy, Sir Louis needed to work hard to remain in the forefront of society, even in the comparatively isolated rural area in which he had his home. He had been elected to the Provincial Parliament for a single term of office, but his parentage had cost him the place in the Federal government which he desperately desired.

Since the beginning of the war Sir Louis had served with the supply service, more latterly in a Stores' depot in France. He had performed his duties well. When a number of Canadian field officers had been wounded in particularly fierce fighting to repel a determined German attack, the Commander-in-Chief had not hesitated to give Sir Louis command of one of the battalions of a Canadian Highland regiment. The Commander-in-Chief believed he was doing a favour for the baronet. After all, a man joined the army to fight, and promotion came far more rapidly on the field of battle.

Major Fowler had also seen the second wave of men suffer the same fate as the first. With a quick glance at his Australian counterpart, he said, 'I agree with Major Ross, sir. Sending more men out is nothing short of murder . . . .'

'You have your orders, Major Fowler.'

Colonel Cameron had difficulty keeping his voice steady. Whether it was from suppressed excitement, or fear, was uncertain.

'Colonel, if you keep this up you'll be the only man in your battalion to survive this battle. That will take a bit of explaining, even to an English Commander-in-Chief.'

While Colonel Cameron was thinking of the implications of his comment Henry said, 'Give me one of your men and do nothing for ten minutes – that won't hold anything up. The battalions on your right are also pinned down by the pillboxes.'

Without waiting for a reply, Henry spoke to a kilted Sergeant who had heard the exchanges between his Colonel and the Australian Major. 'Sergeant, I want a volunteer and a supply of grenades. I intend putting the nearest pillbox out of action.'

'I'm your volunteer, sir – and there's a pouch of grenades right here . . . .'

The Sergeant picked up a heavy pack and Henry motioned for the volunteer to follow him. He brushed past the Canadian Colonel without looking at him; he did not want to give Cameron an opportunity to prevent him taking the action he had planned.

The soldiers of the adjacent battalion had suffered the same fate as Colonel Cameron's men, but their Commanding Officer had no intention of throwing away the lives of any more of his men. He applauded Ross's briefly explained plan of action but suggested he wait until a reply was received to his own request for material with which to lay down a screen of smoke between the advancing troops and the pillboxes.

Ross declined to wait. Even if sufficient material could be found to produce a screen of smoke, the strengthening wind would probably carry it away to one side too quickly for it to be effective – and Colonel Cameron's patience would expire long before such a plan could be put into action.

'Then I'll order the machine-gun unit we have with us to open fire on the pillbox while you make your way towards them. It won't put the Hun gunners out of action, but it might draw some of their fire while you work your way forward. Beyond that, I can only wish you luck.'

The Canadian machine-gunners succeeded in holding the Germans' attention until Henry and the Sergeant had wormed their way on their stomachs through the mud to within no more than seventy yards of the concrete stronghold. Then, from two of the slits around the sides of the hexagonal-shaped pillbox, bullets began to spit in converging streams aimed at the two soldiers.

Both men dived for the cover afforded by a shell-hole and the German bullets clawed at the earth above them. To his disgust,

Henry discovered they were sharing the small crater with the bodies of two Australian soldiers. They had been dead for some time and were probably ill-fated members of an earlier patrol.

'Now what do we do? Stay here until nightfall?' The Canadian Sergeant put the question.

'Colonel Cameron won't wait that long. We move on. Come here and help me dig.'

The crater in which they were sheltering was one of many pitting the muddy ground of the 'no-man's-land' between the lines of the warring armies. Henry had noticed that the wall of earth between the crater they occupied and the adjacent one was no more than a foot thick.

Using their bare hands, the two soldiers were able to dig away enough earth to enable them to slip into the next crater without being seen from the pillbox. They moved to a third crater in a similar manner and a long burst of machine-gun fire which churned up the lip of the first crater was an indication to Henry that their progress had not been observed.

From the third crater they were able to wriggle through churned-up mud and remain out of sight of the occupants of the low-sunk pillbox. They were so close now that if Henry could have been certain of his aim he might have lobbed a grenade through one of the slits from each of which protruded the tip of a machine-gun barrel. Luck had accompanied them so far, but the final few steps would provide the crucial test of the venture.

By cautiously scooping away a few handfuls of earth at the edge of the crater in which they now hid, Henry was able to observe the pillbox, although he was aware he ran the risk of being seen. Fortunately the men inside still had their eyes and machine-guns trained upon the shell-hole where they had last seen the two Allied soldiers. Even as Henry watched, one of the two machine-guns began firing once more, the bullets churning up the ground at the rim of the crater.

While the machine-gun was still chattering, Henry spoke in a hoarse, nerve-strained whisper to the Canadian Sergeant. 'Hand me some of those grenades.'

By the time the firing ceased, Henry had stuffed grenades into most of his pockets and when he spoke again it was in a low voice that would not carry to the Germans inside the pillbox. 'When the firing begins again we'll get ready to go. The moment it ceases run like hell for the pillbox, heading round to the rear. With any luck, the men won't be manning any firing-slits there. Lob in a couple of grenades and duck down. I'll try to do the same on this side. If we succeed we'll do the same to the next pillbox along the line. That should give your regiment a gap they can do something with.'

The Sergeant nodded, without saying a word. Moments later one of the machine-guns inside the German pillbox began firing once more.

All the time the staccato sound was clawing at the air the two men waited. Then suddenly there was a new silence and without a word both men rose and leaped from the shelter of the shell-crater.

It took only a few long strides to reach the pillbox, but during those moments Henry felt that every soldier in the German army must be peering at him along the barrel of a gun. He need not have worried. Unknowingly, he and the Canadian Sergeant had chosen their moment well. As Henry had anticipated, the Germans were not manning the two machine-guns that pointed towards the rear of the pillbox which guarded any approach to the heavy, iron entrance-door, built into the side of the concrete strongpoint. In addition, the machine-gun that would have been pointing directly at the two men as they broke cover from their crater was being re-loaded and the other gun could not be swung to fire upon them at such short range.

Crouching beneath the machine-gun aperture, Henry pulled the pins from two grenades in quick succession and lobbed them inside the pillbox as the Sergeant did the same on the far side.

The shrieks of terror from inside the strongpoint lasted only a few seconds before the combined explosions of four grenades rocked the ground on which Henry crouched and smoke belched forth from the narrow gun-slits on every side of the pillbox.

After this day's battle, army statisticians would estimate that the machine-guns of the German army had accounted for 20,000 casualties in the Allied ranks – but death turned inward upon this particular machine-gun team.

'Well done, Sergeant. Now we'll deal with that one.' Henry jabbed a finger in the direction of the next pillbox, temporarily hidden from view by the remains of a broken low wall that had once delineated the fields of a Flanders farmer.

'Why stop there?' The Canadian Sergeant felt a wild exhilaration as a result of their success. 'If we keep this up we can knock out the lot.'

They were the last words he spoke. Less than a minute later he was lying dead in the heavy, evil-smelling mud of the Flanders field. Henry Ross lay beside him, gasping in pain.

Major Ross had carefully noted the exact position of every German pillbox opposing the line recently held by his Australian regiment. What he did not know was that new trenches had recently been dug, linking many of the strongpoints. They were manned by a regiment newly arrived from Germany. The shots that laid the Australian and Canadian low were the first fired in anger by the young Germans peering anxiously over the parapet of their hastily dug trench.

THIRTEEN

Great Britain 1916

The telephone rang unheeded for many moments on the desk in the large office of the Supreme Court building in Jefferson City, Missouri. It was answered reluctantly by a frowning Judge Roderick MacCrimmon. The Judge was working on a complicated case involving land rights claimed by the parties involved to go back beyond the Civil War. It involved ex-slaves and slave-holders and the outcome would receive wide publicity. It needed to be sewn up as tightly as a meticulous judge could make it and Roderick MacCrimmon was annoyed at the interruption. He had told his secretary that he was not to be disturbed for any reason whatsoever.

'Hello!' Roderick MacCrimmon's sharp greeting exposed his irritability.

'Have I caught you at a bad moment, Rod?'

The voice in the telephone earpiece caused Judge MacCrimmon to straighten up automatically, his irritation forgotten.

'Mister President! I'm sorry, sir. No, I'm working on a judgement I have to hand down – but not before Monday.' It was now Thursday.

'Is it important?'

'It won't change the history of the United States, but it's important to the parties involved.'

'Point taken, but, look – I need to see you right here in Washington. What I want you to do for me *might* just change the history of our country. Can you hand the judgement over to someone else to deliver?'

'I *could* . . .' Roderick MacCrimmon wondered what could be so important that President Wilson should want him to drop everything and go to Washington. He had known the President for many years.

Wilson had been his tutor in jurisprudence when he was studying law in Princeton. Roderick MacCrimmon had also helped with Woodrow Wilson's campaign during the last presidential election. 'Can you tell me what it's about?'

'Not over the telephone, Rod – but it might well be the most important thing you or anyone else will do for America in this decade.'

President Woodrow Wilson was not a man to exaggerate. It was more in his nature to understate an issue. If he said a matter was important then Roderick MacCrimmon would not doubt it was so.

'I'll call in Judge Henwood and be with you tomorrow, Mister President.'

One week later, Judge Roderick MacCrimmon was on board the transatlantic liner *Mauretania,* en route from New York to London, England. His mission was a personal one on behalf of the American President, its object nothing less than a bid to persuade the British government to lift the blockade they had imposed upon German ports and the ports of countries sympathetic to the German cause.

President Woodrow Wilson was by inclination and upbringing an Anglophile, but he had witnessed the horrors of war at first hand whilst living in the South during the Civil War. He was determined to keep the United States aloof from the conflagration in Europe if it were humanly possible.

Despite such considerations, the American President allowed Great Britain and her allies to obtain vital commodities from America and he was keen to maintain the goodwill of his countrymen towards the British cause. However, the blockade of German ports was hitting the pockets of the cotton growers of the Southern States and they were squealing. If they made enough noise, the fickle tide of American opinion was likely to turn against the Allies. President Wilson was anxious this should not be allowed to happen.

It was not a matter he could put through official channels without offending the Germans and those United States citizens of Germanic origins. There was to be a presidential election in 1916, and present indications were that it would be a close-run race. Woodrow Wilson could not afford to alienate any section of his heterogeneous countrymen. It was a measure of his regard for the Missouri Supreme Court Judge that he asked Roderick MacCrimmon to travel to London in an attempt to find a satisfactory solution – albeit a clandestine one – to the problem.

It had been almost a hundred years since Hugh and Robert Mac-Crimmon, Roderick's great-grandfather and grandfather, had left the shores of Great Britain, and Roderick MacCrimmon was the first of the family to return there. He viewed the busy port of Southampton with great interest as tugs eased the huge bulk of the *Mauretania* alongside the jetty. He knew the story of his grandfather's departure from Glenelg because the son of the founder of the American branch of the MacCrimmon family had kept a diary until the day he died in battle during the Civil War. Bound in fine leather, the diary now occupied pride of place on the bookshelf in Roderick MacCrimmon's Ozark ranch home in Missouri, the ranch where Hugh MacCrimmon had settled.

When a covered gangway was trundled across the jetty to link ship with shore, an immaculately dressed young man was escorted on board and shown to Roderick MacCrimmon's cabin. The man was Richard Cobham, Personal Secretary to Britain's Prime Minister, Herbert Asquith.

Comfortably lounging on the leather upholstery of a Rolls-Royce's back seat, on the road to London, Richard Cobham brought the American up to date with the progress of the war in Europe. There was not much to tell. Firmly entrenched in their strong, defensive lines, the two great armies faced each other across a shell-torn no-man's-land that had witnessed slaughter on an unprecedented scale.

As Richard Cobham's narrative unfolded, Roderick MacCrimmon formed the opinion that the war was going badly for the incompetent British Generals and their absurdly confident French counterparts. Between them they seemed intent upon killing off a whole generation of British and French manhood.

When he later suggested as much to Prime Minister Asquith, the British leader admitted that the losses were appallingly high, but strenuously denied that his military leaders were to blame.

'Unfortunately, we and the Germans are equal to each other in every respect but sea power. However, should a country with huge resources in both arms production and manpower enter the war on our side the balance would tip in our favour. In such an eventuality, the war would be brought to an end and many hundreds of thousands of lives would be saved.'

'By "a country with huge resources", I presume you are thinking of the United States of America?'

Britain's Prime Minister allowed himself a pale smile. 'Such a description would seem to be recognisably accurate, at least.'

'President Wilson saw the horrors of war at first hand as a child in Georgia and South Carolina. He has no wish to go down in history as the President who sent his young men to die in a foreign land. It's your war, not ours, Prime Minister.'

'Sadly I must disagree with you, Mister MacCrimmon. We are fighting this war on behalf of all who value integrity, decency and the standards upon which our civilisation is founded – and we are paying a very high price for those principles. It is surely not unreasonable to expect others to make some sacrifices?'

'You're expressing a point of view, Prime Minister. A great many men in my country – a great many *voting* men, do not share your sentiments. They put forward equally strong arguments on behalf of Germany's involvement in this war.'

'Such arguments will be defeated by the very country they support. The Hun exposes more of his true character with every week that passes. Why, you know yourself that had your President not delivered a very strong protest, the Germans would still be sinking unarmed passenger vessels and causing great loss of life among innocent women and children. Those are not the actions of an honourable nation.'

'The machine-gun erased the word "chivalry" from the vocabulary of war, Prime Minister – but since you have brought up the subject of the war at sea, I must tell you that I am here at President Wilson's request to discuss that very subject – and I fear it is *your* country's actions that are causing him the greatest concern.'

Prime Minister Herbert Asquith nodded, saying nothing. He had guessed that this confidential meeting had been requested to discuss Great Britain's blockade of German-controlled ports. America was traditionally sensitive about interference by Britain with its seaborne trade. It had been the primary cause of a war between them in the previous century. He also knew how important it was to keep Germany starved of imports that could mean the difference between defeat and victory for those countries involved in the war.

'Your naval blockade of European ports is causing much discontent to our cotton growers. I think it is no exaggeration to say that if your embargo is not lifted the economy of the South will be ruined, causing great hardship to tens of thousands of people, both black and white, and having serious repercussions for the government of the United States.'

'I appreciate this, Mister MacCrimmon, and your people have my deepest sympathy. Unfortunately, we are engaged in the most terrible war this world has ever known. It is a war we *must* win if the lives of all our peoples, yours and mine, are not to change drastically and unacceptably. The inconvenience being experienced by your cotton growers is as nothing when compared with what might happen should Germany and her allies win this war.'

'Cotton growers are not interested in what *might* happen. They are concerned with *today*. They are losing money, Prime Minister – a great deal of money. This is what they see happening *now*.'

'Might I remind you of the situation in which Great Britain – and the rest of Europe – found itself during the Civil War which you just mentioned. The United States imposed a blockade upon the Confederate ports and prevented their cotton from coming to England. As a result, many thousands of people employed in this country's cotton mills – tens of thousands – were without work for the duration of a war which was not of *their* making. Great Britain is setting no precedent by conducting such a blockade, Mister MacCrimmon.'

'I don't doubt the truth of your argument, Prime Minister. I'm merely pointing out that the men affected by your blockade have a great deal of influence in my country. They might even affect the outcome of next year's presidential election. Should a candidate declare his intention to stop all exports to Great Britain until you lift your naval blockade, it may prove popular enough to ensure his election to the presidency. A President elected on such a promise would surely be far more harmful to your country than a concession from you to our cotton growers?'

'You put forward a thought-provoking argument, Mister Mac-Crimmon. I am most grateful to President Wilson for sending you to London. I will need to discuss the matter with my Cabinet, of course, but I have no doubt we will be able to come up with a solution that will satisfy your cotton growers, please our friends, and confound the enemy.'

Suddenly, Herbert Asquith's smile was backed by a warmth that had not been present before. 'My Private Secretary tells me your family has its roots in the west coast of Scotland: Glenelg, I believe? Have you been there?'

Roderick MacCrimmon shook his head. 'This is my very first visit to Great Britain.'

'It's a beautiful part of Britain, Mister MacCrimmon, possibly the most beautiful. I've made arrangements for Richard to take you there, just for a couple of days. You'll not regret the experience, I assure you. On your return I hope to have a message for you to take to President Wilson that will prove satisfactory for everyone.'

Great Britain's guarantee of a minimum price for the season's bumper crop proved acceptable to America's cotton growers. The agreement was greeted with great relief by all who had the interests of Anglo-American relations at heart. Furthermore, proof of the importance to Britain of maintaining a close relationship with America was not long in coming.

Germany, still convinced it would win the war, behaved towards the United States with Teutonic arrogance. In spite of the strong feelings engendered in America by the sinking of unarmed merchant vessels earlier in the war, Germany resumed its campaign of uninhibited submarine warfare.

In April 1917, such policies reaped their inevitable reward. The United States of America declared war upon Germany. From this time on the outcome of the war was never seriously in doubt. The question was no longer whether Germany would lose the war, but *when*.

Roderick MacCrimmon's visit to Great Britain also had consequences that were less well-publicised than the outcome of his main mission. The Missouri Judge fell in love with the Glenelg peninsular. Here, as nowhere else in the British Isles, he felt at peace with the world about him. It was more – far more – than a sense of the beauty of the Highlands. It was almost as though he had at last come home. He was welcomed by the Highlanders as they would have welcomed a family member returning from exile to the new world. They showed him gravestones in the small cemetery, their carved lettering weather-worn now, but their ill-spelled homage to past generations of MacCrimmons still clearly distinguishable.

The residents of Glenelg showed Roderick MacCrimmon respect, too. It was a respect that had been handed down through generations of villagers to whom a 'MacCrimmon' represented all that had been good with 'the old ways'.

When Roderick MacCrimmon borrowed a set of pipes from a local piper at a Glenelg gathering and proved he possessed at least some of the skills of his ancestors, he added a new legend to the many told of the MacCrimmons of Glenelg.

Roderick MacCrimmon was shown the site of his old family home, long since pulled down, and the ruins of the homes of those who had been dispossessed in favour of a Lowland Scot's sheep.

He was also taken round the empty great house of Ratagan. In the hall, its beauty faded and stained with damp, the guide, a sprightly man in his seventies, pointed to the huge fireplace and said to Roderick MacCrimmon, 'Yon's where your ancestor Hugh, probably the best piper Scotland's ever known, threw the great war-pipes, presented to him by the last of the *real* Camerons. He threw them in the fire at the height of a great party and swore a MacCrimmon would never again play for a Cameron. Then he walked from this hall without so much as a glance behind him and went away to America. My mother was a young skit of a servant-girl working in the kitchen of this very house the night he did that and she would often tell us children of the uproar it caused, and of the fury of Cameron of Glenelg.'

'Did she say why he burned the pipes?'

The old Scots guide frowned. 'She wasna' too sure, but it was something to do with the Clearances. Aye, that would be the reason. The Clearances caused a deal of grief in these parts.'

'Who owns the house now?'

'It was sold soon after the son of the last great Cameron set off for Canada. It's changed hands a few times over the years, but it's still known to everyone hereabouts as Cameron's House. The present Cameron is a "Sir" and living in Canada, I do believe.'

Roderick MacCrimmon went over the whole house and was reluctant to leave. In fact he visited it once more before leaving Glenelg after his brief stay. In London the Prime Minister's office was able to trace the present owner of Ratagan, who lived in London.

The owner did not wish to sell his house on the Glenelg peninsular, even though he had not visited it himself for years, and had no intention of doing so. However, by the time Roderick MacCrimmon left London to return to America, he had leased Ratagan House on behalf of the United States government for the duration of the war, and had obtained approval for it to be renovated at the expense of the American government and used as a convalescent home for wounded colonial officers.

Much to his regret, Roderick MacCrimmon was unable to attend the official opening of Ratagan House as a convalescent home, but he was represented at the ceremony by no less a personage than the American Ambassador to Great Britain.

The opening ceremony was performed by Abigail Cameron, wife of the last surviving Cameron of Glenelg. Of French-Canadian extraction, the baronet's young wife was at last able to ward off the hostility which had smouldered for more than a century as a result of the actions of an earlier Cameron of Glenelg.

In her soft, French accent, Abigail apologised for the absence of her husband, explaining that he was 'somewhere in France', fighting with a Canadian regiment, the men of which, like himself, were descended from Highland Scots who for a variety of reasons had been exiled to North America.

After the official opening, Lady Cameron toured the house, meeting the many officers who were already in residence here. Among those to whom she was introduced was a Major Henry Ross, DSO, MC, who was recovering from severe wounds to his left arm.

Suitably sympathetic, Abigail asked the Australian officer how he had been wounded.

Looking at the very attractive girl before him, Henry Ross bit back the explanation that his wound was an indirect result of her husband's inflexibility and incompetence.

'I was wounded at Passchendaele, ma'am – when I was serving with your husband's regiment.'

For an unguarded moment Abigail appeared taken aback, but recovering quickly, her expression suddenly changed to one of pleasure.

'*Really!*' Looking more closely at the identification on the shoulder of his uniform, she said, 'But you're Australian!'

'That's right, ma'am. I was seconded to the Canadian regiment for only a few days. Unfortunately they decided to attack while I was with them.'

'I do not think you are really serious about it being "unfortunate", Major. You are wearing two medals that are only given to very brave men. Did you earn either of them while you were with my husband's regiment?'

Henry Ross nodded and for the second time refrained from saying what he really thought.

'I thought it might be so. Perhaps we will have time later to talk about your bravery.'

It was no more than a passing comment, similar to many others she had made and would make that day, but as Henry Ross's glance followed her down the long line of recuperating officers, he found himself wishing there might have been time to talk more to her. He also wondered why such a woman had married a man like Sir Louis Cameron.

The next day Henry Ross was walking from Ratagan towards the village of Glenelg. The path twisted and turned as it pursued its course along the loch edge and as he followed the path around a huge standing rock he almost bumped headlong into Abigail Cameron.

'I'm sorry . . . .'

'I'm sorry . . . .'

They spoke in unison and immediately laughed.

'It's the Australian officer, isn't it? Major Ross?'

'Henry Ross, ma'am. I thought you'd returned to London.'

'That had been my plan, but this is such a delightful part of the world I decided to stay for a few days. I've taken a room at the inn at Glenelg.'

'Are you on your way to Ratagan?' Henry felt very much at ease talking to Abigail. She was also by far the most attractive woman he had spoken to for a very long time.

She shrugged. 'I'm not really on my way to anywhere. I was just walking, enjoying the beauty and the silence.'

'And now I've come along to destroy that silence.'

'That is not what I said, Major Ross. I have enjoyed the silence, but after a while it becomes painful. It is nice to talk to someone again. But where are *you* going?'

'To look around the village of Glenelg. Many years ago the Rosses were evicted from the Glenelg peninsular and my particular ancestors were sent to Australia. I'm curious to know if there's anything around to show they once lived here.'

'There is,' Abigail replied immediately. Observing his surprise, she explained, 'For centuries Ratagan was the family home of the Camerons. I've been doing the same as you, looking around to see what there is of their past in the area. In the churchyard are many – how do you say, "tombstones"? Yes, tombstones, bearing the name of a Ross. Some are of very young children and are dated about a hundred years ago.'

'That's the sort of thing I'm looking for. I'd also like to enquire whether anybody knows where the family used to live.'

There was a lull in the conversation before Abigail said, 'I wish you luck with your enquiries, Major.'

She had already taken a couple of paces along the path that led to Ratagan when Henry called, 'Would you come along with me, if I promise to spend only half my time looking for Rosses – and the other half for Camerons?'

Abigail turned and looked at him for so long he thought he had overstepped the bounds of etiquette. After all, she was married to a Colonel and had a title . . . .

'I would enjoy that very much, Major.'

'Great, and so will I . . . ! But I'd enjoy it even more if you'd call me Henry.'

'Very well . . . Henry.' She gave him a smile that seemed to indicate she was looking forward to the day ahead as much as he now was. 'Let's set off on our quest for Rosses and Camerons.'

There were many gravestones outside the small Glenelg kirk commemorating long-forgotten members of the Ross family, and memorials inside to generations of Camerons. None bore a date later than the second decade of the nineteenth century.

'I can understand my ancestors all leaving together,' mused Henry Ross. 'The land they occupied was needed for grazing, but it surprises me that the Camerons should have disappeared from the scene at much the same time. They were the landlords of Glenelg.'

'I believe the Cameron of the time was the black sheep of the family. He was given the option of a baronetcy and exile, or face prosecution for debt. He chose to go to Canada. I don't think his wife helped very much. Rumour suggests she was able to spend his money twice as fast as it was earned. It seems the Camerons of Glenelg have rarely been successful in their choice of wives.'

Something in the way Abigail said the last statement made Henry turn to look at her quickly. He was in time to catch the slight shrug that accompanied her words and the fleeting expression of unhappiness that crossed her face.

He might have pursued the matter had not a woman entered the building at that moment. She had come to prepare the kirk for the Sunday service, still a few days off, but she was quite ready to let conversation take priority over her duties. When she learned the identity of the two visitors to the kirk she spoke of 'the fine Laird, Charles Cameron', and 'those poor Rosses', as though their departure was a recent event and not something that had occurred at least a hundred years before. Eventually she said they should both go along to the manse, the home of the minister of the little church. The minister was away attending a conference, but his housekeeper was very elderly and knew more of Glenelg history than 'any of those overpaid professors in Edinburgh who tell you all about a place without ever going and speaking to a soul who lives there'.

The cleaning-woman's view of university historians might have been more than a little jaundiced, but she was correct about the minister's housekeeper.

Nellie Gunn was a busy and sprightly seventy-three-year-old – 'Four years older than the minister himself, although to look at us ye'd swear I was twenty years younger!'

She was extraordinarily knowledgeable about the history of Glenelg and its peoples, and embarrassingly frank about her views.

'Aye, I remember well the talk of the Rosses when I was a wee girl, here in Glenelg. My grandmother used to scold us with the warning that if we never behaved we'd likely end up being "transported like the Ross men". Father and two sons, she said. The only men ever to have been transported from Glenelg.'

Henry knew that Abigail was looking at him, but he did not meet her gaze. Instead, he said to the old housekeeper, 'It was always known we were the descendants of convicts, but no one ever came out with any details.'

'No, and if it's *facts* you're looking for then you'll not find them by searching the records of the court that had them sent away. Ross – *Angus* Ross, I think it was – yes, Angus it was for sure. He was guilty of no more than making certain his children never starved, but the records will not show *that*. They'd have been written up by one of James Cameron's men – and his is a name you'll find no one around here will have forgotten. It was James Cameron who turned his people from their houses and brought in the sheep. No, there's no one hereabouts will either forget or forgive what he did to Glenelg. His father, the great Charles Cameron, would have been turning in his grave. Glenelg's not recovered to this very day.'

'Did you know that James Cameron was murdered in Canada, and the murderer — or *murderess* as I believe it to have been — was never caught?'

'Murdered, was he?' Nellie Gunn made it sound no more serious than if he had sworn at a servant. 'That will surprise no one.' With a surprisingly shrewd look, the old woman said to Abigail, 'But you'll only be married to a Cameron. Would he not come to Glenelg with you?'

For the second time that day Henry gained an impression that Abigail was embarrassed at the mention of her husband.

'Louis, Colonel Cameron, is in an army hospital. That's why I came here in his place to perform the opening ceremony at Ratagan.'

Now it was Henry's turn to be surprised. No mention had been made of the Colonel being wounded, but Nellie Gunn was talking again.

'Glenelg will be pleased to hear a Cameron is serving his country. From the occasional word that comes back to us, there's not been a Cameron for a hundred years who's served anyone but himself.'

After this blunt assertion, she turned her attention to Henry Ross. 'Have you seen what they've done to the house that used to belong to the Rosses?'

Henry's interest quickened. 'I don't even know where it is, and I certainly didn't expect it still to be in existence.'

Nellie Gunn sniffed loudly. 'It wouldn't be recognised by any of the Rosses who left it, all those years ago – but I mustn't be uncharitable. The owners are English, but Captain Farrell has recently been killed in action and his wife and her father are up there now packing things up. She'll be moving back to England again, I've no doubt.'

'I didn't realise your husband had been wounded. I'm sorry.' Henry made his apologies to Abigail as they walked together along the steep-sided valley of Glen More, away from Glenelg.

'He *hasn't* been wounded.' The tight-mouthed reply came out clipped.

'But you told the minister's housekeeper . . .'

'I told her he was in hospital, and so he is – at least, he *was*. I doubt if he's still there.' Abigail looked at Henry, her chin high. 'He left the front suffering from – battle exhaustion.'

'When?'

'Two days after his regiment went into action at Passchendaele.'

Henry opened his mouth to speak, but closed it again. He could not speak his mind to Abigail. Colonel Cameron would not be the first officer to be sent away from the front after only a couple of days in battle. However, it was rare for the 'sick' man to be such a high-ranking officer. In reality it was a fear of battle that sometimes affected the younger, less-experienced officers. Many recovered sufficiently to return to the front after a short while, usually after a discussion with an officer of more senior rank. Others, the minority, were considered mentally unsuitable to lead men into battle. They would spend the remainder of their army service being shuttled from hospital to hospital, examined by numerous medical specialists, and always aware of the contempt of their fellow serving officers.

'Will he return to the front?'

'No. He's probably on his way to London right now.'

Henry Ross was puzzled. He would have thought Abigail would want to be with her husband, but he reminded himself it was really none of his business.

Suddenly, Abigail came to a halt. 'Look, Henry, Louis and I haven't really had much of a marriage for some time now . . .'

Henry Ross held up his unwounded hand in a gesture calculated to silence her. 'You don't have to explain anything to me. I was being unpardonably inquisitive, please forgive me. I'm enjoying your company very much indeed, I wouldn't want to do anything to sour that.'

'I'm enjoying your company, too, Henry. That's why I'd like you to know the real situation. Louis and I are Catholics so we can never do anything to change things, but he goes his way, and I go mine.'

'I'm sorry, Abigail. I really am. That's no way for two people – a married couple – to live.'

'It isn't entirely the fault of Louis. My family have money, Louis has a title. My father thought these two considerations added up to a very desirable marriage. I must admit I was so dazzled by the thought of being *Lady* Cameron that I gave too little thought to what marriage was really about.'

Abigail suddenly looked so young and vulnerable that Henry reached out a hand and squeezed her arm sympathetically. 'We all make mistakes in our lives, Abigail. Most of us come away from them having learned something for the future. You've been unlucky. You have to carry the result of your mistake with you wherever you go, and for as long as your religion dictates you must do nothing about it.'

Much to Henry Ross's dismay, Lady Cameron's eyes filled with tears. 'I thought you'd understand. It's something I've never mentioned to anyone else, not even to my family. I think they know, but it's not the sort of thing we discuss.'

She looked at him and grimaced. 'Now I've embarrassed you. I'm sorry, Henry – but look, isn't this the house that was once the Ross family home?'

It was the cottage to which Nellie Gunn had directed them, but it was certainly not the primitive hut Angus and Ailsa Ross had once known. It was still a single-storey building, but it had been considerably modernised. The turf roof had been replaced with tiles from the south and an extension had been built that was twice as large as the original cott.

'Do you think your ancestors would recognise it?' Abigail had put her confession behind her and was making bright conversation.

'I doubt it, but they would certainly have enjoyed living here.'

As they were speaking a man came from the house and stared at them for a few moments before advancing along the path and asking, 'Can I help you? Are you looking for someone?'

'We're looking for the past,' Henry smiled, and introducing himself and Lady Cameron, explained his interest in the house.

'How fascinating!' The man looked from Henry to Abigail and back again. 'You'll be one of the wounded officers from Ratagan? Please come in . . . but perhaps you'll allow me to go in first and explain who you are. My daughter has recently lost her husband in action and the sudden shock of seeing an officer in uniform might upset her.'

Henry protested that they had no wish to intrude, but the man insisted that if they waited for a few minutes he was quite certain his daughter would be delighted to see them.

The daughter looked pale and drawn, but both she and her father made Henry and Abigail welcome, especially when it came out in conversation that Henry's Australian regiment had relieved the regiment in which the woman's husband had served only days after he had been killed. She was sympathetic about his wound too, commenting that he might also have been killed.

Before they left that afternoon, the woman explained that she was leaving Glenelg the following day and returning south to live with her parents. Glenelg held too many painful memories for her.

Later that evening, walking away from the cottage, Abigail expressed her sympathy for the young widow they had just met.

'Yes,' Henry Ross agreed, 'war seems to have a habit of claiming those who have so much to live for.' He shrugged. 'Yet those of us who wouldn't be missed seem to survive. It doesn't seem fair, does it?'

'You mustn't speak like that, Henry. You have a whole lifetime ahead of you. So much to do.'

'Perhaps. Right now I don't want to look too far beyond tomorrow. Will you still be here, at Glenelg?'

'Yes, I'm staying on for a day or two.' She did not add that the decision had been made at that very moment. Abigail had intended leaving Glenelg the next day. She did not want to analyse the reason for her sudden change of mind.

'Can I see you? Perhaps we could take a picnic lunch into the hills?'

'I would like that.' Suddenly Abigail knew she had made the right decision. She *would* enjoy spending the day with Henry Ross.

'That's splendid!' Henry, too, suddenly felt the world had something to offer him that had not been apparent that morning. 'I'll see you back to your inn now and pick you up in the morning sometime between ten and eleven.'

The next day fulfilled its promise in every respect. The weather was superb and the countryside in which they walked was breathtakingly beautiful. They both talked a lot, but not about the war or their personal problems. They talked of Australia and of the Canadian town where Abigail had been brought up. They talked of happy times and of memories that were pleasurable to think about.

By the time they came down from the mountain each felt they knew the other as they had never known any one else and there was a reluctance to bring the day to a close. Because of this feeling, Abigail was not surprised when, instead of returning directly to Glenelg, Henry took her down a steeply winding path that led to the upper reaches of Glen More and eventually past the cottage where they had spent the previous evening.

To her surprise, Henry turned in at the cottage and led her up to the front door.

'Why are we coming here? The owner was going away today, she told us so herself . . . .'

Instead of replying, Henry opened the unlocked front door and motioned for her to step inside.

'Do you think we should? What would the owner say?'

'The owner says you are probably the most beautiful woman ever to set foot inside this cottage, either now, or in the far-off past when it was the home of the Rosses.'

'The owner says . . . ?'

'I was up early this morning. I came here and made an offer for the cottage. It was accepted and I handed over a cheque there and then. The paperwork formalities have to be completed, of course, but the cottage is back where it ought to be: with a Ross, and I'm very, very happy you are here to share this first moment with me, Abigail.'

She knew he was going to kiss her, and she made no protest, no attempt to stop him. Indeed, her response left him in no doubt of her own feelings. At this moment all reason, all the standards of the society in which they lived, were left outside where they belonged, in a world at war, a world in which love was being overwhelmed by death and hatred.

In the darkness of the cottage's small bedroom, Henry's voice was husky with spent emotion as he asked, 'What do we do now, Abigail? Where do we go from here?'

'Shhh!' She raised a hand and held a finger against his lips. 'We don't have to think about that now.'

He fidgeted uncomfortably and drew her closer before he spoke. 'I'm afraid we do. I go before a medical board tomorrow. They'll find me fit for duty once more.'

Abigail pulled away from him. Raising herself on one elbow she looked down at him, but could not read his expression in the faint light that came through the curtained window.

'What will that mean?'

'It means I'll be sent back to France again. That's where my regiment is.'

'Oh no! Haven't you done enough? You've risked your life and proved yourself. Can't you stay in this country? Shall I ask my father? He knows someone high up in the War Office . . . .'

'What will you tell him? That we've fallen in love and want to be together for ever? To hell with the Kaiser and the war – and Sir Louis too?'

'That isn't fair, Henry. I - I think you've done enough – but yes, I do think "to hell with the war". I've found you and I want to be with you. Is that so wrong?'

'No, of course it isn't, but don't get upset. Not tonight. Even if the board does find me fit enough to return to duty it won't all happen in a matter of hours. I'll probably be here for at least another week and then spend another week or two in London – can you be there? Who knows what might have happened by then? It's said that if the Germans carry out their threat to wage total war with their submarines the Americans will come into the war on our side. If they do, the war could be over in a matter of months. Then we could come up here and spend the rest of our lives together.'

Abigail held his naked body close in the darkness as she whispered, 'I'd like that, Henry. I'd like that very much.'

Henry Ross had been back in France for two months when Abigail Cameron's doctor confirmed she was probably about three months pregnant. For a further month she was undecided about her course of action. She hesitated about telling Henry; he had enough problems to face. The Germans had launched an offensive, hoping to destroy the Allies before America entered the war and their troops reached Europe. The Australian regiments were engaged in some of the fiercest fighting. She could not tell Sir Louis, although her condition would soon reach a stage where it could remain a secret no longer.

Then fate took a hand and it seemed to Abigail that at last the gods had decided to take her side.

Two German Gotha bombers flew on a surprise night raid over London and deposited their cargo of bombs over the St John's Wood district.

Casualties were comparatively light, no more than fifteen inhabitants of the city being killed when one of the bombs exploded on a popular brothel. Among the victims were seven prostitutes – and Colonel Sir Louis Cameron.

Sir Louis was buried with full military honours in a London cemetery close to the scene of his last and closest encounter with 'the enemy'.

It was another week before Abigail finally found the courage to write a long letter in which she poured out her heart to Henry Ross. She told him of her feelings for him and the joy she felt at carrying his baby inside her. She did not demand that he marry her and only hoped he would be as happy as she was that their love had produced the miracle of new life. He must not feel he had to do anything about the baby – *their* child – but she wanted him to know and hoped he would share at least some of the joy she felt.

For five weeks Abigail watched for the postman from the window of her parents' London home, reaching the front door as he dropped the mail through the gleaming brass letter-box, praying that among the mail lying on the carpet there would be something from France.

One morning it came – but it was not the reply she had been hoping for. Instead, it was a brief, scribbled note that sent her to bed for a month and had her parents and friends fearing she would never recover.

Then one day she rose from the bed and, pale and silent, resumed her life in preparation for the birth of her baby. Her family would never know what it was that had almost taken away Abigail's will to live. Yet, had they been able to look in upon her room late at night, they might have seen her grief as she held a letter in her hand, the letter she had sent to Major Henry Ross, DSO, MC.

It had been returned to her with six words scrawled on the envelope in a careless hand. Six words that had ended a dream: 'Killed in action. Return to sender'.

FOURTEEN

England 1940

Not until the Generals, Admirals and politicians of the warring countries had sacrificed thirteen million combatants was the 'war to end all wars' brought to its exhausted conclusion at 11 a.m. on Wednesday, 11th November, 1918.

The peace, purchased at such an appalling price, never even came of age, lasting just two months short of twenty-one years. On 3rd September, 1939, a woefully ill-prepared Great Britain once more took on the armed might of Germany.

For much of 1939 it seemed as though this war would be different from the earlier conflict, and that it would remain far from Britain's shores. There were sinkings by U-boats, of course, and troops were locked in fierce battle in obscure corners of Europe. Yet apart from a tightening of belts as rationing bit into the way of life, and the disruption of families as men were conscripted into the armed forces, there was an air of unreality about this war. In the public houses of London old men spoke scornfully over the rims of their beer glasses of 'this modern army', making such comments as, 'Things weren't so easy in *our* army. We had to *fight* to earn our pay.'

So convincing was this 'phoney war' that many children, evacuated from the large cities with labels attached to their lapels and gas masks slung over one shoulder in 1939, were brought home again in the early months of 1940.

Then, almost overnight, the whole situation underwent a dramatic change. The armies of Germany, spearheaded by formidable armoured divisions, swept into France. Scorning the borders and neutrality of smaller nations, they by-passed the 'impregnable' defences behind which the French deemed themselves secure from the enemy.

The people of England awoke one morning to the realisation that the enemy would soon be standing on their watery doorstep, hand poised to strike the nation's door a blow it would surely not withstand. Meanwhile, the remnants of the armies of Britain and France stumbled towards the northern coast of France, unable to halt the onslaught of the world's mightiest fighting machine, and teetering on the brink of annihilation.

Then, in a bold and courageous operation that caused the free world to catch its breath and wonder at its daring, a fleet of small boats set out from the ports and estuaries of England, all heading for the small French port of Dunkirk. Yachts, pleasure craft, tugs, even river craft and open boats hardly larger than dinghies, crossed the Channel to the war-torn beaches. Defying German submarines and dive-bombing Stukas, they ferried soldiers from the beaches to the waiting ships.

When the ships could carry no more men, the little boats took on board every soldier they could find and set sail for England. Many paused on the way and somehow made room for the survivors of sunken rescue ships. A number were themselves lost in the cold, grey waters of the Channel with nothing but a few fragments of splintered driftwood to mark their demise.

By the courage and daring of the men who manned these small boats a whole army was brought to safety. One hundred and twelve thousand French and Belgian fighting men, two hundred and twenty-five thousand British soldiers and a few Royal Air Force pilots were ferried back to England. Most of the unfortunate fliers had been shot down before they could reach the crowded beaches that presented sitting targets for every warplane in the German air force. These few pilots were often subjected to the bitterness and frustration of soldiers who had endured days of being shelled, bombed and strafed, more often than not without ever seeing a British fighter aircraft.

One such pilot was a young man, no more than twenty-two years of age, with reddish hair and an air of great weariness about him. On his heavily stained blue Royal Air Force jacket was a curved shoulder-flash that bore the woven word, 'CANADA'.

Pilot Officer Sir James Ross Cameron was lighting a cigarette from the stub of another when a soldier, as haggard and battle-weary as himself, stopped and stared at him accusingly. Only a few hours before the soldier had seen two-thirds of his company mowed down by a squadron of Messerschmitt fighters playing a deadly game of follow-my-leader along the crowded beaches of Dunkirk.

'Where were you blokes when those German sods were shooting us up like we was pheasants at some gentlemen's shooting-party? You'd have thought we had no bleedin' Air Force the way it was on the beaches.'

'Soldier,' Sir James Cameron's soft Canadian accent made his voice sound even quieter than usual, 'when those German "sods" were shooting up the beach, I was down there being shot at, the same as you, reminding myself that "gentlemen" don't shoot at sitting birds. For the rest of it, I reckon you're the lucky one. When you get back to England you have only to explain the loss of a rifle. I need to find a reason why I'm not bringing back the brand-new Hurricane fighter I took off with.'

The young pilot's reply brought smiles to the faces of men too weary to laugh out loud. An army officer standing nearby on the crowded deck, his right hand hidden in a heavily bloodstained bandage, had overheard the exchange. Easing his way through the crowd to where the pilot leaned against a stanchion, he said sympathetically, 'I suppose you weren't the pilot who was having a scrap right over Dunkirk town two days ago? I saw a Hurricane shot down by three German fighters. The pilot baled out and landed in a ditch just to the west of the town.'

'That was me,' said Sir James, ruefully. 'I'd have been better off getting the hell out of there and heading straight back to England the moment I saw the Germans.'

'Well, if it's any consolation to you, one of the Germans never made it back either. You must have hit something vital during the fight. Just before you landed in the ditch he did a wide turn inland with black smoke pouring from the engine and came down about a mile back from the beach.'

Sir James Cameron became suddenly animated. 'Are you sure?'

'As sure as I am of seeing you bale out and landing in that ditch.'

Dragging a notebook and pencil from a pocket, Sir James peered more closely at the insignia of rank displayed on the army officer's shoulders and he suddenly looked at the soldier with a new respect. '*Brigadier?* I beg your pardon, sir – but might I have your name? If I can convince them back at the airfield it was one-for-one they might view it a little more favourably. You see, it was my first operational sortie . . . .'

The Brigadier grinned. 'Then you did well, lad. I've known officers senior to myself who've never fired a shot at anyone in anger, let alone made it count. Your station commander may not agree with me, but the boost you gave to the men on the ground when they saw that Hun aircraft brought down was worth a dozen Hurricanes – and you may quote me if you wish.'

The escape of so many able-bodied fighting men from Dunkirk unleashed the full fury of the German High Command as the *Luftwaffe* turned its attention upon the British Isles. The first targets were south coast ports and it became increasingly apparent that this was part of a 'softening-up' process in preparation for a German invasion.

By the end of July 1940, Sir James Cameron was a Flight-Lieutenant and leader of his flight. Since Dunkirk, he had downed four German aircraft, lost another Hurricane, and been awarded the Distinguished Flying Cross. Well liked among his fellow pilots, he was known as 'The Tartan Baronet', obliquely comparing his skills to those of Baron von Richthofen, 'The Red Baron', the famous German air ace of the First World War.

Sir James had also suffered the loss of a great many of his friends in battle. This was an aspect of the air war which was causing great concern to Fighter Command and to those conducting the war. It was becoming increasingly apparent to everyone from Prime Minister Winston Churchill down that the war would be won or lost by the men who piloted Great Britain's pitifully few fighter planes.

At the height of the summer of 1940, Germany too realised that Fighter Command must be destroyed, if their dreams of invading the British Isles were not to be thwarted for ever; the Luftwaffe was ordered to switch its attention from the ports to the airfields.

*

Flight-Lieutenant Sir James Cameron had just landed after helping to break up a fiercely defended formation of German bombers over the white cliffs of Kent, when the air-raid warning sounded.

At first he paid no attention. The airfield was not far from the south coast and German bombers often strayed nearby. Then, from somewhere frighteningly close, there came the earth-shaking 'crump!' of an exploding bomb, swiftly followed by another.

Sir James's first thought was to reach his Hurricane, currently being refuelled and rearmed within sprinting distance of the hut where he was being debriefed. Snatching up his flying-helmet, the Flight-Lieutenant ran from the building, leaving the startled debriefing officer gathering his papers preparatory to diving for the air-raid shelter.

Running awkwardly in his flying-suit, Sir James had covered almost half the distance to his Hurricane when the aircraft erupted in an explosion that sent pieces of it flying into the air. As he came to a halt another explosion, closer this time, sent earth and stones flying in all directions. He suddenly realised that if there were more bombs to come from this particular German bomber he was likely to be a casualty.

There was a concrete-built underground air-raid shelter nearby with a number of hastily abandoned vehicles around the entrance. James just made it inside before another two explosions rocked the building, sending blinking light bulbs dancing on their flex.

'You look more as though you're dressed to be on the other end of a bombing raid.'

The laconic statement was made in an accent not unlike Cameron's own as the owner of the voice moved along to make room for him on a wooden-slatted stool built against the wall of the shelter. All around were a pale-faced mixture of men and women belonging to the air base's ground staff.

'I'd have been up there among them if they hadn't reached my Hurricane before I did. From what little I saw before I dived in here there won't be a plane left in one piece by the time the raid's over.'

Another explosion shook the shelter, although it appeared to be farther away this time, and somewhere in the distance the steady and monotonous 'crack' of anti-aircraft guns delivered reassurance that all had not been lost above ground.

James looked curiously at his companion. Beneath the man's open overcoat he could see the insignia of a pilot's wings above the left breast-pocket of his tunic, but he had never met this man in the squadron mess and his accent intrigued him.

'I'm James Cameron, Flight-Lieutenant in 145 Squadron. I haven't seen you around here, are you just visiting?'

'No.' The stranger gripped the other man's hand. 'I arrived here a few minutes ago – just in time to experience my first bombing raid. I think I'll be with your flight. The name's Hugh MacCrimmon, Pilot Officer Hugh MacCrimmon.'

In 1939, Hugh MacCrimmon's future seemed assured. His father, Roderick MacCrimmon, a well-respected Republican Senator, had already settled much of the vast Ozark ranch on his son, affording him a substantial private income. It was anticipated that when Hugh completed his studies at law school he would follow the path carved by his father, entering politics via the Supreme Court of Missouri.

When war erupted in Europe it did not come as a complete surprise to anyone in the United States. The probability had been discussed in clubs and at political meetings throughout the country for years. The only uncertainty had been when, where, and who would be involved.

Some Americans felt that their country had a moral obligation to enter the war immediately, but most believed they should stand aloof of the conflagration. After all, the ancient countries of Europe had been doing battle with each other for centuries past. They were best left well alone.

Hugh MacCrimmon disagreed with the isolationists. Adolf Hitler, the unbalanced Fiihrer of Germany, was obsessed with the idea of leading a master race in conquest and determined to exterminate the European Jews. It was unthinkable that the people of a great country like the United States of America should sit back and close their eyes to what was going on in the rest of the world.

Roderick MacCrimmon, older and wiser, advocated that America bide its time as it had in the First World War. Such a course of action had enabled the country to rise above all others in wealth and influence. His sympathies were entirely with Great Britain, seemingly doomed to be the lone bastion of freedom in a conquered Europe, but he was a United States Senator. His country was America. He realised they could come out of this war as one of the most powerful nations the world had ever known.

Father and son would spend many hours discussing the European situation during Hugh's vacations. But Roderick's duties took him to Washington for long periods whilst Hugh was kept busy with his studies – and Europe was many miles away across the wide Atlantic.

Hugh MacCrimmon passed out from law school in the early summer of 1940, an event that coincided with his twenty-fourth birthday.

At the Ozark ranch a grand party was thrown to celebrate the double occasion. Among the vast gathering were friends Hugh had made at law school, political colleagues of his father, neighbours of the MacCrimmons and all of Missouri's 'society'.

Prominent among the latter were many girls of marriageable age. Hugh MacCrimmon was probably the most eligible young bachelor in the State and mothers had spared no expense to ensure that their daughters would not be overlooked at this, the party of the year.

'What does it feel like to be pursued by the most beautiful girls in Missouri?' The light-hearted question was asked by Laura Mac-Crimmon as she took hold of her brother's arm and led him away from a mother and daughter combination that had monopolised his time for far longer than was acceptable at such a gathering.

'I feel like a fat turkey at a butcher's convention, the day before Thanksgiving,' declared Hugh ruefully. 'It's not so much a birthday party as a marriage market. Some mothers are quite blatant about what they're doing. I'm sure that woman you've just rescued me from would have offered me a bargain deal throwing in *both* daughters had I expressed the slightest interest in either of them.'

'Hugh!' Laura was more amused than shocked. Seven years junior to her brother, she adored him. 'It's your own fault for being so handsome – and rich too, of course, as all those mothers know.'

'I suspect that good looks don't come into the reckoning,' said Hugh, honestly. 'You be warned, young Laura. Your turn will come

— unless you scandalise Missouri by running off with one of the ranch-hands.'

They had reached the porch of the house as they talked and Hugh, who rarely drank, took a lemonade from a serving table and turned to gaze at the expensively dressed men and women gathered on the lawns.

'Look at them, Laura. None of them care that while they're here enjoying themselves men and women are fighting and dying by the thousands in Europe. Did you see the newspapers this morning – the photographs of the beaches at Dunkirk? The Spitfire being shot out of the sky by half-a-dozen Messerschmitts?'

'AH that's in Europe, Hugh. We're right here, in America. You can't fight other people's battles for them. Besides, this is your birthday – and we're having a party to celebrate your graduation. You mustn't spoil it for Dad. He's been planning it for months, you know. Besides, he's got a very special present for you and I think he's getting ready to give it to you.'

Discreetly directed by the servants, people were beginning to drift towards the direction of the bandstand, where the musicians were filing away from their seats. Roderick was moving the conductor's podium towards the edge of the platform, to a position where he would best be seen by the guests.

When he was satisfied with the positioning of the podium and the microphone of a public address system had been blown into by at least a half-dozen people, Roderick MacCrimmon called for silence.

'Ladies and gentlemen, it gives me very great pleasure indeed to see so many of you here today to celebrate two occasions in my life that have given me great pride, and great joy. One is the anniversary of my son's birth – which occurred more years ago than *I* care to admit to – a son of whom I have always been very proud . . . .'

Pausing until the applause died away, Roderick MacCrimmon continued, 'The second occasion we are celebrating here today is my son's graduation with a law degree, and I must confess he made it with far more marks than I ever managed to accumulate in an examination.'

This time there was both laughter and applause, which lasted until Roderick held up his hands for silence.

'As many of you already know, the MacCrimmon family have been in the United States as long as Missouri itself. My greatgrandfather – Hugh's namesake – came from Scotland to this very ranch, indeed this very *spot* on which we are all standing, a hundred and twenty years ago. In a rough and raw territory, his son – my grandfather – was a frontiersman and a sheriff who administered the law with a six-gun tucked in his belt. I have often wished the State would let me do the same . . . .'

Again there was laughter, as Roderick continued, 'Both those great men fought in the Civil War, and Brigadier Robert MacCrimmon died fighting for a cause in which he believed passionately: justice. My own father continued that tradition as an attorney during this State's most lawless days, and later as a judge. I like to feel that during my own career as an attorney, Supreme Court Judge, and Senator, I too have added a little to what they began. In seeing my son graduate and become an attorney, I have achieved my dearest wish.'

In a dramatic gesture, Roderick pointed his finger to the skies. 'I sincerely believe that up there three generations of MacCrimmons are looking down on this scene with all the pride I am feeling right now.'

Turning to where Hugh stood with Laura and their mother, Roderick said, 'Son, for you the sky is the limit and to prove it I've bought you a very special graduation present.'

Raising his voice unnecessarily and causing an ear-piercing screech on the amplifying system, the ranch owner called, 'Okay boys, wheel it out now.'

Someone in the crowd began to sing 'Happy birthday to you.' As the assembled guests joined in, a crowd of ranch-hands appeared from a huge barn in a paddock beyond the lawns. Between them they were pushing a brand-new single-engined Piper aircraft.

'There you are, Hugh, I told you the sky was the limit. Now, let's see you take her up and show us how you earned that pilot's licence while you were at law school.'

It was a superb present, even by Roderick's lavish standards. After embracing his father and kissing his sister and mother, Hugh made his way to the new aircraft, walking between two hastily formed lines of applauding guests.

The engine started at the first attempt and the loud roar quickly drowned the squeals and cheers of the party guests. Taxying out to the field that had been especially levelled for use by aircraft, Hugh waved once and then opened the throttle and took off, leaving the partygoers rapidly dwindling in size behind him.

Once in the air, Hugh quickly remembered what it was he enjoyed so much about flying. It was being on his own in a place where no one could interrupt his thoughts. Climbing up through a thin, wispy patch of cloud he entered a world where he was the only being. It was a beautiful, unreal and magical world. Here Hugh felt real happiness. He truly loved flying.

Up here in the sky he could think, too. Really think, and not merely echo the thoughts of others. It was ironic that here, today of all days, he should reach the decision he knew ought to have been taken long before. A decision that would inevitably hurt those who had given him so much.

Hugh waited until all the guests had gone home before he told the rest of his family of his plans. It was the early hours of the morning and they were gathered in the small, private den at the rear of the house. This was the oldest room in the building and it was believed that at one time it had been the *only* room in the house. That had been when the first Hugh MacCrimmon arrived to claim his empire in the Ozarks.

'I hope you've enjoyed your birthday, son.' Roderick beamed across the room. 'I guess I'm speaking for every one of the family when I say that *we* certainly have.'

'It's been a wonderful day, Dad . . . .' Hugh hesitated, reluctant to bring the world crashing down about his father's ears at such a time. 'But there's something I need to say to you all, something important.'

Roderick was about to make a flippant remark about his son perhaps planning a secret marriage, when he saw the expression on Hugh's face. Putting down the coffee cup he was holding, he said, 'I think you'd better tell us about it, boy.'

Looking from one to another of the three people he loved more than any others in the world, Hugh said, 'I've decided to go to England, to join their Royal Air Force as a pilot, if they'll have me.'

His words produced a moan of anguish from Joan, his mother, and a gasp of surprise from Laura.

'When did you decide this?' The question came from Roderick.

'I've been thinking about it for a long time but haven't had the courage to do anything about it. I believe we Americans should be doing something to help England out right now. I realised when I was flying my new plane for the first time just what I had to offer – but I'd say it was *you* who really made up my mind for me, Dad. It was something you said in the birthday speech you made.'

'Me? I'm not with you . . . .'

'You were talking about Robert MacCrimmon, who came from Scotland with his father to settle in this land. You said he died in the Civil War – died "fighting for what he believed in". You also said you hoped you'd added to what he began. I want to do the same, Dad, and for the same reasons. I intend fighting for what I believe in. By doing that I feel that I too will be adding something, something special, to what they began.'

Looking at each of his family in turn, Hugh's eyes went back to his father. 'I'm sorry, I hope you aren't too mad at me.'

'Mad?' Roderick looked at his son with an expression that caused Joan to move quickly to his side and seek his hand. 'Yes, I'm mad! Mad that I'm too old to come with you and do the same. I'm proud of you, Hugh. Proud as hell!'

When the siren announced that the danger of more bombs had passed, Hugh MacCrimmon followed Sir James Cameron from the concrete shelter. Outside, the airfield was a scene of smoking destruction. Hangars had been razed to the ground; piles of rubble lay where once there had been buildings; shattered aircraft tilted at impossible angles and over all hung a pall of smoke, drifting from still-burning buildings.

Among the casualties of the raid was the car which had brought Hugh and his luggage from the station. Amidst the tangled wreckage of the vehicle Hugh recovered his shaving-gear, intact, and while the Flight-Lieutenant helped him pull a few items of clothing from the wreckage, Hugh asked, 'Does this happen often here?'

The baronet shrugged. 'This is only the third time we've been raided, but it seems far more serious than the other raids . . . .' He broke off as a Hurricane, wheels down for landing, roared along the length of the runway before accelerating and gaining height once more.

'The runway's been hit. Here, bring this along with you.' Shoving the recovered clothing into Hugh's arms, Sir James waved down a small camouflage-painted van and after giving an order to the driver, called for Hugh to climb in.

They drove out to the runway where a great many men were standing around a number of craters. Engaged in animated conversation, the only common factor among them seemed to be a great deal of shaking of heads.

Leaping from the still-moving van, Cameron said, 'What are we all doing? *Talking* isn't going to get these holes filled in. Where are the spades? Come on, there's work to be done.'

One of the airmen, a Corporal, said, 'We're going to need a bulldozer to fill in these holes, sir . . . .'

'We've no time to wait for any machinery, start using shovels. There are aircraft up there waiting to land and their fuel won't last until a bulldozer arrives. Fill in all the craters in a straight line from the dispersal point to the old west hangar. That won't take long and it will give our planes a strip on which to land – and take off. There's a war to be won and I'm damned if *I'm* going to let the Luftwaffe keep *me* out of the air. Get these men working, Corporal. As soon as I find a plane that's serviceable I intend taking off to find out what's going on. Jump to it, now!'

By the time the two pilots drove away, the airmen were working feverishly with shovels to repair the bomb damage on the runway at least.

Filled with admiration for the manner in which his companion had injected a sense of urgency and direction into the airmen, Hugh asked if the other man was a career officer.

'Me?' Sir James spoke as the van bounced over pieces of rubble which had been blown across the road from a bombed building fifty yards away. 'I doubt if the Air Force would accept me for a regular commission. I'm one of life's natural layabouts – a *colonial* layabout, to boot. I inherited my father's title before I was born, managed to sell most of the family's Canadian land-holdings at a loss, and generally proved myself a mere child in the wicked world of trade and commerce. If it wasn't for this war I'd no doubt be selling matches and bootlaces on a street corner somewhere. How about you? What persuaded an American neutral to give up the soft life and come to fight a war – and if you tell me it's the money I won't believe you.'

Before Hugh could give his companion a reply the van pulled up sharply and James said, 'Don't bother to give me an answer. I guess we all have our own reasons and they all come down to the same thing. This is a war we just *have* to win. Come on, it looks as though the officers' mess is still in one piece. I'll introduce you around — if anyone's there.'

The officers' mess was about a hundred yards from where the van was forced to leave them. On the way they passed a building that had been severely damaged in the raid and a number of men were working feverishly in the ruins. Just as they reached the spot the body of a young woman wearing the uniform of the Women's Auxiliary Air Force was lifted gently from the ruins. Nearby five forms lay hidden beneath blankets.

'Is there anything we can do to help?' James put the question to a perspiring Sergeant who seemed to be in charge of the rescue party.

'Not here there ain't, sir, but when you get back up in the air you can shoot one of them Jerry bastards down and say it's one for the girls we've lost 'ere. We've got out twelve so far, half of 'em dead, and we reckon there's another fourteen still inside.' He fell silent as the body of a WAAF was carried past. There was dust in her blonde hair but it was still possible to see that that she had been a pretty girl.

'Don't 'ardly seem fair, do it, sir? I got one just a bit younger me'self. No doubt some mum and dad doted on 'er, pridin' themselves they've brought 'er up the right way. And for what – for this? Get back up in the air as soon as you can, sir – the both of you. You won't be flying alone. Everyone of us 'ere will be up there with you, in thoughts, at least.'

As the two pilots walked away towards the mess, Sir James said fiercely, 'This bloody war! Why did they have to get women involved? Isn't it bad enough that there are so many men dying?'

They were questions to which he expected no answers and he led the way in silence. Here orderlies were at work sweeping up broken glass, and when he spoke to them, Sir James's fierce, questioning mood had gone. He was once more the carefree, happy-go-lucky fighter pilot that had been personified in the British press.

'What will you have to drink, Hugh? I can recommend the whisky. My mother is staying in Scotland and she's persuaded one of the Highland distillers to keep the messes of Fighter Command well stocked with their produce.'

'I'll just have a soft drink – but shouldn't I be reporting to someone?'

'At a time like this? The Commanding Officer will be looking around the airfield assessing the damage and the Wing Commander is probably stooging around looking for a place to land. Here, let me introduce you to those men who *are* here – but hide that drink of yours. Non-drinkers frighten pilots, they're afraid it might be catching . . . .'

There were only six other pilots in the mess. Two had slight wounds that had grounded them, two were new pilots who had arrived, like Hugh, just in time to be caught in the raid. The others were, like Sir James Cameron, experienced pilots.

The new pilots looked as though they had come fresh from school and in the course of a brief conversation Hugh was appalled to learn that the younger and more nervous of the two had no more than forty hours' flying experience on Hurricane fighters. By way of contrast, the two veteran fighter pilots had clocked up hundreds of hours in recent weeks alone. Looking at them, Hugh thought he had never seen men who looked more weary.

They had been talking for perhaps half an hour when an orderly came hurrying to the mess, seeking Sir James.

'Message from the Ops room, sir. There's a raid developing – a big one, just east of Sheerness. There are no telephones working so the Ops officer can't tell you personally, but he says he can do with any extra planes you can put in the air. It's chaos everywhere at the moment. Our planes have put down wherever they can. No one seems to know where anyone is. Can you get any planes off the ground, sir?'

'How many aircraft are fuelled and ready to go?'

'Seven, sir.'

'We have six pilots – tell the Operations officer that's how many we'll put up.'

Hugh felt an incredible excitement, as well as a sense of apprehension. He had anticipated a period of settling in, of learning how things were done in a front-line fighter squadron. There was to be no such period. He was a trained pilot – trained to fight. This was what he was being expected to do – right now.

One of the young pilots said suddenly, 'But I don't have a flying-suit.'

'A fighter plane doesn't need a suit to fly it, just a pilot. You stay with John in the air.' James indicated the first of the two experienced pilots. 'You,' he pointed to the younger of the two newcomers, 'fly number two to Jeremy. Hugh, you'll come with me. When we get in the air I want you to stay on my tail the whole time and keep your eyes everywhere. Your duty today is to protect *me*. Mine is to shoot down German bombers – and that's something else to remember. We're up there to down bombers, not fighters. Their fighters are up there to stop us. Come on.'

A small truck took them to their aircraft. It travelled so fast over the rubble-strewn ground that it was impossible to talk. Everyone needed to concentrate if they were not to be catapulted from the vehicle.

Once at the aircraft the pilots strapped on their parachutes and donned flying-helmets. Hugh felt as though he had ten thumbs and there was a brief moment of panic when he tried to start the engine of his aircraft only to find it agonisingly sluggish. What if it wouldn't start? What if he failed to get off the ground on this, his first patrol? Suddenly the coughing engine spluttered into life and the splutter became a full-throated roar.

From the cockpit of the aircraft beside him, James held up a gloved thumb and the Hurricanes began taxiing out from the dispersal point in a ragged line.

The take-off was bumpier than anything Hugh had ever experienced when flying from the ranch fields in Missouri. As his aircraft bumped and bounced along the narrow strip of designated runway the airmen filling in the bomb craters kept at their task until the very last moment before scattering frantically.

One of the Hurricanes failed to make it into the air and over the radio Hugh heard a despairing voice wail, 'Oh hell! Sorry, Blue Leader. My horse has broken a leg in one of these bloody potholes. I'll come and join you in the spare Hurricane. Don't wait for me, I'll catch up with you later.'

Now there were only two experienced pilots and three novices flying their first mission. It was a flight leader's nightmare, but as the unpartnered novice pilot was brought in to fly behind Hugh, Cameron's voice over the radio was as even as though they were in a classroom discussing tactics with the aid of a blackboard.

As they headed eastwards from the battered airport, gaining height all the time, Hugh gradually got the feel of his aircraft and he experienced the thrill he always had from piloting an aircraft. But this was no birthday Piper. The Hawker Hurricane was a 328-mph warplane powered by a 1030-horsepower engine. Peering through four ports in each wing were eight 0.303mm Browning machineguns, carrying 2,400 rounds of ammunition, all of which could be exhausted in fifteen seconds if an excited pilot kept his finger on the firing button too long.

'Blue flight, vector fifty degrees to port. Keep up, Blue Two, you're lagging behind. We don't want to lose you.'

Blue Two was Hugh: opening the throttle he caught up with the others and immediately there was another message from Cameron. 'Bogeys dead ahead. Climb! Climb – but stay with me!'

Just before the nose of his Hurricane came up, Hugh saw the sunlight glinting on what seemed from this distance to be a swarm of metallic bees. They were German bombers and flying in awesome numbers. Surely five aircraft could not attempt an attack on them . . . .

But other Royal Air Force squadrons were already falling upon the German bombers. Climbing above the enemy formation to attack, they in turn were set upon by hordes of Messerschmitt 109 fighters. As Flight-Lieutenant Cameron's diminutive flight climbed towards the bombers his pilots could see the aircraft of the opposing forces twisting, diving and climbing in desperate battle.

'Blue Leader from Blue Two, bandits right above us!' Hugh shouted the urgent warning as he saw the Messerschmitts turning high above the five Hurricanes.

'Well spotted, Blue Two. Watch your tails . . . . Here they come.' The radio call was distorted as the flight leader turned his head to watch the enemy fighters, at the same time putting his aircraft into a dive.

Hugh put his Hurricane into a tight turn and followed Cameron in his dive; the young pilot officer behind him was slower to react and as Hugh came out of his turn he saw the lone Hurricane out on its own, well to their left.

'Blue Three, close up – close up for Christ's sake . . . !'

The next moment it seemed Messerschmitt 109s were everywhere, and one of them was on the tail of the inexperienced pilot who had joined the squadron only that day. Hugh seemed to watch for minutes, whereas in reality it was all over in seconds. He actually saw the cannon shells striking home around the cockpit and engine of the Hurricane. As black smoke poured from the engine, the Hurricane flipped onto its back and fell towards the ground in a lazy, spinning dive.

The Messerschmitt straightened up and crossed Hugh's path, and in that instant all his instructions were forgotten as he closed on the enemy fighter and his thumb jabbed at the firing button. Pieces of the enemy plane splintered away and flew past him. There was a sudden flash of fire and the German fighter tumbled from the sky.

Hugh felt an incredible feeling of elation: he had shot down his first enemy aircraft. He had scored a kill! Suddenly he felt the Hurricane judder as shells thudded into the fuselage somewhere behind him. Instinctively he pulled on the joystick and as he performed a looping climb, engine racing, a Messerschmitt flashed beneath him.

As he straightened out, Hugh realised he had lost the others in his flight, but the battle was still raging around him. He attacked two bombers, scoring hits but causing no serious damage to either — and then his ammunition was spent. He had learned another lesson that came early to fighter pilots – guns needed to be used sparingly and effectively, if a fighter pilot was to perform his duties efficiently.

Hugh turned his Hurricane for home, and had a sudden sinking feeling. Where exactly *was* home? He only had the vaguest idea, but by flying on a reciprocal course to the one taken to reach the scene of the battle, he hoped his luck would hold.

It almost did. Just when he was beginning to have grave doubts about his primitive navigation, he spotted an airfield beneath him. He tried to call the airfield on his radio but received no reply. Remembering that the airfield had been bombed only hours before, it was hardly surprising; radio and telephone would still be out of action.

The runway stretched invitingly beneath him – and Hugh never paused to wonder at the speed with which it had been brought back to full operation.

He made a perfect landing before it struck him that nothing here was remotely familiar, unless it was bomb damage – and even this appeared to have been put to rights extraordinarily swiftly.

Taxying from the runway, Hugh found a control tower where he did not remember seeing one before. When he was close to the building someone ran in front of the aircraft waving his arms excitedly. When Hugh brought his aircraft to a jerky halt, the man, wearing overalls, climbed onto the wing and signalled for Hugh to slide back his cockpit.

When Hugh did so, the man shouted above the engine noise, 'Is your aircraft badly damaged? Where are you from?'

'No, it's been hit, but I don't think there's anything wrong . . . .' With an increasingly sinking feeling, he added, 'Is this – isn't this Tangmere?'

'Tangmere? No, mate. You're at the wrong airfield. This is Ford, a Naval Air Station. Tangmere is a few miles over that way.' The mechanic waved an arm to the west.

'Oh! Er, thanks very much.'

As the man climbed down from the Hurricane, Hugh slid the cockpit shut and carefully avoided looking towards the control tower as he taxied back to the runway and took off again.

*

By the time Hugh arrived back at his own airfield, many of the pilots who had been absent upon his arrival had returned. Telephone communications had been restored – and news of his navigational error had reached the airfield ahead of him.

Proof of the amusement it had caused came when he taxied his aircraft to the dispersal point from which he had taken off. There were a number of new and roughly printed signs directing him to the debriefing room. One carried the instruction, 'Yanks should follow the arrows upon leaving the debriefing room in order to reach the mess.' Another declared, 'If lost, stand still and scream. Flight-Lieutenant Cameron will come and take your hand.'

Once inside the debriefing room, Hugh's 'kill' was confirmed. He would have savoured the moment more had the chalked-in name of Pilot Officer Crabb not been erased from the list of pilots while Hugh was studying the large blackboard on which the names and flights of pilots were entered. Crabb was the young pilot who had notched up only forty hours flying-time in Hurricanes.

Hugh entered the mess to a chorus of 'Show him to the bar' and 'Hope you tied a ribbon to your Hurricane, Yank, or you'll never find your way back to it.' Hugh's discomfort was not improved when Flight-Lieutenant Cameron took Hugh to one side and gave him a roasting for not staying with him when he had taken evasive action at the scene of the air battle.

However, when he had said all that was necessary, James smiled at Hugh's crestfallen expression. 'I've said all that needed saying, Hugh. I expect you to remember next time – and not many pilots can claim a confirmed kill on their very first operational flight. Come over and meet the Wing Commander. He says he's never met a flying Yank before. By the way, before he tells you any different, you'll be flying as my number two again on the next sortie. Stay a bit closer to me and we'll make it a permanent arrangement.'

After a few weeks of operational flying it seemed to Hugh's battle-weary mind that he had never done anything else. The whole business of flying had become automatic. You flew, you fought. You saw men die. If you were lucky you shot down the enemy. You returned to the airfield, refuelled, re-ammunitioned and flew and fought again. On good days you managed to snatch some sleep in between sorties. On bad days you did not. On really bad days you slept only to wake in a sweat because the pilot struggling in vain to open the cockpit of the burning Hurricane was you. And all the time there was a constant feeling of numbing tiredness that grew worse with every passing day.

One day, without any prior indication that it might happen, the Germans stopped bombing Fighter Command's airfields and switched their attack to civilian targets. The raids were even heavier than before, but now the Luftwaffe was unloading thousands of tons of bombs each day on London and its civilian population.

This change of policy, although welcome to the near-desperate head of Fighter Command, was quite inexplicable. Had the attacks on the fighter airfields continued, it was probable that a few more weeks would have seen Fighter Command put out of action, and so changed the whole course of the war. As it was, the hard-pushed aircraft factories were able for the first time to turn out fighter aircraft faster than the Germans were destroying them. In the corridors of the Air Ministry there was a glimmer of hope. Unlikely as it had once seemed, there was now a real possibility that the war in the air might be won by the pilots who were driving themselves to the limits of human endeavour.

Each night, when Fighter Command's squadrons of near-obsolete aircraft took over the impossible role of intercepting and shooting down German bombers in the darkness, the pilots who had fought during the day tried to relax and to forget. It was not easy, even for those who drank themselves into near-unconsciousness. There was always the moment when a pilot looked for the man with whom he had been drinking the previous evening, only to learn that he was no longer there. Each day, it seemed, new, eager faces outnumbered the tired and familiar ones.

Those who survived were honoured by the country they served, in proportion to the successes they achieved in the air. Hugh, with seven downed German aircraft to his credit, now wore the ribbon of the Distinguished Flying Cross, while two pale-blue rings circling the sleeve of his uniform jacket marked his promotion to Flight-Lieutenant.

Sir James Cameron was a Squadron Leader, and he had been awarded a second Distinguished Flying Cross. To these medals had been added the blue and white ribbon of the Distinguished Service Order. With fourteen enemy aircraft to his credit, Sir James was one of Fighter Command's foremost aces.

Sometimes, when bad weather prevented the *Luftwaffe* from mounting bombing raids against the British mainland, both men would explore the nearby English countryside together. But such occasions were rare. Sir James felt it was his duty to spend as much time as possible with his squadron, to enable the new pilots to get to know him.

More often, Hugh would go for a walk by himself. He had found a small English public house where he liked to sit in a corner drinking a half-pint of cider and thinking his own thoughts. Always shown great respect by the countrymen, he became known as 'The Quiet American'. Whenever he entered the inn his particular corner would be vacated to make room for him and his silence respected.

One day, when cloud and intermittent rain gave the British fighter pilots a welcome respite, Hugh was thinking of going for one of his walks when there was a knock at the door of his room and Sir James entered before Hugh could answer. The Squadron Leader was in high spirits.

'Get your glad rags on, Cinderella. You and me are off to the ball tonight.'

'Translated into a Canadian's version of English, what exactly is that supposed to mean? A rough translation will do.'

'It means that our estimable Group Captain has agreed to loan me his car, in which I intend taking you to London to gain a little culture. I have tickets for the theatre. The show's not in the West End, but it's theatre, nevertheless. I've also arranged for us to be introduced to two of the chorus girls afterwards.'

'If you'd mentioned the introductions at the beginning, I'd be ready by now. As it is, give me five minutes and I'll be with you.'

Sir James believed in doing things in style. His first call in London was at the Savoy Hotel. Leaving the Group Captain's MG sports car to be watched over by an ageing doorman, he led the way to the dining-room. It was early evening and he announced that they would eat before going on to the theatre.

The menu was decidedly limited but, as Hugh pointed out, there was a war on and they were lucky to be offered anything. A bigger problem came when James tried to procure something special to drink. He was informed that, unfortunately, the hotel was temporarily out of alcoholic drinks for everyone but their residents.

After a few minutes of futile argument, James asked to speak to the head waiter. When he arrived at the table it was apparent from his expression that he was prepared to support his wine waiter's stand. However, before he could say anything at all, James said, 'Señor Raffari? Harry O'Connor asked me to give you his best wishes.'

For a moment the formidable head waiter frowned, then his expression cleared, although there was a hint of puzzlement in his eyes. 'Harry O'Connor, the bellboy?'

'That's what he was here. He's now a Sergeant-pilot in my squadron. As soon as he knew I was bringing my friend here to celebrate the award of his DFC he said I must ask for you and present his compliments.'

The head waiter's glance had switched to the medal ribbon above Hugh's left breast-pocket. Then it moved back to Sir James Cameron. 'You too have the DFC – *two* if I am not mistaken. The DSO too.'

Turning to his waiter, the head waiter had a great deal to say in rapid Spanish. When it was over, the junior of the two men was sent scurrying away by a gesture that might have been used to shoo flies from a dish of food.

Beaming at the two airmen, the head waiter said, 'I will personally serve you.' Looking quickly about him, Señor Raffari stooped towards them and spoke in a whisper. 'Today a few brace of grouse were brought in from Scotland. We are cooking two now, for someone *very* important – but a secret, you understand? I think perhaps one should be enough. As for something to drink . . . . Ah! Here comes Juan now.'

The wine waiter appeared carrying an ice bucket, the contents hidden by a cloth draped over the top. When the bucket was placed on a stand between the two men, discreetly hidden from the few other guests, the cloth was removed to reveal a bottle of champagne.

'It is a *very* good vintage, gentlemen. Accept it, please, with the compliments of the management.'

The meal was all it should have been, and enjoying some of the champagne afterwards, Hugh was glowing pleasantly, more relaxed then he had been since leaving America.

Driving away shortly before dusk, Hugh complimented Sir James on the choice of hotel and his success there, adding, 'But who's this Sergeant-pilot O'Connor? There's no one in the squadron by that name.'

'There was,' said Sir James unrepentantly. 'But he never quite made the grade on Hurricanes. Didn't like being in an aircraft on his own. Made him jittery. He transferred to Defiants, on night-fighter duties.'

The Defiant, a somewhat ponderous fighter, carried a gunner in a turret behind the pilot. The night-fighter squadron was stationed on the same airfield as Hugh and Sir James.

'We owe him one. I'll have a drink sent across to his mess for him tomorrow.'

Skilfully steering the small sports car around a square of fencing guarding a bomb crater that extended for half the width of the road, Sir James shook his head. Without looking at Hugh, he said, 'There's no need to go to that expense, Hugh. Just say a prayer for Harry when you're next on your knees. I telephoned his mess to talk to him before we left today. They told me he was shot down over London last night. Came down in a lazy glide that ended when he hit the side of a block of flats. That's the trouble with Defiants, once inside you need a tin-opener to get out again without help.'

'I tell you I *haven't* made a mistake. Here are the two tickets. The address is on them, "The Kingsland Theatre, Hackney Road" – and look over there, on that wall. It's a poster advertising the revue. *This* is Hackney Road – but where's the theatre?'

It was dusk, and past the time when they should have taken their seats for the 'Star-Studded Revue' advertised on the poster, but this was the third time the two pilots had cruised the long length of Hackney Road in the Group Captain's car without finding the theatre.

'There's an air-raid warden, pull over and ask him.'

An elderly man wearing navy-blue battledress and a tin hat with the initials ARP printed in white on the front was walking along the road towards them. Pulling in to the kerb, Sir James leaned from the car and asked his question.

'The Kingsland Theatre? You won't see anything there tonight, mate. No, nor any other night, neither. Got a direct hit three nights ago. Lucky it was a Sunday and the theatre was closed. Any other night and there'd have been a few hundred in there watching. Good show it was, saw it myself on the first night . . . .'

From near at hand there came an explosion that seemed to shake the houses all about the street. It was quickly followed by two more.

'Hello! They've beaten the siren tonight . . . .' Even as the air-raid warden was speaking a siren began whining, the sound increasing to a deafening crescendo even as more explosions occurred nearby.

'That's the air-raid warning, gents. You'd better park the car off the main street. Put it just around the corner here. You'll find the shelter down the road a little way, in the basement of the woodwork factory. Hurry up now, there's some old 'uns along the road who are a bit deaf. I'll need to tell 'em what's 'appening.'

The explosions sounded dangerously close and the two airmen decided it would be advisable to follow the warden's advice. Tucking the car round the corner, in a small, cobbled cul-de-sac, they joined a steady flow of civilians heading for the shelter.

The cellar beneath the woodwork factory was about a hundred feet long and fifty feet wide. It was crowded with people, most of whom staked their claim to a few square feet of floorspace by laying out bedding and placing children on their selected spot.

Even down here, with the babble of conversation all about them, it was possible to hear – and feel – the explosion of bombs falling on the city above their heads.

Somewhere a small baby began to cry: it was a sound that set listeners' nerves on edge. Close to the two airmen a young boy sat nursing a set of tartan-decorated bagpipes. When it became increasingly apparent that the falling bombs were far too close for comfort and Hugh could feel the tension rising in the shelter, he approached the boy.

'How about giving us a tune on those pipes? Something we can all sing along with.'

The boy shook his head. 'I can't play 'em, they're my grandad's. He usually gives us a tune during raids. He ought to be here by now . . . .'

'Here, let me have the chanter . . . .' From the underside of the pipes, Hugh detached a section of the bagpipes that resembled a recorder played by children in school concerts. Placing it to his mouth, he began to play a tune. The women who had cheered when he took the bagpipes from the boy immediately joined in and they were followed by others.

For half an hour Hugh played, until the explosions and tremors from outside seemed to have moved farther away. The young boy's grandfather had by now arrived to claim the ancient Scottish musical instrument. As he took the chanter from Hugh amidst applause from the occupants of the shelter, he said, 'You'll be a piper yourself, I'm thinking?'

Hugh nodded. 'Legend has it that the MacCrimmons have been pipers for as long as there have been bagpipes in Scotland.'

'Why didn't you play the whole instrument?' queried Sir James. 'Why only the chanter? Had you played the pipes it would have blotted out the whole raid.'

Hugh shrugged, with a faint air of embarrassment. 'There's a superstition in the MacCrimmon family that the pipes must never be played for a Cameron. No offence to you, James, it goes way back in time, to the days of the Highland Clearances, I believe. It's only a superstition, but . . .'

He shrugged again and James Cameron nodded. There was not a pilot in either Bomber or Fighter Command who did not believe he was clinging to life by a very fragile thread. Not all were superstitious, but few would disregard it altogether, just in case.

'Where in Scotland did your family come from?'

'Glenelg, it's on the west coast.'

'That's interesting. Do you know I am a Cameron of Glenelg? As a matter of fact, my mother is staying in a cottage in Glenelg right now. It must have been one of my ancestors who upset yours, all those years ago. I'll have to write and ask Mother if she knows anything about it.'

At that moment a large, pot-bellied man made his way to where they were seated on the floor with their backs against the wall and stood none-too-steadily looking down at them. The colour of his face and the flammable odour of his breath left neither pilot in doubt that he had been drinking.

'What are you doing here? Why aren't you up there shooting down Germans instead of playing a penny-whistle – or whatever it was, down here in a shelter?'

The slurring of his words confirmed Hugh's suspicions, but he replied mildly enough, 'It was a chanter, not a penny-whistle. As for shooting down Germans, right now that's a job for the night-fighters.'

'Pah! 'Scuses, that's all it is. 'Scuses.'

An elderly man had come up unnoticed in the faint light illuminating the underground shelter. Addressing the pot-bellied man, he said, 'How is it *you're* not up there fighting for King and country, Bill?'

The unsteady man turned his head to look at the newcomer, and apparently recognised him. 'Oh, it's you. You know why I'm not fighting. I'm too old. Besides, I'm not a well man. Haven't been since I was gassed in the last war.'

'No doubt as an ex-serviceman you'll recognise the medal ribbons they're wearing, Bill. Unless I'm mistaken they have three DFCs and a DSO between 'em. That don't sound to me like men who haven't been up in the air fighting Germans.'

Addressing Sir James and Hugh, he said, 'You bomber pilots?'

Both men shook their heads and Hugh replied briefly, 'No, we fly fighters.'

'Do you now?' It was evident that the newcomer, at least, was impressed. 'How many Jerries you shot down between you?'

'Twenty-one at the last count,' said Sir James. 'Most of 'em bombers, like those raiding London tonight.'

'There you are then, Bill. You can go back to your missus and tell 'er you've been talking to two 'eroes who've shot down twenty-one bleedin' Germans. That's something to boast about, eh?' With a quick wink at the two pilots, the older man led his drunken companion away.

'You *really* shot down twenty-one German planes?' The question came from a not unattractive young woman who moved closer from the shadow of a nearby pillar. Behind her, smiling shyly, was a girl who must have been in her mid-teens.

'That's right,' declared Sir James, eyeing the young woman speculatively, 'and tomorrow we'll both be up there fighting Germans again.'

'I wish *I* could fight 'em,' said the young girl fiercely. 'My brother's in a prisoner-of-war camp in Germany. They captured him at Dunkirk. He won't be free until we've beaten 'em.'

The older of the two women must have been in her early twenties. Since stepping from the shadows she had not taken her eyes from Sir James; now she said, 'My name's Pat.' Briefly switching her glance to Hugh, she said, 'My friend is Jean. She's going to join the WAAF soon. Why don't you tell her what it'll be like?'

Shifting her glance back to Sir James, she added, 'But not here, though. Old Grandpa Buchanan will be playing his pipes in a couple of minutes and you won't be able to hear yourself talk. Come back to our house.'

'What about the air raid?'

'You don't need to worry about that. We've had so many raids we've learned what to expect. The first half-hour's the worst, the bombs are likely to fall anywhere then. But the Germans are aiming for the docks. Once they've found their target they concentrate their bombing there. I'm glad we moved from the Isle of Dogs last year. If we hadn't, we'd have probably all been dead by now.'

Hugh shrugged in response to a questioning look from Sir James. 'Why not? We never planned to spend the night in a shelter.'

Outside in the street the sky to the south was an angry red, painted by flames that must have reached hundreds of feet into the air.

'They've hit the sugar warehouses,' said Pat, matter-of-factly. 'It means they'll be cutting down our rations again soon.' She had linked arms with Sir James and in the red-hued darkness the younger girl's fingers found Hugh's hand and clung to it.

'Your friend's got Canada on his shoulder. Are you Canadian too?' She squeezed his hand as she asked the question.

'No, American.' Hugh was not used to having girls pick him up in such a fashion and he was not sure how far he should go to respond to the girl's kittenish gestures of affection.

His reply brought a gasp of delight from his companion and another squeeze of his hand. 'I was named after an American, a film star. Do you know any film stars?'

'I've met a few.' This was less than the truth. Hugh's father knew a great many of the stars who were household names. Most had spent holidays on the MacCrimmons' Missouri ranch, but Hugh was reluctant to excite even more hero-worship from his affectionate companion. 'How old are you?'

'Old enough. Tell me about some of the film stars. Have you met Clark Gable, or Cary Grant? I've always wondered what they're really like . . . .'

When Sir James entered the 'front' room of the little terraced house and pulled back the curtains, the early-morning light of a grey dawn reached reluctantly into the tiny room.

On the sagging settee, Hugh put a finger to his lips as he gently disentangled himself from the sleeping girl beside him. Tiptoeing from the room, the two pilots entered the kitchen and closed the door behind them.

'Don't tell me you spent the night in *there!* Why didn't you go upstairs? Pat said there's another bedroom.'

'In America we have a name for men who take advantage of young girls, however eager they are to be seduced.'

Sir James grinned. 'Seems I got all the luck.'

'You don't need to brag about it, these houses have thin floors. It didn't make my self-denial any easier. Does your lady-love have the strength left to make us a cup of tea, or do we make one for ourselves before we go?'

'Neither. We get out as quickly as we can. It seems Pat has a husband. He can't join the army because he suffers from asthma, so he's a police "special", working nights. He's due home soon.'

Outside the house, Hugh shivered. Autumn was in the air and especially noticeable at this time of the morning.

Some of the bombs had fallen much closer to the shelter during the previous night than either Hugh or James had realised. They twice walked past the woodworking factory before they realised where they were. The reason for their confusion was immediately apparent: a number of bombs had fallen on Hackney Road and the adjacent streets.

Once they had located the shelter it was an easy matter to find the place where they had left the Group Captain's car, but their good luck ended here. A heap of rubble and a rope stretched across the road blocked their entrance to the cul-de-sac, and a special constable guarded the ruins.

'I'm sorry, sirs, but you can't come in here. We think there's an unexploded bomb in one of the gardens over the back. No one's allowed in until the bomb disposal squad's been to have a look at it.'

'But, I left a car here last night.'

'A *car*? There won't be much of that left, I'm afraid, sir. Must have been a land mine came down here, I reckon. Whereabouts was it?'

James Cameron raised his hand to point, but lowered it again. He knew where the car had been. It was at the spot where at least half of a three-storey house had collapsed into the street.

'It doesn't matter. Will the buses be running? We need to get to Victoria Station to catch a train back to our airfield.'

'If you walk right the way along Hackney Road you'll come to Kingsland Road. Buses are running along there, I know. But I'm going off duty in a few minutes. Why don't you hang on for a bit and come round to the house for a cup of tea before you go. My wife will be happy to make one for you. She might even rustle something up for your breakfast. Always happy to do her bit for anyone in the forces, is my Pat . . . .'

FIFTEEN

Glenelg 1940

On 11th September, 1940, Sir James Cameron's squadron suffered fearful losses. Intercepting a huge build-up of German bombers to the east of the Thames estuary, they discovered to their cost that they were defended by at least six hundred German fighters. In the ensuing combat the squadron lost eight Hurricanes and five pilots. One of the aircraft shot down was being flown by Hugh. He managed to bale out successfully and, despite bouncing off the roof of a lonely Kent cottage, came to earth with nothing more serious than a sprained wrist.

The squadron had been in action with little respite since the fall of Dunkirk, and this latest disastrous battle prompted Fighter Command to pull the survivors out of the front line and send them to an airfield in the north-west of England to enjoy a brief period of rest while the squadron was re-formed.

The airfield was in Westmorland, on the edge of the Lake District so beloved by the English poet William Wordsworth.

Hugh had hardly settled into his room at the North Country airfield when Sir James entered in his usual breezy fashion. 'Come on, Hugh. Throw a few things in a bag and forget everything else. I've a car ticking over outside waiting to take us on a spot of leave.'

'Don't tell me someone's been foolish enough to loan you another car?'

A sheepish expression crossed Sir James's face. 'No, I had to buy this one. Paid cash, too.'

'Are you surprised?' Hugh grinned. 'Give me ten minutes and I'll be with you. Where are we going?'

'The ancestral home, Glenelg. I thought it was time we both went there to see the place. I've just telephoned to Mother. She's expecting us.'

Outside the mess a huge open sports car with a bullet-shaped tail was parked with engine running beneath the long green bonnet. So slow and powerful was the tickover it sounded like the engine of a deep-sea fishing-boat.

Sight of the car stopped Hugh in his tracks. 'It's a *monster*. What is it?'

'It's a Bentley, so they tell me. It's been parked in one of the hangars since its owner disappeared on a sortie over the North Sea.'

'But it will drink almost as much petrol as a Hurricane!'

'Ah! That's all part of the deal. It has a tank filled with petrol and there are spare cans packed into every inch of storage space. There's so much of it we're going to have to strap our suitcases on the outside.'

Hugh looked at James suspiciously. 'Where did all this petrol come from – a refuelling bowser?'

'Don't ask awkward questions — I didn't. Strap your suitcase into place and we'll be on our way. I told Mother we'll be with her for dinner tonight.'

'How far is it?'

'I don't know. Two, three hundred miles, perhaps.'

The roar from the large-bore exhausts of the massive three-litre Bentley sports car rattled the glass in the windows of the Glenelg cottages as it drove into the village. Leaving the narrow single street behind, the big motor car nosed along a still-narrower track that followed the course of the eighteenth-century military road through the Glen More valley.

When they reached the old Ross cottage, Abigail Cameron ran from the house to meet her son. She hugged him to her with all the love of a mother who had been living for too long with the fear of never seeing him alive again.

After she had smothered her son with affection, Lady Cameron turned her attention to Hugh and her hug for him was only slightly less demonstrative. Hugh warmed towards her immediately.

As she linked arms with both men and walked towards the cottage, she said, 'Tonight I am the happiest woman in Scotland – and the most fortunate. Who else can boast of having two such hand-some young men beneath her roof?'

The years had taken nothing from Abigail's French accent. It was as charming to the listener as it had been to Henry Ross in this very house more than two decades before.

Later that evening, they were talking about the connections both families had with Glenelg. Lady Cameron volunteered the information that the great house of Ratagan had once belonged to the Cameron family, adding, 'I was asked to perform the opening ceremony when it became a convalescent home for servicemen during the last war. It was a very proud moment.'

'Then we have yet another joint link with Glenelg and the past,' declared Hugh. 'It was my father who persuaded the American government to put up the money to convert Ratagan to a convalescent home after he'd been here on a visit. Who owns the house now?'

'An Englishman. He lived there for a while when the war was over but he has not been near the place for very many years. I think it must be in as poor a condition now as when your father first saw the house. It is very sad. But tonight we do not talk of sad things. This is a *happy* time. The happiest I have known since the war began. Come, I have had the best cook in the village make a special meal for you – by courtesy of a Glenelg man who is an excellent poacher . . . .'

For two days the young pilots enjoyed the tranquillity of the Glen More cottage as all the horrors they had experienced in recent months became a little less real. They fished a little, slept late and generally relaxed, all luxuries that had been denied them for too long.

Then a telegram arrived for Sir James, brought to the house by an elderly postmistress riding an ancient bicycle. Scorning the confidentiality of her office, the woman told Lady Cameron of its contents while the telegram's addressee was still slitting open the envelope.

Sir James was ordered to report back to the squadron forthwith.

'Do you think they're sending us down south again?' asked Hugh, following James inside the cottage.

'I doubt it. If they were, we'd have both been recalled.'

'True. But I'll come with you anyway.'

'No you won't. You'll stay here and keep Mother company until your leave is up. It will be good for both of you.'

'Of course you must stay. If I can't spoil James I will spoil you instead. I have spent a fortune buying black-market goods for you. Would you have me waste so much money?'

Abigail tried to make light of the anguish she felt at being parted from her son again so quickly, but did not quite succeed. Hugh felt he owed it to her — and to James — to remain in the Glen More cottage for the remainder of his leave.

When the echoes of the Bentley's large-bore exhausts had faded from the mountains surrounding the glen, life in the cottage became much quieter for Hugh, yet he felt strangely unsettled. He still believed he should have returned to the squadron with his friend.

On the last full day of his stay there, Abigail made Hugh some sandwiches, supplied him with a well-used map of the local area and sent him off to enjoy the solitude of the countryside around Glenelg.

Walking eastwards, following the line of the old military road, the beauty of the mountains soon closed in around Hugh. Only a high-soaring eagle brought a reminder to Hugh of his part in the conflagration sweeping through Europe and threatening to consume Great Britain.

After pausing to eat his sandwiches on a rock-seat on the slope of a high, steep-sided mountain, Hugh walked on. Soon he found himself on the rocky shore of a loch named on the map as Loch Duich. Ratagan was not far away and Hugh headed towards the house that had once been at the heart of life on the Glenelg peninsular, and from which the future of the MacCrimmon family had been decided.

The house was wonderfully impressive, although slightly smaller than Hugh had imagined. Both house and gardens had a sad, neglected air about them – but there was something else. It seemed to Hugh that this house, so intertwined with Glenelg history, was waiting for something, or someone. There was such a powerful atmosphere about the house that Hugh tried the door, not certain whether he really *wanted* it to be open. It was.

Once inside, Hugh marvelled at the wonderful, large fireplaces, tall, diamond-paned windows and the ornate staircase sweeping down in an elegant curve to the grand entrance hall. He fell in love with the rooms and the view they afforded over Loch Duich to the mountains that extended inland for as far as could be seen, and beyond.

Hugh had no idea how long he had been looking around Ratagan when he heard a noise coming from somewhere at the back of the house in the area where he imagined the kitchen and pantries to be. It sounded like a door being closed and then he heard the sound of footsteps, light and quick.

Puzzled, he made his way quietly towards the source of the sound and in a corridor he saw a young girl aged no more than seven or eight walking towards him.

Hugh was more surprised to see the child than she was at his unexpected presence.

'Hello!' She spoke cheerfully, as though there was nothing out of the ordinary about meeting a stranger in a supposedly empty house. 'We're playing hide-and-seek, are you?'

'I didn't *think* I was,' declared Hugh. 'Are you hiding, or seeking?'

'Hiding. Andy's the finder.' The small girl suddenly looked serious. 'I don't really think I should be hiding in here.'

The small girl's doubts were confirmed almost immediately. A young woman appeared at the end of the corridor and seemed only momentarily more surprised than the small girl at finding Hugh in the house.

'Mary, I said you weren't to come inside the house. You must only hide in the gardens.'

'Sorry.' Turning to Hugh, Mary said, cheerfully, 'Bye.' Then she ran past the young woman and disappeared around a bend in the corridor.

'I'm sorry if I'm trespassing. It was just that I've heard so much about the house – I wanted to see it for myself.'

The young woman smiled. 'We're all trespassers really, but I love this place. I bring the children here whenever I get the opportunity. We're picnicking in the garden right now.'

Hugh wondered where this young woman's husband worked for them to live in such a remote area. She somehow seemed too smartly dressed to be a fisherman's wife. He was probably in one of the services.

'You'll be Hugh MacCrimmon?' The young woman put it as more of a known fact than a question.

'Yes – how did you know?'

The ready smile appeared again and he thought she had the sort of mouth that was used to smiling. 'There's little happens around here that isn't immediately known to everyone. I'm Ailsa Ross, from Glenelg.'

They shook hands in a purely formal gesture and she said, 'Have you looked around the house yet?'

'Most of it. It's certainly a wonderful place.'

'I think everything about it is just perfect, the house, its setting, the view. It's wonderful, despite the fact that it once belonged to the Camerons. Do you know much about the place?'

Hugh shook his head. He thought Ailsa Ross's soft accent was the most attractive he had ever heard. He wanted her to continue talking.

'Then I'll give you the grand historical tour – if you've the time.'

'I have, but what about you . . . ? Your children?'

There could have been a hint of amusement in Ailsa's expression as she said, 'They'll be all right. My sister came with me. She lives in London but she's brought her children to Glenelg to escape from the bombing.'

Hugh expressed his sympathy with Ailsa Ross's sister, adding that the RAF were doing all they could, but at the moment were able to do little more than knock holes in the vast aerial fleets of the Luftwaffe.

Ailsa Ross rested her hand on his arm in a warm, apologetic gesture. 'I wasn't implying any criticism of you, or the RAF. Everyone, my sister included, has nothing but praise for you. You're putting your life on the line every single day. Without you Hitler would have invaded the country long before this. Everyone knows that.'

They had been walking as they talked and now they entered the great hall of Ratagan. Stopping before the huge fireplace, Ailsa Ross asked, 'Do you know the story linking your family with this?'

When Hugh admitted he did not, she told him the story of another Hugh MacCrimmon who had defied the then Cameron of Glenelg on account of the Ross family, and had thrown his pipes on the fire declaring that never again would a MacCrimmon play for a Cameron of Glenelg.

'It would have been a brave decision in those days,' she added. 'The Camerons were all-powerful and he would never have forgiven your ancestor. By registering his protest in such a manner Hugh MacCrimmon sacrificed his own future at Glenelg.'

'So *that's* where the legend originated. It's been handed down through the family that we must never play the pipes for a Cameron.'

'You mean, the MacCrimmons still play the pipes?'

'Every eldest son since that first MacCrimmon set off for America. But what happened to the Rosses? I don't recall any of them settling near us in Missouri.'

'Angus Ross and his two eldest sons were transported to Australia. I believe they eventually did very well there. The younger members of the family and their mother made their way to Glasgow. They never made any fortunes, but they at least managed to remain respectable.'

'And that's the branch of the family to which you belong?' Hugh wondered once again about this woman's husband, the present-day Ross. Whoever he was, Hugh conceded, he was a very lucky man. Ailsa Ross had dark red hair and green eyes and her looks would have attracted attention in any company.

Suddenly they both heard a woman's voice calling for Ailsa from somewhere outside the house.

'That will be my sister getting worried about me. Mary will have told her she left me in here with a man.'

'Then you'd better go outside and put her mind at ease. I know how reputations are gained and lost in small communities like Glenelg.'

Ailsa Ross extended her hand to Hugh and as he shook it she said, 'If you like I'll send you a copy of the research I've done into the families who lived on Glenelg at the time of the Clearances.'

'I'd like that very much.'

'Good! I can get your address from Lady Cameron. There's a great deal of interesting gossip about her, by the way, but I won't include that. She's very well liked hereabouts. She and Sir James are quite unlike the Camerons that went before them.'

Ailsa Ross had reached the corner in the corridor before she stopped and looked back at Hugh.

'Would you prefer to have a boat ride back to Glenelg instead of walking? There's room for you.'

Hugh told himself that he was being totally unreasonable to have to *think* about whether he wanted to travel in a boat with this woman and her children.

'Come on, you'll enjoy seeing the view from the boat. Roddie – that's the boatman – says it's the only way to approach Glenelg.'

'Won't your children mind? And your sister . . . ?'

There was just the faintest hint of mischief in her smile as she said, 'With a boatload of chaperones my reputation should be quite safe, were we to be seen by the most malicious Glenelg gossip!'

'Then I'll be delighted to travel with you.'

Outside the door, Hugh was introduced to Ailsa's sister, Flora. Older than Ailsa, Flora gave Hugh an approving glance and said, 'You'll have to tell me your secret, Ailsa. Whenever I go into empty houses I never find anything except dust – and spiders. But it's time we went. Roddie just called up from the boat. The tide is turning and it's time we were on our way. I sent the children on ahead.'

Not until they rounded a final bend in the steep path leading down to the sea-shore from Ratagan did Hugh see the children the two women had taken on the picnic and the sight brought him to an abrupt halt.

'Is something the matter, Mister MacCrimmon?' This time there was no mistaking the mischievous smile on Ailsa Ross's face.

There must have been twenty children in the boat and by no stretch of the imagination could they have been the offspring of the two sisters.

'The children, I thought you were talking about your own . . . .'

'Mine? Oh no, I'm not even married. Two of them are Flora's, the others are from the village. I'm their teacher.'

When Hugh awoke the morning after his visit to Ratagan the realisation that he must return to his squadron that day weighed heavily upon him. His friends would have been astounded at such a change in his attitude. They looked upon Hugh as a fighter pilot who was so dedicated to his profession that he had foresworn drink lest it dull his proficiency in the air.

But now he had met Ailsa Ross.

The young Glenelg teacher had come to the Glen More cottage late the previous evening, bringing with her documents relating to the researches she had made into the Ross, MacCrimmon and Cameron families.

The visit had been quite unexpected. Both had enjoyed the boat trip from Ratagan to Glenelg and were reluctant to part company, but those children whose mothers had not come to the jetty to meet them had to be returned to the school. They had parted, with Ailsa promising to send the results of her researches to Hugh when his squadron returned south to Tangmere.

The reason she gave for changing her mind and bringing them personally that same evening was that she had discovered she had more copies already prepared than she had previously realised, but Lady Cameron took one look at her guest and Ailsa together and suddenly remembered she had promised to visit the home of a near-neighbour that evening.

The evening passed all too quickly as they pored over family trees and neatly written pages of information, heads close together. By the time it was over Hugh had learned far more about his own family than had ever been passed on by his father. He knew something else: Ailsa Ross was a girl he would not easily forget. Neither did he want to.

Later that evening, as they walked together along Glen More, with the moonlight throwing the mountain peaks into relief and turning the waters of the river to beaten pewter, they talked not only of the history of their families but the present too. By a common, unspoken consent, neither made any mention of the future. They both knew that tomorrow Hugh had to return to his squadron. The next day he would begin once more to fight the daily life-or-death battles in the war-torn skies over London and the southern counties of England. In a sphere of conflict where a fighter pilot on active duty had a tragically brief life-expectancy, Hugh would be fighting on borrowed time. There could be no looking to the future for him – not yet.

Their farewell in the darkness of the Glenelg night reflected this. Hugh kissed Ailsa goodnight, but with none of the passion of which he was capable. It was more a promise – a hope.

Walking back to the Cameron house alone, Hugh tried hard to think ahead of what life would hold for him if he were spared to see the war through. He found his mind was incapable of making such a giant and improbable leap. Instead, he began wondering whether Sir James Cameron would still be with the squadron when it moved back south to Tangmere.

The next morning, Lady Cameron walked with Hugh to the jetty in Glenelg. From here a fisherman was to ferry him to Lochalsh, on the other side of the loch. There he would catch a train which would take him on a devious route to the Westmorland airfield.

As they passed by the school Ailsa ran from the building.

'Hugh, I've something for you, something rather special. I hope it will bring you luck.'

She held out a silver band about the size of a napkin ring and an inch or more in width. It was highly decorated with raised silver thistles and carved leaves. It was also slightly misshapen and badly tarnished on one side.

'What is it?'

For a brief moment Ailsa's glance went to Lady Cameron before she said, 'You remember the story of Hugh MacCrimmon throwing the pipes onto the fire at Ratagan?'

Hugh nodded.

'This is the silver ring that decorated the neck of the chanter on those very pipes. It was rescued from the fire by a servant, Alex Dewar. One of his descendants, Maggie Kennedy, lives in the village. She's an old lady now but I remembered her showing the ring to me some years ago. I went to see her this morning to ask if she'd sell it to me. I wanted to give it to you as a present. When she heard who it was for she refused to take any money for it. She says it belongs to you, by right. Take care of it, Hugh, you're the second brave Hugh MacCrimmon to own it.'

Abigail Cameron had walked on alone towards the jetty. When she looked back and saw Ailsa in Hugh's arms it reminded her of another time and a male member of the Ross family. He too had been a brave and very special man.

Hugh arrived at the Westmorland airfield just in time to bid farewell to James. The Canadian baronet had been promoted to the rank of

Wing Commander and posted to the De Havilland aircraft factory. Here, he was to carry out flight tests on a revolutionary new twin-engined aircraft. Made largely of wood, the new aircraft was designed to straddle the barrier between fighter and fast, light bomber. In addition the aircraft, to be called a Mosquito, was expected to prove ideal for reconnaissance purposes.

'I think someone up there in the Air Ministry has had a brain-storm,' declared James, explaining his move to Hugh. 'Can you imagine a modern fighter made of *wood?* They'll be giving us paper aircraft next. But if they keep giving me promotion at the present rate I'll finish up an Air Marshal and be able to indulge my fantasies too.'

Apologetically, he added, 'I tried to persuade the powers-that-be to promote you and give you the squadron, but it seems they're a bit wary of your Yankee roots. Now, if you'd take out British nationality, I'm sure I could do something for you . . . !'

Hugh was genuinely sorry to see the departure of his friend, but there was little time to dwell on it. The squadron was returning to Tangmere the next morning and the Hurricanes were being armed for combat. There was a very real possibility that they would be diverted into action during the flight south.

That night, before turning in, Hugh wrote three letters. The first was to Abigail Cameron, telling her that he had seen James. He assured her that although her son would probably not be able to tell her of his new posting, he was well and likely to be out of the combat area for the foreseeable future. The second letter was to Ailsa Ross and in this Hugh was able to express some, but not all, of his feelings.

The third letter, very much longer, was to his parents in Missouri. He told them of his brief holiday in Glenelg, of Ratagan — and he went into great detail to tell them about Ailsa Ross. As he put the stamp on the envelope he smiled, well aware how his mother would react to the story of his meeting with Ailsa. It would take all his father's powers of persuasion to prevent her catching the first ship across the Atlantic. She would be convinced that her only son was about to disrupt the matrimonial plans she had begun to make for him on the day he was born.

*

The squadron was not thrown into action on its flight south, but the desperate battle for command of the skies over England was still raging. The squadron was called upon to make an evening sortie within hours of arriving at Tangmere. It almost proved to be Hugh's last. The squadron took to the air to form part of a huge 'Wing', a new defensive ploy aimed at meeting the enemy in great strength. It provided a formidable defence against the waves of German fighters escorting the bombers, but some of the more experienced pilots were not happy with the new tactic. They complained of being forced to circle for as long as ten minutes waiting for other squadrons to join up with them, wasting precious minutes and fuel which should have been utilised in attacking the enemy.

However, on this occasion no one had cause for complaint. The various squadrons comprising this particular Wing were in position very quickly. The large formation wheeled and gained height, heading not for London, as was customary, but towards Bristol, where a heavy raid was expected. As the vast formation of fighters flew north-westwards it gave the pilot of each Hurricane and Spitfire an unaccustomed sense of security to look from his cramped cockpit and see the sky about him filled with British fighter planes.

It was a shock to the German pilots when large numbers of British fighters dived out of the sun into the massed ranks of German bombers. It came as an even greater shock when the escorting fighters peeled off to deal with their attackers only to learn that the RAF had held enough fighters back to deal with *them*.

The British fighters intercepted the German aerial armada over the outskirts of Bristol and many of the bombers immediately jettisoned their bombs and turned back, flying south and east in a bid to escape the guns of the British fighter planes.

Hugh came down through the bombers and fired a quick burst at the spindly shape of a Dornier 17. His bullets hit the target, but there was too much confusion in the crowded sky to observe the results of his attack.

He chased another bomber heading southwards, but was forced to break off the attack when a determined Messerschmitt 109 came to the rescue. For four or five minutes, the two fighters weaved a deadly pattern in the sky as each pilot attempted to fix the other aircraft in his gun sights.

The German pilot was the first to break off the inconclusive duel, aware that his fuel was running dangerously low. He headed southwards towards the sea, clearly visible only a few miles away.

Hugh was well clear of the main battle area now, but he still had plenty of ammunition left. He had already turned to head for Bristol again, when far beneath him he saw the shadow of a twin-engined aircraft racing across the green fields of the coastal countryside. Looking for the source of the shadow he suddenly saw a Junkers 88 flying low and fast, heading for the sea.

Hugh put his Hurricane into a steep, banking dive that would bring him down above and behind the German, but he had been spotted and as he dived, the German plane went up in a steep climb, gaining sufficient height for the pilot to take more effective evasive action.

The Junkers 88 was the fastest of all the German bombers used to raid Britain, and this one had a skilful pilot. In spite of all Hugh could do, the two aircraft were well out over the sea before he was in a position to make an attacking run on the other aircraft.

They were both close to the water now and Hugh brought his Hurricane down at an angle that he hoped would send his machine-gun bullets into the bomber's cockpit. Once again, the Junker's pilot took successful evasive action. But this time, as the bomber climbed away from the sea, using every ounce of power provided by the 2,400 horsepower of its two engines, Hugh allowed his Hurricane to come within the sights of the gunner in the exposed belly turret.

The gunner was as skilful as his pilot. In the space of two seconds, forty 7.92mm machine-gun bullets had perforated the engine cowling of Hugh's Hurricane. As the Rolls-Royce engine coughed in protest, a fractured pipe sent hot, black oil pumping over the perspex screen in front of Hugh as though it were an artery pumping out the fighter's life-blood.

Hugh yanked back the cover, breathing thanks to God that it had not jammed. He was so close to the sea that everything needed to work like clockwork. It did. As he freed himself from his harness the Hurricane's engine died and the aircraft banked almost lazily to one side. In the moment before the nose tilted downwards and the aircraft dived seawards like a shot pheasant, Hugh leaped clear.

His parachute opened with a jerk that took his breath away and a moment later he plunged into the sea. For some minutes he floundered in the water until he was able to struggle clear of his parachute and puff air into his life jacket, praying it had not been damaged in the escape from the Hurricane.

The fighter was nowhere in sight, it must have struck the water and sunk while he was still suspended from his parachute. He was relieved to see that the Junkers 88 had also disappeared from view. It was not unknown for a fighter pilot to be shot as he floated helplessly in the water.

After the noise and frantic action of the past half an hour, the silence of the open sea was almost painful to the ears. There was no sound at all, nothing to hear or see anywhere around him.

Suddenly, Hugh realised the predicament he was in. Only the crew of the German bomber knew he had baled out from the Hurricane and they were unlikely to inform anyone but their own squadron intelligence officer. If rescue came at all it would be sent by the Germans. If . . . ?

Hugh had a sudden moment of panic and used his hands as paddles, frantically gyrating in the water, searching the low horizons. The sea was empty – and was likely to remain so. This was not the comparatively narrow confines of the Channel, where both British and Germans were on the look-out for the slightest movement. He had ditched in the approaches to the Atlantic, where ships followed no regular sea lane and few aircraft would come searching the waters.

It was a frightening thought, and Hugh refused to dwell on what might happen to him. The water was already beginning to feel cold and he began to tread water, to keep the circulation going in his legs. Soon it would be dark and he knew that was going to be the worst time of all.

Hugh did not remember seeing the dawn arrive. It had been the longest night of his life. He could not feel his numbed legs now. Although he was willing them to move, he no longer knew whether they were obeying him. He realised too that he was suffering periods of unconsciousness, or fainting – he did not know which. And his mind was beginning to play tricks on him. During the night he had heard strange sounds – sounds that could not have been. Voices from the past, from his childhood. And once he thought he had heard Ailsa Ross, calling for him to come and look at Ratagan once more.

The cold now was numbing and Hugh realised that the blank periods were lasting longer, but he could not do anything to remain conscious.

The strange sounds returned. Voices – the sound of a deep, throbbing engine. He imagined someone was in the water beside him, supporting him, lifting him . . . . Suddenly the realisation came to him that this was not in his mind. A bottle was being forced between his lips and he was choking on the unfamiliar taste of whiskey – Irish whiskey.

Lying on a bunk being rocked by the motion of boat and sea, Hugh did his best to grin back at the swaying men looking down at him. They were dressed as fishermen, and the smell of fish that pervaded the cabin told him he was on a trawler. An Irish trawler.

'Was it yesterday you say you were shot down? Jesus! Ten minutes in the water wid' you was long enough for me. And what would you have done if we hadn't found you?'

'I'd have died.' Hugh found it difficult to force words between lips that were sore and cracked as a result of being exposed to salt water and a cold wind for more than fourteen hours.

'You'd have done that for sure,' said one of the fishermen, 'but we *did* find you, so we need have no more talk of dying. Give the boy another drink, Brian, his insides'll be as cold as a bucket after all night in the water.'

Hugh put up no argument against drinking alcohol. He was not certain he wanted to be an abstainer any longer. Besides, his stomach *did* feel 'as cold as a bucket'. He was convinced that his whole body would need at least a week to warm through.

The fisherman held the bottle to Hugh's mouth and kept it there until he began choking. He would have raised his hand to brush it away, but his limbs had not begun to respond to his brain's commands yet.

'We've a small problem.' The fisherman who had ordered Hugh to be given more whiskey appeared to be the skipper of the fishing boat. 'We've another two days of fishing before we return to harbour.'

'Where's harbour?' Hugh asked painfully.

'Ballydonegan, in Eire. It's not a place you'll be knowing. But where do *you* come from? You're not English?'

'No, I'm American.'

'I'd ask you what you were doing fighting for the English if I didn't have two brothers who are doing the same. Both would as soon fight *against* the English, but they say they find the Germans easier to hate.'

A sudden grin crossed the Irish fisherman's face. 'I'm looking forward to seeing the look on the face of the Chief of Ballydonegan's *Garda* when we turn you over to him. He's the only one of his family who's *not* in America. He'll not know whether to lock you up, or stand you a round. As for notifying your ambassador, will it be the British, or the American? He'll need to consult with his headquarters, that's for sure, and he's avoided doing that for years!'

Hugh's presence in neutral Ireland, in uniform, caused a diplomatic furore, but the circumstances of his arrival in Ballydonegan made him a local celebrity immediately. Lodged free of charge in the town's most comfortable inn, men travelled from miles around to meet him and shake his hand, many boasting of relatives who had 'made good' in America.

Not until eight days after he had been shot down did Ulysses Cuddy, an official from the United States Embassy in Dublin, arrive in the small town in a chauffeur-driven limousine. After hurried introductions, the diplomat insisted that Hugh change into an ill-fitting suit of civilian clothes, and then he drove him away doing his best to pretend that the crowds of cheering residents were figments of his imagination.

Cuddy made no attempt to hide his displeasure at being forced to leave behind the pleasures of the city of Dublin in order to come to Ballydonegan to collect Hugh.

'The thought of driving all the way back over those atrocious roads makes every bone in my body groan,' he complained. 'As for the uproar this incident has caused! We haven't had the official German reaction yet, but if the *unofficial* one is anything to go by it's likely to prove a major embarrassment to the United States government.'

'Perhaps I should have stayed with my plane when it went down,' commented Hugh, sarcastically.

'It would have been better had you not been flying the aircraft in the first place. We're a neutral country. It's damned embarrassing for the government to have to issue apologies for our nationals who're fighting in someone else's war.'

'Denmark, Norway and the Low Countries were neutral too. Invading them didn't embarrass the Germans, why the hell should we care what they think? As for the United States, if we're so damned moral we'd have come into the war when Britain did. We're going to have to eventually, anyway.'

'That will be for the President to decide. My problem right now is how best to handle your particular incident.'

'Easy, when we reach Dublin put me on a ship to England. I'll forget we've ever met, if you will.'

Ulysses Cuddy was beginning to annoy Hugh. It was doubtful that he had ever seen a man die in battle, and probably never would. All that seemed to matter in his restricted little world were the rules of chessboard politics.

The two men spoke little during the remainder of the six-hour journey to Dublin and when Hugh was ushered in to the Ambassador's office at the United States Embassy, he braced himself for more recriminations. Much to his relief, Ambassador Costello greeted him as though he were an old friend, for reasons which he made immediately clear.

'It's good to see you, Hugh.' Rising from beyond a huge polished desk, the Ambassador advanced with hand outstretched. 'I went to college with your father. Matter of fact, he was on the telephone to me no more than an hour ago. I called him when we learned you'd been brought into Ballydonegan, of course, to let your family know you'd been picked up. You'd been posted as "Missing, presumed killed". I can't tell you how happy and relieved they all are that you're safe and well.'

'Thank you, Ambassador. What's going to happen to me now?'

'Your pa would like to see you safely back in Missouri, but what do you want to do?'

Hugh was surprised to learn that he had a choice. After all that Ulysses Cuddy had said to him he thought he faced some form of action by his government – that they might even revoke his passport.

'I'd like to return to my squadron as quickly as possible.'

'That's what I thought you'd say. Officially, I must register our country's disapproval of you fighting for another power, although, as a US citizen, you are entitled to do whatever your principles dictate. Unofficially – I'm damned proud of you, Hugh, and I know your father is too. I'll have you booked on a ferry as quickly as possible.'

'What about the protest by the Germans? Ulysses Cuddy was telling me about it . . .'

The Ambassador grunted. 'I'll let Ulysses deal with that. It will keep him and his German counterpart busy for months. By then anything might have happened.'

Hugh returned to Tangmere to a sadly muted welcome. Indeed, there were tragically few faces he recognised. By a strange quirk of fate it was probable that the Junkers 88 gunner had saved his life by shooting him down over the Western Approaches.

The squadron had borne the brunt of a last all-out effort by the Luftwaffe to destroy Royal Air Force Fighter Command. The German High Command were aware that failure would mean an end to their plans to invade England. During the fierce battles to stem the Germans' last desperate onslaught, more than half the squadron had been killed or seriously wounded. Among their number was Sir James Cameron's replacement: the new Squadron Leader had been shot down in the same battle that had claimed Hugh's Hurricane.

Although the weary pilots did not know it at the time, the Battle of Britain – as these few desperate months came to be known – was already won. There would be many more raids, many more sorties by the Hurricanes and Spitfires of Fighter Command, but Hitler's plans for the invasion of England had been shelved, never again to be seriously considered.

For a few brief weeks in the summer and autumn of 1940, no more than three thousand fighter pilots held the whole future of Great Britain in their battle-weary hands. They did not loosen their grip until they had elbowed the danger aside.

Hugh flew five sorties in the two days after his return to the squadron. On the third day the squadron was kept on standby, but the call to take to the air never arrived and in the late afternoon the order came to 'stand down'. Having a whole evening stretching before them was an unaccustomed luxury for the pilots, and most decided to go off the airfield and celebrate.

Hugh had settled down to writing a letter home, the first since his return to duty, when an orderly came to his room and told him he was wanted on the telephone in the mess.

It was Sir James. To Hugh's delight, his friend informed him he was spending the night in the nearby town of Chichester and insisted Hugh should join him there.

When Hugh arrived at the inn where James had suggested they meet, it did not take him long to locate the Canadian baronet. He was in a corner of the bar, surrounded by pilots, engaged in 'flying talk'. Surprisingly, Lady Cameron was with him, apparently delighted to be in the company of so many young pilots.

She greeted Hugh with an almost embarrassing warmth, repeating again and again how relieved she had been when James telephoned her with the news that Hugh had been picked up from the sea. Her eyes filled with tears of genuine concern when he spoke of his ordeal of spending the whole night floating in the sea with no apparent hope of rescue.

She was still talking to him when James leaned across the table and said quietly, 'There's someone else here who's equally relieved you were picked up, Hugh.'

When he turned around, Hugh saw Ailsa Ross standing somewhat uncertainly in the centre of the bar-room, seemingly unaware of the admiring glances cast in her direction by the customers, who were mainly Royal Air Force officers.

Her uncertainty vanished as Hugh's astonishment turned to unmistakable joy. When he took her in his arms a raucous cheer went up from the customers of the inn.

'Come on, you two, the landlord's given us one of his private rooms.' James put an arm about each of them. 'Let's get away from the lascivious ogling of men who would be more at home in the Navy instead of the RAF . . . .'

To a chorus of good-natured catcalling, Hugh and Ailsa left the bar, accompanied by Lady Cameron and Sir James. In the room put at their disposal by the friendly landlord, it seemed that everyone wanted to talk at once and, gradually, the reason for Ailsa's presence in Chichester emerged.

James had learned the moment that Hugh had been posted missing, and had telephoned the news to his mother. She in turn had informed Ailsa. So upset was the Glenelg schoolteacher that Lady Cameron had telephoned her son each day in the hope that he might have more news. As days went by, hope faded until they received the astonishing news that Hugh had been landed in Ireland after being plucked from the sea by Irish fishermen. The incident had caused far more of a diplomatic flurry than Hugh had known at the time. England, with the enemy only a few miles away across the Channel and battered by constant day-and-night bombing, sorely needed something to boost its morale.

It was felt that Hugh's story would provide such an injection of hope: here was an American neutral fighting with the Royal Air Force, rescued by Irish neutrals and returned to fight again for Great Britain. It indicated that although Great Britain might seem to be fighting alone, other countries in the world, ostensibly not involved in the fighting, were not only sympathetic but also prepared to do something to support its cause.

Churchill himself was keen to have the story known, but he was eventually dissuaded, with considerable difficulty by his advisers, who were themselves being subjected to intense diplomatic pressure.

In the event, although the story was not told in its entirety, news of the incident was allowed to 'leak' to the press and was gleefully quoted in many gossip columns.

Ailsa had been so excited when the news of Hugh's return was passed on to her by Lady Cameron that she left her sister in charge of the small Glenelg school and caught the first available train to Chichester. Lady Cameron, needing little excuse for a chance to be with her son, telephoned him to say that they were heading southwards.

The streets of Chichester had echoed to the tread of fighting men since the victorious legions of Rome settled in the area in the first century AD. It had also known the softer footsteps of countless lovers, and tonight Hugh and Ailsa made no sound as they walked through the blacked-out streets of the ancient city.

They walked in silence until they sought shelter from the softly falling rain beneath the ornate market cross at the heart of the city.

'On the way here in the train I had a sudden fear that you might not be pleased to see me, that . . . there might have been someone else. One of those attractive WAAF girls in the bar, for instance.'

'If that's an oblique way of asking if there's anyone else in my life, the answer is "No". I've always strongly disapproved of fighter pilots who allow themselves to become emotionally involved while they're in a front-line squadron. It isn't fair to the girl, and even the slightest distraction can mean the difference between life and death to a fighter pilot in action.' Hugh tightened his arm about Ailsa. 'At least, that was the rather pompous attitude I had before I met you.'

'Perhaps it's the reason why you'd survived for so long, only to be shot down the first time you went into action after meeting me.' Ailsa's voice sounded very small in the darkness.

Hugh's arm pulled her to him once more. 'I was shot down because the Junkers I was chasing had a superb gunner. Anyway, it isn't the first time I've been shot down. It happened to me on my very first sortie and again in between.'

Ailsa shuddered in his arms. 'What did you think about – when you were alone in the dark, in the water?'

'At first it was how cold the water was. Then my mind went numb – I think it must have been for hours at a time. When I was able to think logically I mostly thought of you. In fact, far from being the reason I was shot down, it was probably *you* who kept me alive in the water. I was determined to see you again. We have so much to live for, Ailsa.'

There was a sound in the darkness somewhere behind them and a young couple rose from a seat in the shadows and moved outside, passing close by.

'We've known each other such a short time, Hugh.'

He smiled. 'You sound just like my mother.'

'What will she say about me? You realise there's so little I know about you?'

'I'm waiting to hear from my mother. I wrote and told her about you the night after I left Scotland. That's how sure I am that you're the girl I want to marry – am *going* to marry. She'll be upset at first that *she* didn't make the choice for me, but that would have happened anyway. Once she gets to know you a little she'll love you as much as I do. You'll see.'

'Do you, Hugh? Do you love me?'

'Yes.'

For a very long time they might have been the only two people in the world, and then Hugh said quietly, 'How long can you stay in Chichester?'

'I must return to Glenelg tomorrow.'

In response to his protest, Ailsa said, 'I must, Hugh. When I heard you were safe I just upped and left Glenelg. I – I had to see you. But now much of the danger of bombing has passed my sister wants to return to Glasgow. She hopes her husband might be able to get home for a while soon.'

'All this madness, keeping people apart who want nothing else from life but to be together. You will marry me when it's all over, Ailsa?'

'I'll marry you any time you want me to, Hugh. War or no war.'

They walked back to the inn very close together, arms about each other's waist. When they reached the door, Ailsa said hesitantly, 'I don't want to go back in the bar, Hugh. Not tonight. There's a back stairway to my room . . . .'

The inn was quiet when Hugh let himself out through the door. So too were the streets. In another couple of hours it would be another dawn. Another day. Yet no day would ever be quite the same again. Flight-Lieutenant Hugh MacCrimmon, DFC, RAF, had done what he had told so many men they were foolish to do. He had fallen very deeply in love and committed his and Ailsa's life to a future that was likely to be short and uncertain. Yet, deep inside him, there was yet another force; a force that made him more determined than ever to help bring this war to a victorious conclusion. He now had a reason for which to live, as well as a cause for which he was willing to die.

Waiting on Chichester station for the train to arrive, the sudden roar of low-flying aircraft set the window panes rattling beneath their crossed strips of sticky paper which were intended to reduce the risk of shattering.

Looking up into the sky, Ailsa saw a flight of Hurricanes pass low overhead, followed quickly by a second flight, and then a third. As they gained height they banked and set a course for London.

Bowing her head and closing her eyes so tightly they hurt, Ailsa prayed as she had never prayed before. She and Hugh had so much to live for.

SIXTEEN

America 1941

Hugh remained with the squadron at Tangmere until April 1941, when he was transferred to a newly formed 'Eagle' squadron, comprised of American pilots who, like himself, had joined the Royal Air Force to fight against the Germans.

The move brought with it a promotion to Squadron Leader, but it also meant cancelling a leave. He had been looking forward to spending a few days with Ailsa. They had not met since their brief time together in Chichester and Hugh felt there was much more he needed to say to her.

Now, instead of travelling to Glenelg, he was posted to West Mailling in Kent, and there followed a lengthy, and largely unnecessary, 'training' period before the squadron became operational – on convoy escort duties.

Daily life in the new squadron was not particularly onerous and once it had settled down to its new task, Hugh was able to take his long-postponed leave and travel to Glenelg to be with Ailsa. The five days he spent with her there were all he had hoped they might be. When he left there was an understanding between them that if the war showed no signs of escalating, they would be married sometime early in 1942.

On 7th December 1941, more than four hundred Japanese warplanes flying from the decks of six aircraft carriers carried out a devastating dawn raid on the American naval base at Pearl Harbor. Using bombs and torpedoes, they performed their mission of death and destruction well. By the time the Japanese aircraft returned to their mother ships, six American battleships had been destroyed along with many other vessels: the wrecks of 149 planes were burning on palm-fringed airfields; and more than 3,500 Americans had been killed or wounded.

The next day, the United States Congress declared a state of war with Japan. Three days later, Japan's two allies, Germany and Italy, formally declared war on the United States.

At West Mailling the stunned pilots of the Eagle Squadron held a meeting to discuss the implications of the entry of the United States into the war. While all were agreed their country could not have stood back from the conflict for ever, it raised a question mark over the part they and the other two Eagle Squadrons would now play in the war. They needed to decide whether to continue to fly as a British squadron, or transfer to the United States Army Air Force.

Had the pilots still been fighting the Battle of Britain, there need have been no discussion. All were men who had joined the Royal Air Force in order to contribute something positive to the war effort against the Germans. Escorting convoys was a boring and frustrating task. They had been performing these duties for months and their only reward had been a Dornier 17 reconnaissance aircraft jointly shot down by Hugh and one of the squadron's youngest pilots the week before.

In sad contrast they had witnessed the sinking of countless ships by the torpedoes of German U-boats, without being able to do anything to prevent such attacks.

The voting was unanimous: they would continue to fly for the Royal Air Force as an operational squadron until the United States Army Air Force established a presence in England. Then they would transfer.

Hugh told Ailsa of the decision when he was able to snatch a rare weekend leave and travel to Glenelg in March 1942. The weather had been unusually mild for the past couple of weeks and, although the peaks of the mountains inland from Glenelg were still heavily capped with snow, it had thawed on lower ground and Ailsa and Hugh walked the loch-side path to Ratagan.

It was an invigorating walk and as they fell in through the unlocked door of the great house their laughter echoed through the empty rooms.

Unwinding a scarf from his neck, Hugh looked about him at the peeling paint, patches of damp about the window frames, and high ceilings festooned with cobwebs. 'It's a comfort to know there are some things in this crazy world of ours that don't change.'

'I believe the spiders are bigger than they were,' declared Ailsa, 'but it's sad to see Ratagan standing empty and unloved. It's survived clan warfare, the Forty-Five Rebellion and the Clearances. Now it's dying through neglect. I could cry about it.'

'You really do love this house, don't you?' Hugh slipped the scarf from Ailsa's hair and kissed her. 'If I thought about it for too long I could almost be jealous.'

'If you thought about it for long enough you'd feel the same way. This house has been at the heart of Glenelg's destiny for hundreds of years. Men have mustered here for wars, have come here to reap rewards for bravery or to be punished for cowardice. Your ancestors and mine had their lives changed by their visits here. Had their words not been spoken in Ratagan neither you nor I would be here right now. Yes, I love the house because I love Glenelg – and because I love you. Without Ratagan nothing, none of these things, would be the same, and neither would I.'

'Then I'll learn to love it too.' With his arm about Ailsa, Hugh walked to the window and looked across the dark, winter-water loch to where a hundred white peaks reared towards a grey sky in a wild and dramatic panorama. 'It isn't going to be difficult.'

When Hugh returned to his squadron at West Mailling he found a message awaiting him. The Commanding Officer of the station wanted to see him most urgently.

It was late at night, but when Hugh telephoned the Group Captain at his home, he was told to get there as quickly as possible. Wondering about the reason for such urgency, Hugh hurried to the CO's home.

The Group Captain, wearing a woollen dressing gown and a pair of well-worn slippers, let Hugh in and showed him to the lounge where he poured them both a large-sized whisky.

When Hugh tried to refuse the drink, protesting that he never drank the night before flying on operations, the Group Captain made a startling announcement. 'Your days of operational flying are over for a while, Hugh. The Air Attaché at the American Embassy

will give you all the details when you meet with him tomorrow, but I
can tell you from what little they let me know that you'll be flying out
of London tomorrow night. Sometime the next day you'll be back
home in the United States.'

Hugh could hardly believe the news. It would be wonderful in
many ways. He had not seen his family since he left Missouri to
come to Britain to join the Royal Air Force – but he had Ailsa to
think of now.

'What do they have lined up for me over there?'

The Group Captain shook his head. 'They wouldn't tell me, but
it must be pretty high-powered. I also had a telephone call from
Fighter Command headquarters tonight. I am to tell you that au-
thorisation has been given for you to transfer to the United States
Army Air Force should you wish. I was also told that if you find any
pilots of your calibre over there who'd like to fight for us, we'll be
delighted to have them. I second that view, Hugh. You're a damned
good pilot and if I thought it was in your best interests I'd fight like
hell to keep you. As it is,' the Group Captain shrugged, 'I hope we'll
meet again some day.'

As he walked back to his room, Hugh wondered how this was
going to affect his marriage to Ailsa. It had been no use asking the
Group Captain, he had told Hugh everything he knew. If there were
any answers to be found they would have to come from the United
States Embassy in London.

At the United States Embassy, Hugh was taken to the office of the
Air Attaché. A full Colonel, the Air Attaché returned Hugh's salute
with a studied casualness, and introduced himself as Colonel Ellis
Capello. 'We've been expecting you, Hugh. Your CO told us you
were visiting in Scotland. I was up there fishing last year. It's a great
country. You have friends there?'

'I hope to marry a Scots girl.'

'Is that so? With a name like MacCrimmon you'll be pleasing
your parents for sure. Me, I should have married an Italian girl.
That's not so easy right now, so I married a Norwegian girl instead.
The family didn't write to me for three months. But I guess your
marriage is going to have to wait a while.'

'It is?'

'It surely is, Hugh.' Rising to his feet, Ellis Capello walked around the chair on which Hugh was seated. Stopping in front of his puzzled visitor, he said, 'You know, we were going to put you into American uniform before you returned to the States – but I'm not so sure now. Letting the men see you in that uniform – with medals – might work a whole lot better than dressing you the same as them.'

'You're way above my head, Colonel. Just who *am* I supposed to be talking to? In fact, what am I supposed to be *doing?*'

'We have two things planned for you, Hugh. First, we're sending you back to the States to talk to air crews who are coming to England in the very near future. We want you to fill 'em with enthusiasm for fighting the war in Europe. It's not going to be easy. They all want to see action in the Pacific, to hit back at the Japs. Those who've been detailed to come to England think they've been put into the second league. What we want you to do is to go on the grand tour and let them know they're wrong. Tell 'em what's going on here. Fill 'em with enthusiasm for fighting Germans. It's not going to be easy – but you can do it.'

'I'm grateful to you for your confidence, Colonel, but you mentioned you had two things planned for me. What's the second?'

'Ah! That's the sugar on the cookie! You may not know it, Hugh, but because you're the son of a Senator, you're big news in the US of A. Every German plane you shot down was reported, the two Distinguished Flying Crosses you were awarded by King George were headlines – and your rescue when you were picked up by those Irish fishermen and carried back to Ireland made you a public hero. If you were to stand for President tomorrow Franklin Delano Roosevelt would need to bow out gracefully to make way for you. No office in the land is beyond your grasp.'

'But — I've no ambition for public office.'

'Everyone *knows* this – and it makes you a more attractive candidate for office in their eyes.'

'That still hasn't answered my question, Colonel. I'm not being put up for President, so what do you have in mind?'

'The rank of Colonel in the United States Army Air Force – and a post as an Air Attaché. Somewhere with a reasonable degree of importance first of all, perhaps – and then you'll take over from me, here in London.'

Hugh discovered he had been holding his breath for some minutes and he let it out as slowly as the need to draw a new breath would allow.

'Do I have any time to think this over?'

Colonel Ellis Capello looked at his watch and grimaced. 'I can probably give you an hour – but most men I know would give their right arm for an opportunity like this.'

'I have plans that include my right arm, Colonel, and I'm not sure I want all the ballyhoo that goes with this "wonderful opportunity" you're offering me. I joined the Royal Air Force because I believed in what the British were fighting for. I wanted to fight with them. I still do.'

'You and I believe in the same things, Hugh – and so too does the President of the United States. You've been chosen to do a job because I and everyone else concerned in this believe you'll do it better than anyone else. It's important to America, and to Great Britain. Very important. Go away and think about it if it's going to help – but an hour's all you have.'

'Can I use an Embassy telephone to call Scotland?'

Colonel Ellis Capello frowned. 'This girl you're going to marry? You can tell her you're not going to be around for a while and will be in touch in a week or two – but I can't allow you to tell her what you'll be doing – or when you'll be flying out of London. These 'phones are as secure as a bat in a paddock. Breathe a word of what you're doing and Göring will have half the Luftwaffe in the air waiting for your plane tonight.'

'Fine, I'll just tell her I won't be marrying her this spring and I'll see her around some time.'

Colonel Capello grinned sympathetically. 'Well, something like that, but if you care to leave me her telephone number I'll have my secretary call her when you're safely in the United States. We'll make sure she knows you're doing one hell of an important job back home.'

'Thanks, but all I need is three minutes of telephone time and I'll make my own excuses.'

*

Hugh's standing as a hero in the United States had not been exaggerated. He stepped from the American Air Force transport plane at the Springfield, Missouri airfield to find a band playing. It took him a minute or two to realise they were playing to welcome *him*. Two Air Force Generals were waiting to shake his hand, together with a sprinkling of State Department officials and his family.

Dozens of journalists were gathered on the tarmac and after posing for them with almost everyone in the welcoming group, Hugh was subjected to a press conference which he managed to stumble through until it was brought to a halt by one of the Generals.

As they left the press behind, the same General said, 'No doubt you'll want to go home and relax for a couple of weeks before you take up your new duties, Hugh.'

'The way I was rushed over here I thought I was on an urgent mission.'

'So you are, but you've had a hell of a time over there in England, boy – if you don't believe me you'd better read the newspapers over the next few days. We'll be giving you plenty to do, make no mistake about it, but you need a break. Besides, if you made a start talking to our pilots right away it would lack the impact we need. We'll feed them with every scrap of information about you and about the battles that have been going on in the skies over Europe. You'll have the big build-up. By the time we've finished they'll be falling over each other to hear you speak and then be eager to get over there and have a crack at the Germans for themselves. Go on home, Hugh. Enjoy yourself for a week or two. When we're good and ready we'll come to Missouri and fetch you and we'll be working the butt off you, make no mistake about that.'

It was a relief to be in the car speeding along the road to home, surrounded only by the family. It seemed that everyone was talking at once, until Joan MacCrimmon said, 'Before your plane arrived I was wondering whether you would be bringing this Scots girl with you.'

Breaking the sudden silence, Hugh said, 'Ailsa's her name, Mother – as well you know. I would have brought her with me had I been allowed to, but the Air Attaché in London told me I couldn't even tell her I was coming home.'

'I'm sure it's all for the best, dear.'

Something in the tone of his mother's voice told Hugh that her mind was already working on her own schemes and he decided it would be better if they settled this most important issue right here and now.

'Had I known about this earlier we would have been married on my last leave. Now it will need to wait until I return to England – but I *am* marrying her, Mother, so don't try pairing me off with any of the girls on the list you've been compiling since the moment they told you at the hospital you'd just given birth to a son.'

Roderick MacCrimmon grinned at his wife's discomfiture and Laura said cheerfully, 'Ailsa's a lovely name. What's she like?'

'She's like no one I've ever met before – and never will again. She has dark-red hair, is tall, very attractive, intelligent – she's something very special.'

'I'm glad you've found someone like that, Hugh. So will Mother be, once she's met her. I wish you could have brought her back to Missouri with you.'

'I will one day. Soon, I hope.'

'I only wish I knew a little more about her,' said Joan unhappily. 'You're a very rich young man in your own right, Hugh.'

'She doesn't know that. All she knows is that I'm an American serving with the Royal Air Force. No more.'

'Hmm!' Joan was not reassured. 'What of her family?'

'She has a sister, that's all. Mind you, she has some interesting ancestors. Some of them were convicted of sheep stealing and sentenced to be transported to Australia. That was about the time the MacCrimmons came to America.'

'You mean — she comes from a family of gaolbirds? Oh my God! What will folk think if they ever find out ... ?'

The laughter in the car drowned Joan MacCrimmon's concern and when it died down, Roderick asked, 'What do you think of Glenelg, Hugh?'

'It's breathtakingly beautiful. *As* for Ratagan House – Ailsa doesn't think there's any place on earth quite like it. I must agree with her, even though the place is criminally neglected it's still a very special place.'

'I couldn't agree with you more, Hugh. I wonder whether it's still owned by the same family ... ?'

The conversation took another turn as they topped a hill and came within sight of MacCrimmon land. From here the conversation was about the changes that had occurred since Hugh had left Missouri for England.

Lecturing air crews who had been selected for a tour of duty in England proved to be a great success – but it also took far longer than anyone had envisaged. This was mainly because the scale of the task increased with every week that passed. Vast numbers of aircraft and men were being sent to Europe. Churchill and Roosevelt had agreed that the defeat of Germany should be the priority for both of them, and already plans were being laid for an invasion that would liberate France and the other occupied European nations.

For more than a year Hugh lectured air crews on what they could expect when they reached England and fought the Luftwaffe for the first time. Then, Hugh asked to be taken off his lecturing duties. He had been away from England for a year. As he pointed out in his request, circumstances and tactics for fighting the war in the air over Europe would have changed. It was senseless sending American airmen to fight in Europe having learned out-of-date tactics.

Hugh now wore the uniform of a Major in the United States Army Air Force and he knew he could not return to England to fly with the RAF – but he reminded the USAAF of the promise made to him by the Air Attaché in London. It was pointed out to him, in turn, that the arrangement was that he should serve in a similar office elsewhere in the world before taking up a post in London.

Promoted to Lieutenant-Colonel, Hugh was sent to Kunming, in southern China. Here he was not an Air Attaché, but had the daunting task of putting together a fighter force capable of protecting the freight routes into China, supplying the soldiers of Chiang Kai-Shek and fighting against the formidable Japanese Air Force.

That Hugh was able to achieve any degree of success at all was remarkable in itself. In the air his pilots fought against the Japanese. On the ground, using improvised and often dangerous airfields, they had to protect even the most essential stores against the depredations of ill-disciplined Chinese soldiers.

Meanwhile, Hugh was also involved in a number of political battles. One of the fiercest was against army officers considerably senior to himself. They considered the needs of the army to be far more important than supporting a few squadrons of hard-pushed fighter aircraft.

Personally too, Hugh found life in China frustrating in the extreme. Mail from Scotland took weeks to find him and all too frequently disappeared altogether.

One of Ailsa's letters that did reach him had mentioned that the owner of Ratagan was finally putting the house in order, although she did not know whether to be glad or sorry. It meant Ratagan would survive, but it also meant she was no longer able to walk through its lofty rooms, dreaming of the past. Nevertheless, she told Hugh, she would continue to take her schoolchildren to the gardens on picnics until ordered to desist by the owner.

Scotland seemed very far away from Kunming and its corruption, disorganisation and endless frustrations. The war in Europe, the 'real' world and Ailsa, all seemed very, very far away.

Then one day, early in 1944, Hugh was working at his desk, trying to ignore the monotonous protest of the fan above his head. It set his teeth on edge, yet barely managed to disturb the hot air of the room. There was a sudden commotion from outside and he looked up to see a tall, bespectacled Air Force Colonel coming through the door.

'You'll be Colonel MacCrimmon,' said the newcomer, advancing with outstretched hand. 'I'm John Holland. I expected you to be waiting for me on the airfield with all your bags packed and raring to go.'

'Go where?'

'You mean you weren't even expecting me?' Colonel Holland took off his hat and ran a crumpled sleeve across his perspiring forehead. 'I should have kept my big mouth shut when I came in through the door. I could have turned around and gone back to the United States without anyone being any the wiser.'

Selecting the only chair that was not heaped high with files for which there was no storage space elsewhere in the room, Colonel Holland sank down, stretching his long legs in front of him.

Glancing at the insignia of rank on Hugh's lapel, he said, 'It seems that news of your promotion's got delayed along the line too, Colonel. I'm your replacement – my papers are here. You're to proceed back to the States and after a spot of leave you'll be taking up the post of Air Attaché in London. I've just ended a tour of duty in England. The way things are coming to the boil in Europe it's going to be one hell of a job – but if you get fed-up with it come right on back to Kunming and let me take your place. I can promise you a vote of thanks from some of the prettiest ladies in London . . . .'

SEVENTEEN

Glenelg 1945

Hugh reached London in April 1944 to take up his new post in the American Embassy. It was to be one of the busiest times of his life, but not as physically demanding as his days as a Royal Air Force pilot during the Battle of Britain. Nevertheless, he was busy from dawn to dusk — and beyond. Plans were far advanced for the liberation of Europe. Details were a very well-kept secret, yet there could not have been a man or woman in Britain who did not realise that an invasion of France was imminent.

One of the first things Hugh did upon his arrival in London was to telephone Ailsa. Her excitement when she learned he was in London immediately dispelled all the doubts he had entertained on the way to England that her feelings for him might have changed.

'Are you coming to Glenelg?' The question was asked eagerly.

'I can't, not just yet. But I'm stationed at the Embassy now. Gan you get down to London? I'll book you into the finest hotel in town.'

There was a brief silence before Ailsa said, 'I can't leave Glenelg right now, Hugh.'

'Why not?'

Ailsa had been bubbling with excitement until now and her change of mood frightened him.

'My sister's with me for a while. Her husband has been posted "Missing in action". We're awaiting more news. I need to stay with her.'

'Of course.' Hugh was disappointed, but he knew that Ailsa and her sister were close and at a time like this she would need comforting. After expressing his sympathy and expressing the hope that there would be good news of her sister's husband before long, he asked about Ratagan.

'It's looking beautiful.' Suddenly Ailsa was enthusiastic once more. 'The men who are decorating the house allowed me inside to see what had been done. It's being furnished too. By the time it's done Ratagan will look the way it must have done at the height of its glory. We still don't know *why* it should be done just now, or whether the owner intends coming here to live, but there's a rumour that all the land around Glenelg has been bought by an Australian – one of the Rosses.'

'Your Rosses? The ones who were transported for sheep-stealing?'

Ailsa laughed and it was a sound he had longed to hear for a very long time. 'All that happened more than a hundred years ago. I don't think they'd be very pleased to have that held against them now. The truth is, I don't know, but it would be rather a coincidence if it were another Australian family by the same name, especially as they already own the cottage where Lady Cameron is living.'

Hugh was surprised to hear that Lady Cameron was still living at Glenelg. He had heard only intermittently from Sir James since leaving England two years before and he asked Ailsa about him now.

'Oh, Sir James is one of the great heroes of the war. He's leading a "Pathfinder" squadron, flying Mosquitoes and picking up more medals.'

Hugh was relieved to learn that James was still alive and well, though surprised to learn that he had returned to active duties. It must have been at his own request. A 'test pilot' usually continued with such work. He would have to try to locate his friend and arrange a meeting.

Hugh and Ailsa chatted for almost half an hour before a frosty-voiced operator came on the line to say someone had been waiting for fifteen minutes to be connected to a Glenelg line, and didn't they realise there was a war going on? Telephone calls should be kept to a minimum length, in case the lines were required for urgent matters.

It did not matter. Hugh and Ailsa had spoken to each other and all was well between them. It would take more than the disapproval of a telephone operator to take away the joy they both felt.

*

Not until three months after he was posted missing did Ailsa's sister receive news that her husband had been wounded and taken prisoner by the Germans. He would spend the remainder of the war in a prisoner-of-war camp, but he was alive. Ailsa telephoned the good news to Hugh, but there was no question of her coming to London in the immediate future.

Two weeks before, the Allied forces had landed on the beaches of Normandy. They were now locked in a desperate battle that was likely to decide the outcome of the war with Germany.

Hugh had twice been to France since the landings and had returned to a London that was being subjected to yet another terror from the air. Unable to match the superiority that the British and American Air Forces had gained over the Luftwaffe, the Germans were now launching pilotless aircraft packed with explosives, aimed at England's capital.

Known to those who lived in London as 'doodlebugs', or 'buzz-bombs', the menacing buzz of their engines had become a familiar sound above the noise of London traffic. Those who listened to them breathed a sigh of relief when the sound of the engine receded into the distance. They were safe – until the next one reached them.

If the engine faltered and cut out, there would be a desperate scramble for shelter. It meant that the flying bomb, known as the 'V-1', was gliding to earth on its short, stubby wings to reap an indiscriminate harvest among the residents of London. It was not the place for a girl from the remoteness of Glenelg.

However, the latest German weapon failed to put a stop to the Embassy parties that were held at the slightest excuse. At one of these parties Hugh met Cornelius Ross, from Australia.

He was introduced to Hugh by one of the Embassy staff who suggested that they both had a common interest in the same part of Scotland. It was not long before Hugh realised that his countryman had been relieved to pass the Australian on to someone else.

Cornelius Ross had been drinking heavily and Hugh suspected the Australian had consumed a great deal of alcohol before coming to the Embassy.

'So you know Glenelg, eh?' Ross pushed his face close to Hugh's in an almost bellicose manner. 'What's your interest there? Business?'

'No.' Hugh had no intention of telling this man about Ailsa. 'My ancestors left there more than a hundred years ago. I was curious about the place.'

'Oh! Mine left at about the same time. Went to Australia. Did bloody well! Even though one of the damned fools married a bar-girl – *married* her! You could lose the whole of Scotland in the lands we own now. Ross Enterprises, that's us. Biggest landowners in Queensland – probably in the whole of Australia. That's why they elected my brother Governor. He takes care of the politics while I look after the business. That's the only way to run things these days. It was different when the first Rosses got to Queensland. You staked out your land and God help anyone who tried to muscle in on you. No pussyfooting around in those days.'

'What's the nature of your business in Glenelg?'

For a few moments as Cornelius Ross glared at him, Hugh thought he was about to be told to mind his own business. Instead, the Australian said, 'I've got property up there and put in a bid for some land on behalf of the company. It's a lot of land by Scottish standards, I suppose, but back home it wouldn't be much more than you'd run a few chickens on.'

Hugh immediately remembered the work that Ailsa said was being carried out at Ratagan. The thought of this man occupying such a beautiful house filled him with dismay. He would appreciate neither its history nor its beauty.

'You a shooting man?' Once again the questioner seemed to be seeking an argument.

'I've been known to go hunting back in Missouri.'

'There you are! Everyone enjoys hunting, but there's little op-portunity for it in Britain. That's why I've bought land at Glenelg. It's a good investment. Shove a few deer on the hills, set a few hundred grouse loose and men will pay the earth for the privilege of going out and shooting them. It's a gold mine, you mark my words, a gold mine. Mind you . . .' Cornelius Ross leaned towards Hugh at a dan-gerously acute angle, 'mind you, a few families are going to have to move out of the more isolated cottages. They're born poachers up in the Highlands, did you know that? Born poachers . . . .'

'You mean you're going to evict men from their cottages? A modern Clearance?'

'And why not? It's not good for anyone to stay up there, stagnating.' He had difficulty with the word. 'The Rosses were "cleared" years ago, and look at me now. It did us a favour. I'll be doing the same for them. Waiter . . . ! Did you see that? Deliberately looked the other way. Waiter, I'll have another drink . . . .'

As the Australian lurched away in pursuit of the waiter, Hugh wondered what his plans would mean for those who lived on the lonely peninsular. He wondered too what Ailsa would think about having a man like Cornelius Ross living in Ratagan.

Hugh learned of the death of Sir James Cameron when he picked up a newspaper. It had been left lying beside his seat on an aircraft bringing him back from yet another trip to France. Unfolding the newspaper he saw Sir James's photograph smiling out at him from the page beneath the headline, 'AIR ACE KILLED IN TRAGIC FLYING ACCIDENT'.

Reading on, Hugh learned that James had died when taking off from an airfield in Oxfordshire. A trainee pilot who had left the ground just ahead of him reported his engine faltering and swung his aircraft around in a bid to return to the runway. His aircraft dropped on James's Mosquito just as it was leaving the ground. Both pilots had died in the ensuing conflagration.

The news left Hugh numb. He had last seen his friend only a week before, when he had come to London to attend another of the Embassy parties. It had been a memorable reunion and during the course of the evening James had suggested that Hugh should accompany him on an unauthorised flight to Glenelg whenever he had twenty-four hours at his disposal.

Back in London, Hugh lost no time telephoning Ailsa. She confirmed that Lady Cameron had already been notified and the whole of Glenelg was in mourning. Sir James Cameron was the first member of his family to be popular with them for a hundred and twenty-five years, and he was to be buried at Glenelg in three days' time.

'You will come to the funeral, Hugh?' Ailsa put the question anxiously. 'You were his best friend.'

'Of course I'll be there.' Hugh and Ailsa had managed forty-eight hours together a month before. They had met up in Glasgow, Ailsa travelling there by train, Hugh obtaining a lift on an RAF transport aircraft. It had been a wonderful reunion, but had not lasted long enough. 'Please pass on my deepest sympathy to Lady Cameron. I still can't believe it. James was indestructible . . . .'

The procession from the small kirk included every able-bodied man and woman who lived in Glenelg, and as the coffin reached the open grave, Ailsa handed a set of bagpipes to Hugh.

There was an immediate stir of excitement among the mourners. Every villager there recognised the silver ring that had once adorned the pipes belonging to the first Hugh MacCrimmon. It was now fitted to the chanter of the pipes Hugh held firmly beneath his arm.

As the coffin was lowered beneath the ground, Hugh played the slow, mournful notes of a tune known as 'Cameron's lament'. It had been written by the first Hugh MacCrimmon and played at the graveside of Cameron of Glenelg, close to the battlefield of Toulouse in Napoleon's France.

As Hugh played, there was not a dry eye among the assembled villagers and when the chill wind that had been blowing all day suddenly dropped, it seemed the whole world was mourning the passing of Sir James Cameron. The villagers knew of the oath the first Hugh MacCrimmon had taken all those years before. This was his descendant's way of paying an exceptional tribute to his friend and he knew it was right to do so. The first Hugh MacCrimmon would have been the first to acknowledge a brave man. He would have understood.

That evening Ailsa and Hugh sat in the Glen More cottage with Abigail Cameron and discovered that life without her son was not the only problem the titled widow had to face.

It came about when Hugh said, 'You'll be staying on here, in the cottage, of course?'

'That had been my intention, but it seems even this is to be taken from me.'

Walking to a roll-top yew desk in a corner of the room, she took out an envelope and handed it to Hugh.

Opening it, Hugh read the contents and exclaimed, 'This is from Ross Enterprises. The company belongs to a man I met recently at an Embassy party. He said he'd bought the land hereabouts and intended stocking it for shooting. He also told me he'd be moving some of the residents out, but I never realised it would affect you.'

'It's a double irony,' exclaimed Abigail sadly. 'I can remember when this cottage was bought by a Ross. A soldier, convalescing at Ratagan. He was a very brave man – just like James.'

'Is that why James's second name was Ross?' Hugh put the question gently.

Lady Cameron looked at him for a moment before nodding. 'Yes. We met when I performed the opening ceremony.'

'I'll write to Cornelius Ross. He's the man I met at the Embassy party. His brother is Governor of Queensland.'

Lady Cameron shook her head. 'No, perhaps it was meant to be.' She gave Ailsa a sad smile. 'You are not the only one to have studied family histories, and time has a habit of repaying old debts. Many years ago a Cameron had the Rosses removed from Glenelg, and I believe the MacCrimmons tried to persuade the then Cameron of Glenelg to allow them to remain. He never succeeded. Now a MacCrimmon would try to persuade a Ross to allow a Cameron to stay on. I'm afraid you'll be no more successful, Hugh.'

'What will you do? Where will you go?'

'Back to Canada. I have a little money, and a property at Lake of the Woods.' She smiled at them. It was a sad, defeated smile and Ailsa could have wept for her. 'One day, perhaps you'll visit me there.'

Hugh *did* write to Cornelius Ross, but Abigail's view of the matter proved prophetic. Hugh had told Cornelius Ross that Lady Cameron had been a friend of Henry Ross at the time he bought the cottage and had, perhaps, contributed in no small way to his recovery from the war wounds he had suffered in World War One.

The reply came not from Cornelius Ross, but from a clerk at Ross Enterprises. It stated stiffly that the matter had been discussed at 'a high level' and it had been agreed there were no grounds for changing the original decision. Furthermore, Lady Cameron had been allowed to occupy the cottage for many years at a rent considerably below that which might have been demanded for such a property.

They were quite certain that all parties concerned would agree that they were not acting unreasonably.

Lady Cameron left Glenelg three months before Hitler committed suicide in his Berlin bunker and his High Command signed surrender documents bringing the bloody war to a conclusion. Before her departure she attended the wedding of Hugh and Ailsa.

The ceremony was carried out in the small Glenelg church and afterwards the wedding bouquet was placed upon the grave of Wing Commander Sir James Cameron, Bt, DSO, DFC & Bar, AFC.

All the members of Hugh's family were present for the wedding and no one was happier than Joan MacCrimmon. She had come to accept that her son had made a wise choice. Joan and her daughter-in-law would now be the best of friends.

The highlight of the day came at the wedding reception. Roderick MacCrimmon laid a small, gift-wrapped parcel on the table in front of Ailsa. No more than four inches in length, he announced to the intrigued wedding guests that it was his present to the young couple — and was especially for Ailsa.

Every neck was craned for a better view when Ailsa opened the parcel, but they were as baffled as the bride when the last wrapping fell away and she was left holding a key. Not a new key, but one that showed age.

When Ailsa looked to Roderick MacCrimmon for an explanation, he smiled. 'It's a very special key, Ailsa. A key to your dreams. A key to the future, and a key to the past. It's the key to Ratagan. I bought the house and had it restored when I was certain in my own mind that you and Hugh would be married.'

Looking towards his son, Roderick MacCrimmon said, 'Buying Ratagan has brought an additional reward – one of which the first Hugh MacCrimmon would be proud. Ailsa has told me his story, and it seems he worked very hard to thwart the man who wanted to clear the people of Glenelg. He failed in his endeavours — but with that key *you* have already succeeded. You see, when I bought Ratagan for you, I went back through all the documents appertaining to the house. I discovered that although the first baronet Cameron sold all the lands separately from Ratagan, he retained certain rights for the house. They included hunting rights.'

A smile of enlightenment lit up Hugh's face and his father nodded. 'That's right. Cornelius Ross might have bought the Glenelg lands, but he will not be able to carry out his plans. The hunting rights of Glenelg belong to you, Hugh and Ailsa. In view of this I have no doubt that Ross will be happy to sell all the land you want for a nominal profit. After a hundred and twenty-five years you will have succeeded in doing what the first Hugh MacCrimmon set out to achieve.'

Roderick MacCrimmon raised his glass. 'I propose a toast to the bride and groom, and to the MacCrimmons — of Glenelg.'